"A good novel will invite you in, gain your confidence and interest, and gather intensity so that you can't put it down. "Atlas Rising" does this exactly. …The premise of "Atlas Rising" in some ways is reminiscent of "Atlas Shrugged," but is less demanding to read - (no 50 page speeches). Still the underlying message is clear and the story builds your interest up to the climax. Overall, a truly enjoyable read."

– Richard L. Bjornseth

"A poignant rendition of things to come. The storyline was very captivating, building with intensity. …A very good storyline relevant to today's society. A good read."

– J Hargis

"Fantastic read! Couldn't put it down, which NEVER happens. I don't have the attention span to complete books, but this was a page turner. Definitely recommended."

– KFBR392

"Good read. Thank you so much. Quite interesting and different. You could really get into the read. I would recommend it."

– By Caton

"I really enjoyed this book for the intriguing, futuristic story and for the subtle political messages of a government gone too far. It was hard to put down. I hope the author writes a sequel."

– Lester Jameson

"This is a must read political thriller. If you care about your freedom and the liberties of your children, or the liberties of all Americans, this book will have a deep meaning for you. I loved it!"

– skymomon

"'Atlas Rising' is a very well-researched and well-written futuristic sociopolitical drama.! I hope you enjoy it, too! Remember to always carry "The Card" ; Don't you dare leave leave home without it."

– Dave Hon

Also by W. C. Augustine

Atlas Rising

For the
COMMON GOOD

W. C. AUGUSTINE

Robb,
I wore Jacket to The Office
This week.
If Someone Turns Me in
For TradeMark Violations
Should I Send Them your
Address or Tele #;
enjoy
Bill

Atlas Rising Publishing
Illinois

For the Common Good

Published by Atlas Rising Publishing.

Cover and interior design by Carol Davis
www.tolgraphics.com

Published and printed in the United States of America

Library of Congress Cataloging-in-Publication Data is available upon
request.

19 18 17 16 15   5 4 3 2 1

ISBN: 978-0-9864355-0-8

1.Fiction, Suspense
2.Fiction, Political

"The natural progress of things is for liberty to yield
and government to gain ground."

Thomas Jefferson

Acknowledgements

I want to thank a number of people who gave their time and perspective helping me edit this sequel. Richard Bjornseth, Susan Clements and Faith Potetti's input correcting mistakes and focusing the story was invaluable. Nan Sevy spent many hours correcting mistakes and giving suggestions. She was the English teacher I should have had in school.

The cover designer, Carol Davis, not only designed the cover but walked me through the maze of getting the book in present form.

As I journey forward in life I gain perspective on the fortune to have had not only two parents growing up, but four grandparents I knew and from whom I learned. This story contains a number of life lessons and wisdom obtained from them.

Without my wife Sue's encouragement to keep writing and her acceptance of my spending evenings seated at the computer rather than in the family room this book would not be. I owe much to her.

Any fool can make a rule,
and any fool will mind it.

Henry David Thoreau

Prologue

In "Atlas Rising" Julie and Andrew worked to avert an apocalyptic asteroid, now they are challenged to stop microscopic tyranny. While earlier they fought to protect life itself, now they must preserve liberty. This time the peril is not state ineptitude, but the divergent goals of the state and the people.

Diverse perspectives on life and a different regard for the individual put two sides on opposite courses. The powers-that-be, determined to do their duty, set a course to do what they deem is best for the common man.

The state's behemoth database of who, what, when and where and expanding capacity to connect the dots put every aspect of life under the state's microscope. Citizens find themselves being measured for a straightjacket. Now technology has provided the final element to control individuals at their very core. The race is on as the state seeks to insert the key for total domination.

Only after a man-made disaster strikes at home does Andrew realize the battle must be fought. With former Atlas compatriots based offshore and others throughout the country Julie and Andrew do what they must.

Knowing there is no retreat; citizens galvanized by their passion for liberty conspire to avert subjugation. Setting up a hidden base in pioneer fashion allows them to evade the watchful eye of the state and orchestrate the plan. It is a battle that must be won.

"The natural progress of things is for liberty to yield
and government to gain ground."

Thomas Jefferson

Chapter 1

October, 2041

Sophie, having taken more calls and helped more citizens work through the maze of health care regulations in four days than any of her colleagues would in five, had a clear conscience. She called in sick and rewarded herself with a day of shopping at the mall. Little did she realize that her transaction card debits at the mall laid her claim of sickness false. The National Security Agency stored the information.

Julie and Andrew Collier pulled their two-seater into the small mountainside town of Mount Shasta after a 500 mile drive they had enjoyed. A warm autumn sun unencumbered by few high wispy clouds joined by a gentle breeze to keep the air fresh made the weather perfect. It had improved throughout the trip, an omen of their stay they were sure.

The trip allowed an unwinding of anxiety, quite the opposite of their last long drive together. They remembered all too well the long drive in '39 to Cheyenne when they planned a nuclear heist.

Andrew's life-long passion of observing the stars coupled with his technical skills had identified a dangerous asteroid. It was Julie who saved Andrew physically and from his complacency. Together they had been instrumental in averting a disaster that they wanted to forget.

Both looked forward to a month long vacation giving them opportunity to digest both the triumph of their endeavors and the heartbreak loss of people close to them. The containment of discontent they had hoped would become a new awakening in the country would also be on their minds, but they agreed to put their disappointments aside. The stay allowed them time to contemplate the future at a place they perceived to be close to something greater.

Halfway through the trip Julie placed her grape in the vehicle's sound system receptacle. They were enjoying the late 20th century composer Yanni's blend of jazz, classical, and soft rock when the Federal Communications Commission overrode entertainment on her grape for an address by the President.

> "Good evening fellow Americans. As I promised before the election I am taking another step to expand the freedoms this government offers our citizenry. Because of the success in our efforts to mitigate the effects of climate change, I am, under the discretionary powers afforded me under the Highway Safety Act, allowing the national highway speed limit to be raised immediately to 55 MPH…
> …make no mistake this administration will do what is in the best interests of the public at large, but will lightly use the hand of the government while preserving freedom…"

The President's speech was shut off as Julie pulled her grape from the receptacle.

"Enough," she said as Andrew increased their speed. "Duh, how obvious. Funny how they still won't admit global warming has stalled since around the turn of the century, but take credit for what they won't admit."

"Well, at least it's something," Andrew added hoping to set a positive tone for the trip.

"Did you notice how he said *freedoms this government offers our citizenry*? How many people know it's supposed to be the other way around?"

"Please, you know we agreed," Andrew said as he tenderly laid his right hand on the back of her hand and slowly intertwined their fingers.

"I know. We both need this getaway."

At the edge of town they pulled into a roadside Holiday-Marriott motel, one of those previously family owned enterprises absorbed into the conglomerate in the early part of the century. It would be later tomorrow before they could find their way to the mountainside cabin.

John Whitehouse had been good to Julie and Andrew. When they moved to Boise he had welcomed Andrew's return as a design engineer at Amalgamated Robotics Company (ARC) and offered Julie a job as director of security. With the refusal of NASA to return Andrew's telescopes and equipment Andrew would have more time to devote to work. They were at Mount Shasta because John had given Julie and Andrew use of his family cabin halfway up the side of Mount Shasta as a wedding gift.

The cabin had been in John Whitehouse's family for three generations, but was seldom used by his family. John saw a month's stay as an appropriate wedding present to his top robotics engineer and the new director of security at ARC.

"Let me tell you about the cabin," John said before they left. "It's an hour's walk from the historic Sisiyou trail. The cabin has no electricity or plumbing. Water for washing must be carried from a nearby stream fed by snowmelt. Drinking water and food are carried in. The only heat is from solar panels on the roof, but given the lessened restrictions you may be able to periodically use the wood-burning stove. The environmental police usually ignore sporadic wood burning in this desolate place anyway. Now having heard this, do you still want the place?"

"Absolutely," Julie had answered.

"What time in the morning can we check in for the permit to occupy the cabin," asked Julie?

"I believe John said 10:00. It's amazing that we need to get a permit to occupy the place."

"Well the place is under control of the Shasta-Trinity National Forest even though the cabin is privately owned."

"It depends upon what you consider privately owned. John says he is prevented from selling the property and the only transfer of ownership allowed is to the U.S. Park Service."

Mount Shasta, a volcano, created nearly 600,000 years ago stood at 14,179 feet, the second highest peak in the Cascades. The cabin was halfway up the Southwest slope from the village of Mount Shasta. The town sat where an unnamed stream joined Big Springs Creek which became Cold Creek and eventually the South fork of the Sacramento River. Private transportation was prohibited on the mountain and supplies could be dropped off only by the Park Service officers.

Before he retired for the night a bald-headed Alcohol, Tobacco and Firearms (ATF) agent in Boise checked the Colliers' vehicle location through its onboard black box to find the vehicle at Mt. Shasta as expected. Their grapes also showed them at Mt Shasta.

Julie and Andrew as most everyone carried multi-purpose communication devices that came to be generically called grapes as in an earlier time another fruit name attached to early technology. The personal link to the world allowed multi-media links in one device. They also contained a sensitive tracking chip that could pinpoint their position within a few feet and monitored all phone calls, inner and outernet searches, file uploads and downloads, and mail. Some people found this oversight obtrusive, some found it prudent for safety reasons and others didn't know or care.

The Colliers' location was not as the bald-headed agent hoped. Since the embarrassment of the fourth of July 2039 in which he was flattened by the illegal gun butt of Andrew's neighbor, Jim, the agent had been on a mission. Orders to vacate Andrew and Jim's arrest warrants ate on him. Catching Andrew, Julie or Jim at illegal activity was his self-defined mission.

Julie and Andrew joined the line at the Park Service center at 10:00. It was 12:30 when they presented their credentials and a letter from John Whitehouse to the attending officer.

"It would've been nice to get some notice you were coming."

"I checked the website and phoned but the only advice I got was to show up early."

"Well you are lucky. You are only the second party needing to have supplies delivered today."

Andrew wondered what the others in line ahead of them were doing but thought better of asking. "Great, we appreciate all the help you can give us."

"I have John's card on file for payment but I will also need both of yours. Come back at 3:00 and the supplies should be loaded and we can take you to the cabin. But if you're staying for a month we'll need to resupply you. We can only haul a week's worth."

"Thanks, we'll be back at 3:00."

Out of hearing distance Julie said, "Wow that went well, perhaps a harbinger of a great month."

At 3:00 an officer led them to an off-road vehicle filled with supplies. "Are we ready?" asked Julie.

"You have your orientation completion certificate with you, right?"

"What do you mean?"

"I can't take you up until you have completed orientation."

"How do we get that?"

"The next session starts at 10:30 in the morning."

Julie looked at Andrew. He shrugged his shoulders and smiled at her. She got his message about the positive thoughts thing and forced a nearly genuine return smile.

After another night at the Holiday-Marriott, Julie and Andrew sat in the orientation room with two other couples. The Mount Shasta Education and Compliance officer conducted the orientation.

"Part of your obligation is to protect the valuable plant life unique to the eco-system."

The officer gave a geological history of the area and the volcano's history including the last eruption in the eighteenth century. He then proceeded to describe varieties of unique plant life including the Chaparral Iris, Giant Blazing Star, Soft Arnica, and Creeping Sage…

"Please forego the temptation to pick any plant species. It is absolutely prohibited and if we find you have picked plants you will be evicted immediately and fined…."

"…You need to realize that a waste placement area is at all locations and waste placement is only allowed in those areas."

A member of another couple attending the orientation asked, "What do you categorize as waste?"

"Put all paper, bottles and food waste in the appropriate trash containers. Human waste is to be only deposited in the HWPAs."

Sensing he has lost them, he clarified, "HWPA's, that's Human Waste Placement Area."

Julie who studied some plant biology in college interjected, "Isn't urine a good fertilizer, it contains urea which is a form of nitrogen and also phosphates and potassium."

"That is true, but it can harm the plant eco-system because high concentrations can burn some plants and those that aren't burned become unnaturally fertilized and will have an advantage over neighboring plants without the fertilization."

"But what about the animals, are they unnaturally discriminating as to which plants they fertilize?"

"Lady, they are part of the natural environment."

Julie started to refute the comment, but backed off feeling Andrew's hand on her shoulder and seeing the look in his eye. But she had to wonder at the rationale that humans were not part of nature; the idea was obviously part of the post-humanist times and took her thoughts further. If humans are not part of nature and nature is all the product of evolution, then is anything human part of something else? Did a materialist just make an unintentional argument for intelligent design?

Her philosophical deliberation was interrupted by hearing the word surveillance, a key word given her security training.

"Everyone here should realize that in addition to random checks the park is monitored by cameras and miniature drones patrol the area on a frequent basis. Enjoy your stay here but remain cognizant of your social responsibility. Expulsion from the park will cost you HCI (Health Care Index) and CSR (Credit Suitability Rating) points."

The officer hesitated briefly and added with a smile, "And any violations cause us a lot of paperwork. Please don't make more work for us."

After a thorough explanation of plant life on the slope Officer Johnson started on the fauna including among others, Mountain Beaver, Bushy-tailed Wood Rat, and the Long-tailed Meadow Mouse.

Following a break for lunch the two couples listened to a description of the water table underneath the alluvium soils. It was hard to miss his admonitions against drinking any stream water.

"Remember the stream water will appear clean and pure; it is not. Anyone needing to be evacuated because of some bacterial agent ingested from the water will, well it would not bode well on her HCI index." Julie couldn't help wondering how the animals survived.

"Your supplies will include a small gazebo type tent. We strongly urge you to use your sun screen and if sitting outside use the tent. Skin burns easily at this altitude and sun burns are considered a voluntary anomaly to proper health care and treated accordingly."

With orientation certificates in hand they rolled a cart to their car and gathered items for the wilderness stay. Before locking the car Andrew pulled his grape.

"What do you think?"

"I think we can get by without these for a few weeks."

"What about your hair brush?"

Julie always carried the hair brush in her purse, pocket or fanny pack. It was the instrument that saved Andrew at O'Hare airport in Chicago. The unique weapon specially designed for her delivered an adjustable dose of Antisolo tranquillizer with air injection.

"Okay, I'll leave it. A bear's claws would do me in before I could get close enough to use it. But you must promise you won't need to be saved."

Once their luggage was searched for prohibited items they were transported to the cabin. Julie and Andrew unloaded the cargo under the watchful eye of a Teamster's Union member. Most of the weight was the reusable glass water bottles.

"Have a great time," she told them pulling away.

"We intend to. Thanks for your help."

Once organized Julie and Andrew headed for a quick exploratory walk before sunset, then settled into wooden chairs on a small cedar porch and watched the sun sink lower in the mountain sky. Andrew pulled his chair close to Julie and without a word they felt in harmony with themselves and nature. With Mount Shasta at their back they watched the sun gradually set over the far off mountain range.

After the sun disappeared Andrew asked, "What shall we do now?"

"We are on what is called a honeymoon."

He smiled and followed her in the cabin.

The sun rose high over the peak of Mount Shasta before they were out of bed. The double bed was comfortable. King and queen sized beds had been prohibited for over a decade. Whether they were a wasteful use of material Andrew didn't care, he was comfortable. Julie did care although it had nothing to do with Andrew.

The first day at the camp was cloudy, and they went for two long walks. They were amazed that a stream a few hundred yards from John's cabin was clear enough to see trout swimming. On the way back to the cabin Julie heard an unnatural buzz, caught a glimpse of a drone out of the corner of her eye and alerted Andrew not be too obvious looking. But Andrew stared in startled awe at a flying object the size of a model plane he had put together as a boy. It made two circles and left.

"Amazing; I've heard about them but this is the first I've seen."

"Yes, kind of creepy. Actually they call them Aerial Citizen Protection Units (ACPU)." Quickly interpreting the glance from Andrew she stopped and didn't add what she was thinking.

Three days into their stay with the sun shining bright Julie gathered the canvas gazebo and headed for the stream. "Let's set the awning up partially over the stream and we can sit and fish."

Andrew hadn't caught the meaning of her words, but he helped her set up the sun protection. With the tent set up and two folding chairs at the water's edge, Julie headed for a maple tree on a rise near the stream. She returned dragging an eight-foot limb from a maple tree and proceeded to strip it of stems and leaves.

"What do you plan to do with that, beat off bears?"

"Well, I'm going to fish for dinner."

She sat beside him, pulled a reel of cord from her pocket and fiddled with the lining of her jacket until she produced a metallic arc about five centimeters long with a barb and sharp point on one end and a loop on the other.

"What the... Where did you get... Isn't that a fishing hook?"

"I picked up the digital blueprints at the speakeasy in Boise last week, and printed it on our 3-D copier before we left."

Speakeasies, reincarnations of the hundred-year-old gathering places that had been havens for illegal alcohol and gambling, were gaining numbers across the country. Near the mid-point of the twenty-first century they had become places to exchange politically incorrect ideas, in addition to find prohibited items and the software to make them. Some speakeasies had been compromised with undercover agents from the acronym alphabet soup of government agencies, but a number of those agents were transformed into double agents.

"Hopefully, the Boise speakeasy is as safe as the one in Midland," Andrew thought out loud as Julie awkwardly tried to attach the cord to the hook.

"You really are going to fish, aren't you? What if we get caught?"

"Well the awning should protect us from those flying snoops. I'll dress what we catch right here and we are allowed a small fire every other night."

He watched her trying to put together some semblance of a fishing contraption and took it from her. "If we are going to do it, let's do it right."

She watched him expertly knot the line into the fish hook and attach it to the maple rod. "I see the engineer in you coming out."

Although she was right about Andrew's innate inclination to make order out of chaos, and efficiency out of slapdash, Andrew wouldn't admit it.

"Not really. When I was young my grandfather took me fishing. It was a great time. I learned much, least of which was how to fish."

Julie thought about what he had said and inquired, "When you said *it was a great time,* did you mean you and him had a great time or something bigger?"

"Both."

"But isn't there something else I need?" she asked.

"Perhaps you can will the fish to offer themselves."

"Don't be funny. You know about fishing. What shall I use for bait?

Andrew ventured to a stand of tall grass and came back holding a grasshopper. "I found a volunteer."

"Was there any pushing and shoving in the volunteer line?"

Continuing their playful banter he answered, "No I just picked who I thought was the most succulent looking."

She handed him the hook. "Do you mind?"

"The lady who has no trouble immobilizing people or dogs with an Antisolo injection is afraid of a grasshopper?"

"I didn't hear you complaining when I rescued you from the TSA agents at the airport."

With the small fire they were allowed that day and a skillet meant for vegetable frying from the cabin, they soon had a pair of two pound trout ready to eat. They were delicious.

Julie scanned the sky for overhead eyes. Seeing none she walked downstream and bent to wash the skillet in the mountain stream.

Andrew remembered the first time he saw her in the jeans she was wearing, now slightly faded but still gently gripping her body and attracting his attention. He had been waiting for her in his car while she shopped for clothes that day. As their quick get-away from the airport left her without clothes other than what she was wearing, he took her shopping. Seeing her that day in something other than his oversized workout clothes caused him to look at her differently. He didn't look at her differently today in one sense, but in another he did.

As she bent to wash the skillet her white knit top raised exposing bare skin in the gap to the top of her jeans. He was glad he met her. Thinking further he was glad that she saved his life, opened his mind to what he denied, but mostly he was glad she was his wife.

"Were you staring at me?" she asked sitting down beside him under the awning.

"Yes, with a body as lovely as yours, why wouldn't I?"

She kissed him. He kissed her back.

The kiss, the fire, real food digesting and the warmth of the day made the cool water look appealing. Julie took her shoes off, rolled up her jeans and dangled her feet in the water.

Andrew joined her. "It's nice here, isn't it? Imagine being the first settlers here, fending for ourselves. Doing what they needed to do. Amazing how they did it."

"I'm sure you could have built a nice log cabin. If fact you probably had an ancestor who was very good at it and passed it down to my engineer husband."

"Yes, I think I would enjoy building a cabin from logs."

"If you could choose, would you choose to have lived back then?" Julie asked.

"Probably, but we don't have that choice."

"Always so practical and reserved, aren't you?"

"Maybe or sometimes," he answered only to wonder if she was suggesting he was too practical. *Maybe she was right,* he thought. Now there was no reason at all for being practical or reserved. He pulled his shirt off followed by his jeans and stood knee deep in the cool steam looking back at her.

"What are you doing?"

"I'm being impractical. We used to call it skinny dipping. Want to join me?" he said as he tossed his underwear on the bank.

"What about...?" she asked as she tilted her head up.

"I don't remember any prohibitions against this. Don't be so practical."

"No, you don't taunt me with the impulsive," she said tossing her bra to the bank.

"Still your turn," he replied looking at the sun glistening off her wet breasts.

"Check," she said as she added her panties to the laundry on the bank.

He reached her, pulled her to him and whispered, "Checkmate."

They were nearly shoulder deep in the stream and oblivious to the humming buzz until it grew in volume. On the mechanical voyeur's second pass they waved at it.

The drone was programmed to investigate and document prohibited activity, nudity was not on the list. As its controlling mechanism was digital, rather than human, it had no interest in nudity and moved on.

With both chuckling at the non-interest of the drone Andrew said, "It's a good thing we can laugh."

"We just as well," answered Julie as she held a double handful of clear stream water and slowly raised it to her mouth and shyly tasted it.

"Are you sure?"

"Yes, the trout seem to be doing well as are the chipmunks and coyote. What do you think the pioneers drank?" Again she scooped up her clasped hands full of clear water, swallowed and challenged him. "Go ahead."

"But, ...you know, what if...?"

"What will be, will be."

They drank mostly from the stream for the rest of the trip and emptied the water bottles on plants.

The day before they were to leave Julie carried her jacket into the woods. Using her jacket to shield any observation she pulled her knife and gathered an assortment of purple Chaparral Iris. Andrew entered the cabin to find a freshly cut bouquet.

"What do you think?"

"Gorgeous, but what are we going to do with them tomorrow?"

"We'll bury them. Let's enjoy and celebrate our last day here. Later they went for a swim and as soon as the sun was down went to bed earlier than normal and stayed late in the morning.

Julie arose feeling unusually fresh with newfound warmth. She couldn't place her finger on the sensation. The clean air and fresh water maybe, but they had been in the remote for nearly a month. It was something she couldn't describe, a type of fullness, completeness. She not only felt close as ever to Andrew, it was more. Maybe it was closeness to nature, but it was her definition of nature, a cycle, yes a cycle of nature.

The park check out process was much easier than the check in. Once their bags were checked for who-knows-what someone might carry out, they were out of the park. After an early dinner they again checked into the Holiday-Marriott and soon retired for an early morning start home.

On the return trip they discussed plans for the week. Julie informed Andrew of new security precautions she was initiating at ARC. Andrew talked of the change in the engineering department's focus toward development of robotic 3-D printers, pneumatic material handling systems and what it meant for the machine shop.

"Something we've put off that we need to do next week is the flu shot. I believe next week is the deadline."

"You know more people are avoiding it these days."

"Why would anyone not want to get the shot? If your health records don't show you've been vaccinated, it's an automatic reduction to your HCI.

"Do you believe everything you hear?"

"Well, no, but…"

Julie interrupted him, "For a fee some doctors can be persuaded to dispose of a dose and mark your records that you have had the shot."

"We're not home yet and we agreed only positive thoughts on this trip."

"I know, I'm sorry," Julie said as she leaned into him and kissed him on the cheek. "It has indeed been a very positive trip."

"Any society that would give up a little liberty to gain a little security will deserve neither and lose both."

Benjamin Franklin

Chapter 2

The White House.

Although the President had been elected primarily because of the recognition he fraudulently received from averting the deadly asteroid in 2039, he did not intend to be a caretaker President. He intended to use the talents that had made him President to manipulate the media he couldn't control outright into advancing what he deemed was in the best interests of society.

Advancing policies that benefited humankind was a noble cause, one that required a strong hand. Given that his lessers would stumble into policies less than advantageous to their own good, directing them was his responsibility. He held his goals worthy of measures some might find outside of the realm of proper governance, but an antidote always resonated within his mind. You must break a few eggs to make an omelet.

As was the case with many other issues, a third of the population believed the Russian version that the National Aeronautics and Space Administration (NASA) didn't have anything to do with saving civilization from the asteroid; a third believed it did and a third didn't care. The President had plans to alter the divergence of opinion.

The director of the Homeland Security Agency (HSA), the National Security Agency (NSA), the Internal Revenue Agency (IRS) and his press secretary arrived at the White House on time to finalize plans for a greater good.

"Are we ready?" asked the President."

"Everything's a go. We've double checked all systems out at sea and have backups in place," answered the director of HSA.

"Are you absolutely sure the thing will fail and I won't be in any danger?"

"Absolutely, but we must make it look real and creditable."

The President asked the director of NSA, "Are you set up to tie that kid from Colorado to this?"

"The evidence has been planted."

"How did we come up with the Hamlin kid studying at Georgetown?"

The director of NSA answered, "Actually he was part of a divide and separate ploy a few years ago. He was in a group of four kids we found to be together at a number of flash demos. We made sure the others didn't get re-enrolled the next semester in college, but we made sure Hamlin was promoted to a better school."

"I have to say the divide and separate strategy works very well. It uses jealousy and suspicion to break personal and ideological bonds and is much more effective than issuing the same punishments."

"An ingenious tactic, I think you were the author of it, correct?"

"Maybe not the author, but I utilized it heavily at NASA. It will be better if we conclude the investigation soon and look competent with it. People don't like uncertainty."

"We'll nail him quickly, sir."

"Okay. Will we be able to connect him with these crazy flash demonstrations?"

Spontaneous demonstrations had become common throughout the country before the successful asteroid aversion propaganda. They were named flash demonstrations because the protesters gath-

For the COMMON GOOD

ered and dispersed quickly. The protest organization was minimal primarily because of the state's ability to track people via grapes, vehicle black boxes and hundred of thousands of facial identification cameras. The flashes were an expression of citizenry frustration at an elite-anointed agenda. It was an agenda sculptured by the proper ideologically credentialed whose moral compass held hope for the greatest good. The President intended to squelch impediments to the benefit of all.

"Yes, we've documented his participation in many of the demonstrations. And from his e-mail, phone, and social media connections we can link him to many others, and we've implanted more links."

"Don't worry about others. We want to singularly place as much blame as we can on him. Naming others only widens the scope of family and friends creating more sympathy. For the others, we'll ramp up the IRS beyond what they've been doing for decades, but let's talk about this first. What about the evidence?"

"We've upgraded his 3-D printing device to print with different materials, added the needed software and created a false printing history. We have also produced records of him purchasing a quantity of materials. The sum of what material is left and what was used will equal the amount he purchased making neat circumstantial evidence from inventory."

Turning to his press secretary who had been his assistant during his tenure as information director at NASA, "Does the media understand how important my speech on extending freedom tomorrow will be?"

"Yes, the networks are already hyping it as an ingenious triangleization policy. Some are saying it is co-opting the issues from the other side."

"Good."

To the director of the IRS, "I want you people to nail anyone associated with these flash demonstrations. Anyone connected to—even two to three removed from—this Colorado boy. I want nailed. It will be a time of maximum leverage for us. The public will demand action. Let's not waste it. I want these throwbacks to another time bled broke from legal fees trying to stay out of jail. I'm tired of 40 years of the IRS pussy-footing around the edges with these people, half-assed using your muscle. Do I make myself clear?"

"Yes, Mr. President."

"And if you don't do it I'll find someone who will."

"I assure you, Mr. President."

"What time does the copter pick me up for Arlington Cemetery?"

"9:00, sir."

"Let no one say that this President shied away from doing what needed to be done even if it involves personal risk. Timorous and faint-hearted behavior caused Lincoln near failure. I will be bold."

The President walked to Marine One at 9:10 appropriately late to convey normality. The number of reporters on the White House lawn was more than normal. Although all national outlets were set-up at the Arlington speech site, his press secretary had allowed unusual access to local reporters from around the country for his White House departure, including Tony Johnson, a reporter from KRMT in Des Moines. It was the first time Tony had been on the White House lawn in any capacity. He wondered if the station news editor would be impressed.

"Will your speech represent a permanent policy change?" yelled a reporter at the President.

Hardly turning, the President shouted an answer back, "We'll see." He ignored further questions and boarded the helicopter.

The pilot and no one else in the helicopter had reason to be anxious. But the President feeling his heart rate elevated felt like a sitting duck. He hoped the gun was in fact loaded with blanks.

The helicopter neared the Potomac less than a thousand feet above the Lincoln Memorial as the President looked out the window. The crew of the helicopter had never seen him do so before.

Ten minutes earlier a ¾ ton pick-up truck with a rack extended three feet above the bed pulled onto the South-bound shoulder of the George Washington Parkway (GWP). An inconspicuous Toyota pulled in behind the truck and picked up the driver. With morning traffic it was a few minutes before the Toyota re-entered the traffic but was well out-of-sight before a Virginia Highway trooper pulled behind the abandoned truck to investigate.

An agent of a special branch of the HSA was on foot in Lady Bird Johnson Memorial Park within a quarter of a mile of the abandoned truck. At the first sight of the helicopter, the agent speed-dialed a number on his disposable cell phone. The signal activated a sequence in the truck. A tube was lifted toward the helicopter, radar locked on the helicopter, fire bellowed from the truck bed and a missile rose from the truck bed.

The co-pilot of the helicopter saw the marine helicopter's defensive laser system engage nearly simultaneously with the radar locked-on warning light blinking. It was all out of his hands.

Although the FIM-92 Stinger missile was only 6 feet long and three inches in diameter it carried a deadly punch in its 22 pounds. The upgraded radar-guided version of the missile was on target to bring the helicopter down. However, the solid fuel ignited prematurely raising a ball of fire in the truck bed and the missile expelled its fuel before it could reach the helicopter. Less than a hundred feet from the President's helicopter, the missile fell to the ground.

Patrolman Joshua Tremble found no one in the cabin of the truck and was looking for the driver when he heard the hum of the electric lift on the missile tube. Noticing the bed of the truck was odd he stood on the bumper and peered in the bed as the missile ignited. Four cars collided on the Parkway as the drivers were distracted by Patrolman Tremble inundated with flames flailing to get away. He died in route to the hospital.

An unusually observant President heard something and stormed to the cabin door. "What's that noise? What's wrong?"

"We were locked on by radar and engaged by a missile, but our defense laser system negated the attack."

Using the words he had rehearsed in his mind the President said, "Is there more coming. Can we get down fast?"

"We'll be down at the cemetery in ten seconds, sir."

Although she didn't know why and how, the co-pilot was mistaken that the laser had taken down the missile. The powerful laser stream missed the missile by ten feet but hit a car on the North bound GWP causing a pile up. Karen Simmons was commuting from Groveton. Through her windshield the laser moved across her body nearly slicing her in half.

As planned the President stayed in the grounded helicopter for over an hour while the news of the event reached a crescendo in the media. By the time the President headed for the outside podium all the networks and cable outlets were locked into live coverage.

"Fellow citizens, forgive me if I sound dismayed and disheveled. The prospect someone, foreign or domestic, has attempted to negate the results of your will expressed in a popular election... well... disheartens me. Frankly, if not for the great work of the Secret Service and HSA I might have been buried here in a few days."

Holding up a binder of paper he continued, "This was to be the speech I very much wanted to deliver today. My hope was to extend liberties in the country by rolling back protective measures taken in the last few years. Unfortunately, given my sworn duty to protect and defend, I can not do that today.

Be assured we will find out who was responsible for this and measures will be taken to make sure never again will someone try to trump the will of the people."

The President hurriedly left the stage for a waiting limo. His press secretary astutely picked up the binder he dropped containing blank pages. A reporter for News You Can Trust (NYCT) network thought it strange that the President for the first time had a hard copy of a speech but quickly put it out of his mind.

The Presidential motorcade return to the White House was delayed by rerouting around accidents on the GWP. In route the President was informed that two people had been killed and a number injured on the Parkway most likely related to the failed assassination attempt.

Unfortunate as the deaths were, thought the President, he and his press secretary planned to make the most of the highway tragedy. The President attended both funerals and spoke at Patrolman Tremble's.

Two days after funerals for the highway victims the FBI director, Bill Silvers, met with the President, his press secretary and directors of the Secret Service, NSA, HSA and the IRS.

Director Silvers gave a report on what the agency had discovered. "The truck used for the mission was stolen with a retrofitted black box. In the truck was found finger prints of Aaron Hamlin, 21 years old, originally from Colorado, now a student at Georgetown University majoring in political science. He has been caught on video at a number of flash demonstrations and is suspected of having a leadership role of undetermined rank. His prints were also found on a disposable mini-grape which we determined was the triggering device in a trash can at Lady Bird Memorial Park."

"How did he get the missile?" the President asked knowing the answer he would hear.

"Frankly, he made it. We found the newest version of a multi-material 3D printer at his apartment and tools used to assemble the printed components in a garage rented by him. In a forensic examination we found remnants of software to print and build the components on his computer."

"That does it! Have you picked him up?"

"Yes, we have but a number of aspects bother me about this."

"Sounds like a slam dunk to me. Let's move on."

"Respectfully, Mr. President, I have reservations. Our investigation has much more to process before we can conclusively give a final report."

"Get over them. I'm turning this over to HSA.

"But Mr. President, I think this investigation falls under…

He was cut off abruptly, "If you will, now excuse us Bill."

The President and remaining officials put together a plan to demonize the participants in flash demonstrations. They also discussed the introduction and sale to the public and congress of a bill written before the election. The bill would be called "The Domestic Safety and Job Protection Act. It would require registration and NSA digital monitoring of all 3D printers and implementation of a tax for their sale and use. It would also prohibit any digital blueprint sale without government certification. As per title the bill would keep the means to ferment trouble out of the wrong hands and save manufacturing jobs which were being lost to 3-D printing.

Bill Silvers in route back to FBI headquarters shared his reservations with the assistant director. "Why would someone plan such an elaborate assassination attempt and be so clumsy as to leave fingerprints in the truck and on the trigger phone. He would have had to scale the fence to get in the park after leaving the truck if he had no help. Someone should have seen him… And failing to wipe the computer clean? We also have witnesses who saw a car pickup the truck driver, but this Hamlin was in the park? Why have I been ordered to shut down the investigation?"

His assistant agreed that it didn't make sense and in an hour was on the phone with the director of HSA.

That evening in a bar not far from Dupont Circle two former college friends met. Tony Johnson, the KRMT reporter from Des Moines and Adam Winhaar, a reporter with NYCT. Even though Adam was younger they had attended journalism school together.

Tony's career started as an engineer with Atlas Transportation, but as a Community Improvement Corp hire he had been relegated to remedial work. He had passed information on to the ATF about his employer's activities which got him fired in exchange for a promise of entry into FBI training. He never received entry into the FBI, so he ended up in journalism school. It was something about the way Dan Barnmore fired him that inspired him. He liked reporting and although Des Moines was his home he hoped to move to bigger markets.

Some considered Adam and Tony from another time when reporters instinctively questioned what politicians said. That required work and an inquisitive, skeptical attitude of which they saw little in their peers. Over drinks Tony wondered why small town reporters just happened to be invited to the White House lawn before a major news event. Adam talked about the written speech in a binder he had never before seen the President carry.

They both thought it ironic that an outrageous act of one person would conveniently allow the President to scrap a plan to lessen governmental controls.

"Was it a gift too good to be true?" Tony pondered out loud.

Adam ignored his question and asked a deeper one. "Why doesn't anyone else wonder or do they?"

Later in the week the Marine commandant who was responsible for the investigation into the incident gave a report to the director of the HSA.

"We have validated that the laser did not hit the missile. In fact it hit the Karen Simmons car. The missile failed because of an internal flaw. It ran out of propellant within just a few feet of the helicopter."

"How close did it come?"

"Within perhaps fifty feet."

The HSA director was taken back momentarily. It wasn't supposed to get nearly that close. What went wrong? But ultimately the outcome was satisfactory, in fact with the two funerals, more than satisfactory. He studied the Marine commandant and said, "Its best we seal this report and it not go further, understood?"

"Yes sir."

Julie and Andrew sat at the breakfast table a few weeks after their return from Mount Shasta. Andrew was eating. Julie was not. They had planned to go to work later and were discussing the reports of Aaron Hamlin's arrest in Washington.

They hadn't made the connection to the Colorado boys who two years previously they rescued from agents at the rest stop. Ethan Alderman they remembered from the group. Aaron they did not until Barry Bradley called and informed them.

"We probably should have done more to help them understand the danger. But who would have thought one of them would have gone this far," lamented Andrew.

"Well we had bigger things to worry about at the time. And do you really believe what we heard on the news? I'm not sure I believe the report."

"I don't know what to believe sometimes. Anyway I'm glad Barry said Ethan is not connected with Aaron any longer. I understand he's working somewhere in Iowa. In fact, Barry also said Eric Hansen, the former NASA director, is also in Iowa.

Julie abruptly got up and trotted to the bathroom. Andrew knew something was wrong and he thought she might have been put off by his *I don't know what to believe* remark until he heard her vomiting.

Her face was flushed when she came out. "Did you get the flu shot?"

"The records show I did."

"Oh, no. Really you should have. I'm sorry you got the virus, but I won't," he said trying to make a point.

"Yes, I know you won't and I don't think I have the flu."

"What's going on?"

"Please, let's not talk about it for a few days."

A week later for the third time Julie didn't eat breakfast and had an upset stomach.

Andrew wanted an answer, "What's going on Julie?"

"Since I see you're sitting. I'm pregnant."

He immediately acquired a *'you're kidding'* look but didn't verbalize it.

After an extended silence Andrew asked, "What are we going to do?"

"We can't ignore it."

"It's time we leave. Let's put together a plan to exit through Canada."

"I agree, it's probably for the best, it's meant to be."

"You know how this happened, don't you?"

"Of course we both knew when you started drinking the spring water at Mt Shasta that it was possible. I have no regrets, do you?"

Andrew walked behind her chair, bent encircling her with his arms and whispered in her ear, "None." As she turned her head he kissed her.

For years all drinking water, municipal or bottled, contained the chemical Phoroppin. It effectively eliminated sperm mobility. The male contraceptive was introduced to limit population growth and control who would be allowed to propagate. In order to conceive a child an antidote to Phoroppin had to be obtained from the state. The application process involved the Health Service Agency's (HSA) calculation of a prospective couple's Suitability for Prodigy Index (SPI). Among the components of the index were the health of the potential parents and their families, education level, unspecified genetic traits, social compliance scores and unknown political considerations.

The United Nations gave nations an annual quota of allowed births. The United States quota was 1.5 births per couple, which would depopulate the country at an acceptable rate in line with post-humanist values. Hopeful would-be parents were given an antidote to Phoroppin from the highest SPI downward until the antidotes produced 95% of the national quota.

The other 5% of births were achieved by a lottery system for the allocation of the antidote. This allowed for some diversity and kept alive the prospect of hope for all couples wishing children.

Fraud to obtain children was becoming more widespread. As marriage was not a requisite to obtain an ample SPI, men who could not obtain a sufficient SPI with their lady of choice hired other men of the right criteria to file for a SPI with the prospective mother. Once the license and antidote were issued the unqualified hopeful father took the antidote and by modern definition an illegitimate child was conceived. In order to control the process and eliminate fraud, Congress for some time had debated requiring all conceptions to be performed artificially allowing verification of the source of the sperm. It had met solid resistance.

Phoroppin stayed in the system two to three weeks. Julie and Andrew knew their four-week stay on Mt. Shasta with Andrew drinking the unpolluted mountain water made her pregnancy possible, but with her in her forties doubtful.

Julie's annual mandatory medical checkup was due in two weeks. There was no avoiding it. Once her pregnancy was exposed without a permit the fetus would be scheduled for termination.

Julie and Andrew confided in their closest friends, Alice and Barry Bradley. Barry, always a source of information through digitally clandestine expertise, validated that terminations were running nearly a month behind the mandating of them. And the requisition of terminations usually lagged a week behind the identification of an unauthorized pregnancy.

"We'll need to think about the timing of our departure," said Julie.

"You know we are going to miss both of you. Perhaps it's time for us to leave also." Alice offered looking at Barry.

"I know how you feel Alice, but I've too much to do here," Barry replied.

As Julie and Andrew started to leave Andrew said, "We'll let you know and see you soon." The hugs lasted longer than normal causing Andrew to realize this would be harder than he envisioned, but necessary.

At home Andrew summarized the timeline. "A week till your checkup, a week until they submit the order and four weeks wait for the procedure. We have six weeks. To be safe I suggest we leave in three. We'll have some time to get our affairs in order."

"But if the wait for the procedure is only one week, we'll be cutting it close. My appointment is a week from today, January 15th."

"You're probably right, let's err on the side of caution, let's leave two weeks from today. I'll notify Torrence we'll be crossing the border the 22nd at the spot he's been using. For safety, I'm sure he'll suggest we head to Poland until things cool down.

"Given the talk at the speakeasy about government agents crossing the border to kidnap expatriates and bring them back, going to Poland makes sense at least for awhile. After we are safe it would be nice to see Melissa and other friends again on the island-boat."

After the Atlas Transportation Company successfully diverted the asteroid from a collision course with earth, most employees including Melissa, Dan Barnmore's wife, discreetly resettled on an island-boat off the coast of Costa Rica. Originally they had dispersed to Russia, Poland and Mexico to avoid prosecution.

The worldwide collapse of individual wealth crushed the large vacation cruise lines. Former Atlas engineers and scientists with advances on consulting work from non-American companies purchased a mid-sized cruise ship at liquidation. Over two hundred scientists and their families became a confederation of individuals on the movable island. They worked and lived outside the purview of nation states. In addition to sustaining themselves with consulting work, the island-boat inhabitants worked on projects to help the freedom movement in the states.

At her annual checkup January 15 the doctor asked Julie if she knew she was pregnant.

"I didn't know, but I suspected," she hedged.

"I don't see a permit on your records."

With no answer the doctor continued, "You know I have no choice but to report this."

"I know." Julie held no grudge; the doctor was doing her job, but more than that she had no choice.

"I am going to perform a sonogram."

"But why?"

"It is just required."

Julie sensed surprise in the doctor's eyes as she watched her study a monitor out of Julie's vision. "What is it?"

The doctor shut the screen off and made some notes avoiding eye contact.

"Please, what did you see?"

"Believe me, it won't do you any good to know."

"Tell me or I'm refusing to leave this room."

Knowing her index score as a medical provider didn't need another incident of a negative kind, she reluctantly said, "I saw twins."

"Wow," was Andrew's only response to the news when Julie told him. He didn't know whether to be thrilled with the news. But if it pleased Julie so it would him.

They had not discussed their imminent departure with anyone including John Whitehouse. Not that they didn't trust people close to them, it was just better to avoid burdening people with information they might need to hide. Alice and Barry were the only ones to know.

They avoided packing until the last minute just in case unexpected guests dropped by. Being too careful was not a risk; getting caught was. Packing two bags apiece would not take long but culling their list of what to take was more difficult than they imagined.

"If a society is to be free,
its government has to be controlled."

Ayn Rand

Chapter 3

Avery was concerned. In order to produce another potential prize-winning lily she needed to prevent rabbits from eating the delicate shoot breaking through the spring soil. The animal repellent she used was forbidden by the Federal Animal Protection Agency (FAPA). She had seen the Aerial Citizen Protection Unit (ACPU) overhead. She was afraid it had seen what she was doing. It had.

Mahaska County, Iowa

It was only the second quinceanera Ethan Alderman had ever attended. The coming out party for Engracia Alvarez should have been more fun than his first quinceanera, because he was sitting beside the girl's sexy older sister, who recently had become his wife. Caridad's purple flowered gown which by the designer's intent fell off a shoulder drew his eyes, among others, to a strong hint of what lay below. It was the first party of any kind that he could claim the most attractive woman in the room as his wife. He was happy to be at the party as part of the family. However, events in the news and the fate of Aaron Hamlin, a former high school friend, weighed on him.

While the women were dancing his wife's uncle, Juan, told him the meaning of Engracia's name was goodwill.

"What does my wife's name, Caridad, mean?"

"You are a very lucky man senor; it means love."

"And my boss, her mother, your sister, Adana?"

"It means skilled expert."

"How fitting she is the most competent person I've ever known."

Ethan Alderman had been a freshman in college when he and three high school friends, including Aaron Hamlin, had been caught painting a dollar sign at a rest stop in Colorado. Had they not been rescued by the chance of Atlas's nuclear escort being there, his life would be different.

His boss and Mother-in-law, Adana Alvarez, wouldn't hear of the event as chance however. According to her serendipity was a matter of providence, not luck.

Mrs. Alvarez had started working at a young age in her father's landscaping business in Illinois. He had crossed the border from Mexico when most traffic was inbound to the US. Hardworking and ambitious her father branched out into construction. Eventually his son, Juan, had taken over the landscaping segment of the business, Andana the construction side.

Andana was as industrious as her father and grew the construction business into a company employing hundreds of people including Ethan. Although her self-reliant underpinnings made it uneasy at times, she played the game necessary to acquire government construction contracts. As nearly all construction was public sector, she put up with the bureaucratic malaise. But with always a mind to efficiency, the excess overhead required for compliances and permits frustrated her.

After being identified at flash demonstrations in the summer of '39, Ethan had found himself expelled from college. He wasn't given an explanation. He was just no longer registered. Aaron was the only member of his group of four who remained in college.

Although Caridad was eight years older than Ethan they met at the University of Colorado in Boulder. He was a freshman; she was doing post-doctorate work in genetic chemistry. On an evening when she was doing research at the digital library, he interrupted her concentration with a sigh. Needing a break, noticing his bewildered gaze into the Organic Chemistry 101 textbook and remembering the help someone had offered her, she helped him. Later they had coffee, found they had an Iowa background in common and soon began seeing each other regularly. She found him to be mature beyond his years. He found her confidence and quest for substance beyond the superficial appealing. Although he had only met Julie once Caridad reminded him of her, the take-charge lady who had directed the group that saved his band of four at the rest stop in Colorado. The innate physical spark between them augmented by their complimentary personalities, background and circumstance soon evolved into a physical relationship that sizzled when they were together and smoldered while apart.

After being skipped over twice for a tenured professorship, Caridad accepted a job as a chemist with the Food and Drug Administration (FDA) back home in Iowa. The second time Ethan traveled to Iowa to see Caridad he met her mother, Adana, who offered him a job. Upon his hiring Mrs. Alvarez told him that his evaluation as an employee would be on performance only. He agreed.

Being close to his family farm was secondary to being close to Caridad. Within a year he proposed; she accepted. He excelled at construction work moving to be foreman and then job superintendant.

Andana left the dance floor and sat beside Ethan not as his boss but his Mother-in-law.

"I'm sorry for the tragic news you received."

"I know Aaron would never have contemplated killing the President. That's not what we were about. We were about changing people's ideas, not punishing people."

Placing her hand on his shoulder she said, "I'm not going to tell you I know how you feel about Aaron, but it's all part of a plan. Often we don't understand the "why", but there is a reason. I know you don't believe what you hear and neither do I or I expect most people."

"But what do we do? There must be something."

"Let the philosophical materialists plan, but they don't know they plan against the current, a higher plan. They think that with more number crunching ability, more control, and managing every aspect of our lives they can create a utopia. But, even if possible, it would be their utopia, not ours.

Just as their materialistic view says big enough computers would allow them to predict what our great grandchildren will be wearing a century from now, they try to bend our future to their will. Ironic isn't it?"

By their definition there is no free will, but then they try to exercise it. They seem to know the future without adequately explaining the past. I'm sorry I'm off on a tangent again and I just wanted to console you."

"Thank you Andana. You did and you always give me much to think about."

White House, January 20

The President received a briefing on a long term project from the NSA director for over an hour. The project offered a long term technological answer to aberrant social behavior. With more antidotes to the anti-social drug Antisolo being smuggled into the country a more effective method to control people was needed.

People arrested for anti-social activities were still placed on social farms where they were held up to three weeks and given the highly addictive Antisolo drug which mellowed their behavior crushing any inclination to question authorities. But an antidote had been developed in Russia to the addictive influence of the drug. The Russians were making money on the antidote and facilitating unrest in the US with their unwelcome export.

"We anticipate the nanotechnology will be ready for trial within two to three years. Followed by full implementation in four to five years," reported the NSA director.

"A time will come when we will need to work with the Food and Drug Administration (FDA) on the project. If you don't have upmost confidence in the director, you may want to think about it. They have a facility close to where we are working on the project in Iowa."

"Good point. I think a change is in order. How confident of security with the project are you?"

"We have taken every measure. Nothing can move within 50 miles of Mahaska County, Iowa, where the FDA and our facilities are located, without us knowing. We monitor all traffic, digital and otherwise, of all project employees and all those once removed. By the way, we have named the project TIP (Tranquility Insertion Project)."

"I like the name. But I want to employ this before I leave office. What better legacy than being known as the President who took an important initiative for the common good. People again will feel good about their government. Think of how much easier it will be for succeeding Presidents to implement beneficial change."

The director hesitated at the door. There's one other issue I need to bring to your attention. You did say you wanted to be personally updated on anything unusual with Andrew Collier, the amateur astronomer who identified the asteroid and worked with Atlas Transportation.

"Yes, what is it?"

"I understand his wife has become pregnant without a permit. The termination is scheduled for February 17. I suggest it be given priority and moved up."

"I shouldn't be surprised that he is trouble, anyone who was associated with that Barnmore guy at Atlas... But we've got to be careful how we handle him now that we allowed him some credit for the asteroid thing."

After a pause the President continued, "We made a mistake; we should have locked him up at the time, but we can't very well change course now. It would be admitting a mistake. Is there any indication he may be thinking about leaving the country?"

"None that we see, but that doesn't mean he's not planning to."

"Who is the guy's wife?"

"Julie, …let's see, formerly Julie Levine, she worked in security at Atlas."

"How high, what did she do?"

"She was just a part-time night security guard." (The director's information reflected Barry's alteration of the records)

"Given what I read on the personality profile of this guy, I still believe he is not inclined to ferment trouble. Guys who marry part-time custodial type help are not destined to be trouble makers. Let's give him a good reason not to. Have the records show the couple applied for a permit and it was granted. Change whatever records you need to make that happen. With a kid running around, it'll make him think twice.

"Actually the report indicated she is carrying twins."

"All the better. She sounds like the kind of woman who will demand a lot of help from her husband caring for twins. Get on it. But alert our people in Boise to keep a close tab on him. We absolutely don't want him leaving the country and adding to foreign propaganda."

Government databases the next morning showed Andrew and Julie with a high SPIs for which they had applied over a year ago. Suddenly Andrew's Health Care Index increased to 62 and Julie's to 74, both above the required 60 for a prodigy permit. Records showed that a permit for prodigy had been issued four months ago. The government, unwilling to vilify someone held as a semi-hero through its own distortions, quietly sanctioned their forthcoming children hoping to occupy them.

Although Julie and Andrew hadn't gotten their traveling bags out, they were organizing what they intended to take out of the country. Clothes were not a priority. Julie had laid out reminders of her parents, a Star of David necklace that her mother wore and her father's

Siddur. Andrew took the founding fathers sketch that his mother had framed from the wall. But they planned to take little as the last couple of miles to the border they would carry their bags.

After all they had been through together Julie and Andrew could not leave without telling their neighbors Jim and Nathan goodbye; telling Orlando, their son, they would avoid and leave the explanation to his parents. Sensing that the neighbors had a topic to discuss Nathan sent Orlando to his room to study. As an intuitive child with a curious nature Orlando, now twelve, hid in the stairway and watched the farewells and a few tears. He couldn't understand what he saw, a strange combination of congratulations and sadness.

"It's going to be tough, without both of you as neighbors. I sometimes think we should join you. And you'll never get to ride in my new nursery truck," said Jim, a little offset by somber goodbyes.

"You bought a new truck?" Andrew said equally uncomfortable.

"No it's another old one, but I've got a kit ordered from Poland to bypass the black box."

"Always the tinkerer, aren't you? We'll someway get together again and we and …well everyone will always be indebted to your help getting the package from Cheyenne and for the use of your old truck, or course."

Nathan suspicious Orlando was not in his room checked once the company left.

"I don't understand," he said.

"Julie and Andrew are thinking about going back to Texas for some time," Nathan lied.

"I hope they don't, I'll miss them."

"Yes we all will."

The bald-headed ATF agent was parked a block away observing Julie and Andrew walking back to their home. Being this close brought back memories of his embarrassment when Jim knocked him down that Fourth of July. Why were Jim and Andrew still loose he continued to wonder? He didn't understand the ways of his bosses, but he followed orders and his orders now were to give close surveillance and keep monitoring the Colliers' traveling bags. He would.

The agents of the ATF, Department of Alcohol, Tobacco and Firearms, had little to do enforcing their original mission. Alcohol was legal but heavily taxed, Tobacco had such harsh ramifications on people's HCI that little was used, and firearms had pretty well been driven underground, literally so in many cases. While the FBI continued to pursue violent criminals, the ATF was primarily focused on the apprehension of violators of social transgressions, often acting as the enforcement arm of regulators as opposed to statute violations.

Barry periodically scanned Julie and Andrew's home, as well as Jim and Nathan's, for listening devices. He had yet to find any. However, at the airport traveling from Texas, small devices had been placed in Julie and Andrew's bags. The devices were dormant unless the bags were moved, hence they couldn't be found by Barry. The bald-headed ATF agent stayed on the street till well past midnight. The bags remained unmoved.

At 9:00 pm Alice and Barry excitedly knocked on Julie and Andrew's back door out of the agent's view. Not knowing who it was the travelers-to-be covered their to-take stack with a blanket and answered the door.

"Good news. You have a permit."

"What are you talking about?"

"I just checked the termination scheduling and could find nothing in your name. Digging deeper I found you have a Prodigy permit dated August 7 but it was issued this morning. According to the records you applied over a year ago and you have an SPI over 80. Amazing you also both have a HCI over 60."

Skeptically Julie asked, "What do you think is going on?"

"I think they've decided to let you have children."

"Why would they do that?"

"I suspect they think allowing the two of you to have children would look good and they probably fear you might leave."

"Could it be a trick?"

"No, they have no idea we have access to those files. If it was a trick it would make no sense to bother with the records. They would just send you a bogus letter."

Alice and Barry left unsure, as were Julie and Andrew, whether they would leave their homeland.

—⁊⁊—

January 22, 2042

Julie and Andrew were undecided until the sun rose after a sleepless night. Andrew had been on the fence but Julie leaned toward leaving. The slight tip of the scale was enough and they started filling their bags.

The bald-headed ATF agent had just ordered fried peppers and eggs when his grape vibrated. It was notification that the Colliers' bags had been moved. The predetermined calls were made and soon fifty agents were on standby.

Andrew pushed the last bag into the small storage area in their car. Knowing the grapes would track them, they were left in the kitchen. Julie pulled their secure cell phone from its hiding place. "Shall we take a last walkthrough the house? Andrew asked.

The ranch home looked nothing like it had when Andrew lived alone in it. Gone was the astronomy paraphernalia strewn all over the family room. It now looked more like Julie's former apartment in Midland. Much of her furniture they had brought here. What little Andrew processed had been damaged by the ATF's search of the premises. Andrew's stuff damaged or not, Julie would have decorated to her style which pleased him. The place had a warm glow of maroon and gold creating a serene atmosphere. Looking at it, for what he expected to be the last time, he was reminded of the feeling he had when he first visited Julie in Midland.

"Remember what happened the first night I saw your touch in decorating and put some Mozart on the speakers?"

Julie shook him from a hesitant daze, "Let's go. We'll find Mozart elsewhere."

At just before 5 am Alice and Barry were watching through their front window as the couple pulled out. Julie caught sight of them waving.

The bald ATF agent followed them heading Northwest on Interstate 84. As he expected, but needed to confirm, the Colliers turned off on highway 95. He notified the Spokane ATF branch to set up a road block north of Bonner's Ferry just south of the border.

Julie and Andrew had just pulled out of the last US town on their route, only four miles from where they would exit the road and walk to the border when the secure phone startled them. It was Barry.

Julie picked up the secure cell phone. It actually was bigger than a grape, more the size of a 90's phone. The size allowed for a vial of hydrochloric acid to be contained adjacent to the interior circuit boards, most of which were designed to encrypt and hide the signals. Upon noticing the cold outside temperature of 19 degrees it displayed, Julie dialed 912852722. The code had to be entered right or the acid would melt the workings of the phone. Anyone in a number of alphabet agencies getting their hands on a secure phone would be disastrous. The code was the inverse of the temperature displayed (91), Julie and Andrew's identity code ATLAS (28527), and the inverse of the date 22. By the fifth ring the code was accepted and Julie answered.

"I've been monitoring your grapes, just in case, and you just got a message from your doctor. I'll feed it to you."

> "Mrs. Collier, this is Doctor Michaels. I don't know how
> this happened but I just received notification of your prod-
> igy permit. Since it already was in the system, it overrode
> the termination appointment. You should have told me
> you had a permit. Anyway I need to run more tests, please
> schedule an appointment soon."

They pulled the car over and listened to the message three times and sat. Looking ahead they could almost see Canada. They couldn't see the road block two miles ahead of them tucked in a swale nor did they notice two ATF cars observing them or others who had parked along side roads.

"Someone obviously wants us to have these children here."

"Maybe that should scare us," said Julie more thinking than talking.

"It's your call," Andrew said gently laying his hand on her not yet extended abdomen.

Thoughts of her father, Dan, unfinished work, and the twins all spun in her mind but when the spinning stopped it was clear. "Turn around, let's go home. It's where we are needed."

As they passed the bald ATF agent, he thought they had noticed him. They hadn't. They were too wrapped up in their decision. After blocking the road for two hours ATF agents dispersed. The bald headed ATF agent was disappointed, bitterly so.

White House

Without reservation the President replaced the director of the FDA with someone he could trust. The President was not a risk taker and understood that limiting uncertainty, particularly the reliability of subordinates, enhanced his control. He informed the director of NSA that he had appointed a close confidant, the Presidential press secretary, as the new director of the FDA.

"I think that is an excellent choice, Mr. President. With operation TIP commencing we need someone we can trust there"

"He's not too happy about uprooting his family but he understands the importance of the assignment. And you should also know that I accepted the resignation of FBI director Bill Silvers. It seems as though the pictures you obtained of him in a skirt hastened his plans for retirement. Funny how the peculiarities of the organization will end as it started."

"I want you to know the assistant director was helpful in setting it up."

"Yes, he's the new director as of today."

Before leaving the NSA director reported that Andrew Collier had nearly been apprehended leaving the country, the President was pleased with his decision-Andrew's yes, but more importantly his.

"So for some reason he came very close but changed his mind. That is good. I don't think Andrew Collier will be giving us any more trouble. Good all the way around; we don't need to explain why he was picked up. I'm guessing that night guard wife of his talked him out of it. Another good sign, she's the boss and that'll mean no trouble from him. What's her name again?"

"Julie."

"See," he said to the director of NSA. "Using our head is sometimes better than force. Besides we can't lock everyone up. Remember you catch more flies with honey than vinegar. Makes sure she gets more honey, give her another 10 HCI points."

At Julie's follow-up appointment with the doctor on her birthday, February 6, she learned she was carrying fraternal twins a boy and a girl.

Julie and Andrew quickly picked names for the babies. They would be named for heroes, Daniel Barnmore who orchestrated Atlas's interception of the asteroid and Sandra Levy whose last minute information allowed its success. Both had given their lives for their heroic effort.

On the fourth of July, three years after neighbors had saved Julie and Andrew from arrest, Julie gave birth to Sandra Levine Collier and Daniel Atlas Collier.

"The greater the power, the more dangerous the abuse."

Edmund Burke

Chapter 4

October 12, 2045
Federal Court Richmond, Virginia

"Will the defendant please rise," the federal district court judge ordered. The jury had found Aaron Hamlin guilty in just two hours the month previous. His sentence would be a surprise to no one as the federal statute was explicit about the penalty.

"I hereby sentence you, Aaron J Hamlin, to death by lethal injection at a to-be-determined federal prison at midnight on June 30 of next year."

A court officer on either side of the defendant steadied Aaron as his knees buckled upon hearing the sentence. It had been no surprise; the judge had no discretion in the sentencing, but it still hit Aaron's withered physique as a ton of bricks.

The four year ordeal of uncertainty, second guessing what he had done and why he was framed worked on his body peeling thirty pounds from a once trim frame. But it was the mental stress that had taken a larger toll.

Given the planted evidence was conclusive his lawyers had little hope of overcoming the inevitable; nevertheless it had been four years since he was charged. His lawyers, chosen for the right political connections, might have lost the case, but they acquired enough publicity to launch successful careers.

Lost in the process was a little noticed violation of the Constitution, the Sixth Amendment guarantying the right to a speedy trial. What was particularly disheartening to those who considered the constitution more than an antiquated irrelevant document was the failure of anyone to even mention it. During the four year ordeal the administration bled all the political benefit possible from Aaron's flasher connections.

The demonstrations around the country had subsided. Called at various times flash demonstrations, mobs, and anti-social protests, they were now called flashes and the participants flashers by the media. Intended or not, it linked the flashers to a craze in the previous century of people who chose to run naked in public for no apparent reason other than the shock effect.

The White House

"It's five minutes, Mr. President."

"Yes, I'm ready." The President responded as he headed toward the press conference. The President who was reliably ten minutes late for scheduled appearances always requested a heads up five minutes before his ten minute late entry. He was not a tardy person, but understood well the need for orchestrating a message.

Media outlets were assembled. They understood the President would give an opening statement. Following there would be seven questions all approved by the White House in advance. Long ago news outlets learned that failure to comply with the new protocol limited their access to news. In the past that would not have deterred

For the COMMON GOOD

aggressive reporters as most news was not made in Washington. It was no longer the case.

"First I want to say a few words about the conclusion of a trial that tested the power of you, the American people, to set the direction of this government. Anti-social elements intent upon regression to a harsh bygone era finally crossed the line by challenging your right to have the people you elect serve you with your best interests at heart. However, despite the treachery shown, my government is not inclined toward vindictiveness. We will, by example, demonstrate a desire for healing and social unification in the country. I am hereby signing papers to commute the death sentence pronounced yesterday on a misguided individual who would have taken my life to 30 years in prison...
First question, please."

"Mr. President, are those seeking to circumvent the ban on non-authorized use of 3-D printers altering two-dimensional printers to function as 3-D printers?"

"Yes, it has come to our attention that is happening. I am proposing a bill for priority in the congress to require all two-dimensional printers be attached to the internet in order to monitor manufacturing on the sly. We will not allow another near travesty to befall the country."

"Mr. President, many people find it hard to believe Mr. Hamlin did not receive some assistance in the plot. Have all investigations into the assassination attempt stopped?"

"Yes, they have. At some point we must move on and come together as a country. I'm happy to work with all my countrymen. If we can work together there is no limit to where we can go for the betterment of all humankind."

Back in the oval office the NSA director said, "Mr President you were right. Although I was skeptical about the clemency thing, immediate polls show people were moved by your empathy and are now more receptive to internet monitoring of all printing."

"It's about the big picture we must never forget that. Never get sidetracked, keep your eye on the ball and, besides why in the world would we want to risk making a martyr of the boy?

Eddyville, Iowa

The committee of microbiological designers charged with annually upgrading the flu vaccine finished a video conference with the Center for Disease Control in Atlanta. It was the designer's charge to design a flu vaccine that would encourage the body to produce antibodies to combat the flu virus. The vaccine needed redesign as the virus naturally mutated. They discussed the challenges presented to them by not having the virus at the Iowa facility.

"Do you have any idea how difficult it is to fashion a vaccine for a hypothetical virus of which we only know the chemical structure without any conception of the phonotypical characteristics? It would be easy to build the virus here without risking shipment and eliminate speculating on its traits," said a frustrated associate vaccine design chemist, Dr. Caridad Alvarez-Alderman, PhD, to her colleagues.

The director of vaccine design echoed her concern. "I know it's a challenge but we understood that from the origin of this project. We have no choice; we'll do the best we can do. Since the Center for Disease Control Center (CDC) in Atlanta evidently finds this imaginary virus so vile they won't even let us test components of its structure, we'll just do the best we can. As we've discussed I think we should develop numerous potential vaccines so they have a variety to test."

"Doesn't anyone concern themselves with the duplication of effort and the laborious design uncertainties that are unnecessary? We have viral security measures that equal any the CDC has."

"Caridad, be careful what you say. I thought we were making progress. Do you see getting a number of vaccines to Atlanta on schedule for them to test?"

"No we'll get it done. Sorry, sometimes I just need to vent."

"Let's talk about how we do that next week."

Caridad shut down her organic chemical CAD software and left the laboratory nearly an hour after most employees of the FDA had cleared out of the facility. It was a nice day for a walk and she sauntered through one parking lot, and bypassed another heading for a small temporary trailer office.

The building complex lay adjacent to the Des Moines River directly across from the small village of Eddyville about halfway between the city of Des Moines and the river's demise into the Mississippi. The complex had originally been designed to process locally grown corn into a variety of products including sweeteners, dextrose, corn oil, lysine food additives and ethanol.

The Food and Drug Administration had taken over the abandoned corn processing facility nearly twelve years ago. Owned originally by a privately held multi-national corporation, the food products had fallen out of favor for nutritional reasons and the ethanol for environmental reasons.

Once the FDA found it necessary to take over the production of a variety of drugs and vaccines from commercial companies who resisted governmental control, the facility fit the need. It sat in a relatively sparsely populated area easing security concerns, was empty and the project had the backing of an important long-term congressman from the state. Retrofitting the abandoned plant was an ongoing operation employing many construction workers and an appropriate number of inspectors.

Caridad approached the austere looking trailer serving as an office for a construction company that employed a thousand, more or less, people depending upon the time of the year. As always she was struck by how out-of-place it was. Supervisors in her building who were responsible for half a dozen people had offices that would make her mother's look like squalor. She took three steps up the weathered wooden steps and opened the aluminum door on the metal sided structure.

"Hi mother," she called.

Wearing the same brown coveralls as her construction workers, Adana greeted her daughter, "How was the day in the white coat?"

"Frustrating, but let's not talk about it."

"It's only frustrating because you let it be."

"I know. When do you want to leave for the Illinois symposium?"

"I think we should leave by 10:00 Friday morning. I promised Julie we'd pick her up at the airport."

"How do you know her again mother?"

"Julie's parents stayed with relatives when they moved to the US from Israel and we had our first landscaping business in the Skokie, Illinois. Even though I was older we had our recent entry into the country in common. We played together and kept in touch over the years."

"Will she be staying in the same hotel?"

"No she is staying with relatives in Skokie. We'll drop her off there and stay at the symposium hotel in Evanston."

"I thought Ethan would be here by now?"

Her answer came as the flimsy door opened and her husband, Ethan, entered. "Hi, honey, what a welcome surprise."

He wrapped his arms around her from behind before she could turn. Turning only her head in his embrace he planted a kiss on her. It deepened and was nearly finished when Ethan's boss and Mother-in-Law admonished them.

"Alright, that's enough. I'm not paying you to kiss my daughter."

"Did you hear from Barry and Jim in Idaho?"

"Yes, they are coming this weekend for hunting, or that is sighting, and bringing Orlando with them. Barry is very interested in the increased security around here and a sighting trip is good cover. Too bad Andrew isn't coming also. I guess he's watching the twins while Julie joins you. Nevertheless, I'm anxious to meet Jim."

"Did you invite the construction inspector to go with you?" asked Adana.

"Yes, I did. Hopefully Barry can get something from him, but if not, he'll owe us a favor. By the way, what is the symposium you're attending this weekend about? Please not too much detail."

"Simply, presentations will be made on random amino acid combination into simple proteins from a historical perspective within the context of early earth history," answered Caridad.

"That sounds so simple and exciting, wish I could be there."

"Don't be sarcastic. The ramifications are important to basic philosophical viewpoints. That's why mother and Julie are also interested."

—ᴥᴥᴥ—

On the Alderman family farm Northeast of Eddyville in Mahaska County, Iowa.

"Walking is more difficult than I anticipated, not something an official with the Voter Empowerment Bureau has been trained to do," exclaimed Barry Bradley as he made way through another patch of shoulder high Big Bluestem grass.

"Orlando and Jim on the other side of the slough aren't complaining and the grass is taller than Orlando," responded Ethan Alderman.

"I'm not complaining, it's just unexpectedly cumbersome walking with heavy canvas pants, and tall boots carrying this crude likeness of a saddle carbine. I feel like an awkward want-a-be cowboy wearing these chaps and heavy boots; at least the cowboys rode and they hunted instead of sighted."

"The heavy pants shed burrs and the boots protect you from errant prairie rattlesnakes, which are becoming more common since reintroduction into Iowa two decades ago. But I do wonder what my ancestors would think of the resurgence of rattlers after their efforts to rid the county of the pest," answered Ethan looking off in the distance at a few buffalos grazing on a loess hill half a mile away.

They stopped and rested waiting for Orlando and Jim to make their way around a wet area containing mostly swamp milkweed the blooms of which made a pinkish peninsula on the prairie.

Ethan continued "The snake, which was a danger to their livestock, is today's feel good attempt to recreate a pristine environment, although denigration of human interests is probably more descriptive of the motive."

"Well let's let it go today, better be careful we don't know how far our voices carry," cautioned Barry. "The inspector is just over the rise."

As they rested on the gentle loess hill, Barry looked to a set of old buildings. "Are those buildings part of the farm?"

"Yes, no one has lived in the house for ten years. We have some old farm machinery in an out building. We should get rid of it but scrap price is all it's worth."

"What do I see two rises over, beyond the set of buildings, whatever it is it doesn't look like it belongs here?"

"It's a carbon reserve. The Department of Transportation obtained a long term lease of a quarter section of what had been a large pork farm years ago. For years replaced railroad ties have been stockpiled there. They can't be burned as they tie up carbon, so they are shipped here for storage. But now the railroad tie dump is property of the Environmental Protection Agency (EPA)"

"How far away is it?"

"It's nearly two miles. Its surrounded by a chain link fence, they say millions of railroad ties lie there slowly rotting. Entry is strictly prohibited, but I played there with a friend during by boyhood summers here with my grandparents."

"Why does that not surprise me?"

"My friend and I dug a tunnel under the fence for entry and had fun rearranging the railroad ties, building forts. It was a great place to get away, no guards or other surveillance, just the fence."

Barry looked through the light mist across the swale toward Jim and Orlando. "I'm glad we came. Orlando is having a wonderful time as close to an alpha male hunting experience as possible. He'll remember it for years. I remember so vividly hunting squirrels with my grandfather as a boy. It never was about shooting squirrels. It was about male bonding, a communion not directly between us but through trees, grass and ants. No barriers existed, just a freedom to be whatever while experiencing complete serenity in life.

Sighting trips with our 3-D image capturing guns provide much of the same experience as hunting did without the hassle of carrying and dressing game. Orlando captured a great image of a red-necked pheasant yesterday. He can preserve the image as a digital anaglyph or hologram, displaying it and passing it on to his children. If this were a real hunt, his trophy would be eaten or taken to a taxidermist only to gather dust and deteriorate in an attic. Change isn't all bad Ethan.

"Maybe so," replied Ethan looking first to check the construction inspector's distance, "but try to tell my father that. This land, once a productive farm, has been in the family for generations. It provided a decent living for the family until my grandfather was mid-aged. Dad was born on the farm but grew up in Colorado; never-the-less, he kept the farm after grandfather died only to see its monetary value decline."

As the demand for farm products declined so did the value of farmland. Eating meat, although still legal, came to be discouraged and taxed heavily destroying the demand for livestock and thus feed-stuffs. Red meat could not be sold in grocery stores, only meat markets, which were zoned at least a thousand meters from residential areas and schools. Red meat consumption in restaurants was banned as it was offensive to some people. Like smoking sections in previous times fish and chicken could only be served in the carnivorous section of restaurants.

Processing grains for fructose sweeteners declined when it was decided soda pop was bad for the public health and punitive taxes were applied. Ethanol production, which at one time consumed over 40% of the corn crop, was taxed rather than subsidized.

Discouraging the use of farm products and eliminating the use of genetically engineered seed effectively outsourced most food production to South America, Eastern Europe and Russia. Over regulation also forced family farms out of business as only mega-corporate farms could comply with the red tape. Finally the fashionable movement to de-humanize the prairie was the last straw for the family farm.

Returning to within ear shot of Barry after they had circled a low swale of mud, Ethan without voicing the reasons stated the condition of farm owners. "Farm owners are pushed economically into granting the feds long-term leases. The Federal Land Use Administration (FLUA) must approve all ownership transactions. It did help when local property taxes were limited to 80% of the federal lease payment. Regardless, I don't see any alternative but turning ownership of the farm to the feds in lieu of paying estate taxes when father dies. I will never be able to pay the tax. In a sense it will be me who loses the family farm."

"Don't go there. We all have responsibility at least three generations," said Barry again nearly out of breath. "You know I hear similar things from Jim. Nathan and him built a successful nursery and now struggle to keep it open amongst the debt and regulation."

"You know Dad told me wet areas like the bog we just circled didn't exist when the farm was productive. Underground tubes called tile made of clay originally then plastic were laid and drained excess water from the soil. But the naturalists couldn't get a stand of swamp grass on drained soils, so they used grant money to tear out the drainage tile."

"I'm certainly glad they did so I can get my exercise sinking in the mud", replied a now sitting Barry with mild sarcasm before inquiring. "Sitting feels good, aren't you tired Ethan"?

"Well, if I am, I'm not admitting it. Father often told of his grandfather who in his 90s would torment kids who would say they were tired by exclaiming he had never been tired a day in his life. Guess I want to be like that. Once this was a land of optimism and a can do attitude. It was settled and worked by men like my great grandfather. People measured themselves by what they produced.

Barry watched Orlando and Jim rounding the edge of pink blooms, the purples of Spider Wort and blue Lobelia on top of a blanket of purple prairie clover. "It's beautiful here but I wonder what the pioneers who first came here would think if they knew we were headed back to what they first saw. The state like many segments of society is headed toward the past."

"I disagree, Barry, nothing ever returns to the past," interrupted Ethan. They both quietly contemplated the thought until they were startled.

A whoofing clamor came from the grass halfway toward Orlando and Jim. A clump of tall switch grass bent toward the wind's desire as a red neck pheasant clamored to gain lift. Its powerful wings beat at the air in frenzy to lift a body proportionately much too big to be carried upward. At ten feet with clumsy control the brilliantly red-necked crusty male bird turned into the wind. In his element now he headed off swooping with the contour of the land.

Unnoticed by the commotion of the bird's takeoff Orlando was pulling up and aiming his image-capturing gun, a near look-alike of the famous or infamous Winchester model 94 saddle gun. Jim patted Orlando's back as they viewed the captured image on the gun's screen embedded in the stock. Orlando was elated rushing to Barry and Ethan to share the image. It was a keeper. The bird was caught in a moment of maximum thrust as it fought to gain height. The sun behind their back, perfect placement and exposure made the digital image and video a keepsake.

"Hey, Orlando you handle the Winchester like a young John Wayne," hollered Barry.

"I've heard Dad talk about him like he was more than an old dead movie star," answered Orlando with an inquisitive look.

"What he symbolized was more. He was born just some 70 miles west of here."

"Barry, you're beginning to sound like Dan," Jim reflected out loud in a softer voice as the construction inspector joined them to inspect the prize photo.

The image capture invigorated fourteen-year-old Orlando for more hunting. Jim and Barry had had enough tromping through the prairie grasses for the day and rested on a fallen, slowly rotting maple tree trunk as Orlando and Ethan continued their hunt joined by the construction inspector.

"Too bad we couldn't talk Andrew into joining us, he would have enjoyed this trip and time away would have done him good," Jim said, now happy to be sitting.

"Alice would have been happy to watch Sandy and Danny for a couple days, but Andrew won't leave them. It seems as though the more Julie becomes involved with the movement the more protective Andrew becomes of their kids."

"I know. Now that Andrew's turned 60, his priority is the children. With the feds watching him, and in some way protecting him, he doesn't want to risk jeopardizing Sandy and Dan's future. Julie, on the other hand, is still on a mission to rectify her parents suffering."

"I think Julie's fervor is more than about her parents, she sees it as an obligation to her children's future," Barry disagreed. "While Andrew is somewhat resigned to making the most of current society for the benefit of the children, Julie sees her activities as an effort to make the country right for her children more than any retribution for her parents."

"Well, I hope they work it out. I know they are having tough times. More than once Nathan and I have heard them arguing across the cul de sac.

"We haven't had a chance to talk. What have you seen in security measures around here? Is Ethan right?"

"I've seen an unbelievable amount of security given where we are. The surveillance equipment became denser about fifty miles from here."

"What do you mean? What did you see?"

"Notice the street lights. The covers should be completely opaque, but in at least half the street light covers you'll notice a circle of clear glass about the size of the old quarter. That indicates a camera. I started noticing it fifty miles from here at the edge of Des Moines. I also noticed I'm getting constant feedback on my electronic sound wave sensors; that indicates listening devices."

"Are we okay here?"

"Of course or I wouldn't be talking, but watch what you say anywhere near a town."

"The question is why here. There must be an answer."

"Yes that's what we must find out."

"I see Orlando is looking up to Ethan, like a big brother," observed Jim watching the two inspect another slough nearly a quarter mile away.

"He's a good role model, Jim. Remember the first time we met Ethan and his band of rebels at the rest stop with our truck loaded with nukes? Julie was probably right, it was risky to save them from the feds, but I'm sure glad we did. He's learned a lot since, not the least of which is caution."

"Nathan wouldn't agree with your characterization of him as a role model for Orlando. He has hopes of Orlando getting into a good college, and well, fitting in so to speak. Ethan's activities, time at a social farm and other behavior prevented him from having the opportunities that his quick mind should have allowed. Nathan fears Orlando taking the same path. We are very careful what we say around Orlando, he is a perceptive boy. Last year his school contacted us twice about his attitude.

Orlando's DNA tests for school entrance indicated he may have a genetic propensity to develop his own critical thinking avenues outside what is socially acceptable, although they don't put it in those terms."

"You mean he can think for himself and not believe all that is fed him."

"Exactly, you put it better; but I'm trying to help moderate Orlando for his own good. Frankly, that's why I brought him here seeking to give him an outlet. At his age I had what was called football to blow off steam, he doesn't.

Do you agree with Nathan that we should protect Orlando by limiting his contact with people like Ethan?"

"I think Orlando should do what he wants. As I heard Dan Barnmore say once, it's important to live. Is living moving to a drumbeat as all birds of a flock will scurry to and fro in unison? Some, like Andrew, take a good part of their lifetime to figure that out, whether Orlando does and when is for him to determine."

Their conversation stopped as the inspector joined them. "I see you guys are resting again."

"Its nice to sit and enjoy the beauty of the land, sitting lets a person take it in," said Barry as he continued the sentence in thought *rather than focus on dealing with the obstacles of the times.*

The inspector was an employee of the Food and Drug Administration at the plant in which Ethan worked. His title was director of facility updating. Both he and the director of facility maintenance served under the director of facility property management. Although he was responsible for updates and changes in the physical layout and equipment at the facility, in practice he was an inspector.

The work was contracted out to a government facilities management company in Chicago. Neither did the Chicago company perform any of the actual construction work or maintenance at the facility, but provided the paperwork and maintained the proper political connections. They subbed the work to the private company run by Adana that Ethan worked for.

"Mind if I join you guys?"

"Sure have a seat on this log and rest your legs. You must get enough exercise moving around the large FDA plant," Barry prodded.

"Well yes and I will soon be much busier."

"A new project coming up?"

Proud of his responsibilities and all too often unable to talk about the tasks that he conscientiously performed the inspector was inclined to talk. "Yes, work will soon be starting on a transportation link with the NSA plant down the river."

"Oh, a new highway?"

"No, nothing like that, an underground link, a tunnel."

"So there's a need to transport something between the plants. It's good to know different agencies are working together. What are they to be moving?"

"It's for using the same geothermal heat source, I'm told," the inspector answered seeking to impress the others with his knowledge, but he actually didn't know.

Thinking he had said enough the inspector changed the subject, "What did you guys think of the historical museum in Des Moines?"

"Thanks for the tickets. We would have never thought or known about the museum if you hadn't given us passes."

"The city council increased our donation to the Des Moines museum last year and well they provided us council members with complimentary passes."

"The town has a unique name, where did it come from?" Jim asked trying to evade the question.

"The town was named Oskaloosa meaning 'last of beautiful' in honor of a Creek Indian princess. The county was named after a Native American chief called Mahaska, which means White Cloud. What did you think of the museum in Des Moines?"

Orlando and Ethan, also looking worn out, joined the others resting as Jim answered, "The museum was certainly eye opening, but rather depressing."

"Its all part of our history but that doesn't mean we need to be proud of it. What we did to the beautiful land, well you could say it was rape, killing the plants, exposing glacial tills and loess soils to erosion, polluting the streams and killing and driving to extinction animals that had lived in harmony with the land for millennia."

"Well whatever happened, look at it now, we are making amends," Jim carefully added as he gave Orlando a *let-it-go look.*

"Got a great image to show you on the other side of the hill where the buffalo are," said the inspector. In matted grass where buffalo laid I got a prairie rattler," said the inspector.

They all circled him to see the image on the gun's stock. "He was maybe three feet long. I was ten feet away and he paid me no attention. Eventually he slid on. I didn't bother him and he had no disposition to bother me. Funny how all those superstitions came to be."

"Maybe he's pretty in a way, but still creepy," said Orlando.

"That feeling is all part of our misinformed learned behavior," replied the inspector. "Its something we all have but must work to rid ourselves. We all have our place here and thankfully we humans have finally recognized that and backed off to allow other species their proper due."

"So we should put everything back to normal as it was before white man came? I discovered on my grape over ten thousand years ago this land was covered by glaciers. How do we know that is not the normal?"

Both Jim and Ethan took a step toward Orlando contemplating how to avoid the conversation going where they feared.

"Well we humans have a responsibility to look out for other species, protect their niche in nature and certainly not take advantage of them."

"But the animals moved in here after the glaciers, why was it all right for them to move in but not us? The Native Americans moved in from Asia. Why was it okay for them to move in but not us? I checked on the red-necked pheasant we are imaging and it's from Russia and not indigonus here, so why do we keep it here then based on what you said?" queried Orlando.

"I think you mean indigenous", corrected Jim.

"I'm hungry," said Ethan trying to help Jim and head off where the conversation was headed. "Let's call it a day and head to town."

"Sorry I can't join you for dinner," said the inspector. "We have a city council meeting tonight."

As they all shook hands and said goodbye the inspector added, "Please, although it's no big deal. I'd appreciate it if you didn't mention the tunnel project. Ethan you'll find out soon enough."

"No problem. I'd already forgotten about it," Barry lied.

Later Jim and Orlando sat across from Barry and Ethan in a restaurant booth. It was busy with local customers. The table had paper place mats depicting the stars and stripes with the new pledge of allegiance imposed on the middle of the flag. After the long day of laborious walking sitting felt good and they quietly read the menus and ordered various vegetable specials.

"What do you think about the project the inspector..." Ethan started to ask as he was cut off by Barry who motioned toward his jacket pocket that contained a surveillance detector.

Barry glanced around the café again before he tore a corner from the place mat, tuned it over and wrote, *"no talk here."* Once Ethan and Jim read the message Barry wadded it and put in his pocket.

"That's Tony Johnson of KRMT sitting over there," Ethan noticed, but didn't verbalize what Barry and he were thinking about Tony's past relationship with Atlas and meeting him at a few flash demonstrations.

Shortly Tony spotted Ethan and approached the table. "Glad to see you Ethan. I want you to know we are having a little get together next Friday at noon in Knoxville to make a statement about all the property that is getting bought up around here. I've got the day off. We should have a good gathering. Hope to see you there."

Not getting a response Tony whispered, "You know flash demo."

"Glad to see you too. But I've got too much work next week."

Tony left the table getting the message that Ethan didn't want to talk. Once he was gone Ethan tore a corner from his place mat and wrote – *"CANCEL—Audio monitor"*. Ethan excused himself for the restroom as Tony picked up his dinner napkin at his table. As nonchalantly as possible Ethan dropped the note near Tony's dinner plate as Tony was looking the other way. Tony not noticing Ethan's passing put his napkin over the note and never saw it.

When Ethan dropped the others off at their motel, Barry suggested Ethan accompany him on a walk.

"What do you make of the tunnel project?"

"I don't know, hadn't heard anything about it. The NSA facility and the FDA plant we work at in Eddyville don't exchange anything that I know of."

"Well there is a reason for it. It makes sense if you wanted to move something unnoticed. And frankly I don't buy the sharing geothermal heating explanation. Geothermal is becoming taboo now as we have decided we have no business disturbing the pristine subterranean."

"I'll let you know if I can find out anything."

"Okay, hopefully Tony got the message. It is very dangerous to have a flash demo anywhere around here with all the security. And there is no doubt that conversation was picked up."

"I'm sure Tony will avoid it. He already has been warned by the news station."

"Disobedience is the true foundation of liberty.
The obedient must be slaves."

Henry David Thoreau

Chapter 5

Joshua liked running a paint brush, not on canvas, but walls; roller, brush, taping edges; he found it all fun. His neighbor enjoyed gardening, planting and caring for flower beds. They traded, each doing what they enjoyed and getting something done they would rather not do. Though they were happy with the arrangement, the government frowned on the avoidance of service taxes. Their Credit Transaction Cards showed Joshua buying paint materials to be delivered to his neighbor's house and his neighbor paying for nursery plants to be delivered to Joshua's home. Information of the purchasing anomaly was stored.

Evanston symposium on early protein development.

Julie, Adana and Caridad sat together during the second presentation of the morning at the symposium. They were careful about any opinions they expressed at the conference. It was widely known that the conference had drawn skeptics along with those who sought explanations for the missing final pieces of the evolutionary puzzle.

Certain ideas and theories were best not spoken in public particularly at an event that was bound to be monitored extensively.

Dr. Stephen Minor, a well-know expert in chance and statistics was presenting on the random probability of amino acids forming proteins.

"...The probability of achieving a random functional sequence of amino acids in the simplest 100-amino acid protein known is small around 1 in 10 to the 63rd power... The probability of randomly acquiring the right configuration of amino acids in a simple cell is smaller. A simple one-celled organism needs at least 250 proteins to function and the proteins need on the average of 150 amino acids to be arranged in precise order. The probability of producing just one of the average sized proteins by chance is calculated at 10 to the 164th power. Multiplying that number by the 250 proteins needed in a simple cell gives us ...well a very small probability...

...Another method to envision random possibilities is to multiply the number per second particles can interact with another as limited by the speed of light times the number of elementary particles in the known universe times the time that has transpired since the big bang. This number, 10 to the 139.4th power, is the number of events that could have taken place in the observable universe since the origin of the universe..."

Caridad seemed to be following the presentation but Adana and Julie occasionally gave each other lost looks as the Professor delved deeper into statistics, but they got the general unspoken message.

At the end of the presentation Dr. Minor agreed to take a few questions. At the microphone waiting in the center aisle was Eric Hansen. Julie recognized the former director of NASA before he spoke; unbeknownst to her Adana also recognized him.

"Dr. Minor you indicated that the probability of a chance configuration of a functional amino acid sequence is small. In laymen's terms what do you mean by small?"

"I can only quantify it in mathematical terms."

"Dr. Minor without using numbers how likely would it be that I could find a single element you might tag somewhere within our galaxy?"

"I'm not an astrophysicist but that would obviously be very, very remote."

"Well, there are 10 to the 65th power elements in our known galaxy and most of the calculations you quoted in your remarks address probabilities much, much more remote, correct?"

"My field is statistical analysis not the interpretation of the numbers."

The question had to be on most minds, but Julie knew that only someone of Hansen's credentials could get away with asking such a question. Although he had run an agency that nearly thwarted Atlas's diverting the asteroid, he had resigned. She found herself wondering about him.

At the lunch break the women were heading through the lobby for a restaurant Julie's relatives had recommended when a voice behind them said, "Adana, is that you?"

Adana turned immediately recognizing Eric Hansen. "Eric, I can't believe it."

"So good to see you."

Seeing Eric noticing the women with her, Adana introduced them. Eric sensed that Julie's face was familiar.

"Eric was the director of NASA for years and now is with the Department of Energy, right?"

"Yes." He studied Julie's face.

"We've met before, haven't we?

Julie wasn't very comfortable but wouldn't avoid the question. "Yes, at a funeral in Houston."

"Oh yes, you were with Andrew Collier at Sandra Levy's funeral."

"Yes, he's my husband now."

Adana sensed the awkwardness of the encounter but wanted to renew an acquaintance and learn what Eric was doing at the conference. "Why don't you join us for lunch, Eric?"

"I'd love to."

Adana caught a less than pleasant look from Julie.

Seated for lunch Adana asked Eric what he did with the department of Energy.

"Actually I'm in charge of subbing out piecemeal microscopic electricity producing research."

"Can you tell us anything about it?" asked Caridad.

"There is nothing secret about it. We are working on ways to generate electricity from glucose, the simple sugar. It is how our bodies get energy by burning the glucose molecule. We are working on methods to shortcut the Krebs's Cycle and produce electricity instead of kinetic energy. We use nature's way of storing solar energy as glucose."

"I appreciated the question you asked at the symposium," Julie stated.

"Thank you. As a former employee of Atlas, I'm sure you understood my reference to elements in the galaxy. Weren't you in security there?"

"Oh I don't understand much about astronomy. I was just a security guard who worked the night shift most of the time," Julie lied.

The spark in her eye told Eric otherwise.

Adana changed the subject, "Here's what I find amazing. We talked about probability this morning in physical terms, but think about the probability of this. I know Eric from high school, and Julie from my time in Skokie. Then the circle completes with Eric and Julie knowing each other from a funeral and Atlas. Added to that coincidence my daughter, Caridad, is a bio-chemist with a professional connection here. We are all sitting at the same table and all have an interest in the subject of this conference, plus we share similar but unspoken skepticism about some settled science."

"You assumed the last part, shared skepticism," replied Eric.

"I haven't heard anyone disagree. Talking about skepticism, the point is: I'm a skeptic of coincidences."

A broad smile over came Julie's face as she remembered an often quote of Dan Barnmore: *'coincidences happen, but only fools believe in them'.*

"What is it Julie?"

"Nothing, what you said just reminds me of someone."

Boise, Idaho

Julie and Andrew had dinner at Nathan and Jim's across the cul-de-sac. They could tell Nathan and Jim were disturbed. Orlando left after dinner to play with friends.

"What's bothering the two of you?" asked Julie.

"It's Orlando. A social worker from DHHS (Department of Health and Human Services) stopped before Orlando got home from school. She said Orlando is in jeopardy of getting downgraded in the socially and emotionally disturbed class, (SED), which they send him to once a week. We've got to be much more careful what we say around him.

"I can't believe it; he is as emotionally mature and astute as any kid I know."

"That's not the issue Andrew. It's about what they call his anti-social attitude."

Later that evening Andrew watched Julie place the secure phone high on a ledge inside the fireplace. She had been in communication with the island-boat off Costa Rica. Part of the conversation had been with Melissa about the twins. Melissa wanted so much to see them, but the secure phone couldn't send pictures and other means were too dangerous. But most of the conversation was about activities around the country.

Andrew had a difficult time rectifying Julie's desire to dangerously get involved against the need to provide security for the twins. The news of Orlando's trouble only heightened his concerns.

"I think having the secure phone in the house is too dangerous."

"Why? We need access to it."

"Let's hide it off the property."

"It wouldn't be as handy when we need it."

"Why do we need it that handy? We must think of the twins," Andrew replied sharply with his voice rising.

"Let's not have this conversation again, it gets us nowhere," Julie countered trying to defuse the ongoing disagreement.

"All right but we need to have another conversation. It's time to get the twins flu shots. Why take a chance? As accident prone as Danny is, an emergency trip to the doctor might cause his blood to be checked for flu antibodies. Without them it would be more trouble than we need and the shot might keep the twins from getting the flu."

"Where do you stop Andrew? Maybe we shouldn't ever tell them the truth about the asteroid. It would be safer for them, right? Maybe we should turn Barry in for what he does, that'd get us health care points and maybe get the twins into a good school."

"You are being ridiculous."

"Oh, am I? Look at yourself Andrew?" asked Julie, her voice rising now.

"Our primary responsibility is to protect the children."

"Well I guess we have different definitions of that," Julie said as she headed for the door.

"Where are you going?"

"To the speakeasy, don't wait up."

Office of the FDA Director in Eddyville

The past press secretary to the President, now director of the FDA, sat in his office. Although the director of the agency normally ran things from Washington, prudence required the director be close to important activities. No one but the director knew that the lady who had access to him at any time was an employee of NSA.

She tapped on his office door but twice before entering, "Sir we have a tip that a flash demonstration will be held in a nearby town tomorrow."

"And where is this insurrection to take place?"

"In a town square about halfway to Des Moines, a town called Knoxville."

"How did you get the information?"

"Our audio monitoring at a café in Oskaloosa picked up a conversation honing on the key words "flash demo". It was between that reporter we've been watching from KRMT and a table of others including an employee of a construction company that works here."

"Who initiated it? Are they all involved?"

"No it appears just the reporter, Tony Johnson. He initiated it and the others seemed to ignore him. They brushed him off. I don't think the others wanted anything to do with it."

"Well we'll sort it all out by seeing who shows up at the flash. As we've discussed I have authority from the top to squelch these things and that's what we will do. Notify the ATF to activate the plan. Make sure they have enough buses. I want our people to make sure no one gets away. We will make these people disappear."

"The measures we have planned should eliminate any evidence of what happens but word will still get out, be it someone watching through a window or just family members missing."

"I know. What would be the point if we just made a group of people disappear without anyone getting the message? As long as there is no proof of what happened, it will make others think twice about seditious behavior."

"Is there anything else, sir?"

"No, go get started on it."

Alone the director typed the words, "Squelch plan activated" and transmitted it on his direct communication device with the White House. His, like many high level government grapes, had been programmed to destroy all messages if necessary, a practice that had been in place for over three decades since its clumsy but successful use by the IRS.

—⟨⟨⟩⟩—

"Hi, honey. How was the sighting trip?" Caridad asked as she heard her husband enter.

"Fine, but my legs are sore from walking most of the day in mud."

"Perhaps you need a nice leg massage."

"Perhaps I miss my wife and that would make the trip worthwhile."

Later in the evening he asked if she had heard anything about a tunnel connecting the NSA plant and the FDA facility. It was a surprise to her.

"Is there any material, ingredients or product moved between the facilities?"

"None that I know of."

"Anything strange going on that you know of?"

"You probably know more about the overall operation than I do. I stay in my department and communication between departments is discouraged."

"Yes, you're right."

"But I did find something very strange in my department today."

His look said continue.

"It's about the vaccines we are working on for this fathom new virus. You know I've been pressing Atlanta to give us more on the structure of the molecule; otherwise the effectiveness of any vaccine is hit and miss. Today we received a segment of the virus structure."

"Is it what you anticipated?"

"Not exactly, I'm the only one in the department who has a background in virus anatomy, strange as that may sound to you; it's a discipline not needed for vaccine development. Actually I left that out of my resume because I hoped to be hired here, not the Center for Disease Control (CDC) in Atlanta. Anyway the partial structure they sent us is not natural."

"What do you mean not natural?"

"I mean it is not a natural mutation of a presently known virus. The structure indicates it is man made."

"What are you going to do?"

"Tomorrow I'll make my observations known."

"I think you should hold off on that. Let's run it by some others."

"I assume you mean some people outside the country."

"Yes, let's not tip our hand that you may know something at least until some people we can trust evaluate the meaning of this. I'll contact Barry."

It was noon Monday morning that Ethan who had traveled home for an early lunch twisted a Phillip's screw from a baseboard in the bedroom. Behind the baseboard was a hole he had carved out in the drywall containing a secure phone that Barry had left him. Barry had insisted that given the extra security in the area he wanted him to have a way to securely be in contact. Ethan was more than a little nervous about putting the code in given Barry's explanation of what would happen if he hit the wrong key. Carefully inversing the temperature, adding his code and inversing the date he contacted Barry.

Ethan had yet to complete passing information from Caridad when static broke out on the connection and ended the conversation. Barry contacted Torrence on the island-boat off the coast of Costa Rica. A return call from Torrence said an electronic storm was interfering with all electric circuits within a hundred mile diameter circle in the Southeast quadrant of Iowa. He promised to get back with Barry as soon as he knew more.

Torrence Jackson had been the CIO, Chief Information Officer, at Atlas, and acted as such on the island-boat. Barry's training had given Torrence the expertise to surf secure databases and with sophisticated equipment on the island-boat much beyond Barry's, he was the go-to guy.

The NSA liaison to the FDA was in Knoxville before 9:00 am personally directing ATF implementation of the squelch plan. As part of the plan five specially equipped semi-trailers marked in various commercial logos parked in an empty lot at the edge of town. Each trailer held thirty heavily armed ATF agents. Their lookouts around the town square reported no crowd at 11:00 but noticeably more people than normal in restaurants and a number of occupied cars parked on side streets.

She addressed the assembled agents. "Our mission is to gather up these flashers as quickly and quietly as possible. Do not use any unnecessary force but do not allow anyone to escape."

"Which is the greater priority, sir?" someone asked.

"No one escapes, do I make myself clear?"

An agent rolled a metallic box out on a two wheeled cart. The box made mostly of lead and much heavier than it looked contained a number of stun guns. The NSA liaison and three ATF leaders put their grapes in the box.

"Where's our camera guy? Asked the liaison.

A tall thin agent stepped forward and placed his camera in the box and the lid was closed.

At 11:30 the Knoxville police received a call from the ATF ordering all officers to return to the station and stay there until informed otherwise, as did the Marion County sheriff's department in nearby Pella.

The ATF captain received notification at 11:50 that people were walking from many locations toward the town square. He turned toward the NSA liaison looking for the final go, "It's on we have movement of people converging on the town square."

"Commence operation squelch now."

The five semi-trailers that left the parking lot heading toward the small town square were pulled by specially adapted road tractors. The diesel tractors had been retrofitted with non-electronically controlled fuel injection pumps and no circuit boards on the trucks. At a great cost internally they resembled road tractors from the previous century.

A small motor retracted the roof cover off a truck bed parked at the NSA plant in Chillicothe at 11:55. Another motor raised a missile-filled tube into the air and it blasted off on its 35 mile route toward Knoxville.

The director of the NSA plant was on the phone with the FDA director in Eddyville as he looked out the fourth story window and described the launch. "Looks good from here."

"Great, hopefully they get the message."

No one else at the plant witnessed the launch as all employees including maintenance had been assembled for a noon meeting, all that is except Eric Hansen, the demoted and discredited former director of NASA. The flash caught his eye as it passed a window. He made a mental note of it but would not ask questions.

As was the norm the assembled group at NSA started the meeting with the pledge of allegiance as it had been rewritten: *(The pledge had been changed more than once since originally written by a collectivist, Francis Bellany, in 1892 ironically to sell flags.)*

"I Pledge allegiance to the flag of the United States of America and to the institution for which it stands, one nation, indivisible with fairness and justice for all."

It took the missile only six minutes to reach its intended place three thousand feet over the town square in Knoxville, Iowa. The detonation of the focused explosive device sent an electron pulse down and out essentially frying all circuit boards within a half mile and disturbing all communications within 50 miles.

At the flash of the explosion the five trucks now surrounding the square emptied of ATF agents who quickly surrounded nearly 400 flash demonstrators. The metal box was opened, grapes retrieved, stun guns were passed out and the tall thin agent took his camera.

Most of the protesters were sufficiently dazed by the explosion and offered no resistance as they were herded into the trucks. Twenty who were shielded from the blast by others tried to get away. All but four including KRMT reporter, Tony Johnson, were hit with projectiles from stun guns and dragged to the trucks.

Four of the non-dazed protesters were wearing clothing designed to thwart the stun guns. The electric charge lit up their clothes but didn't slow their attempted escape; however their belief that the special clothes would save them was in error. Four to ten rounds of live 223 caliber ammunition apiece did. Within fifteen minutes of the electronic blast all the protesters, dazed, stunned or dead, were packed into five trailers pulling out of Knoxville.

Added to the apprehended group were a few onlookers who had made the mistake of venturing out. Others saw through windows but, thanks to the electric pulse, no photos or videos recorded anything. As expected word-of-mouth would eventually spread, and questions would be raised as to what happened to the protesters by family, but no evidence existed.

Ethan had yet to put the secure phone away when it flashed (for security reasons it did not ring). After entering the code he answered.

"Ethan, do you see anything unusual going on there?" asked Barry.

"Adana just called and said all the company's grapes had quit working for a time but all is fine now. What's going on?"

"It seems as if an electronic pulse of some kind caused a lot of temporary static and a town not too far from you is like off the map now."

"What caused it?"

"We don't know, but do you remember where Tony said that flash was to occur?"

"I think he said Knoxville."

"That's what I was afraid of. Keep your eyes open and contact me tonight."

Five trailers pulled onto an airfield between Knoxville and the NSA facility that was used by NSA and FDA personnel. It was closed for the day. The occupants of the trailers were herded toward two cargo planes. Many sought to know where they were being taken. No answers were given. As all had recovered from the concussion daze of the explosion they were not orderly and became less so with the lack of explanation. Most of the captured flash demonstrators not knowing their intended fate, but well aware of four dead comrades, ran in all directions.

The careful plan had called for this exchange to take ten minutes; it took over an hour as about a third of the group took stunning rather than be driven like sheep. Only fifty ATF agents accompanied the trailers to the airstrip and they soon ran out of stun darts. Tony Johnson was stunned a second time in an hour. Some flashers turned on the agents seeking to take their stun guns.

A supervisor told the tall thin agent with the camera to forget filming and help. The cameraman chased two fleeing flashers.

Emily Scholtus and Darrell Greene made a bee line for a small stream near the airport perimeter chased by an ATF agent as others headed in all directions. The agent having expended his stun darts reluctantly readied his lead firing weapon. Realizing they were followed, Darrell motioned for Emily to hide in some reed canary grass at the stream's edge. He hunkered down behind a clump of giant fox tail as the agent approached. Darrell leaped for the agent but the distance was too great. The agent spun quickly with his short barreled automatic and put three bullets in Darrell's midsection.

The agent bent over Darrell and watched him take his last breath. *Orders, this wasn't what he signed up for,* he thought as Emily brought a half decayed piece of Maplewood down on his head. Before she could take his weapon she heard voices.

"Over this way, I saw one of us chasing someone."

Emily headed back for the Reed's Canary grass at the edge of the water and submerged herself leaving only her face out of the water amongst the grass. She heard more gunshots erupt on and around the tarmac as she laid under water. The mêlée soon ended when many more TSA agents thinking they had no choice in preventing an escape opened fire.

Two agents found the first agent recovering from a mild blow. "You stopped him. Did what you had to. Was he the only one?"

The agent looked up at the others. His head was clear now but he didn't answer.

"Did any get away?" the agent asked again as the other walked to the water's edge.

"No, only him."

The NSA liaison's driver pulled on the tarmac after the firing had ended. She found agents standing around listless not knowing what to do.

"What the hell happened here? Who is responsible for this?"

The lead agent answered, "We didn't have a choice. Your instructions said not to let anyone escape at any cost."

Another agent looked at his gun as if it were burning his hands and threw it as far as he could in disgust.

Ignoring him the liaison asked, "How many?"

"We've got 14 wounded and 9 dead flashers." He hesitated before continuing, "And one dead and 5 wounded agents."

"So the flashers fired on agents."

"Frankly, not so. Our agents were hit by misses and bullets exiting the flashers."

"What a rebellious, uncouth lot they are. Look at this. You did the right thing. There is no place for such behavior in these times. Let's be rid of them. Load them up. And you who threw your gun shape up or you'll be among them."

Emily carefully rose from the water and made her way to where she last saw Darrell. He was gone. The only sign was blood stained grass and a camera. She picked up the camera crawled on her stomach to where she could see the revolting spectacle. Not a novice to using a camera she caught the ATF agents forcing the remaining flashers on the planes, the dragging of the wounded and dead and the howls of the wounded.

In five hours the two cargo planes crammed with far more than anyone intended landed at Guantanamo Bay in Cuba. In route two wounded flashers died on one plane. On the other plane, three flasher doctors working in cramped quarters only lost one.

The head count of flashers was found to be off by one at the unloading of the planes, but it was written off as a counting mistake in Knoxville. It was also the easy explanation.

The Guantanamo Bay renovated prison would make the perfect place to keep those who couldn't be controlled and posed a risk to a major project for the greater good.

"The man who asks of freedom anything
other than itself is born to be a slave."

Alexis de Tocqueville

Chapter 6

*Lois attended Georgetown University. It wasn't often she knew many
in her classes. The fact that convicted would-be assassin Aaron Hamil
shared two classes with her she didn't know. The government did and
had the information stored.*

Julie requested a conference call with Barry Bradley, Torrence
Jackson and Ethan and Caridad Alderman in Iowa. Andrew listened
on the attached speaker but didn't comment.

"I understand the official explanation of the communication static
and electronic malfunctions in Iowa is a natural occurring magnetic
storm. Torrence, what do the astrophysicists there think the chances
of that are?"

"Nearly zero, such an event would be the first time in history and
it was emitted from a singular source."

"Barry, tell the others what you found in Iowa."

"The surveillance is much denser, I'd say many times denser there than anywhere in the country except Washington."

"Where is it centered?" asked Torrence.

"Around the FDA and NSA complexes."

"What have you found out about the planned flash demo you were invited to Ethan?" asked Julie.

"I don't know if it took place or not, but I do know Tony Johnson is missing as are a number of others that I suspect might have attended the event."

Torrence added, "And we know the burst of electric energy was centered over the town where the flash demonstration was supposed to happen."

"Caridad, do you know anything going on at the FDA plant that would require the activities that we are seeing?"

"My focus there is narrow and they have all activities very compartmentalized so I don't know what's going on in most departments. But I have to say the work I'm doing is out of the ordinary."

"How so?" Julie inquired.

"Probably doesn't mean anything but we are developing a vaccine for an unknown virus which isn't natural."

"What do you mean isn't natural?"

"From what we can see of the virus, I believe its man made."

"Is someone expecting a bio terrorist attack?"

"I've seen no chatter about that," answered Barry.

Caridad added, "It wouldn't make sense, if someone was producing a virus for a bio attack, how would we know the chemical structure of the virus? It is unlikely they would give us the viral blueprint as a warning; we wouldn't know; unless, that is, it was produced here? And if we knew someone was producing a virus for a bio attack, why wouldn't we go after the source and stop it rather than develop an antibody?"

"Good point, Caridad. I think we need to get more people in the area and find out what is going on."

They all agreed including a reluctant Andrew. Julie asked Caridad to stay on the phone.

"Caridad, the vaccine you are developing is for this spring, right?"

"Yes."

"Given what you know, would you recommend vaccination? I'm thinking of the twins."

"I well don't know. The vaccine will offer no protection against any known viruses or potential close mutations, but would be effective against this hypothetical virus."

"So?"

"Sorry I can't answer the question."

"Let me ask you this way. Are you going to get a shot?"

"No."

With the phone put away Andrew asked, "You want to go to Iowa, don't you?"

"Someone must find out what is happening."

"Under what auspices would you be there?"

"That, I would have to work on. You haven't said what you think about it," she said while bracing herself.

Andrew leaned back in the chair and found his eyes settling on the framed drawing of the founding fathers hanging on the wall, Franklin, Jefferson, Madison et al. He had known this day would come for some time. It was the spirit in Julie that he had fallen in love with. Not that he could, but it wouldn't be fair to her for him to squelch her yearnings which ultimately were her needs. If he could subdue her, what would it do to his feelings for her? He loved her for her. For his love to survive he needed her to be Julie.

"I would expect you to be as careful as possible and I'll miss you."

She sat on his lap and kissed him as passionately as she had for a long time. Danny and Sandy both watched and giggled. Soon they all laughed.

—✺—

The White House.

The director of NSA, CDC and the FDA joined the President in the Oval office. The first item on a full agenda was an update on the flash roundup in Iowa from the NDA director.

"Our people were successful rounding up the demonstrators. None got away and no evidence was left. To date nothing has showed up anywhere except rumors. In fact the rumors have been less than we expected, maybe not enough to discourage others.

All told 17 flashers and two agents were killed. The agent's deaths are attributed to training accidents. Not exactly what we wanted but in the big picture what difference does it make? And the ATF agents involved in the roundup have been transferred to Cuba guarding the prisoners where we will have opportunity make them aware of the hazards for disclosing what happened."

The President interrupted, "Sometimes bad things must happen for the greater good. As much as I'm concerned about the loss of life, the divergence from the projection bothers me. You projected no loss of life. What does that say about our planning and control? We are contemplating a much bigger operation than that, which can not go wrong."

"Mr. President what happened completely validates what we know to be true about these rabble rousers. They are a fanatic band of misfits that have no respect for authority. To tolerate them is to invite anarchy in our midst. If there was a miscalculation on our part it was the fervor of these throwbacks."

"You've got a point there."

The President turned to the director of the Center for Disease Control (CDC), "I see some skepticism in your eyes, talk."

"Well, Mr. President, history is littered with people who have underestimated the fervor of fringe groups that shouldn't have been consequential."

"Yes, maybe, but no one in history has had the technology we do and we have people's best interests at heart, which the bulk of important people understand. And I know your background is history, but the notable make their own history which we shall. What are your projections of the percent of the population that had flu shots last year?"

"Mr. President, We believe between 80 and 85% had the vaccine."

"That is unacceptable, given its good for them and the risks they take from us if they refuse. Do our mandates mean nothing?" Looking to the NSA director he asked, "What percent of the population do we need to receive TIP to acquire the control we need?"

"Theoretically, if we had the nano-controllers randomly in 80% of the population we would be good. We estimate that only 10% of the population is active trouble makers. This analysis would mean the non-vaccinated part of the trouble makers is only 2% of the population. Although another 40% may sympathize with them, they'll never cause us trouble.

The problem is who get shots. It is not random. We estimate that of the malcontent's 10% portion of the population only half get shots. Given this premise the nano-controllers would only get in half the malcontents. It would only allow us to control half their numbers."

"As I feared."

Again the President looked to the CDC director, "Will you have enough of the flu shot inspiration agent ready?"

"Yes, Mr. President the virus will be ready by spring."

"How will it be spread?"

The director of NSA answered, "Canisters will be put on air transports and for a week they'll fly lower than normal."

"How lethal do we expect this virus to be?"

"Mr. President based upon our tests about a tenth of a percent of the unvaccinated. Given the population of 350 million and an estimated 85% vaccinated, that would leave 52 million unvaccinated and vulnerable. If it is lethal to a tenth a percent of the unvaccinated, it would project around 50 thousand deaths, mostly the old and very young."

Sensing some Presidential skepticism the FDA director injected, "As horrific as the number sounds, it is not more than traffic and gun deaths in a year. And those deaths strike middle aged productive people harder than those in their waning years. But more importantly, it would play havoc with the unvaccinated trouble-makers and insure nearly everyone getting vaccinated next year when the

Tranquility Insertion Project (TIP) nano-controllers are ready to be incorporated into the vaccine."

Work had started twenty years ago on a non-drug method of controlling restless behavior in people with a number of anxiety-related diseases. Progress slowed when the pharmaceutical companies were taken over, but a number of scientists directed by NSA had made progress. They developed nano-technology that would stimulate the production of GABA (Gamma-Aminobutyric Acid).

The man-made machines were just a few nanometers in diameter. Given that a nanometer is a billionth of a meter and a human hair is 80,000 to 100,000 nanometers wide, the machines were much too small to be seen but by the highest powered microscopes.

Releases from the floating microscopic machines in the bloodstream stimulates GABA production in the brain producing an inhibitory (calming) and feel-good or relaxing action in adult vertebrate. Higher amounts of GABA cause sleepiness, tingling and flushing.

The NSA facility in Iowa had incorporated into the GABA stimulating nano-machines switches that could be activated by high frequency waves. By broadcasting a code of frequencies authorities could neutralize passion, thus anti-social activity in a population. The nano-machines would allow authorities to sedate the population when the need arose.

Besides receiving a signal capable of opening and closing a switch in the nano-machines, the machines are to bounce the signal back allowing tracking of the nano. In effect, with enough computing power the machines would enable authorities to track everyone anywhere anytime. With tens of thousands machines in the bloodstream they would be impossible to dispose of without completely bleeding out the body. With insertion of the nano-machines in the population, control would become a matter of interpreting information rather than gathering it.

Also the nano-machines were being programmed to permanently increase GABA production if the machine sensed a host carrying DNA with the MAOA-L or the D4-7 Allele gene variant. The

MAOA-L gene, called the warrior gene, causes its carrier to be more willing to take risks and increases critical analysis aptitude. The D4-7 Allele gene commonly expresses itself in exploratory and novelty seeking activity.

Americans continued to carry more of these genes inherited from pioneers who did not immigrate to America randomly; hence the advantage to European governments with more compliant populations.

The nano-machines harness the same energy source as the body, using glucose as a parasite would. The simple sugar fuel source eliminates the need for batteries and gives it life as long as the body functions. They are also designed to resist being sorted out of the blood stream as they move through the kidneys.

The Tranquility Insertion Project (TIP) encompasses producing the nano technology and building the micro-machines at NSA's Chillicothe, Iowa plant. The final part of TIP involves getting the machines into citizens' blood streams by adding them to the flu vaccine produced at the Eddyville plant.

"How sure can we be that the fatality rate of the non-vaccinated will be a tenth of a percent instead of 2 or zero? As sad as 50 thousand deaths would be, in the big picture it would be worth the cost. But do we absolutely know it won't be 0 or a million? I can't abide the higher end of deaths but we certainly need a few thousand to make a point and insure everyone is vaccinated next year. In the long run it will save lives, and we're charged with the long run health of this country."

"Mr. President, a tenth of a percent is our opinion but we can't absolutely say without a trial test."

"How or where could we run a small test and validate it?"

"I've an idea sir," offered the NSA director.

"Go ahead."

"We've got the 378 flashers at Guantanamo Bay. If we can ever release them, it will be years. They are in tight security. No one knows what happens there. They would be a perfect test sample."

"What about the TSA guards holding them?"

"Let's inoculate them with the vaccine we are developing. We can test that as well," added the FDA director.

"Okay, let's move. I want this done and TIP implemented long before I leave office."

—ɷ—

Caridad was one of three organic chemists at the FDA facility on a video conference call with the FDA director and viral researchers with the CDC in Atlanta. A woman was with the FDA director she didn't recognize, but learned later it was the NSA liaison. The chemists felt their work's importance vindicated by the presence of the director, although Caridad thought it was usual as she had never met the director.

The Atlanta people agreed with the FDA chemists that vaccine number three would produce the most effective antibodies for the mystery virus. Having chosen the vaccine for production, their work on this project was over. And Caridad expected it to go into full production immediately. She was surprised when the director ordered only 500 doses produced.

It took a few days to produce the 500 doses in the research lab that could have been produced in the full production plant across the complex in minutes. Instead of being given a packing address as was the norm, it had been requested to send the brown cardboard box to the administration building.

Caridad personally packed the box and put normal red bio-warning tape across the top of the box. The tape roll was empty before she completed wrapping the box; she reloaded the tape dispenser and wrapped it again.

The next morning her grape buzzed. It was Ethan.

"I'm working on a project in the administration building cafeteria. Want to join me for lunch a little early?"

"Sure I'll be right there."

It was a sparse crowd in the dinning room near the main hallway at the early hour. Caridad talked about their next project having to do with measles and Ethan said he would be home late as Adana was meeting with the building inspectors about a new project and she wanted him to attend. They avoided any other discussion.

Caridad was about to leave when she noticed a shipping clerk pushing a cart of outgoing boxes down the hallway. The box she had packed the day before with the extra red tape caught her eye. The clerk parked the cart beside the men's rest room door and left it.

"Excuse me," she said to her husband and headed for the cart.

The box was covered by another which she moved and read the shipping address on the box with the extra red tape. She immediately noticed international postage and the address, Guantanamo Bay, Cuba. She had started to place the box back when a man approached her.

"Lady, you are not authorized to handle outgoing shipments."

"I'm not, well actually this box was about to fall off and I caught it before it did."

"Where is the shipping clerk?"

"I don't know."

Seeing the commotion and recognizing the man as the building inspector who had sighted with him on the farm Ethan approached. "Hi, I want to introduce my wife Caridad."

"Oh, glad to meet you... and... thanks for grabbing the box."

The shipping clerk returned from the rest room. "Do you know you are to never leave outgoing shipping out of your sight?"

"Yes sir, sorry."

"Well, glad to meet you again Mrs. Alderman. I had a good time sighting with your husband."

Outside Ethan asked, "What was that all about?"

"I'll tell you later."

That evening on secure phones the normal attendees were on a conference call.

Ethan who had just got home in time for the call reported of learning about a tunnel construction project that had to be completed within a year.

"That confirms what the inspector told you Barry. Does anyone have any idea what the purpose of it is?"

No one had any ideas but Ethan said, "I was tempted to ask the inspector but it is better to not show much curiosity. However, I was surprised at the urgency they have for its completion."

"Well that's why I need to get to Iowa, said Julie. "How's the work coming on my credentials Barry?"

"I should have everything in place within a week. They are hiring new security personnel at the NSA plant. And I'll see to it that your application is moved to the top of the list, but travel may be a problem, air travel anyway. Your iris and finger prints won't be recognizable in regular channels to any identity but your new one, but the Transportation Security Agency (TSA) has links to its old database and will identify you as you. Double identity will throw off alarms all over an airport."

"She has a way to get around airports," Andrew quipped jokingly.

"Not this time I'm afraid."

"Okay, I'll need a way there without taking our car which is black boxed."

"We were planning on a trip to Colorado next month and since you'll be staying with us, if you can get to Boulder you can ride back with us. We can move the trip to next week," offered Ethan.

"That will be great. Is there anything new to report from the FDA, Caridad?"

"Yes, I don't know what it means but I think it is important. The new vaccine we've developed, we only produced 500 doses of it and it is headed to Guantanamo Bay, Cuba after going through the administrative office rather than normal channels."

"So what vaccine are they producing for this year?"

"Same as last year, I guess, since we've not given the production department the new vaccine. They will start shipping last year's around the country soon."

"Do you have any idea of why your small batch of the new stuff was sent to Guantanamo Bay?"

"No, I don't."

"That could be important. Torrence, contact the Russians I think they still have some contacts in Cuba."

—ᴍ—

White House

"Mr. President I think all things considered the Hamlin kid should be sent to Guantanamo Bay. It is more secure than anywhere in this country and it is set up as a facility for permanent residents. No one ever need know where he is and it will ensure he is quiet forever."

"But what about putting him in contact with other flashers he may know?"

"What difference does it make; none will ever leave the place?"

"I guess you are right, so be it. How close are we to running the little experiment we talked about?"

"Two weeks sir. The vaccine was given this week to guards and other personnel. Full immunity will take that long. The virus will be shipped next week."

"Ask not what the government can do for you.
Ask what the government is doing to you."

Anonymous

Chapter 7

Des Moines

It had been six months since Darrell Greene moved into Emily Schotus's studio apartment. Although the lease hadn't run out on his studio, they had plans to find a one bedroom flat and talked of marriage. Now he was gone, not herded in a plane but dragged in, permanently gone, gone as in dead and no body to mourn.

His mother had called the previous evening and Emily lied saying she didn't know where Darrell was. "Is everything okay?" she had asked implying Emily and he might be having a quarrel. Emily didn't have the nerve to tell her and wouldn't have known what to say if she did. She was scared, scared because she had been there, scared because she had escaped and struck an agent and scared because she had a camera chip she didn't know what to do with. But she was scared mostly because anyone, particularly someone she loved, could be taken with no cause, explanation or acknowledgement.

Upon getting back to her apartment from Knoxville she had wiped any fingerprints off the video chip, packed it in two sealed plastic bags and buried it in the adjoining apartment building's flower bed. It was better to not have it in her possession she decided.

But after a week of not hearing anything of the episode she dug up the chip, plugged it in her TV and watched the video of the events in Knoxville filmed by the ATF agent followed by what she had captured on the tarmac. She watched it three times through. Any hope of finding an answer or invalidating her memory was vanquished. It was nearly more than she could do to view glimpses of Darrell on the video taken by the ATF agent she had battered on the head.

She had filmed the events until the planes took off and hid again in the canary grass until the agents finally left. When it finally felt safe she retrieved the camera from under a log where she had hidden it, pulled the memory chip from it and started walking. Within a mile she thought of leaving the camera behind but if they found it without the chip they would know someone had it. Thinking it safer if the camera was never found she walked another mile, found a broken steel fence post in a farm field and used it to bury the camera.

Her grape still didn't work eliminating calling for help, but she didn't know who she would call if she could. Some miles from the site a farmer who was headed to Knoxville picked her up.

"Are you sure you want to go to Knoxville?" he asked.

"Yes, I'm to meet someone there."

"After whatever happened there at noon, I wouldn't advise it if you don't need to. I'm only going to check on my sister. I can't reach her on the grape or telephone. Seems as though nothing is working there after that electric burst of some kind."

"What do you think happened?"

"I don't know but someone knows about it. Look there is another one."

Emily looked in the direction he was pointing. She had seen two earlier but thought they were turkey vultures. Looking closer she saw they were man made. A chill went up her spine thinking they still were vultures.

There was little traffic in the town. Dropped off at her electric car she found it wouldn't run and smelled of burned wiring insulation.

She was not alone; she soon found as nothing in the town seemed to work. It was the next evening before she made her way back to the Urbandale suburb of Des Moines.

Emily had not revealed to anyone the existence of the video and didn't know what to do with it. In some respects she knew it would be the smartest thing to destroy it, but she couldn't bring herself to do it. Someone should know what happened. No hints came from the news she had watched frequently, only talk of a natural electrical storm in Iowa. It was no electrical storm that she had ever heard of. When would the others be back? When would news of Darrell's demise get out? She missed him. Was it all actually a bad dream? The scratches on her arm were real as was Darrell's blood on her jeans.

Who would she give the chip to? The people she would trust with the chip were gone. She decided she would carry on at her job as a physical therapist and decide later what to do with the chip, if anything. Far too much was happening now for her to digest.

Guantanamo Bay, Cuba

The prison facility had been used, closed and reopened more than once in the last half century. Each time it was reopened the security was tighter. Three hundred special NSA security agents ran the facility. The guards included the former ATF agents who escorted the prisoners from Iowa. They were now NSA agents. Meals were all outsourced, delivered twice a day in a truck.

The NSA guards were specially picked based on extensive psychological testing which identified the least risk-taking, most prone to following the system. They alternated monthly deployments at the camp which left 150 on duty at all times. Their special employment status afforded them full retirement at 90% base pay after ten years. It was not something they would jeopardize.

The former NSA district director, now warden, made it clear to all the guards that loss of pension would be the least of their worries should they leak anything about where they were or anything about the camp. Anyone violating the rules would immediately become a prisoner at the camp instead of a guard.

Prisoners were frustrated getting no answers about how long they would be captive, but the guards knew no more than they. Neither would be told that the powers that be had no intention of them ever leaving or any word ever getting out as to their whereabouts.

After hearing rumors vibrating through the barracks that a new prisoner had arrived, no one was more surprised than Tony Johnson to find Aaron Hamlin in the exercise yard.

"Long time Aaron."

"I'd like to say I'm glad to see you, but not glad to see you here."

"I have to be frank with you, you being here, I suspect, may not bode well for the rest of us. We had hoped this to be a short term stay, but I suspect yours won't be."

"Why are you and the rest here?"

"We were all picked up at a flash in Iowa. They were waiting for us."

"What did they charge you with?"

"Charged us with nothing, just herded us on trailers, then planes and flew us here. We resisted and the ones you don't see came here in body bags," Tony said going into further detail about what happened.

"I guess I'm not the only one locked up for no reason," Aaron said watching for the reaction from Tony.

"We didn't believe you had anything to do with the assassination attempt, but as you were able to stay in college and Ethan was booted, frankly, we suspected you of turning."

"Glad to hear you use suspect in a past tense. What's it like here?"

"The guards know nothing. We are up to four hours a day in the exercise yard and promised we'll have unlimited daytime access if everyone obeys the rules."

"Does anyone know you and the group are here? Can you get any messages out?"

"We haven't figured out how."

A NSA guard behind tinted glass in a tower watched the conversation between Aaron and Tony through binoculars. He and his partner traded off between the binoculars and staying within grasp of the 50 caliber machine gun's handle. As proximity to the machine gun required less work they both preferred the other do observation. Little did they anticipate need to use what they referred to as the mowing machine.

"The new prisoner and the guy he is talking to obviously know each other."

"You better go report it."

"Yeah, when I get back you can hold the binoculars. My arm is sore from that flu vaccine they gave us a couple weeks ago."

"Oh, oh, I feel so sorry."

"Shut up twinkle toes, at least I took it and didn't waste credit points paying to doctor to dump it because I'm a wimp."

Before the guard with the message got back to the tower, a meal-carrying panel truck pulled into the secure area between the two outer rows of parallel sixteen foot high chain linked fence.

Each fence was topped with barbed wire as the norm for a prison fence, but not normal was the rigging of motion detectors between the second and third fence linked to spray nozzles of deathly gas. More than once had an armadillo tunneled under the fence unwittingly killing him and causing sickness of prisoners downwind. The prisoners got the message and dropped plans to tunnel under the fence into no-mans land.

The too-loud buzzer sounded for meal time. Prisoners lined up outside the dining hall while the guards watched Cuban workers load the food on carts in the inspection area. A veteran food service worker, Adelmo, orchestrated the meal delivery to the inspection area. All plates were taken from carts, put on a conveyer for inspection and moved on the conveyer through two fences and a wall to the dinning hall. Guards watched every step of the process and the Cubans never got within two walls of the prisoners.

Adelmo Perez was working in the footsteps of his father in more ways than known. His father had delivered food to the base for military units stationed at the bay compound and later to early prisoners. Many of their co-workers had wondered how the Perezes came to live somewhat better than others. Actually they cleverly covered up how much better their life was than others. Russians having a need for intelligence outside of Cuban channels for information about the base employed the father and later the son.

As the meal was being served the guard relayed his observation of the new prisoner knowing another prisoner to the prison commandant. "You were right reporting this to me. We will be asking them questions. And by-the-way after dusk we will be conducting a test on the nozzles in the second fence corridor, don't worry it will not be poisonous."

As he promised shortly after dusk nozzles sprayed a fluid containing a man-made viral substance in the entire donut parameter between the first and second fences ensuring the drift would reach all whatever direction the wind was blowing. Only the guards were protected.

It was two nights later that a tunnel project started. Knowing entry into the space between fences would be deadly, the plan was to tunnel under all the fences from the basement of the dinning hall. It would require a 400 foot underground tunnel and the dirt would need to be carefully spread around the yard.

The plans for its construction had been on hold until ramifications of Aaron Hamlin's appearance became clear. Confident they would not be held for a short time in a facility with someone who allegedly attempted to assassinate the President, the risks seemed smaller. Though none of the prisoners had had any prison experience inside or outside, they knew short-termers were not mixed with long-termers. They had discreetly voted and it was nearly unanimous.

In addition to the human watch towers that might have been considered lightly-manned for a maximum security prison, the prison employed a variety of electronic surveillance apparatus. Foremost was a small 360 degree convex mirror system on top of a flag pole in the center court. The inconspicuous device only measured three inches in diameter with a sophisticated camera pointed toward the mirror. It sent a downward focused video feed of a complete circle, which software unwrapped, giving those in the commandant's office total sighting of the grounds from one camera. The prisoners wrongly believed the obvious surveillance cameras, which deceivingly showed a gap in coverage, would allow a difficult but discreet route to the dining hall.

On the second night of digging they had breached the plane of the first fence. Unbeknownst to the diggers sensors buried in the ground which sensed vibration triggered an alarm in the commandant's office.

Night guards monitoring the prison had advised the commandant of the first entry into the dining hall some nights ago. It was his decision to let them dig until they breached the second fence allowing them to stay busy wasting their effort. He was not surprised when awakened with the news of the second fence breach. Guards quickly stormed the basement and seized thirteen working the shift, seven men and six women. They were taken to a lock up.

Within an hour six relief diggers, who had not heard of the fourteen's capture, entered the basement. They were added to the thirteen in the lock up under the commandant's office.

The next morning the commandant met with all but a few of the guards. He explained the demonstration plan for the containment of future anti-social behavior.

"This is not a random sample of our citizenry we have. These people have shown complete disregard for the bond that holds our society together. We are charged with containing that threat. But we must do so in a manner that discourages future escape attempts.

I have been given full authority to use whatever means necessary to fulfill our mission. Our demonstration will ease our work here and ultimately deter further hardship on the prisoners. Let's all repeat the pledge before we go to work.

"I Pledge allegiance to the flag of the United States of America and to the institution for which it stands, one nation, indivisible with fairness and justice for all."

The door opened allowing light to enter the basement. At the bottom of the steps were two cells, each six by eight feet without any furniture, only a five gallon bucket. Eight women had been placed in one cell, the eleven men in another. The nineteen prisoners were relieved when their cell doors were opened and they were escorted outside. All had expected a longer stay of discomfort including the indignities of such confinement.

Merrine and Noah were among the nineteen who had been locked in the basement of the commandant's office. They had been married eight years and it had been six since they applied for a prodigy permit. Although they retained hope, their SPI was nowhere close to the permit level, primarily attributable to NSA records at the Utah Data Center recording their attendance at flashes. They abhorred any kind of violence as their grandparents had a century earlier and like them demonstrated against what they considered an oppressive establishment. Noah waited for Merrine on the stairs and they walked up to sunlight together. They would not be separated again.

The other prisoners had been formed up at the far side of the courtyard facing the three consecutive gates linked to the three parameter fences. The gates were all open. Nineteen captives were escorted to within fifty feet of the first open gate leading to freedom.

On speakers around the courtyard bellowed the commandant's voice. "Those who seek to dispute your condition and seek freedom, even after your prior treacherous behavior, we offer you this opportunity. The gates are open."

The nineteen scanned the courtyard. Few guards were seen. No shadows were apparent in the tower by the gates which was common in the early morning sunlight.

"I don't like it," someone said in the group.

Someone else yelled at the others lined up opposite in the courtyard, "Come join us."

Many took steps forward until a string of armed guards formed a picket line in front of them.

The silence became eerie. No one moved. Finally two men started taking slow steps toward the gate. At the first gate opening they stopped and summoned the rest to join them. Again there was silence.

The commandant stood in the tower, looking over the assembled prisoners, beside an agent manning a mowing machine. In the tower 90 degrees to the right waited another mowing machine operator.

Impatience getting the better of the commandant he instructed the operator, "Its time to coax them."

The machine operator swept the barrel of the 50 caliber machine in an arc about twenty feet in front of the nineteen captured would-be escapees in a practice swing. Once the arc was established he looked at the commandant. The commandant shook his head and the operator squeezed the trigger and retraced the arc in two loops.

The 706 grain bullets traveling at nearly 2600 feet per second plowed the ground in front of the standing group. Hitting nothing hard enough to ricochet the bullets they stirred the soil underneath into a rising cloud of dust. But they also sent a gauntlet of rocks and pebbles toward the group, knocking many down with cuts and abrasions and putting two eyes out. The group instinctively stepped back and huddled together, but stood still. Another swoop of the machine gun added to their injury.

Two guards standing by the dining hall stepped forward, one with his hands to his side with palms up as if to ask, *what's this about?* The two stepped back when one of the machine guns pointed in their direction.

Noah held Merrine as they both seeped blood from lacerations. Both were able to walk as their wounds, nasty as they looked, were superficial. Others were now running many struggling with limps. They headed for the outer gate. "Let's not run," Noah said as he steadied his wife.

As the first two escapees crossed the third and final open gate, the commandant said, "Now!"

The first two escapees collapsed onto ground already soiled with their body parts. The operator in the other tower joined in the mêlée making short work of the group. As blood and body fragments made a pink cloud around them, Merrine and Noah Weiland held each other never knowing who succumbed first.

Many of the remaining assembled prisoners including Tony couldn't hold what remained of the previous day's dinner in their stomachs. Neither could many of the guards.

Adelmo Perez twice watched the video feed from the 360 degree mirror that Russian technicians had tapped into before sending it by encrypted route to Russia. He too felt sick.

The next day a few prisoners felt a sickness coming on. The following day even more became sick. They attributed it to the trauma of what they had witnessed. They were wrong.

"The greater dangers to liberty lurk in insidious encroachment by men of zeal, well-meaning but without understanding."

Louis Brandeis

Chapter 8

Jayden was an organized person. He seldom lost anything, least likely phone numbers. He kept most anyone he had talked to or texted on his grape caller contact log for years. Little did he know that the NSA also kept track of whose numbers were on his call log. They included three people who had been identified by security cameras as having attended flash demonstrations.

Fortunately for Julie she had not only decided to travel light but to use shopping bags for what she took. Anyone seeing her carrying traveling bags might be suspicious and they could not risk Caridad and Ethan picking her up at home. Their inadvertent avoidance of the traveling bag containing an electronic bug might have been coincidental.

Andrew loaded the twins and shopping bags into the cramped half seat of their car and drove Julie to the shopping mall recently re-named for a community organizer. It didn't escape Julie or him that it was the parking lot where he had waited for her while she shopped for clothes some years ago. The significance of her coming to him then and leaving him now weighed on him.

Julie opened her door and reached for each of the twins giving them a hug they didn't understand before gathering her two shopping bags. Andrew noticed a tear in her eye as she kissed him goodbye. He also felt one coming as he watched her enter the car with Caridad and Ethan.

—ɷ—

The director of security at the NSA complex in Chillicothe, Iowa had been given authorization to beef up its security personnel numbers. The facility already had twice the security of any other NSA project of similar size the security director knew, but he wouldn't question the authorization as it put more people under his direction bumping him into a higher pay grade.

He was authorized five more hires. A complex system of test scores, experience, social attitudes and unknown factors rated a long list potential hires in order of best fits for the openings. As their supervisor the security director could avoid hiring the top five on the list, but he would need to document a good reason and doing so would draw attention to himself. He had no reason to do either.

The third name on the list was Julie Levine-Collier's new alias, Julie Archibald. It was primarily Torrence at the island off Costa Rica who had corrupted the list of applicants and altered Julie's records to put her third on the list. Putting her first wasn't necessary and potentially could draw unnecessary attention.

In a motel room overnight on the route from Idaho to Iowa Julie cut her thick brunette locks and covered her head with a blond wig, similar to the one she wore as a phony TSA agent when she saved Andrew. Her beautiful blues eyes she covered with brown contacts which also altered her iris print. In Iowa she would be Julie Archibald. Although warned, Caridad and Ethan hardly recognized her the next morning.

Temporarily Caridad and Ethan made a place for Julie in the living room of their one bedroom apartment, having already notified authorities of taking in someone to help with the payment to the housing authority. In two weeks a small studio a few blocks away reserved for NSA personnel would be open to her.

In the week of orientation for the job, Julie learned primarily that security was more focused on information leaving the facility than someone getting in. The threshold for bringing an employee in for questioning was very low they were warned, unusually so given Julie's understanding of government security protocol. They were not told they would be monitored off work. She would need to be careful.

The first day of real work she was given her assignment. A tunnel was to be built to connect with an unidentified facility. It was to be constructed by subcontractors. It would be her job to monitor the workers both on and off the job. She was given a list which included Ethan Alderman.

"We couldn't have been luckier about my assignment," Julie told Ethan that evening over for dinner. "I'll be watching you," she said with a laugh.

"Well I for one don't believe in luck," observed Adana.

"Remember I told you at the Chicagoland conference how you sound like someone else I knew." Julie told them about Dan Barnmore's belief in a helping hand guiding serendipity.

"I've no choice but to move to the studio they furnish me but I certainly can't keep the secure phone there. I'm sure the place is thoroughly bugged."

"You can leave it here hidden with ours."

"No, we can't have two together and chance losing both. I'll find a place to hide the phone."

They soon used the secure phone on a conference call with Andrew, Barry and Torrence. "I heard back from the Russians today. They have something for us. They are sending it tomorrow."

"What is it about?"

"Guantanamo Bay."

Barry asked, "Have any more shipments been made to the base?"

"I can't tell you about more shipments, but I think not since we haven't made anymore of the vaccine," answered Caridad.

"Speaking of vaccine Julie, the clinic called me with a date tomorrow for the twins. I can't put it off again," Andrew stated.

"What about it Caridad, has anything changed your mind?" asked Julie.

"No. It's the same as last year's."

—⟋⟍⟋—

Alice, Barry's wife, had fixed lunch early for the twins as Andrew was due to pick them up at noon. She had become very close to the twins watching them during the day as Julie and Andrew worked. The arrangement was convenient, offered an excuse for the two couples to be together frequently without raising eyebrows, but most importantly in Alice's world gave her a motherly attachment she had unknowingly missed. She dreaded the twins turning four next year requiring their attendance at day-long preschool.

Andrew had the twins at the clinic prior to the 1:00 appointment. It was not an uncommon practice for physicians to fake giving the flu shot to patients with proper consideration. Julie and Andrew had met the physician at the local speakeasy more than once.

What little money that still existed had no value as it had been outlawed some years ago and registering an exchange of credit points on the TAC (Transaction Account Card) was not a safe alternative. Hence Andrew offered the physician an IOU made out for 20 United Nation Credits (UNC) and signed it. The physician could trade it to someone else for services and eventually someone would present it to Andrew for the trade of services or the physician could use it for barter directly with Andrew. A system of floating IOUs had become a type of black market currency.

The physician drew two doses of vaccine, put them in the sink, made the proper notations of vaccination on his report and showed them the door. On their exit he placed the IOU in his pocket Andrew had left on the counter, later that evening the doctor exchanged the

IOU at a speakeasy for drink. The next time Andrew was at the speakeasy he had one drink but two were charged to his TAC and he was given his IOU.

Andrew returned the twins to Alice, "I have a favor to ask. Just got a call from the laboratory, I need to go in, some problem with a security robot. I know you probably looked forward to time alone."

She interrupted him, "No not at all. You go to work. I had nothing planned and frankly was missing them."

Andrew thanked her twice before he left realizing how lucky Julie and he were to have such a great friend and caregiver for the twins.

That evening across town the bald-headed ATF agent, who had tracked Andrew to the border before being disappointed, lay in bed with his roommate of six months. He was using his roommate, another ATF agent, to bring down one or hopefully both of his primary targets, Andrew and Jim. Presently the blond agent was working at Jim and Nathan's nursery doing odd jobs in order to glean incriminating information.

"You've been working at the nursery, what now, four months?"

"Your mind is back to business quickly tonight, why?"

"Failure to get anything on those two is bothering me, they shouldn't be loose. Any news at the nursery?"

"Yes, I've sent numerous samples of the plant stock material and nothing has tested positive for genetically engineered animal retardants."

"Does the customer tracking still correlate with the records?"

"Nathan and Jim took off for a couple hours yesterday and I went through their financial records again, everything they have matches their government filings."

At Nathan's insistence, primarily to protect their son, Jim and Nathan had quit using illegal seed stock and had done everything to the letter of mandates. It was frustrating Jim, but Nathan was sleeping well.

"I'm working on another route to get Jim. The son of his, Orlando, is borderline SED. Just a couple more outbursts at school and he'll be gone.

Besides separating about 10% of students as specially challenged for additional help and the gifted 3% of students in high schools for advanced placement, schools separated about 10% of the students in a category called Socially and Emotionally Disturbed, (SED). SED students were prescribed medication to mellow antisocial behavior. Washington had funded a new program to give the SED students further help. Those most challenged SED students, who had multiple antisocial complaints filled against them with the Department of Health and Human Services (DHHS), were separated from their families and taken to intensive retraining schools. Many parents welcomed the relief from dealing with problem children, others did not.

"Oh, so they've got a son that's a social misfit."

"Yes, that's one way to put it. I think it's time for you to leave the nursery and get a job with ARC where Andrew works," the agent stated looking coldly up at the ceiling from bed.

"What can I learn there at an entry level job? A big company like that I won't get close to the books."

"I know but maybe its time to use your good looks. Its time to trade in your garden aprons for some eye-appealing dress clothes."

The blond agent was thirty-five but could pass for twenty-five. Her body was trim, helped by the extensive ATF training regime. Whenever they were out her supervisor noticed all the heads she turned. He smiled thinking some guy might think given her petite stature that he could get aggressive with her and learn that looks, particularly her looks could be deceiving. Her blond hair was not natural. The color didn't match her eyebrows and a darker color showed through on the side it was cut shorter. She wore her hair in the asymmetrical style of the times, shoulder length on one side and above the ear on the other side. In earlier decades her hair style would have been considered outside the norm or just weird, but in these times when people sought avenues to express individuality the spectrum of hair colors and styles was broad.

"What do you have in mind?"

"According to the employment bureau, Andrew's wife was reassigned to the Company headquarters in Harford. The guy might be getting lonely."

"How far do you want me to go?"

"How far do you want to go in the agency?"

With appropriate leverage in two weeks the blond had a data entry job on the third floor of the Boise ARC building. Andrew worked on the sixth floor, but she always rode the elevator to the seventh floor and returned. Surveillance had determined to the 90th percentile the times Andrew would arrive and leave the office and visit the cafeteria. The blond agent worked harder at her real job running into Andrew than entering data.

After meeting on the elevator numerous times and exchanging pleasantries, the blond asked if the empty seat beside him in the cafeteria was taken. Andrew was not looking for companionship, but she was lovely, in a green dress cut squarely in the style of the times, the helm with square cutouts on the side and a little shorter than normal. The top strap was cut in a sharp line down to a 90 degree turn across the slight rise of her breasts. The top two buttons of the dress were undone, but the look, although gently alluring, was not audacious. It was a look that suited her having a somewhat less than average endowment.

In Iowa Julie was dressed in running clothes. Before her evening walk-run routine, she made her way to the basement with laundry. It was her plan to do laundry nearly every day or at least when ever she needed to retrieve her secure phone. In a utility room off the laundry she reached up above the plate on the foundation behind an uncovered batting of 8 inch fiberglass insulation and retrieved her secure phone. Hiding it in her studio or her storage locker was much too dangerous.

Once the proper codes were entered she saw she had four missed calls from Torrence since last evening. The phones only identified missed calls they did not take texts as having written communication even with the secure hydrochloric acid protected phone was a risk. She sat on a park bench at her turnaround place on the recreation trail.

"Torrence, what's up?"

"Our contact in Russia got back to us. Their person monitoring the Guantanamo Bay compound says the newly renewed prison facility is holding Americans."

"How many? Who are they?"

"I'm getting there. By the meals being delivered they estimate 3-4 hundred. We don't know who they are but they are definitely Americans. Most tend to be 20-50 years old, there doesn't appear to be any older people."

"Am I too quick to speculate where they may have come from?"

"Isn't that about how many were expected at the flash in Iowa where the electron storm took place?"

"Yes, but we have no witnesses. It's as if it didn't happen. Those demonstrations get canceled sometimes, but we can't find anyone who we would have expected to have been there."

"I haven't told you the worst part. It appears the special NSA guards who are running the place, machine gunned twenty inmates in cold blood in front of the other assembled prisoners."

"Can they validate that or is it second hand?"

"They have a video of it and will hand deliver it."

"Oh my god, do they have any clue why it happened?"

"No, they are working on it but say the security is super tight and they don't want to compromise their agent."

"We've got to find out what happened in Knoxville. Notify Barry and keep me informed. Wait. Also see if the Russians know anything about a vaccine being used at the prison, anything unusual with flu vaccines."

Julie hung up and thought for a few minutes before calling Andrew. She quickly filled him in on what she had learned.

"We have found the Russians a reliable source of information but I find it hard to believe. I can't imagine even the NSA going that far without some reason, justifiably or not."

"I couldn't reach Barry tonight. Go see him and see if he can get me a list of the names of anyone we know of who attends flashes in Iowa."

"You know there is no written record but I'll see what he can come up with. You know Ethan will be the best source."

"I'm headed there now."

"I'm sure you'll find out what happened but be careful. The twins miss you and I miss you."

"And I miss you. Did you take the twins to the doctor?"

"Yes and I followed your advice."

Caridad buzzed Julie into their flat. Julie engaged in small talk while holding her index finger in front of her mouth as she scanned the room with an electronic eavesdropper detector she picked up when she replaced the secure phone.

With all apparently clear she filled them in on the news from Torrence. They were aghast."

"I need the names of people who might have attended the flash in Knoxville. She got twenty names of regulars at demonstrations. Anthony Johnson's was among them.

Guantanamo Bay

There had been little interaction between the prisoners after the morning massacre. No announcements came from the guard staff other than a lockup in the barracks. The commandant had already communicated very forcefully. Although they had always been reluctant to talk openly inside, preferring outdoors, no one had anything to say. All were lost in their thoughts.

The next morning the loudspeakers announced that the courtyard would be open six hours and, barring anymore trouble, all daytime hours in a week. No one celebrated the relaxation in rules and they were slow to trickle outside. All traces of the killings had been covered up including a darker, less sun bleached dirt where blood had flowed. Three inmates never made it outside that day as they weren't feeling well.

The following day seventeen didn't make it outside. They were running fevers, and vomiting with headaches. Anthony theorized that trauma affected people in different ways. No one disagreed with him. But the next day half the prisoners were sick.

The NSA personnel didn't attempt to isolate anyone, partially because they lacked the facilities. The house doctor examined many prisoners and diagnosed it as the flu. Eventually 243 of the 367 prisoners left alive got the flu including Aaron Hamlin. Most recovered within three days and found the illness no worst than any flu they had experienced.

However, after a week 26 remained very weak. Some were given fluids, but as they all had very low Health Score Indexes (HSI) and prisoners weren't afforded better coverage than their indexes warranted, recovery was slow.

Eventually five succumbed to the illness. Aaron Hamlin was among them. The four year trial had drained him physically and made him perhaps the most vulnerable.

Three NSA guards also caught the virus but recovered quickly. The prisoners were aware that they had not received the normal mandated flu shots, but most had refused them in the past. Actually they drew no conclusions as the variation of those getting the flu with and without the vaccine in the past wasn't apparent.

Observation via the 360 degree camera told Adelmo that few prisoners exited the barracks for days, guards entered the barracks wearing masks and five bodies had been removed from the facility. His thoughts ran toward the possibility of food poisoning and any potential blame toward his food service. He passed the information on to his Russian contact.

At the Russian intelligence center in Moscow note was made that an unknown illness at the US prison had sickened many prisoners and apparently killed five.

—◊—

ARC building in Boise

Andrew was working on updates to ARC's newly redesigned pneumatic robotic material moving system. Although using air to move material had been done for many decades, ARC had taken the concept to a new scale. It fit ARC's mission to build the best, most innovative material handling robotics. Deeply involved in a project, as was often the case, Andrew had nearly skipped lunch and entered the cafeteria just before closing.

He had just sat when his occasional lunch partner sat across from him at an empty table in a nearly deserted dinning room.

He clearly noticed her figure as she bent forward putting her plate on the table and steadying herself as she raised a leg over the seat bench that more closely resembled a picnic table than a dinning table. Although Julie had lost most of her added weight gained during pregnancy few women matched the physical appeal of this woman. No man would miss the exposure of cleavage and more than a little thigh as she wrestled herself onto the bench.

"Eating late today also, I see,"

"Yes, I lost track of time on a project," she said knowing it would match his reason for a late lunch.

"Do you like working here?"

"Yes, I do but I don't really have any friends around here."

"You'll find friends, attractive as you are," he replied before realizing that she might not have been referring to male friends.

"I know I will. How long has your wife been away now, a month?"

"It's been three weeks and yes I miss her."

"I love to cook and it is so boring cooking for myself, why don't you come for dinner this weekend?"

"I have the twins to think about."

"Have your nanny watch them for one evening, what will it hurt?"

Her foot startled Andrew. He felt her warmness as her instep half encircled his ankle. The softness told him that the black heel she had sashayed up to the table in was gone. It reminded him of flirting he missed. And it reminded him of Julie.

Andrew stuttered momentarily and awkwardly cleared his mouth. "You are a very attractive 30 year-old I would guess. I have to ask you why would you be interested in a married man born in 1984?"

"I've always had an attraction for mature men, particularly engineers who build things and make a difference in the world."

"You forgot the married part."

"Don't be such an oldie, your wife chose to leave you, didn't she?"

Regretting that he had obviously told her too much in earlier lunch conversations he countered. "Yes, but she will be back."

"Of course, I only invited you to dinner."

Wishing to return the flattery and avoid the wrath of a scorned woman he added, "You are a very nice and attractive lady. I appreciate the interest more than you'll ever know." Seeing the disappointment in her expression, he added, "If I were ten years younger and single I would enjoy the chance to have dinner with you. However, I know two new engineers that I would like to introduce to you."

She wrote her telephone number on a pad and handed it to him. "Just in case you change your mind."

On the way home that evening Andrew stopped at a grocery store to buy food to make his own lunches for a couple weeks. Later that evening he called Julie.

Seeing Andrew had called, Julie returned the call on her secure phone. "What's up?"

"The twins are doing fine. Work may have a tie-in with where you are. Sales told me we have an order for our new pneumatic materials system at a NSA run plant in Iowa."

"Do you think it is in Chillicothe?"

"I don't know, but how many NSA operations that need to handle material are in Iowa? I've got John looking into it."

Sensing a slightly different tone in his voice, she asked, "Anything else going on there?"

"Yes as a matter of fact, I received a dinner invitation from a woman at work today."

"Do you know her?"

"Not really. She's sat beside me at lunch a few times and seems to always be running into me."

"Is she good looking?"

"Yes, she happens to be very good looking."

"What did you tell her?"

"I told her I was too old for her."

"Why don't you go out with her?"

"Well the invitation was at her place. And I don't want to encourage anything."

Didn't know her, very good-looking, young, a come-on- the wheels were spinning in Julie's head. She knew Andrew was probably under limited observation of some kind and she was gone, it was a perfect opportunity and it smelled but she didn't want to throw cold water on her husband although he was also probably suspicious, "I hope you were kind to her."

"I was. But I do miss you."

Even though she might have interpreted his comment as a veiled threat, Julie didn't take it that way. "I'll be back before long. Tomorrow I'm taking a trip to find out what happened to the fathom flash in Knoxville."

"Be careful honey."

Thinking a little hint of jealousy might be in order, Julie asked, "What color is her hair?"

"Blond."

"As am I," she thought.

"The Constitution is not an instrument for the government to restrain the people, it is an instrument for the people to restrain the government – lest it come to dominate our lives and interests"

Patrick Henry

Chapter 9

Liam's blood analysis at his mandatory annual health check-up had never shown nicotine in his blood. He thought he was crafty as he never had a cigar six weeks prior to his exam in order to avoid a HCI demerit for smoking. However, an aerial Citizen Protection Unit had identified smoke emanating from his patio. They were a year away from making the connection and deducting 10 HCI points.

Julie looked for answers close to her studio apartment in Oskaloosa before heading out of town the next morning. Knowing flashers were apt to be working during the day that evening she knocked on the doors of two people on her list to find no one but noticed mail stacked up. At the third name on her list in town she also found no answer to the door bell.

Leaving, Julie spotted a lady across the street. As Julie approached her, she asked, "Looking for the Weilands? No one's seen them for a few weeks."

"Do you have any idea where they may have gone?"

"No. Are you family?"

"No, just a friend, has their family been looking for them?"

"Yes, Noah's mother has stopped by twice and Merrine's family also. No one has any idea where they may have gone."

"Do you know where I might contact either of their families?"

"Merrine's brother left here an hour ago and said he was headed for a coffee shop around the town square, you might catch him there."

Julie parked on the west side of the town square that featured an ornate band gazebo in the center of the block. Sidewalks like spokes in a wheel connected the gazebo to the perimeter sidewalk around the square. Most of the green benches lining the spokes of the town square were occupied for the Thursday evening band performance. The sun setting over the buildings west of the street created shadows on the ground and bottom half of a bronze statue of Mahaska, an Indian chief. The upper torso of the statue in a Napoleonic pose was brilliantly illuminated by the orange rays of the sun.

She entered the coffee shop soon finding a man dressed as the neighbor described. "Hello, I'm Julie Collier," using her real name, "Your sister's neighbor told me I might find you here."

"Grant… here," he started to pronounce his last name, caught himself and stopped.

"I was looking for your sister and her husband."

"May I ask why?"

"I'm a friend of Ethan Alderman. He told me your sister and husband may have attended an event in Knoxville a few weeks ago."

Grant didn't respond for some time gazing into the reflection of the fluorescent light off the liquid in his glass. In that moment curiosity overcame his fear and he replied. "I don't know for sure but I suspect they attended an event in Knoxville and haven't been seen since. Why do you want to know?"

"Let's just say I'm trying to find out what happened."

Thinking officials would already know what, if anything, happened and not acknowledging any connection to the event he continued, "I don't know what happened other than the electrical storm and anyone I know that might have attended the event is missing."

"If I learn anything I'll let you know."

"I would appreciate that."

Julie walked out the coffee shop door to be engulfed by music from the city band playing "My Country 'tis of Thee". She looked toward the square. The sunlight was gone; it was all in shadows. The meaning was not lost on her.

The next morning Julie called in sick and headed for Knoxville, a small town west of Oskaloosa. Dusty cars not moved since the storm still sat on the street. As the flash was supposed to take place in the downtown area, she asked a number of employees in various shops what they knew of the day. No one knew anything. Most everyone became defensive with many anxious to put distance between her and them.

She met a 50-something lady on the street and visited about the weather and further tried to warm her up by complimenting her on the nice town. "Are things returning to normal around here?"

"You mean after the storm?"

"Yes."

"They'll never be back to normal."

"Were there more people than normal downtown that day?"

The lady gave Julie a quizzical look and started to say something but her expression changed to skeptical. "Glad to meet you but I must get home."

Julie's next stop was the Des Moines area. Ethan had been trying to reach Tony Johnson for some time to no avail. The former local reporter had not been seen on KRMT news since the event and no mention was made of his absence. Ethan had given Julie his parent's address in Urbandale.

His parents were delighted to see Julie hoping that she might know something. Disappointed she didn't, they were baffled and worried about his disappearance but didn't know anything. Julie asked if they knew anyone she might talk to.

"Last week a young lady stopped here and asked about Tony. She seemed anxious to talk to someone who had connections. We asked what she meant by connections but she wouldn't say and left. But she did leave her name and address."

It was dinner time when Julie rang the buzzer to Emily Schotus's studio apartment.

"What do you want?"

"Tony Johnson's parents gave me your name."

"OK, so?"

"I just wanted to talk."

"I'll come down."

They walked across the street to a park bench. Julie told her she was curious about what happened to people in Knoxville. "Do you know anyone that might've been in Knoxville the day of the electric storm?"

Emily studied Julie's face carefully. "Who are you?"

Julie never liked to be reckless but she needed information and she sensed Emily was the one person she had met that might know something.

"Do you know Merrine and Noah... I can't remember their last name or where they are from?" Julie asked holding back information.

Understanding Julie was as careful but needing to reach out as she was, she answered, "You mean Merrine and Noah Weiland of Oskaloosa?

"Yes, that's them. "Do you know an Ethan... what's his name?" Julie continued her ploy revealing little seeking confirmation that Emily wasn't a plant.

Emily didn't answer. Julie felt her skepticism and picked up her grape. Now was the time to gamble; it felt right. She dialed Ethan.

"Hello, Ethan."

"Hi," he answered somewhat skeptical as Julie had never called him on her grape.

"Someone here with me I want you to say hi to, introduce yourself." Julie handed the phone to Emily.

"Hi, I'm Ethan Alderman. Who is this?"

"Emily Schotus."

Julie took the grape from her and disconnected. It was worth the chance but she knew the grape connection would end up as one of multi-trillions stored at the NSA data center in Camp Williams, Utah. More than enough information was stored there to completely monitor and thus control all interaction in the country. Fortunately, although progress was being made, the analytical capacity of the would-be controllers, as yet, couldn't utilize the mountains of information.

"Who are you?"

Julie looked a last time into Emily's eyes for a hint of deception before she took a step.

"I'm Julie Levine Collier, but as far as anyone here knows I'm Julie Archibald. You've probably heard of my husband Andrew Collier."

"You asked if I know of anyone who was in Knoxville that day. I was there."

Emily told Julie everything about the day she could remember. It was painful, but a relief to let someone know. Doing so didn't eliminate the sorrow but in some slight way gave her hope.

"What happed to the camera chip?"

"It's buried in the next door Trumpet Lily bed. Come inside I'll fix something to eat and after dark I'll retrieve it for you."

It was late when Julie entered her studio apartment in Oskaloosa with the chip. She never knew that Emily had made two copies hiding one in another flower bed and one in a bag of mementos of Darrell and hers at her sister's place.

The sun was nearly up before Julie put the chip away. She found no surprise as the video matched the description of events as Emily told it, but seeing and hearing made it more profound.

Julie was tempted to place a secure call to Barry and Torrence before she headed for work but refrained. Too much traffic to the laundry might be noticed, but the day went slow at work.

At the mid-point of her evening walk she described to the conference call participants what she had discovered about the now non-phantom flash. She went into as much detail as possible about the video.

Torrence drew the same conclusion as others, "No doubt the prisoners at Guantanamo Bay are flashers from Iowa. With the video of their apprehension and the camp video the Russians have of the murders, we've got powerful material. But I'm getting some resistance from Russian intelligence on providing the camp video."

"Why, they've always worked with us?" asked Barry.

"They claim they don't want to waste it. They would rather keep the evidence for release when it could have the maximum impact. They went through some rigmarole about when they were a controlled society our help was minimal."

"I need to get this video chip out of the country to you guys on the island-boat and we certainly can't send it electronically. Can you get a courier to me?"

"I agree we've got to move it by hand. Can you make some copies?"

"Done and I think we just as well share it with the Russians, maybe it'll help them see the time is right to expose what they have. Torrence, how are your people on the island-boat coming along with the idea to infect the NSA data site in Utah with a worm?"

"They are making headway on a novel plan. That's all I better say."

"As time goes on they will figure out how to use more of the information they have stored and I'm sure there is enough in there to provide us all with a ticket to Guantanamo Bay."

"Believe me we know and our little island is not that well-equipped to deal with the US navy."

—ɱ—

White House

"Mr. President we have the report on the virus test in Cuba. Over 68% of the prisoners showed signs of the flu virus. Of those around 8% were seriously ill for a few days and 1% perished," reported the NSA director.

"So how many died?"

"Five, sir."

The NSA director knew the President, as skilled as he was, did not excel in math nor liked to get deep into numbers. Using discretion to round the percentage to 1% served the purpose minimizing the loss of life.

Nevertheless the President looked at the CDC and FDA directors and observed, "If I recall you predicted a much lower fatality rate."

The FDA director interjected defensively, "Mr. President the good news is the vaccine worked very well. Only one percent of the NSA guards came down with flu symptoms and they were mild."

"Am I to believe that we can expect a higher fatality rate in the unvaccinated population than we expected? How many deaths would that project to?" queried the President.

Not answering his question the CDC director said, "We must realize that the prison sample is not a random sample of the population. They are stressed, particularly so given the unfortunate escape incident of which I was just informed. I would expect the result in the total unvaccinated population to be much less."

"How much less and how many are we talking about? Originally you estimated 50 thousand."

"As I said before it is not a random sample so I don't think we should put much credence in the results, but we estimate the results could indicate a maximum of half a percent of the unvaccinated population."

"Quit dancing around with numbers. Please answer my question. How many?"

The CDC director was more restrained in fudging the numbers than the NSA director. "Half a percent of the unvaccinated population would be 150 thousand at the most, Mr. President. But we need to remember, although the prisoners may be stressed and more susceptible to disease their numbers didn't contain old or very young people."

The director of the CDC had no particular ideology, but one overwhelming goal of self aggrandizement with a healthy anticipation of risks. He was very good at hedging his position against any potential risks. He positioned himself well.

Frustrated at his inability to get a straight answer, the President waffled luring others to make his point, "As much merit that our goal has, is it worth taking the kind of chance we are looking at? If it were found out we were responsible for anything close to what we are talking about,... well... I need say no more."

"But Mr. President without the motivation of this flu increasing vaccination numbers next year, our TIP effort will be ineffective. Getting our machines in people who we control today is a wasted activity. It is the marginally controlled people TIP was conceived to bring into the fold. Those who flaunt what is best for them; well we can't be responsible," ranted the NSA director, fearing a loss of years of work and the potential for nearly unlimited power flowing through his fingers."

"How narrow is the sphere of people who know anything about this?"

"Bottom line, Mr. President, only nine people including you know the total scope of TIP. The people in Atlanta believe the virus they are making attacks a harmful virus. Those at the FDA plant believe they are producing a vaccine for a common flu virus mutation. While at NSA anyone below my staff believes the nano-machines are designed to kill harmful plants in cropped areas; that being why the plant is in Iowa. But most importantly strict compartmentalization in each of the facilities has kept work on various components separate and outside the scope of other departments."

The CDC director added, "And, Mr. President, if any one was able to put the pieces together at one plant, no plant knows what the others are doing or the relationship."

"What about that tunnel between the plants in Iowa?"

"It's just common ductwork for geothermal heating."

"It is a tough decision. I'm gong to need to spend some time on it."

"You know that the timetable is such the air transport planes with the virus will need to move within ten days."

"I know. I'll make a decision within a few days," the President said.

Eating dinner alone in the third floor family quarters the President felt a need to talk to someone. Details of TIP and the virus had been discussed enough back and forth. It wasn't details he needed. It was something deeper. Widening the small scope of people who knew of the plan was not an option, but he needed to be okay with whatever decision he made.

The first lady had traveled to the national high school science fair. It had become her project to increase interest in studying the sciences. He didn't expect her home until late.

The President and first lady had a complimentary relationship. She placed higher value on the ability of people to make decisions regarding their own welfare than did the President. He felt people needed direction for their own good. His proclivity to control extended to their personal relationship; hence they found structured, limited interaction best.

The first lady entered the family quarters near midnight. Although the day had been long the handsome navy-suited woman's posture remained perfect. The President was awake when she entered her bedroom. When he guessed she had enough time to be in bed, he tapped on the door.

"Yes, I'm home. But it is the sixteenth of the month."

As in other aspects, their conjugal life was structured. On the 10th, 20th and 30th of the month if both were in the White House one would visit the other's room. He had no intention of breaking their routine, but wanted a sound board.

"I just need someone to talk to."

"Come in."

He sat on the edge of the bed in his Presidential robe. After an exchange about their respective days, he said, "I have an important decision to make. The rewards will be great but as normal in such tradeoffs risks are involved."

After an extended discussion about the responsibilities of leadership in which she didn't ask any details and he didn't volunteer any, she said, "You know this has always been a nation of risk takers, it's who we are and it's what built this country."

"Thank you," he said and kissed her forehead before heading to his room.

She had no idea what she unwittingly approved.

Center for Disease Control, Atlanta, GA

When the idea of utilizing a man-made virus for the ultimate benefit of humankind was in the early stages of contemplation, the director of the CDC started working on implementation. His tenure as a public employee had benefited from putting in place operational details in anticipation of future political decisions. Nearly two years before a call would come to release the virus the director had the method of disbursement in place.

The Department of Transportation (DOT) owned and operated all airports, train stations and gasoline and electric filling stations in the country. All aspects of the maintenance of their facilities were in the purview of the department including cleaning and janitorial services.

As the areas controlled by the DOT were widely accessed by the public-at-large, the CDC contended that for public safety reasons the DOT should follow CDC guidelines in disease prevention. Hence the CDC had started providing the DOT with a CDC approved concentrated cleaning solvent for use at airports, train stations and car filling venues. The solvent's label called for the concentrated solvent to be mixed with twenty parts water.

In a warehouse and chemical blending plant outside of Atlanta a forty thousand liter tank sat nearly full of a medley of cleaning chemicals. Monthly the entire contents of the tank were robotically placed in four-liter plastic jugs, stacked on pallets and shipped around the country for DOT's use as a concentrated cleaning solution. This month the huge vat had the normal mix of chemicals but lacked a few hundred liters of being filled.

On the day before the jug filling process started, employees were given the day off. Waiting on the outskirts of the CDC campus complex a few miles away was a fiberglass tank containing billions and billions of a new virus. As viruses went it was of medium size, approximately 50 nanometers in diameter. Although they were nothing but micro-particles containing genetic material and a protein coat, this one had deadly potential. It had been grown in a medium replicating itself until the virus was concentrated in the fiberglass tank.

The fiberglass tank had been held under a 24-hr. security watch until the CDC director received a call from Washington. Later that day the tank containing what was later called the H2N46 virus was loaded on a truck. It left the building the next morning.

The next morning CDC workers in full hazardous waste suits topped off the big tank with the contents of the truck. Although the ingredients of the tank included an anti-bacterial, the virus, not bacterium, had been designed to be impervious to the chemicals in the tank. The next day the disbursement into jugs started.

Elizabeth Moore, the former President of the United States, lived in Vermont after her tenure in the White House, but she kept in touch with many of the people she had appointed. As time passed she came to look with question on some of the decisions she had made, and regret at some of her appointments.

The President called her once a year, others more often. Her appointment for NSA director remained on the job. With time his fervor matched the unbridled passion she had seen in the President when he was information director at the National Aeronautics and Space Agency (NASA). With age she noticed her conviction of having all the answers diminished.

"I can't tell you all the good things that are happening and being planned," boasted the NSA director to her.

"Give me a hint. With my arthritis acting up again I need something positive to dwell on."

"I shouldn't but you are one of us. Good things are happening in Iowa that will eliminate a problem which tormented you and still harasses us."

Elizabeth Moore having worked with the President and the director of NSA knew that he would not be exaggerating the consequences of the "good things happening". There was no doubt that whatever was being orchestrated fit their definition of the greater good. But it was their definition and they knew no limit on the means to apply.

The former President of the United States (POTUS) in many respects couldn't understand why she should concern herself. It was for good. She didn't know the facts. Given knowledge she probably would've approved whatever was happening, at least then she would have. She had much to lose. With a permanent HCI of 99 she was guaranteed a long healthy life absent any incurable genetic anomaly. Her lifestyle was opulent and her reputation was untarnished. Life was wonderful, almost.

Trying to solve the riddle of what was planned she narrowed down her speculation to the NSA facility in Chillicothe, being the only one in Iowa, as the "happening" he referred to and either the Russians, Poles, Ukrainians or the flash demonstrations as the problem.

It was inconceivable that anything could be produced at a NSA plant that could deter the spontaneous flashes. They were being at the very least contained by propaganda. However, what might be produced to deter the Eastern Europeans scared her. Surely no one wanted war, but it was the most logical explanation she could think of.

Her initial training had been legal and she had started her government career as an assistant prosecutor. She would not betray those she had worked with and mentored, but she would not withhold exculpatory evidence. Part of her said she needed to at least cause someone to look.

The question of whom to render a hint of direction she pondered as much as her speculation about what was happening. Any opposition in Washington was a light version of the people in power. They all basically drank from the same well of privilege. Opposition outside of Washington was nothing but a disconnected, leaderless group of phantom protestors. The fact they were leaderless she recognized was a good part her doing. Anyone attempting an organizing effort was given much to deal with, starting with the IRS followed by more acronyms than they could handle.

She knew of one connection to the NSA plant in Iowa, albeit a strained one. Eric Hansen had resigned when she asked him to participate in the asteroid cover-up. His conscience having gotten the better of him infuriated her at the time. But time had a way of softening her. She decided to see if it had him. As a project manager of subcontracting work for the Department of Energy he worked at the NSA plant. It was her connection.

"Hello Eric."

"Madame President, good to hear from you."

"I wasn't sure you would answer my call."

"Of course I will. We had a disagreement. I'm okay with that. I did what I needed to as did you."

"Well, in retrospect I'm not so sure about my side. But we did what we thought was right at the time. You know I really believe that 99.9% of people do what they think is right. That does not mean it is, but to them given what they know and their circumstance, they believe it is. Have you ever done something you were absolutely sure was right and later regretted it because of new information or just a reassessment of all the balls in the air?"

"Of course I have."

"I heard something I want to ask you about. It may be gossip, but is something being worked on in your area that might effect Eastern Europeans?

"Not out of the ordinary that I know of, the normal spy gadgetry."

"Isn't it strange that you with the Department of Energy are stationed at a NSA facility?"

"It all has to do with security. The work I'm doing with subcontractors in micro energy development is very high security and I have the highest clearance."

"Anything otherwise, out of the ordinary?"

"There is one department here doing work on agricultural nanotechnology, something to do with killing fungi on plants. It seems a little out of our scope but so is what I'm doing and we are in Iowa."

"Anything to do with the flash demonstrations?"

"Not that I know of."

"Could you do me a favor by finding out what you can about any special projects, and oh, be discreet about it?"

"Sure," answered Eric wondering if he was being set up.

"One other favor, this is touchy and I never suggested this, understand? Do you ever have any contact with the amateur astronomer who ended up working for Atlas Transportation before we broke them?"

"You mean Andrew Collier, no?" He didn't mention that he had attended a seminar with Andrew's wife.

"I don't have any contacts, you know… I won't say it, but I sense he may."

"What do you want me to do?"

"It wouldn't look that unusual for you to talk to him since you have something in common. You might suggest that if he knows anyone who might be curious about let's say unusual activities they might investigate the NSA plant in Iowa."

"Wow, I understand, but that, well from you surprises me," he answered carefully not promising anything.

"Good the call was not wasted."

"I'm glad you called."

—ɯ—

Julie hadn't planned on using her secure phone in the evening, but found two missed calls from Andrew.

"Hi Andrew. How are the twins?"

"They are doing fine. Alice loves watching them and they adore her, but they miss you."

"Well I miss them too."

"And I miss you."

"Likewise, I wish I could be home."

"You planned to only stay about this long. When are you coming home?"

"There's a lot going on here and much I don't know. The more I learn the more I feel something is happening here."

"I agree, that's why I want you home. It's dangerous there, particularly with what you are doing."

"Andrew, you know I can't leave now. I miss you and the kids very much, but someone must find out what's happening. Who will do it if I don't?

"You put too much on yourself. We have to think of the children."

Maybe not his mind, but she could usually read the inflection of his voice. "I sense something else is going on Andrew, what has you concerned?"

"OK… I got a call from Eric Hansen today, remember him?"

"Of course, I met him at the micro-biology conference in Illinois. I've seen him a few times in the building here, but he doesn't recognize me with my disguise."

"He called me today and said if someone had a curious nature, they might be interested in what was happening at the NSA facility in Iowa."

"How strange, he works there as an employee of DOE. So he seems to be sending a message through you thinking you will pass it on."

"That's the way I take it and that's why you need to leave. It's too dangerous. Remember people there ended up in Guantanamo Bay."

"What did you tell him?"

"Nothing, of course; I said I didn't know anyone who would be interested in what happened in some small town in Iowa, I said I had my hands full in Idaho."

"I guess I'd have said the same thing, nevertheless that's all the more reason I have to stay."

"I'm not surprised, but I had to try."

"We've gone through this before Andrew. I'll be home when I can."

After Andrew had put the kids to bed he poured himself three fingers of Glenfiddish and sat in the backyard patio, the place where his telescopes once were. He missed the telescopes also.

As if they knew he needed company Nathan and Jim seeing his patio light on knocked on the gate and entered the patio. "Hi, thought you might like some company this evening."

"Sure, glad to see you guys." Andrew filled his neighbors in on the developments in Iowa. And that Julie wouldn't be coming home for some time.

"I wish I could go and help her. I need to be doing more than minding Impatiens," said Jim immediately catching a look from Nathan.

Changing the subject Andrew asked, "How's things at the nursery?"

"About the same but we did rid ourselves of a headache a few weeks ago."

"What's that?"

"You mean who's that. A blond we hired last year quit. A bit of good luck there, we tried everything we could to encourage her leaving, had given up and one day she just quit."

Giving Nathan, who handled hiring at the nursery, a glance Jim continued, "Good hiring decisions are so important these days because once you hire someone you are stuck. It'll cost more in legal fees to release someone than keeping them on no matter how incompetent they may be."

"Where did she go?"

"Don't know, don't care."

"Those who torment us for our own good will torment us without end for they do so with the approval of their own conscience."

C S Lewis

Chapter 10

Lucas was a careful person. Unlike others he used a mixture of public transportation and his own car to attend flash demonstrations. Using his car he parked at least a mile away and walked. He suspected last year's IRS audit was not random, but would withhold judgment. Little did he know that the proximity of his car and bus camera facial identification of him had been scrutinized by NSA. The information was passed on to the IRS. The auditors would visit him again later this year.

Boise, Idaho July 4, 2046
Alice and Barry Bradley hosted a combination 4th of July celebration and birthday party for the twins. Orlando, Nathan and Jim were in attendance in addition to Andrew and the twins.

"Too bad Julie couldn't make it," said Jim getting a stern look from Nathan. Nathan had advised him earlier to avoid mentioning Julie's absence as it was a topic Andrew would rather not discuss.

Before Alice could change the subject Andrew brushed it off. "Well she's headed to a fourth party in Iowa and she called earlier and talked to the twins."

"Why do we use that big phone instead of the grape when we talk to mommy?" asked Sandy.

"We just like to use the old time phone," lied Andrew.

"Can you play ball with us Orlando?"

"Sure Danny. Let's flip a coin to see who plays whom. Loser plays the Cubs, winner the Rockies."

Once the kids were playing in the backyard, Jim asked, "Do Julie or you have any idea what is happening in Iowa?"

"Not really, but the flashers being taken to Guantanamo Bay, the extra surveillance, and whatever is happening at the NSA facility, have to be somehow tied together."

"The surveillance, and getting rid of people who might notice things certainly lends credence to something happening no one is supposed to know about," observed Barry.

"I just wish I could help, maybe replace Julie in Iowa," added Jim.

"I know you are just itching to get into trouble, aren't you? You should remember your days in the SEALS are over," retorted Nathan.

"Since moving was brought up, I'll soon have my twenty-five years in at the agency and be pushed out, not that they'll miss me, because I don't really do anything. Consequently, Alice and I have been talking about where we want to be, maybe it's not here, perhaps on a boat off Costa Rica."

"How would that affect your access to government information?"

"That's been the part of my work for the last six months setting up avenues to access anything from anywhere. And I'll remain as a part time consultant at the Bureau of Elections which will give me a legitimate route to enter the system."

Alice started to expand on the pluses and minuses of moving but was interrupted by a late arriving guest.

"John, we're so glad you could make it."

"Sorry for being late. My flight was delayed. A thunderstorm delayed the flight and I spent three hours at the Des Moines airport. I've been thinking about your great barbecues all afternoon."

"What were you doing in Des Moines?"

"Andrew knows, but we are getting a contract for a pneumatic material handling system at a NSA facility there. I usually have someone else make these arrangements but it is big enough I needed to finalize the deal."

Jim looked at Barry who gave him a cautionary look, but Jim knew better than mention the warning Andrew received about the facility with John or Orlando back from playing ball. "Are you going to need to send engineers there?"

"Oh, yes, someone will need to oversee the installation."

After dinner Alice brought a red, white and blue cake to the patio with four candles on each side. The twins sitting on either side of the cake soon had the candles out and were eating cake less carefully with the frosting than would be required indoors.

"What did you wish for?" asked fifteen year old Orlando.

Sandy quickly replied, "I wish mommy was home."

"Well that's a good wish better than the wish a creep girl made at her birthday party last week."

"What was that?" asked John.

"She wished that our country hadn't been so mean to the indigenous people here and exploited people around the world, and polluted the environment, been so militaristic and set such a bad example for the world. I told her she was listening to too much BS in school."

Jim put his arm around his son beaming with pride. Nathan sought to blunt the support he was getting from his other dad, "Yes, and you were asked to leave the party also. I thought you liked her."

"Not any more."

Oskaloosa, IA

Adana Alvarez was known for her 4th of July parties. Her large backyard slopped down to a small stream with a bike path on the other side. Thunderstorms rumbled far in the west sapping any breeze and smoke from two grilles filled the yard on the warm humid Iowa afternoon.

Adana's family, a few neighbors and Julie feasted on burritos filled with smoked pork. Caridad had brought homemade Valentina sauce and Mole for the lighthearted.

After dinner they sat on the deck trying to catch a breath of air and noticed many on the bike path stopping to absorb the smell of the barbecued meat hanging in the air.

"Julie we have a tradition at all holiday gatherings to spend time talking about what the day means to us, whether it's Christmas, Easter or the 4th.

Adana's husband went first and told of the times after they had migrated north the day was marked by firecrackers. He said as a kid it was looked forward to perhaps as much as any holiday for the thrill, although dangerous, of doing what was frowned on other holidays and now strictly forbidden.

Caridad talked about being grateful that her grandfather had come from Mexico while this country still offered opportunity. "It was amazing he was able to find his way here when many couldn't. It is too bad today children do not understand what it was like then as today more people move in the other direction."

Ethan was next. He tried to pass but Adana wouldn't hear of it, but he was short. "I don't know. I'm not much for speeches."

"Just say what is in your heart."

"On this day I prefer to think about of the ideals the country was founded upon and forget how it is now."

Julie said, "I am just proud to live in a country that, as tough as all seems in these times, I'm blessed to find freedom-loving people like you to spend this day with."

A neighbor who worked at the FDA plant as an assistant supervisor of the mass vaccine production line said, "Well, I don't know what to say." Then thinking of something safe she said, "Let's remember why it happened nearly 300 years ago. I'm glad we don't have a King

George to master over us. Thank God the revolutionaries ridded us of that line of tyrants."

Adana was last but she was quiet obviously contemplating. Caridad turned to Julie, "I want to warn you mother loves these talk sessions and I'm sure she is extemporaneously about to let loose with pent-up thoughts that will go on and on."

"I can't wait to hear what she says."

"I was going to say something about hope. People, who had the foresight to rebel against the norm, had hope. They weren't thwarted by being accused of anti-social behavior, or even the prospect of the gallows. But what our neighbor just said caused me to rethink and put things in perspective. Something I hadn't thought about. The founders revolted against a king but more than that against an oligarchy of the privileged headed by a monarch.

Let's think about the monarchy. The system had been a fact of life and untouchable for many generations. Today we think of the establishment credentialocracy as impermeable. The monarchy only existed as long as the masses willingly allowed it. Ask George III, Charles I, or Nicholas II about their invincibility or Louis XVI as he walked the stairs to the guillotine."

"Be careful what you say," warned a neighbor.

"I'm just talking about history. Bear with me I'm thinking of more comparisons." She hesitated for a few moments and continued.

"The Hapsburgs of the Austrian-Hungarian Empire used taxes to sponsor composers writing beautiful music that the masses could not enjoy. The Mozart sonatas and operas were entertainment for the privileged. Today Washington subsidizes the arts for enjoyment of the elite regardless of the tastes of common folk. Do you see a difference? They control media programming by many means as other industries without regard to the most efficient method of distribution known to mankind, the market. Why? Because it serves them as past economic systems served others.

In the monarchy peasants and lower classes were expected to clear the roadway on the approach of aristocracy in carriages. Today millions traveling through airports are expected to leave freedoms at the terminal door while government officials and crony-capitalists are unburdened in private aircraft. It's for our good they say.

Monarchs commissioned artists to paint portraits of royalty. Commoners didn't have access to the paintings. The portraits added no value to the average life, but at least the paintings did not mock the commoner. Today a myriad of art works, which are subsidized through the National Endowment for the Arts by working people's taxes, purposely ridicule working people and their beliefs. Major campaign benefactors of the elite in the movie industry joy in debasing the common American as immoral, and imbecilic.

In another area monarchs controlled information other than word-of-mouth. Printing unapproved articles was to invite a treason charge followed by an ax. Today what percent of the sanctioned news do people believe? Again the channels for dissent are cut off.

Even after Heidelberg invented the press few could read. Many in the aristocracy considered a literate population dangerous. Today schools regularly fail to prepare students for the job market. Increasing amounts are thrown at schools with little regard to productivity. And yet I have to teach new construction workers how to measure. Working people's money finance student loans and grants for many curriculums, which add little or no value to a student's earning capacity. In private industry warning labels such as "This curricula may or may not add to your quality of life, but most likely will not add to your earning capacity" would be required.

Whatever the similarities in practice between medieval governess and the present a difference comes to my mind.

The royalty tended to be self-absorbed. They protected their rule and taxed to secure their lifestyle, but other than what the commoner might do to affect them, they didn't care how the commoner lived. As long as the privileged were secure in their wants, they sought no further control over average Joe. Seeking more control only distracted from their pleasures. Today the ruling class is obsessed with controlling how others live. They look upon it as their duty to do what is best for their lesser humans.

What does it all mean? I guess at some point we need to look deep within ourselves and determine whether we have the will and courage to preserve what was given to us. I'm sorry if I sound preachy and I don't mean to be a downer. Let's get on with the party."

Ethan passed another round of beer from a cooler to the group.

"Well you've certainly given us something to think about," said the vaccine supervisor.

"Yes she has," said Julie and continued. "I want to add another difference between then and now. Medieval rulers didn't have access to the technology for monitoring and controlling people's lives. King George, whatever his motivations might have been, didn't have the means of the ruling today."

Alone later Julie said to Adana. "Your words have done a great deal to motivate me and confirm that I am doing the right thing. I miss my husband and kids and I know it is hard on them, but I don't have a choice. When we came into this world there were no guarantees, we were given certain abilities and weaknesses. We found ourselves in places, meeting people who influenced us, all to learn certain lessons. As individuals we have no reason to believe the combination of our strengths and yearnings we've acquired have come together out of happenstance and every reason to believe they haven't.

The lesson I heard from you resonates with a message I often heard from Dan Barnmore: *The biggest job most of us have is discovering what we are here for. And the biggest waste is not using our resources to that end.*"

"He was obviously a very tuned-in man."

As Adana and Julie continued to speak of profound and spiritual matters, the others broke into groups, Caridad and the supervisor of the vaccine production moved to the yard.

"I hope you enjoyed Mother's party."

"I wouldn't miss it. This is our third year here."

"She does sometimes get carried away talking."

"Don't apologize for her, I enjoy it. I may not agree with everything she says, but it doesn't offend me."

"I never get to talk to anyone in mass production. I'm pretty much confined to development. How was vaccine production this year?"

"It went smoothly, given that we started behind schedule. Getting the new formula late from your department made it a challenge."

"You used the new formula? I was told you would produce the same vaccine as last year."

"No, we were a week late starting the assembly line. I didn't mean to insinuate anything about your department," she added noticing a disturbed look on Caridad's face.

Caridad was little help cleaning up as the party ended. In her mind she rolled over the implication of what she had heard. Before Julie left she summoned her.

"I heard something tonight that I think you should know about."

"Yes."

"I found out that the vaccine mass produced for the general population was not the same as last year. They used our new formulation."

"Okay, does that mean something?"

"Yes, they used the new vaccine formula we produced for the non-naturally mutated virus."

"I've got to rendezvous with a carrier to pick up the video chip of the flash arrest in the morning. We've both had more than enough to drink; let's meet before work in the morning to discuss this."

At 5:30 Julie left her studio apartment traveling a different direction than she did in the evening. She headed South toward Edmundson Park, rather than North toward William Penn University. She wore a white top with purple running shorts and met man wearing a green top and black shorts running the opposite direction. The clothes each wore matched what they were looking for, the face they would never see again.

Julie stopped and sat on a bench in the park and quietly surveyed the area. She saw no one and at the five minute mark she laid an important ¾ inch square chip in the grass an inch interior of the right bench support. She continued her run. Five minutes later the man in a green top rested on the bench for five minutes before leaving with the chip.

This was the last stop on his undercover route which had carried him from Mexico through Oklahoma City and Wichita where he dropped off secure phones operating on a different circuit than the Boise/Iowa group. Torrence and other former Atlas people on the island-boat off Costa Rica had developed multiple secure phones (SP) circuits to enable them to communicate with Atlas linked groups around the country. But for security the circuits all needed to route through the island-boat.

It was his third venture back into the country after he had left as a teenager with his parents for Poland. His father, an engineer with Atlas, left at the collapse of the company, took his family and acquired joint Polish citizenship before rejoining his colleagues on the island-boat. He drove a vehicle that had the black box altered to prevent NSA tracking. After picking up a chip he headed toward Canada.

Starting in 2015 all new vehicles sold in the country were required to have a black box installed. It was similar to what had been used in aircraft for years. The argument for the inclusion of a box was safety. In the event of an accident a determination could be made as to the cause and the box could sense the shock of an accident alerting authorities and medics immediately. It did save lives. It also allowed authorities to track all vehicles anywhere all the time.

The vehicle driven by the courier contained an early version of the Polish made black box disabling retrofit. It successfully gave the vehicle the identification of local vehicles commonly using the road it was on. However, if the vehicle it was mimicking passed within a few hundred yards, a red flag went up at the NSA data center in Utah which was transmitted to NSA headquarters in Fort Meade, Maryland.

While at a fueling station in Austin, Minnesota red flags went up in Utah and drones were scrambled to follow both vehicles from which emanated the same signal. Within an hour ATF agents acting as the enforcement wing of the NSA were on the road following both vehicles. One vehicle pulled into a garage in a residential section of Owatonna, MN. Soon fourteen agents using a heavy ram burst through the door of the home. After two days of intensive inquiry they released the occupants.

Torrence was alerted by a warning from a program at the island-boat that tracked the courier and ATF activity in its immediate area. The courier's SP buzzed on interstate 35.

"You are being followed. Vacate the car immediately and ditch the chip and phone."

The courier quickly pulled the car to the shoulder and headed for tall grass on the roadside, but before he lowered himself in the grass he saw two black vehicles stop behind his car. Lying in the grass he drew a pocket knife from his clothes, sunk the three inch blade into the sod, twisted it enough to create a slice in the sod and pushed the video chip to the bottom of the hole.

He had run fifty feet before an agent saw the grass moving, "Over there, someone's running."

The courier knew there was no escape. He held his SP and hit an incorrect sequence. The SP started sizzling before he could drop it. He was able to move twice before he was surrounded.

Authorities found what was left of a plastic molded device with remnants of silicon components. They speculated that it was a communication device. The courier was quietly sent to Guantanamo Bay.

—∿—

After successfully dropping the chip Julie met Caridad for breakfast. "What do you think?" Julie asked.

"We know this; the vaccine that was mass produced for the population was developed to combat a virus that is not natural. And we have reason to believe a disease at Guantanamo Bay played havoc with the prison population killing a number. And we know that a 500 dose sample of the new formula vaccine was shipped to Guantanamo Bay weeks before the outbreak."

"Is it possible the CDC knew of a possible foreign biological attack, had you develop a vaccine for it and tested it at the prison? And used the vaccine to immunize the guards?"

"Do you think counter espionage has uncovered a virus a foreign power is planning to use on us?"

"No, possible but doubtful. If the government knows about it, why wouldn't they attack the source? That leaves one logical explanation. The CDC developed the virus, had you develop a vaccine, tested the virus and vaccine on inmates and guards and saw a reason to distribute the new vaccine to the population."

"Exactly, they are most likely spreading the virus. And guess, people of what inclination are least apt to get vaccinated."

"Oh, my God. It's people like us."

"It makes sense, but who would have ever thought. Could they go to such lengths?"

"It's all in Alinsky's strategic playbook that they go by, what I think is rule number 10: *do what you can with what you have and clothe it with moral arguments.*

Neither spoke for a few moments before Julie burst out, "Vaccine, do you have any?"

"Yes a few doses, at the lab."

"Go in vaccinate yourself and bring it out. I want to borrow your car. I'm heading to Idaho."

Caridad took her insulated lunch box to the lab that morning. Once she had filled it with all the vaccine it would hold she headed for her mother's trailer office. Her mother, father, Ethan and Julie were waiting. She vaccinated them all.

"Have you reached Andrew yet?"

"No."

"Take ten doses and the car. Please be careful."

It was six pm Mountain Time before Andrew noticed his SP had five missed calls from Julie.

"I see you called five times, what's happening?"

I'm in central Nebraska heading your way. Where are the twins?"

"Right here with me. I just picked them up from Alice. What's going on?"

"I'll be there mid day tomorrow. Don't leave the house or be in contact with anyone until I can get there and explain."

Andrew wanted to ask more, but he could tell from Julie's tone it was not the time. And he was glad she was coming home regardless of the reason.

The next morning Andrew called John Whitehouse, his boss's assistant answered the phone. "Is John in?"

"No, he called in a few minutes ago and said he wasn't feeling well."

"Just tell him I'm not coming in today and hope he gets to feeling better."

"A government big enough to give you everything you want
is also big enough to take away everything you have."

Barry Goldwater

Chapter 11

It was past noon when Julie pulled into the driveway. Andrew and the twins met her at the door.

"Mommy, Mommy."

"I'm so glad to see you sweeties." A twin clasped to each of her legs as her husband embraced and kissed her.

"Did you bring us something from Connecticut? Danny asked. The twins had been told the ruse for everyone's protection.

"I can't believe you're back, but from what I picked up on the phone there is a reason other than our smiling faces." It didn't come out quite as Andrew intended.

Julie ignored the tenor of his remark. She could see from his facial expression he regretted it and kissed him before he could apologize. "I've got to get you and the kids vaccinated now. I'll explain later."

"But what's going on. Vaccinated for what?"

"Things have changed. Just roll up your sleeve," she said as she pulled a syringe out and drew vaccine from a bottle.

Andrew complied thinking *if he couldn't trust his wife, whom could he trust.*

"Get some alcohol. I only have one needle and I need to sterilize it before the twins."

By the time he returned with alcohol, the twins surmised their mother might not be finished with the needle and disappeared. They weren't hard to find.

"This will not endear them with their mother, you know."

"I don't care."

Finished with the needle, Julie explained the urgency of the vaccination. Andrew was somewhat skeptical that all the pieces fit together in the manner Julie assumed, but he had never seen her wrong when she showed this much zeal.

"Do you know anyone who has come down with the flu?"

"No, well yes, when I called off work today John's assistant said he was ill."

"And he was at the 4th of July party with you?"

"Yes, but he came in late on a flight from Iowa."

"We must vaccinate others who were at the party. Call Barry and Nathan."

"Hi Andrew. I see a car in your driveway, company?" inquired Nathan.

"Not exactly, it's Julie. What time will Jim and Orlando be home?"

"Around five, I'll come over now and say hi."

"No. I think it better that you don't. Could you have them come home earlier?"

Andrew hung up the phone and turned to Julie. "Let me distribute the vaccine. You need to spend some time with the kids."

"I know, but I think it is safer for me to go. I was vaccinated yesterday morning and according to Caridad within a few hours I will start to get some immunity although it takes two weeks to get full immunity."

Julie explained the situation to the Alice and Barry and vaccinated them first. She was waiting with Nathan when Jim pulled in the driveway with Orlando.

"This had better be important," said Jim knowing it was as Julie explained the reason for urgency. They had sent Orlando to his room but he overheard the conversation. Nathan was surprised when Orlando came down from his room unannounced and asked for the vaccination because Orlando did not like needles.

"Why did you tell them you had to leave school early?" Nathan asked as Julie vaccinated him.

"I told them it was none of their business."

"You didn't."

"Ya and when they kept asking I told them maybe I was going to paint some dollar signs around town."

As in the previous century young people used graffiti to protest. Three generations earlier it was the peace symbol. Like the peace symbol was then, the use of the outlawed dollar sign was as much anti-cultural as political.

"You can't do that, Orlando."

"Yes, I did. You should have seen the looks on their faces."

"Sit down we're going to have a talk," Jim said as Julie gathered her stuff and excused herself.

"How much did you hear?"

"I heard Julie say we needed to get vaccinated because of something the authorities did."

"Well we don't know that; taking the shot is just playing safe. But really Orlando we all must be careful about what we say. We can think what we want, that is our freedom, dream, be Walter Mitty all you wish. But in the long run saying things that ultimately will hurt us is foolish."

"It's funny you say that. The constitution you gave me to read; the number one thing is the free speech amendment. It must be important if they put it first."

Jim jumped in trying to be professorial. "The first amendment has always had practical limitations. The proverbial exception being; you don't have the right to exclaim fire in a theater and cause people to be injured. Today society has taken it further to mean you don't have the right to say things that counter the common good. Now we may not agree with society's definition of the common good, but until we can change it, we must live by the rules."

"I haven't painted dollar signs on buildings. But what's wrong with displaying a symbol that means liberty. It's funny those green notes everyone says are worthless, but everyone I know tells me their parents have some hidden away like you do."

"Let me put it another way," said Nathan. "You know your dad and I love lilies. There is nothing more beautiful than the six petals of brilliant color on an aromatic Oriental Lily. But some people prefer Iris. Irises grow in clusters like a commune; lilies grow on a single stem. Think of the symbolism there. But we can't tell customers we don't sell Iris because we prefer Lilies. We would soon be out of business, then how many lilies would we sell?"

Orlando quietly thought for a time and said, "I get it. I'll be more careful."

The three hugged and Jim said, "You know we love you for your independence."

Julie reacquainted herself with the twins, read them a story until they were asleep and headed for the bedroom. Andrew was already in bed. "What is that look for?" she asked as she undressed.

"Can you blame me? It's been a while since I've shared a bed with a woman."

"That's good."

Julie sensed Andrew's restlessness and glanced at the clock projecting 4:41 a.m. and 71 degrees on the ceiling. Although still lacking sleep from the previous all-night drive she asked him, "What's wrong?"

He didn't answer but bolted for the bathroom.

Behind the closed door she could hear him disposing of dinner and her fears were confirmed.

Julie was up when he returned. He pulled a travel bag out of the closet. "I think it best that I get out of here and not risk exposing the twins any more than I have. I'll check in at the hotel."

"I understand but let's do it the other way. You've touched everything in the house. You stay and I'll take the twins to the hotel. If they haven't been exposed they'll be in a clean environment."

"Guess that makes more sense."

Julie threw a few items into the bag with some of the twin's things and woke them. "We are going on a fun trip kids."

"Aren't you coming Daddy?"

Keeping his distance Andrew replied, "No, I'm not feeling well. Go with Mommy you don't want to get sick."

Julie looked at Andrew. They both felt the same urge to hug one another in perhaps a token after-expression of the passion they had shared a few hours earlier, but both knew better.

By noon the next day Andrew wasn't feeling any worse but neither was he better. He called the office to check on John's condition to find him back.

"You're back, glad to hear it."

"Yes, just a 24-hrs bug of some kind."

"Well, I've got it now."

"Sorry, but it doesn't amount to much."

Andrew called Nathan and found out Jim had come home mid-morning ill. "I don't think it is serious John is back to work already. We probably overreacted."

"Well better to be safe than sorry."

Julie was pleased to find out John was well and Andrew was no worse. Nevertheless they decided it best to keep the twins isolated for another couple days. "I've got my hands full occupying the kids, but at least we're getting reacquainted."

Alice had a mild case, Jim was better in 24 hours as was Andrew. Nathan, Orlando and Barry showed no symptoms. But Barry reported that the local hospital's occupancy was up considerably.

The bald-headed ATF agent and his blond roommate were about to leave for work when his grape beeped. He had routed the motion detector in Julie and Andrew's travel bag to notify him through his grape. They soon had tracked the bag to a local motel, room number 214. The motel was a two story horseshoe-shaped configuration wrapped around an outdoor pool. The agents got a room opposite 214 and soon had a camera set up focused on the window overlooking the pool. For two days and nights they watched Julie and the twins anytime the drapes were opened. The bald-headed agent had walked the second story perimeter and left a listening device on the window ledge enabling them to monitor conversation inside the room.

After hours of tedious listening to children's stories, the agents discovered what they thought to be a marital spat was only an effort to keep children from getting the flu. Again the listening device in Andrew's suitcase had led them down a blind canyon. The bald-headed ATF agent was more frustrated than ever.

Andrew had been feeling fine for over twenty four hours when Julie came home with the kids. "I'm sorry perhaps it all was a false scare."

"No, I don't think so. Look how many we know who got sick albeit mild. And not all cases are mild. Barry found that the hospital occupancy continues to rise."

It was the middle of the night when Julie and Andrew were awakened by Sandy crying. She had a fever. They were not alarmed as no one Julie had vaccinated had more than a light case of the flu. The vaccine even with short periods to build antibodies appeared to help. At midmorning Daniel also showed signs of the flu.

The twins' health had not improved in the amount of time it took Andrew to shake it. Nathan had also come down with the flu, although everyone else they knew was fine.

On a secure conference call that evening they discovered Adana's husband contacted the virus. Caridad was better, her dad wasn't.

Barry and Torrence independently found hospital occupancy rates were up throughout the country. Only at hospitals around Washington D.C. were rates not up.

"It all makes sense," said Caridad. "Where would you expect the greatest complicity with a government mandate?

"You're right," Julie answered and was interrupted by Torrence.

"I see on our news tracking monitors the President has scheduled time to address the nation in an hour."

"Fellow citizens, as I'm sure you are aware the annual flu outbreak this year has exceeded those of recent years. Many of our citizens have suffered mild to serious effects. The good news it that very few people who were immunized have suffered. The DHS and CDC strongly mandated vaccination because they have the best interests of the population in mind…

Those who ignored the best advice of experts have not only jeopardized themselves but the put the rest of us at risk as the virus grows and becomes more vibrant in their bodies…

Nevertheless, I have instructed the DHHS to spare no funds to treat those who have become infected with the preventable disease by their own obstinacy…

"Did I just hear a parent tell the children I hope you learned your lesson?" inquired Barry.

"That's a good way to put it," answered Andrew before they signed off.

Two days later the twins were no better. Julie and Andrew took them to the clinic. In normal times without an appointment a two hour wait was common, this day it was over three hours before they saw a doctor.

After examining the twins the doctor said, "I think they'll be over it in a couple days, but keep a watch on their temperatures. They are 100.1 and 100.2 now. If either gets above 101 take them to emergency. Otherwise give them as much fluids as they can keep down."

Julie and Andrew kept the twins cooled with wet towels and gave them all the water they could hold down. Beside the twins, of those they knew, only Nathan and Adana's husband remained sick. But chatter on the news was of an unprecedented epidemic with anchors hardly covering their glee at having the public's attention.

Early the next morning Sandra's temperature exceeded 101, Daniel's was slightly higher. They headed for the emergency room.

The twins were placed in a room meant for three patients, it now had six. They were given fluids intravenously and antibiotics to stave off secondary infections. For three days and nights they remained the same, a few degrees up and a few down. Julie and Andrew never left the hospital except for a quick trip home to shower and change.

On the fourth day Sandy improved. Her temperature was normal and she was released that afternoon. Danny had not improved. Julie and Andrew alternated between home with Sandy and the hospital with Danny for two more days. Julie was home and Andrew joined her for a shower and meal before Julie was to alternate at the hospital for the night when Andrew's grape buzzed.

"This is the nurse on your son's floor. I think you should get here immediately. Your son is having trouble breathing. We are putting him on a respirator."

They were at the hospital within a few minutes after dropping Sandy at Alice's. A doctor met them in the hallway as they headed for the room, "Your son's O2 level is at 50 if we can't get it up soon, well it doesn't look good."

"What can we do?"

"We are doing all we can. I tell people to use their own methods."

Julie and Andrew both placed a hand on Daniel's head and asked for help from a source not trained in medical schools. His blood oxygen level didn't rise. The doctor and nurses were losing hope; experience told them that Daniel's prospects were dim.

"I can't believe this is happening," said Andrew.

"Andrew, believe me we don't know what's happening."

Eight hours later Julie sat in a chair close to Daniel holding his hand and felt a mysterious presence. It was the presence of her father, she didn't know how she knew but she did. It felt comforting and he moved toward her and Daniel, then toward Daniel. She felt the fine hair on her arm pulled toward them. And then they were gone.

Andrew had sensed something from Julie and stood on the other side of the bed as the green line on the monitor went flat. "He's gone."

"I know."

—∿—

Two days later a memorial service was held. Sandra was back to normal, other than being stricken by confusion about where her twin was. Alice stayed home to comfort her. Neighbors and friends gathered. Jim and Orlando were particularly sad; undoubtedly wondering if the same fate would meet Nathan who remained in the hospital. Ethan and Caridad stayed in Iowa with Adana caring for their dad.

During the eulogy the non-denominational cleric stated the boy's full name three times, Daniel Atlas Collier. Each time Andrew felt his spine flinch with the words. Julie turned to him as they left the funeral home, "I guess we've lost two Dans."

"Yes, I guess we have," Andrew replied in as many words as he had spoken since they left the hospital.

Parked a block way from the funeral home were the bald-headed and blond ATF agents. They watched Julie and Andrew and Jim and Orlando leave the funeral home.

"I think it's terrible. Whatever you think, I feel sorry for them," she said.

"Sorry for them, no way. I feel sorry for the little boy, but it's their fault. In the best of worlds we would be arresting both the parents for child abuse. And look, there come Jim and his misfit kid. His other father is in the hospital in a coma. I hope they are enjoying their time together."

"You enjoy this, don't you?"

"Look at it this way. If I'd been allowed to do my job right in '39 none of this tragedy would have happened."

At home Andrew started for the door saying he was going to get Sandy, but Julie stopped him. "We need to talk. You can't imagine how sorry I am."

"So am I."

"If I only had a clue, I wouldn't have kept you from vaccinating them. Will you ever forgive me?"

"Forgive you? You think it's your fault? No, it's not your fault; it's my fault for not having him vaccinated. I took him to the doctor. But no, if anything it's my fault for getting complacent. It's everyone's fault for allowing this travesty to continue. It's John Doe's fault in Cleveland for turning his head and allowing this tyranny to imbed itself. Its Jane Smith's fault in Kansas City for thinking it was cute to play the system and live off the work of others without realizing there would be consequences.

There is no go along, get along. To go along is to reduce oneself to servitude to the mercy of the self-anointed. But there are those directly responsible and I will not rest until they are held accountable, if that means doing it by my own hands."

Julie held Andrew as his pent up emotions continued to vent.

"In my own short sightedness, trying to protect the children, I lost sight of the big picture. There are no halfway measures. We comply completely, leave our freedom and souls at the door and bow at the feet of those who believe themselves to be morally and philosophically superior to us or we fight."

"I know."

They stood at the door embracing each other in tears for some time before they felt fit to retrieve Sandy.

Alice met them at the door; Sandy was playing in another room. "Alice had trouble keeping composure but said the obligatory, "Let me know if there is anything." But she meant it.

"There may be Alice. We've a lot of thinking to do."

While Julie and Andrew were trying to explain to Sandy where her brother was, across the street Jim heard more of a pounding than knock on the door. He answered to find the bald-headed ATF agent staring at him. Beside him was the DHHS social worker that had warned Nathan and him of Orlando's behavior.

"Is Orlando here?" asked the social worker.

Orlando had entered the room hearing the commotion.

"Please come with us Orlando."

"What's this about?" Asked Jim trying to remain calm.

"We have a regulatory warrant for Orlando to be taken to a Training Center for the Socially Deficient (TSD) in Omaha.

Although the bald-headed ATF agent was ready for a physical re-action, his pleasure at the look on Jim's face slowed his reflexes. Jim's lunge at him took his breath and Jim's fist landed solidly between his cheekbone and jaw loosening three teeth before a taser from the blond stunned Jim into convulsions.

Orlando took flight and jumped off the landing from the kitchen back door but into the arms of two waiting ATF agents.

Jim's head was not clear but he realized he'd been handcuffed when he heard Orlando plead to pack some clothes.

"No, we find that anything brought from home is distracting and interferes with training."

Soon Jim was locked up for assaulting an officer of the law and Orlando was headed for Omaha.

"We still find the greedy hand of government thrusting itself into every corner and crevice of industry, and grasping at the spoil of the multitude… It watches prosperity as its prey and permits none to escape without a tribute."

Thomas Paine

Chapter 12

The morning after the Danny's funeral Alice and Barry visited Julie and Andrew. They would have preferred it to be a consolatory visit, as uncomfortable as that was, but they knew they had to share what had happened across the street. They knew Julie and Andrew had not learned of more bad news in the neighborhood.

"Thanks for coming Alice. You and Barry are such great friends."

"We are here for you."

"I know and Andrew and I have much to contemplate. And frankly, we need to make plans, but we've a few things to work through yet. We may be asking something of you."

"Well you know we mean what we say, but we should let you know about well, unfortunately more bad news in the neighborhood."

"Nathan, oh no, not him too."

"No, no, Nathan is fine. Well no, he is still in a coma but no change. It's Orlando. The DHS picked him up last evening and took him to a TSD in Omaha."

Oh, no, my…"

"How's Jim?"

"He's in jail. The bald-headed ATF agent that has been on your cases was there at the pickup and Jim worked him over for a second time. They're holding him for assault of an officer."

"Did he hurt him good?"

"Andrew, please."

"I'm going down and bail him out now," said Barry.

No one said anything. They wondered what more there could be. Alice and Barry headed down the sidewalk, but Andrew stopped them. "No Barry, let me bail him out. You need to keep your distance. Using your transaction card to get him out would bring scrutiny on you. We can't afford the authorities to start watching you too closely."

"But you've got Sandy, same for you."

"No you are more important to the cause. They won't bother us."

Andrew's statement confirmed a conversion in his priorities to Julie. She knew him well enough to understand that he didn't change easily, but once he did his pursuit was relentless.

White House

From the Atlanta headquarters of the CDC the director reported to the President who had the directors of the NSA and FDA in the oval office.

"Our estimates were on the low side as to the number of fatalities, although we believe the worst of the epidemic is over."

"How many fatalities will we have?"

"I still believe it will be within the range of from 100 to 300 thousand, in which a high percent are older and the very young."

"I thought you talked about up to 50 thousand."

"If you check the log of our analysis I believe you will see we said as high as 150 thousand," the director said very timidly.

"Let's cut the ass covering, what will the final total be?"

"We are still compiling numbers and many are still in critical condition."

"OK, give me your best guesstimate; how many when this is over."

"Our best estimate is it could approach 300 thousand."

"Why is it above the range of your estimates?"

The director ignored the insinuation that the death toll would be outside his upper range. "Two reasons; based on our analysis, fewer people were immunized than we anticipated. Actually of those vaccinated the percent that caught the flu was within our estimated parameters. Additionally of those not vaccinated the virus hit them harder than an extrapolation of results at Guantanamo Bay."

"What he's saying is the overwhelming majority of the suffering was the result of a self-inflicted wound. It was voluntary victimhood. If the public places railroad crossing lights and cross arms at a railroad crossing and someone chooses to ignore them, is it the public's fault?" interjected the director of NSA trying to set the tone.

The President spoke quickly. "Enough, enough with your convoluted reasoning. I know what you are trying to do, but a third of a million people is a hell of a tragedy. It's something neither I nor anyone would have sanctioned. It's absolutely terrible."

The President turned and looked out the window in silence for some time. The others knew better than to speak given his tone. Finally the President continued in a mellow and cautious voice, "But others have sat in this chair and entered wars unaware of the suffering they had unleashed as I was unaware of this.

No one expected this. But there is some truth to what you said. People will not refuse vaccination next year. Nevertheless, I think having planned on an upper limit of 150 thousand fatalities as being acceptable and yet enough to push people to get vaccinated for the success of TIP; that's what the number should be. I suggest it may be very difficult to compile the actual numbers, it will be cumbersome and time consuming, but ultimately the official record will show no more than 150k perished. It will be around 150k."

"I understand, Mr. President. The record will show as you suggest."

—ℳ—

ARC (Amalgamated Robotics Company) Boise location

Andrew met with John Whitehouse, VP and manager of the Boise location. "I understand the robotic pneumatic system for the NSA plant in Iowa is a go."

"Yes, it's a deal, but the project really won't require anything new from your people in design engineering as we have the components on hand. The push will be in engineering adaptation for installation and it will be paramount that it be completed on time given the penalties for tardiness. The late penalties exceed any government work we've done, so its important to someone."

"That's what I wanted to talk to you about. Send me to Iowa to oversee the project."

"I didn't mean to overstate the installation challenges. I believe we have many project managers who can handle it."

"You don't understand. I want to go. Julie is going back and I think I can be useful there."

"I thought she was there incognito. You sure wouldn't be; someone could recognize you."

"Send a couple new engineers with me. I can supervise the work off site. No one will know but what I'm here."

"Would you take Sandy?"

"We're working on that."

"Let me think about it."

Andrew had already made up his mind to go whether doing work for ARC or not.

Later that evening Andrew asked Julie, "When are you headed back to Iowa?"

Before she could answer he continued, "I'm going also."

"How? Why?"

Andrew explained the conversation with John. "It fits; no one knows more about the robotic system than I. I designed many of the components and we need to find out the connection of the NSA plant with what is happening there. I'm not staying here doing nothing anymore, and waiting for what they will do to us next. I told you that last week."

"How can we take Sandy with us?"

"If we are not successful and the country continues on the path it is on, is this where we want her? I've been doing a lot of thinking. You and I have to stay here because it's in us. We could have left when Atlas folded, could have gone when you were pregnant, but we didn't because we felt a need to be here, we haven't given up. But is it right for us to subject her to a future that frankly isn't bright? If we would have left when you were pregnant we would still have Daniel. As painful as his death is, we shouldn't subject Sandy to a possible future like Orlando."

"How would we send her, to be with whom?

"How many times have we heard Alice say she doesn't know why she is here? Sandy adores her and it is mutual. She is a child Alice never had. In the long run it would be better for her. Unless we get locked up we will see her again. But if we do get locked up, which, let's be honest, is certainly possible, it would be better if she was not here."

"It's a big step Andrew. What you say makes sense, but she's our daughter."

"That's right, it's why we should think about her long term future. I'm not going to stay uninvolved like I was. What good did it do Daniel? Are you going to stay home and be a mother? I'm not asking you to, but the most important thing parents can do for their children is providing for their future. If the trends don't stop, there will be no future for her in this country.

That evening they were invited to Alice and Barry's for dinner. Jim stopped by on his way to the hospital.

"You know part of me wishes Nathan wouldn't wake up. Finding out what happened to Orlando will be a blow I don't know if he can withstand."

"Is there any change at all?"

"No, I'm meeting a doctor at 7 for consultation."

"We are thinking of you and Nathan. But I want you to know I may not be staying here. It is possible I'm going to do installation of a robotic system in Iowa."

"I don't suppose that is a coincident. What about Sandy?"

"Alice, that's what we came to talk to you and Barry about. I know you have talked about leaving the country. And I know Melissa would welcome you on the island-boat."

Alice and Barry agreed to think about the proposition of Alice leaving with Sandy.

Jim sat at Nathan's bedside, held his hand, talked to him and pried his eyelids open as he had been doing seeking a response of some kind. If he could just identify a muscle twitch or eye movement it would give him hope. He found none. Satisfied that Nathan was still in a respirator sustained coma Jim met with the attending physician.

"Nathan's prognosis is difficult Jim, I would give the odds of him coming out of the coma at around 20%; that is the best estimation I can make. The good news is if he comes out of the coma he should be fine as the rest of his bodily functions are normal."

"What's the bad news?"

"Nathan has been on the respirator a week. The DHHS has mandated that all flu victims be categorized as voluntary recipients of the virus. It's the non-vaccination thing; I can't do anything about it. Consequently there are limits to the care available and his Health Care Index (HCI) has been lowered."

"So what does that mean?"

"They are limiting intensive care to twelve days."

"So even though there's a decent chance he will come out of it, they're just going pull the plug and let him die?"

"I'm sorry."

Jim stood so quickly his chair fell backwards. Its aluminum back pinged of hollow as it struck the floor and bounced. The noise startled the doctor and the vibrations it caused kept ringing in the doctor's ears. When he cleared the ringing from his ears Jim was gone. The doctor was glad as he didn't know what to say.

Jim rejoined his neighbors and shared the news from the hospital. As bad as they felt for Nathan and Jim the ramifications were also clear for Sandy. Julie and Andrew's eyes locked on each other. Both realized their decision had been made.

"Perhaps we could get Nathan out of the country for treatment."

"How? Carry the respirator? It's not easy to cross the border if you can walk, let alone carry someone."

"Are you serious about going to check out that NSA facility Andrew?

"Yes, I'm going. But I'll need to find a place to hide out and work remotely."

"How are going to get there undetected?" asked Jim.

"I haven't got that far."

"I'll take you. My truck has the Polish retrofit box and won't be detected."

"But you are on bail. You'll soon have a court date."

"So, I'll be convicted and go to jail. From what I can ascertain no one gets out of the TSD they sent Orlando to until they are twenty one, and if Nathan's gone, I just as well be on the run. I can transfer enough credit points to compensate you for the bail from the nursery. Besides, you'll need some protection. We made a good team a few years ago and if Nathan, well. I'm not staying here."

"What about the nursery?"

"The nursery had been a good part of my life but it's not my life."

The families broke up for the evening. At the door Alice said Barry and she would have a decision for them the next evening.

Back home Julie said, "I'm going to leave the day after tomorrow. I need to get back and we need to find a safe place for you. Unfortunately, you can't stay with me, I'm identified there as a different person and single. It would be too dangerous to change my identity. Let's set up a conference call with Caridad and Ethan tomorrow evening. Until then I'm spending all the time I can with Sandy. This isn't going to be easy."

As planned they gathered the next evening. Alice had reached a decision; she would take Sandy to the island-boat off the coast of Costa Rica.

"You don't know how much we appreciate your doing so; we wouldn't have considered asking anyone else. I know it was a difficult decision for Barry and you, as it was for Andrew and me."

Sandy sat on Julie's lap as Barry plugged the secure phone into a speaker for all to join the conference call.

We're so sorry to hear about Nathan's condition," said Melissa with Torrence on the island-boat.

"About the flu, we've done research on flu fatalities around the country. It seems the CDC has forbidden reporting fatalities through normal channels. We can't trace how they are tracking the information. Nowhere in the administrative chain are numbers being fed to the CDC; it's like the numbers magically appear from the department head."

"Are you saying the fatality number is a fabrication?" asked Julie.

"Well the official numbers do not match what we've discovered. Our contacts at dozens of places around the country through informants in hospitals have given us raw, but real data. Our statistical analysis of the sampling indicates half a million people have perished."

"Oh, my God," exclaimed Caridad expressing everyone's thoughts.

"Can anyone give me a plausible explanation for what happened, other than it was orchestrated?"

When no one answered Julie continued, "Although it has been the policy to shrink the population by controlling births, I think there was another reason for initiating the flu epidemic. We've got to find out."

"I think the answer lies in the NSA facility there. Our tip indicated that and other leads point in that direction," observed Andrew.

"Ethan I'll be back in Iowa late tomorrow, have you any ideas where Jim and Andrew might hide out for an extended period? Andrew is recognizable and Jim will be on the run."

"I've got an idea I'm working on."

It was before daybreak that Julie entered Sandy's room and kissed her goodbye. She knew she must leave before Sandy woke. "This is hard Andrew. We will see her again, won't we?"

"Yes, we will. It may not be in this country but we will see her again."

They both thought about the implications of what he had said but neither commented. Andrew regretted the way he had phrased it, but chose to let it pass.

With a parting kiss for Andrew who carried her traveling bag to Caridad's car, Julie was soon gone.

The bald-headed ATF agent was rousted from bed by his grape's warning that the Collier's traveling bag had been moved. He dressed quickly but the car had left before the blonde agent and he arrived. He assumed Julie was heading back to the company headquarters in Connecticut, but would follow-up later to be sure.

Andrew met with Jim two mornings later after an evening call with Ethan. Jim had spent the night at the hospital with Nathan.

"Do you remember the sighting trip you went on the farm in Iowa with Ethan and Barry?"

"Sure we had a good time."

"What do you remember about a railroad tie stockpile and the abandoned farmstead?"

"The railroad tie stockpile was huge and looked out of place. It had a chain link fence we walked around. Ethan says he played there as a boy."

"I know this sounds strange but Ethan says the abandoned farmstead would make a great place to hide out for a couple guys and the tie stockpile would allow hiding electronic communication devices if the guys were handy and had some pioneer blood."

"Would be kind of like starting from scratch wouldn't it?"

"I suspect we could build a log cabin from ties and conceal it pretty well with other railroad ties. We'll have plenty of room in your truck for tools. Barry wants to send communication equipment and I've got a new type of solar panels I've been experimenting with in the backyard."

Barry and Alice joined them and were brought up to speed on the plans.

"What are you going to do with the nursery?" Alice asked.

"The selling season is nearly over; I'll just let it go. I most likely will have to anyway, whenever the trial takes place, I'm sure I'll get time for whacking the agent. Without Nathan and Orlando working…, but more I just can't envision running it without them around, too many reminders; I'll just walk away."

"What do you think of the plan, Barry?" asked Andrew.

"I see too much risk in the plan. With Jim on the run and you recognizable, neither of you can be upfront about renting and living in the house. What if a housing or occupant inspector shows up? It will be obvious someone is there. And as crafty as you guys are I don't think living in a log cabin you construct from railroad ties will cut it. Another thing the communication gear we're talking about, can you two set it up and operate it? The communication gear, if configured properly, will allow us a major down and uplink with the island-boat. Torrence would like it to be the main connection with the country."

Andrew suspected where Barry was headed but asked, "What do you suggest?"

"I'll move with you. I'll rent the house and get legitimate relocation and occupancy permits. I can provide cover and help you with the communication equipment. It would also open up the possibility of Alice visiting with Sandy, because she will be crossing the border under the auspices of visiting her sister in Canada as she has in the past. It wouldn't be unusual to visit her husband at his new location with her niece."

"But we're leaving in two days. It'll take you weeks to get a relocation permit."

"You forget what I can do to their records system. I'll get the permits within a week. You'll need to hide out until then."

Andrew looked at Jim, who nodded. "Okay Barry we want you with us."

They soon started prioritizing a list of what would be taken in Jim's fourteen foot covered truck bed. Tools; solar cells, batteries and electronic communication equipment were first on the list, but Jim had more to add.

At the nursery Jim ignored numerous operational questions from employees that had built up in his absence. He had already emotionally divested himself of the business. It would soon be the government's to administer. In a greenhouse he gathered part of Nathan, Orienpet and Trumpet lily bulbs that Nathan had hybridized and varieties of impatiens Nathan had worked on for generations. He would keep part of Nathan.

With everything in the truck he wanted, Jim carried five gallons of the herbicide Roundup to the injector on the robotic sprinkler system that Andrew had designed. It would kill everything in the greenhouses. Seasonally the employees would soon be out of work regardless. The state would confiscate only part of his property. The genetics carrying Nathan's and his work were in the truck. Like a parasite the state had lived off his work while making it ever more difficult to feed their insatiable appetite. They could find another host.

"I would prefer to leave before midnight," Jim told Andrew. "The life support will be shut off exactly at that time. Frankly, I don't want to be around. I'm not into mourning a body that has lost what made it human. I can think about his spirit and have whatever relationship is possible anywhere as his spirit will not be tied to a cluster of void carbon molecules.

My plan is to go to the hospital midday and stay until ten. Come say your good bye early evening then leave me time alone with him. I'll be standing at the hospital door at 10:10, pick me up with the truck and we'll be on our way."

"Are me and Auntie Alice going to be gone a long time?" Sandy asked Andrew as she helped him pack her clothes. She had taken to calling Alice aunt which neither Alice nor Andrew discouraged

"Yes, you will be gone awhile. We have some friends who can't wait to see you."

"Why haven't they come to see me then?"

"Because that's the way it is. You know Mommy and I love you. We want the very best for you; that is why we do what we do."

"Will I be going to see Danny?"

"No, we told you we must wait a long time to see Danny, but he watches us."

"Sometimes I try to talk to him. Is that silly?"

"No. I think that is a good thing to do."

Andrew crawled into the truck with a few tears in his eyes, but resolute and sure of the path, although not the destination. But he hesitated before leaving the driveway and entered his family room to add something to the truck he could not leave behind, the drawing of the founding fathers in his Mother's walnut framed handiwork.

Another tearful parting took place in the hospital. At 10:00 Jim pulled an electric circuit breaker used to switch off the lights in the nursery from his pocket. It was set to break the 110 volt circuit in 100 minutes. He unplugged the respirator, plugged the circuit breaker in and the respirator to the circuit breaker.

Although the state controlled most everything, Jim decided in this case they wouldn't. Yes, they could decide that Nathan's life was not worth sustaining even given a 1 in 5 chance of him fully recuperating. They could penalize him by letting his life slip away because he violated a mandate. In effect, your most important material possession, your life, was at their discretion. To live was to be at their pleasure with a person in perpetual indebtedness to the state's blessing of life. But they could not dictate the hour, or minute the unfettered spirit would leave. Nathan would be pleased with that.

Jim caressed Nathan's cheek with his hand. He held it for nearly a minute. Before he pulled his hand he thought he felt a slight twitch. Probably his own heightened blood flow in his hand, he surmised, but he would hold on to the thought that it was Nathan's farewell.

Chapter 13

Addison had an inquisitive mind. At some point in her life she decided she would leave the world with as few stones unturned as possible. Her political viewpoints were varied and fluent, but she always sought information. As such she regularly logged into inner and outernet news feeds from around the world. She continued to be amazed at the disparate ways a world event could be viewed. She would have been surprised to know the NSA monitored her grape connections to unofficial news sites and viewed it with alarm.

Eric Hansen had thought a great deal about the strange call he received from the former president. Originally after passing on the information to Andrew Collier, as she requested, he intended to forget what she said about something important happening at the NSA facility in which he worked. But he couldn't.

Collier had been an amateur astronomer, but NASA had confiscated his equipment. NSA certainly didn't look at the sky; they focused on observing people, mostly citizens. Since Collier was involved with Barnmore's Atlas Company, many thought he had ties to the underground. Was the former President trying to lead the meager resistance somewhere? That seemed a reasonable deduction, but was she earnestly giving them a tip or participating in setting a trap?

As director of NASA he had compartmentalized the agency, but for efficiency reasons. The compartmentalization at NSA seemed to be more focused on keeping anyone from seeing the big picture. If only for his own satisfaction he would find out what was going on at NSA. But it wouldn't be easy, he had casually asked people in the building what they were working on and been given cold stares. Not surprising, he thought, as he, too, had been discouraged from sharing his work focus. He would need to approach it differently.

At noon in the building cafeteria he scanned for tables occupied by a mature, scholarly looking person, someone who fit the profile of scientist. An unkempt, wrinkled shirt, unattended hair might be a cliché, he thought, but not necessarily wrong. He gingerly approached a table that was occupied by one man. "May I join you?"

"Certainly."

"I'm Eric Hansen, and you are?"

"Todd Gerald."

Eric ate his lunch making small talk with Todd, conversing about the weather and the local soccer team's exploits.

Wednesday he met Mary Wilson and Friday Scott Hampton in the same manner.

Saturday he searched the name Todd Gerald, found seven in Iowa, two within fifty miles of the facility and one Dr. Todd Gerald, MD, PhD who had written numerous papers on the suppression of antibody production to transplanted non-organic substances.

The one Mary Wilson who fit the criteria had acquired a PhD studying radio wave transmission connection to nano-technology. Mr. Hampton had a masters degree in vascular physiology.

His curiosity only heightened, Eric met three others the next week, a PhD geneticist, Melinda Rhoads, who had developed methods to mass produce nano-technology and a researcher on stimulation of Gamma-Aminobutyric Acid, our natural valium.

The weekend found Eric at home sketching diagrams of the top level expertise he had found.

Stimulation of feel-good hormone
Geneticist
Antibody suppression for Non-organic objects
Radio wave transmission to nano-technology
Mass production of nano-technology
Vascular physiology

He added to his list the field he was managing, the conversion of glucose to electric energy, and found none of the people he met had a background in intelligence gathering, the purview of NSA. Most were in the fields of biology or nano-technology.

Eric plotted the components on a large board like detectives would do on old crime shows. The parts started to fit together.

It wasn't long before he drew a supposition. If you made the assumption that all these experts in their respective disciplines were working on a single project, you could draw some conclusions. You didn't need a geneticist to listen to grape conversations, a vascular expert to track vehicles, or an antibody suppression specialist to ID faces from hundreds of thousands of cameras in public places.

NSA was working on radio controlled nano-technology that would produce a feel-good hormone in the vascular system with energy from glucose and they intended to mass produce it for a genetic specific application. Was the simplest answer correct as Occam's Razor predicted or was the explanation too simple?

It was 11:00 pm, the supervising nurse on call entered Nathan's room. She had her instructions. The doctor would not be in. It was never easy; sometimes she had delayed her orders for a few hours but doing so never made it easier. The next time she entered the room it would be to terminate the connections.

His heart rate was up marginally, the O2 level was slightly higher. She checked his blood pressure. It too was closer to normal. She contemplated calling the doctor, but thought better of it as the last time she had done so it had caused him to be short with her.

In exactly an hour she returned to shut off the machine. Strange she thought noticing that the respirator was not cycling, but she flipped the switch down anyway and pulled the breathing tubes from his face. Task completed she left. She couldn't help that he had no family or friends with him. She would let him go in privacy and monitor his demise from the control center.

Although a beeper, that would notify the center when his heart stopped, hadn't sounded she periodically glanced at Nathan's vitals. In an hour his vitals had improved, she entered his room.

She laid her hand on his forehead then gripped his hand. "Nathan can you hear me?"

She felt something and repeated, "Nathan can you hear me?"

His hand gripped hers. "Oh my God."

Within five minutes the doctor on call entered the room and examined him. "Move your left foot Nathan." He did.

"Are you awake?"

Nathan mouthed "yes."

By daylight he was looking around the room, conversing with nurses and trying to roll over. The staff placed multiple calls to his home with no answer.

At his suggestion they called Alice. "I think Jim made all the arrangements before he left," she told them.

"You don't understand, he is out of the coma and will be released this afternoon."

"We'll be there soon." Alice gathered Barry and entered Nathan's room to find him sitting.

"I know Jim left, he told me he didn't want to be here when I passed. I understand. I could hear him but he didn't know I could. Where is Orlando?"

Getting no answer, he asked, "Did he go with Jim?"

"No, he's alright but not here right now."

"I wasn't here either for awhile after Jim left; I traveled far down a path. It wasn't like I was walking, more like floating toward a destination I did not know. Actually it was more like I incrementally changed form rather than traveled. It was an alluring place, maybe not a place but a light or energy. It was so inviting, so serene and gentle, but it wasn't my time and suddenly I saw a nurse with her hand on my forehead and soon I could no longer see her from out of my body but I felt her grip my hand."

Late in the afternoon Alice and Barry took Nathan to their home and, as gently as they could, explained what happened to Orlando. Nathan surprised them by not being upset, like he already knew.

"I'm calling Andrew on his secure phone; we'll let Jim know the good news."

"No, don't. Jim is okay now. He's doing what he needs to… I'll contact him in time, but not now."

The hospital cleaning staff sanitized the room for the next patient and carted the respirator away, but not before noticing it was plugged into a box attached to the electrical outlet. Not knowing what it was, they threw it in an accessory box in the equipment room.

Rural Iowa

Ethan was waiting at the abandoned farmstead as Jim and Andrew pulled in from the long drive. He directed them to a metal covered building with an earthen floor. Stored in it were a number of old farm tillage implements, a metal frame on wheels under which hung round steel blades called a disc, and another metal frame on wheels with C-shaped shanks tipped with a sharp point and a series of tine-like spikes sharpened by friction with the soil known as a field cultivator.

"Keep you truck parked in here out-of-sight."

He showed them the house. The front door was ajar, some windows were broken, and a raccoon had left evidence of his habitation. Resident spiders occupied the corners of most rooms. But it was sound, pretty much as they expected.

"I told you it wasn't much. There is a rural water line connected but I better wait until Barry shows up before I get the water turned on, or the electricity. I assume you have a supply of water and food."

"We do; the truck is full and the place is fine. We'll spend most of our time in the railroad tie yard until Barry arrives."

"Remember there is a security camera at the main gate."

"Got it, Barry is going to take care of that but until then we'll burrow under a fence and be careful not to create a path."

"Well let me know on the SP if you need anything, Caridad and I will be out in a couple days."

Jim retrieved a shovel from the truck and planted bulbs from the nursery on the South side of the out building. Andrew carried a few necessities in the house giving Jim time alone with the remnants of Nathan and Jim's work. Jim was cleaning his shovel when Andrew approached and saw a number of freshly dug and filled holes.

"It's a good place for them."

"Yes, it is."

Early the next morning they were inside the railroad tie dump's fence surveying the huge pile. The ties had been picked up with a long armed cherry picker and released high on the pile from which they rolled in a haphazard manner. From a distance it would have resembled a gigantic pick-up-sticks game. The pile was laid out in a c-shape stacked as high as forty feet around the center which was twenty high.

The railroad ties were 7 by 9 inches and most were 8 1/2 feet long, but a few switch ties were 16 feet in length. Some were oak, other's Eucalyptus, commonly called gum, in various stages of rot and decay. The oak ties weighed nearly 150 pounds. Softer gum ties weighed less. The ties were black as they had been treated with creosote, a preservative. Beside the belief that stockpiling tied up carbon from the atmosphere, creosote had been declared toxic to the environment. It was considered safer to stockpile both the carbon and toxicity than dispose of them by burning or burying.

For the COMMON GOOD

The ties reminded Andrew of a novel Dan Barnhouse had given him years ago. In the novel the heroine, Dagney, had run a railroad. He wondered how many of these ties she may have laid in the prescient novel. After discouraging people from reading the novel backfired, authorities ignored it; so people thought, but the NSA kept track of who purchased copies.

They decided the area inside the tall arc of the pile was the place to build. It would be easier to reach the ground and offered a canyon-like hideaway. The first day they removed enough ties to get to the ground. They laid ties side-by-side with tools moved to the compound from the truck until they had a 16 foot square floor. Stacking the ties flat in rings twelve high, they built walls 7 feet high. They staggered the joints and alternated the laps at the corners to give the structure stability as pioneers had a log cabin.

"I remember Julie, on our honeymoon at a cabin in the wilderness, asked me if I would have liked being a pioneer and building a log cabin and the idea struck me as intriguing. Funny now here I am."

"A little difference though, they had round logs to work with that weren't necessarily straight. They would have loved working with these."

"You've got a point."

It took the two builders a week get the structure together. They fashioned a roof, covered it with a camouflage insulated tarp they had brought and laid ties haphazardly over the roof, against the walls and around to structure to hide their work in a myriad of randomly resting ties.

Ethan and Caridad stopped at the house twice leaving water and food and checking on their progress. For safety Jim and Andrew had minimized moving between the house and the wooden structure. When necessary to travel back and forth with supplies or tools they carried a six foot square piece of insulated tarp Alice had sewn for them. Upon hearing the buzz of a vulture drone they covered themselves hiding from both regular and infrared cameras.

Jim and Andrew stayed away from the main gate to the RR tie dump; its surveillance camera they would leave for Barry to handle.

Some of the small electronic and communication paraphernalia of Barry's they had moved to the structure but the solar panels of Andrew's and the bigger communication gear they left in the truck awaiting Barry's arrival.

In the '20s a European private/public conglomerate had placed a number of small CubeSats in geostationary orbits over North American to form Out-net links to facilitate communication between US and European interests. As the technology became obsolete and hampered monitoring by the respective governments, use of the CubeSats declined. A Dutch company purchased the CubeSats for little and sold space on the CubeSats to companies. Companies generally purchased the encrypted space to enhance communication between company locations.

ARC, Andrew's employer, had leased space on the CubeSats for years. The technology was the determining factor in John Whitehouse approval of Andrew's move to oversee the robot installation in Iowa. It would allow Andrew to monitor the installation without being on site and communicate with Boise. However, a simple tweak addition to ARC's encryption allowed Andrew and Barry to use the link for much more. With Barry's arrival they would start putting the pieces together.

Preparing the farm house for occupancy would explain Ethan and Caridad's many trips to the country. With Ethan's help Andrew and Jim replaced broken windows and stashed two extra windows and a door in the truck for later use in the RR tie structure.

The following evening Caridad and Ethan arrived with cleaning supplies and Julie. Andrew greeted her with a hug and noticed she had brought blankets and a paper bag of clothes. "Planning on staying, but a paper bag instead of a suitcase?"

"I started to put things in the suitcase, but it didn't feel right; hence the bag. I'm here for the weekend, or is this a guy-only location?"

After laughter, Ethan warned them, "I've filed for the occupancy permit. The inspector will inspect the house next week. It can be cleaned but must not look like anyone is living here. We'll be back here Sunday evening to pick Julie up, but from Monday until the inspector comes, you guys can not be here."

The group huddled around a speaker plugged into the SP in the farmhouse with Alice, Barry and Nathan on the other end in Boise.

"How's my little girl?"

"She's fine playing in the other room. I'll get her once we have covered business."

The conversation determined that Barry would arrive on Friday, but until the permit was issued he would stay with Caridad and Ethan. Alice and Sandy would leave Wednesday for Canada the same time as Barry headed for Iowa.

At Nathan's request, the Bradley's didn't bring up the subject of Nathan, but Jim asked, "I just wonder, how is… er I mean, how did things go?"

Barry looked at Nathan who was shaking his head 'no'. "Don't worry Jim… things went just fine."

The others drifted away as the words: Mommy, Daddy, and little girl were used a lot.

Later Andrew pushed what had been on his mind, "I've got to make contact with Eric Hansen. I suspect he knows much more than he revealed in the telephone call. He initiated the conversation, it shouldn't be unexpected if I follow-up."

"I think that is too dangerous. First place, although you have a disguise, you could be noticed and do we absolutely know it isn't a trap?"

"How do you suggest we contact him?"

"Remember I met him at the conference in Illinois. I have legitimate credentials for being here. It wouldn't seem that unrealistic if I ran into him. Let's find out his routine so we can make it look coincidental until we are confident it isn't a trap."

"Legitimate? Your credentials show you as Julie Archibald. He knows you as a brunette, not a blond."

"Andrew, I think I'm much more adept at security issues than you. Do I question your engineering?"

Andrew reluctantly acknowledged she was right. Before dark Julie said, "I want to see what you guys have done with the railroad ties."

Andrew gathered his sleeping bag and a camouflage insulated tarp, Julie grabbed her blankets and the brown bag of clothes. They both looked at Jim.

"I know. I'll see you in the morning."

Surveying the construction Julie said, "I guess I should have expected as much with an engineer and a handyman working together. You're getting a chance to be the pioneer you talked about at Mt Shasta."

"Do you think this will suffice as a secure communication center?"

"I think it's perfect."

"For what else?" he asked as she felt his arms encircle her from behind.

—◊◊◊—

Boise, ID

The bald-headed ATF agent had been busy. Another group of dollar-sign graffiti misfits had sprung up in Boise. He hadn't forgotten about Julie's travel but had yet to confirm the suitcase had arrived in Connecticut. Logged onto the ATF web tracking site he found the suitcase was in Iowa. A stop at relatives or friends in route he thought, he would check back in a few days.

—◊◊◊—

"What are you going to do Nathan?" quizzed Alice.

"My experience in the hospital has changed the way I view this world. It is taking time to sort out. Big things look small now, as some former small things I now find are overriding. I sense the need to put more emphasis on the total landscape of life rather than the parts that we get hung up on. What will I do? I don't know, but like Jim, there is nothing for me here with Orlando, Jim and the nursery gone. At first I was hurt by Jim leaving. But finding myself alone here in the same situation as he expected to be in, I understand why he left. He couldn't stand the thought of being here without Orlando or me, neither can I."

"You must tell him."

"I know, I will, but not now. If I went to Iowa I would only be in the way. If Jim knew I was here he would be torn between doing what he needs to do there and being here with me. Alice would Sandra and you like a traveling companion?"

Alice and Barry looked at each other. "Sure but what then?"

Once I'm situated out of the country. I'll contact Jim. Perhaps Melissa can find something useful for me to do on the island-boat and it might be helpful if Sandra and you had an escort."

"We are leaving Wednesday."

"I know, I'll be ready."

With his small car packed with electronic gadgetry Barry told Alice and the others farewell. The cargo would not cause alarm as Barry was now a former government employee to be engaged in part-time communication consulting. Alice and he planned on her returning from Canada to Iowa after all were situated at the island-boat. Returning from a long visit with her Canadian Aunt would be expected and Barry's wife with him in Iowa would raise fewer flags.

Nathan was carrying identification as a Canadian citizen who had been visiting his cousin in the states and Sandra was his daughter. Identities produced by Barry allowed them easy access across the border. The three were met by an escort from the island-boat five miles north of the border and taken to Vancouver. In five days traveling through Mazatlan, Mexico and San Jose, Costa Rica, they arrived at the converted cruise liner anchored ten miles off the Costa Rica coast in international waters.

Melissa, Dan Barnmore's wife, was expectantly waiting for them. She took to Sandra immediately as Sandra did her. Sandra became an instant celebrity on the island-boat as everyone had an opinion whether she looked more like Julie or Andrew. Sandra was fascinated that everyone seemed to know her parents. The questions: "How do you know Mommy, How do you know Daddy?" were heard for days around the ship. Sandra, perceptive for being shy of five years old, found that the circle of her parents' acquaintances was much wider than she had known.

"Government control gives rise to fraud, suppression of truth,
intensification of the black market and artificial scarcity.
Above all, it unmans the people and deprives them of initiative;
it undoes the teaching of self-help."

Gandhi

Chapter 14

The suitcase remained in Iowa and Andrew, Julie, their kid, Jim, Nathan and two neighbors, Barry and Alice Bradley, had disappeared from Boise. A judge issued an arrest warrant for Jim. Nathan had unexpectedly recovered only to disappear. The nursery's old truck was gone as were the Bradleys and Nathan's cars. The nursery had been abandoned and government property acquisition personnel reported greenhouse plants were dying. The bald-headed ATF agent was livid; it had happened under his watch.

Pre-occupied with tracking down graffiti punks on orders or not, he had let them slip away and would need to answer for it. He made sure his black shirt collar was straight, his merit metals were in place and braced himself for his supervisor's tongue lashing.

"Let me get this straight, you send fifty agents on a goose chase to follow this suitcase to the Canadian border a few years ago when they appear to be out for a drive, you place an agent at the nursery for months to no avail, and then you transfer her to follow Collier for nothing. And now they all disappear and you have no idea where they are. All you know is a suitcase is in Iowa."

"But Madame, we had no indication any of them…"

"And the only ones you can account for in those families are one dead kid and one social derelict locked up in Omaha."

"Send me to Iowa with a few agents. Someone is around that suitcase."

"So you can mess up again? Absolutely not, not without more information."

The berated agent left the regional director's office. Chewing someone out made the regional director feel good. No discredit would come to her as none of the shortcoming would be passed on to Washington. She had learned some time ago to only report operational activities after they were successful.

For the ATF agent it was not over. Three vehicles had disappeared. A record of those vehicles would be at the NSA data center in Utah. Although the information might be buried, with enough work on his part, he would find out where they went.

Literally trillions of pieces of information on who went where when, who called whom, who mailed what to whom, and who was on a street at a given time in front of hundreds of thousands of surveillance cameras were stored in Utah. No flags had been placed on the vehicles, but the information from the vehicle black boxes was stored.

Although the analytical abilities of state computers to glean suspicious behavior were immense and increasing, the volume of information was overwhelming. But it was there. With enough tenacity an agent pushing NSA database investigators relentlessly could find out. The bald-headed ATF agent was motivated.

Iowa

Jim checked the farmhouse cautiously Tuesday after occupancy inspectors normally quit for the afternoon. He found a leaf that he had placed in the upper door jam had fallen, indicating entry by someone. To be safe they stayed away from the house until Ethan had verified the permit had been issued the following Tuesday.

Barry arrived Friday and moved in late Tuesday with permit in hand. The next morning they took him on a tour. Although they had kept traffic in and out of the railroad tie dump to a minimum, it wouldn't have taken an accomplished tracker to discover someone had been entering the facility. Acquiring safe access through the main gate was a priority.

Barry tapped into the camera circuit that covered the gate from a ladder on the backside. He used a system similar to what he had deployed in the Cheyenne nuclear warhead warehouse. The software he downloaded caused the camera to recycle a previous hour's video every other hour. The hourly cycling would allow them to move in and out the gate unnoticed every other hour. It was set such that the odd hours were safe. Even hours they had to stay away.

Jim had logged the appearance of vulture drones for a week. They were obviously programmed to work a grid; seldom did less than 90 minutes pass between sightings. They had the truck ready to move when the vulture drone disappeared. With the camera recycling and the gate open they pulled the truck as close as possible to the structure and unloaded solar panels and communication gear. In thirty minutes the truck was parked back in the farm machine shed.

For the rest of the week the men laid out solar panels, wired them to batteries and communication gear. Linkage to the CubeSats was through an outdated 36 inch parabolic dish once used for TV satellite reception. It was painted in camouflage and nestled between railroad ties.

In the 16 foot square cabin interior were desks made of ties, batteries, solar lights, a large screen monitor on a wall with hookups for grapes and notebooks. It was beginning to look like a command post in the wilderness. Once powered up they would no longer need to rely upon bulky secure phones. They would have secure access to the inter and outernets, the ability to send and receive files and mail, but perhaps most important a direct link to the island-boat.

Barry installed motion detectors around the cabin structure and the farmhouse. Only one person was supposed to inhabit the farmhouse. Andrew and Jim alternated sleeping in the cabin or farm house. Whoever spent the night in the farmhouse slept by the back door allowing fast exit.

Saturday they finished their work. Solar panels were charging the batteries and all was ready for Monday's startup. ARC had made arrangements for use of part of the company's ban width on the CubeSats designated for use of the pneumatic robotic installation and maintenance. It was to commence Monday morning, but they would use it for much more.

Sunday Adana joined Caridad, Ethan and Julie bringing an assortment of food to the farm for a picnic. As Ethan owned the property, Barry was leasing it and they could describe the others as relatives or friends, this made the get together safe.

Andrew was taking Julie for a tour of the cabin center as they came to call it when she altered the subject, "I discovered Eric Hansen also jogs in the morning,"

"So you are planning to accidentally run into him?"

"That's the idea. We've got to find out what he knows, but we can't tip our hand, as I'm sure he will be cautious also."

"Just be careful. It could be a setup."

"I know."

Upon Julie and Andrew's return to the farmhouse they heard Adana questioning Barry.

"So tell me more about this company ARC, Amalgamated Robotics Company, how big are they?"

Andrew answered, "They are a big publicly traded company headquartered in Hartford, Connecticut. We, in Boise, are primarily the research and design division."

"And Barry says the division head, John Whitehouse, set this link up or allowed you to use this link?"

"Yes, he is trusted. He knows it will be used for other activity."

"How about the people in Connecticut?"

"Well, no. or I don't know."

"Let me ask you this, how big a player is ARC becoming in robotics?"

"We, or they, are gaining market share all the time. Competitors are struggling."

"Let's step back a minute and look at the big picture. ARC, a large company, is growing and gaining market share. We like to think that is because they are innovative and efficient, that's the way it is supposed to work. But in reality if they are smothering the competition and getting government work it has more to do with something else.

"You had a business once Andrew, did you go out of business because you didn't have enough demand or because you didn't produce a good product?"

"Well, no. I sold it to ARC because they were better at other things."

"Precisely, there is a synergy at work in the country between government and big business. Government creates regulation and barriers to competition and entry in certain industries and favored companies reward those clearing their way with their compliance to the state's will and contributions to the right people. It's a mutual aid society.

Don't think the company executives in Connecticut are motivated by how well the installation of your robotic system goes. In the big picture it doesn't mean anything to them. Gaining influence by playing the game better than others or showing their commitment to the present ideology is far more rewarding, and thus motivating. Their careers are not tied to efficiency, they're tied to compliance. The gain from uncovering a resistance operation would far outweigh a major uptick in sales, cost control or certainly a successful robotics installation."

Andrew looked at Barry, "What do you think?"

"She's got a point. We've put a lot of work in this. We don't know what is happening here but we know it is something we must uncover. If we are found out, all of us ending up at Guantanamo Bay would be the least of it. The signal is encrypted by the company and we have altered it somewhat, but it is possible if the company is checking they may find something amiss.

"What do you suggest?"

"Let's contact Torrence. His people can develop a more sophisticated encrypting system to overlay the present one such that our traffic won't be noticed. It should only take a few days."

"Thank you, Adana. You're right, caution is imperative. In the meantime Andrew can startup the legitimate ARC communication tomorrow and it will allow us to test everything," Julie summarized.

Julie discovered Eric Hansen lived on the opposite side of Oskaloosa. As she jogged in the morning on the western loop of the community recreation trail, he had been jogging on the eastern loop. Her observation had found him living near North Park Avenue and jogging south to University Park. Julie found it interesting how joggers habitually used the same routes.

She double checked her fanny pack to make sure she had the hair brush, took her blond wig off and had slowed to a walk as Eric reached the point he usually turned around. The timing was perfect he was slowing down and noticed her before she spoke.

"Eric, is that you?"

He stopped and briefly studied her. "Yes, you were at the Evanston conference, ah… Julie, right?"

"Yes, that's right. Are you still studying cellular evolution?"

"I'm but a novice. What a co-incidence meeting you here. What brings you here?"

"I don't believe in coincidences and, I expect, neither do you."

Julie had decided prudent straight talk was the best route to build trust without revealing anything. "I've been jogging on the other side of town. But after your call to Andrew… well I think we should talk."

"Oh, I see. I was just passing something on for an acquaintance. Is Andrew still in Boise?"

"What difference does it make where he is? But we're curious, what if people were interested in learning more?"

"Why would anyone think I would know more?

With her disguise at the building where they both worked she doubted that Eric would ever recognize her, but Julie knew she had to take a chance. If she ever met Eric again this would be the only time she could be confident he wasn't carrying a listening device. "Eric, I know you directed us to pay attention to a facility you work at and it is in proximity to another facility that was involved in the murder of thousands of people. And we know a tunnel is being built linking the two."

"What do you mean the murder?"

"Many more people died of the flu than reported and we have reason to believe it was not accidental."

Eric Hansen's wife had contacted flu. She had survived but it had been a long battle to recovery. She had always had an aversion to taking medications or vaccines, to her detriment he often told her. His limited knowledge of biology had caused him to wonder how such a deadly virus could spread with a huge majority of the population vaccinated. He sat in silence for a period then felt the same inner directional pull he had when he resigned as director of NASA.

"Come with me, let's jog for a few minutes."

After crossing highway 92 a forested area lay to their left. "Follow me," he said.

Once they were obscured by brush from the path he asked her to leave her fanny pack.

Julie knew this was a critical moment, but also knew Eric could not have anticipated her visit. It was a good sign that he also suspected her of being bugged, but nevertheless she only reluctantly left the fanny pack containing a hair brush capable of incapacitating a man his size and stepped away with him.

"Now raise your top."

"What? Why?" she said incredulously until his reasoning struck her. She raised her white closely knit top revealing her torso partially covered by a running bra.

"Turn around."

She did allowing him to assure himself she was not wired.

"I have information that someone should know, but I want to know what you know about the flu."

"We know by extrapolating the deaths in localities across the country many more than acknowledged died of the flu. I can tell you more once I hear something in return."

"Okay… I've discovered a wide variety of specialists work at the NSA facility including one of the world's experts on mass production of nano-technology."

"I suggest we meet at the same place in 48 hours and compare more notes."

"Agreed"

They both left feeling comfortable with the other, but planned to verify the information they had received.

The tunnel being dug connecting the NSA and FDA facilities was of a horizontal oblong shape designed to contain two tubes each less than a meter in diameter and lying side by side. As the tunnel was dug molten quick-forming plastic was forced by pressure into the earthen hole encasing the hole in the ground. An ARC designed and built robotic pneumatic system would send capsules five-foot in length in both directions. Compressors on both sides of the tunnel were being installed to send the tubes floating toward the other end. Robotics loaded and unloaded the capsules in basement rooms of both buildings, which were off limits to all personnel.

Tunnel workers had no idea what the product to be moved was or from where in the building the containers would come. Those packaging the nano-machines would place containers on a conveyer and it would disappear through a gate in the wall. Those on the receiving end had no idea where it came from as a door would open delivering a container. ARC had two technicians on site, one at each end of the tunnel instructing subcontractors. Neither the ARC technicians nor the subcontractors knew what the other was doing. One pair worked on the pneumatic system, the other pair on the elevator delivery system.

The technicians sent data to Andrew constantly and received his feedback. He relayed the information to the ARC Boise plant. In order to send the large amounts of data securely, an uploading station was needed; hence the use of CubeSats. Local transmission from the site to Andrew was not a corporate security issue, but sending the data to Boise was. ARC was concerned about corporate theft of proprietary information both in and out of the country.

From the start of transmission Monday the uplink and communication devices worked as planned by ARC personnel.

It had taken a week of continuously sending high priority requests for information but the ATF agent on a mission finally got someone at the NSA data center to send him the information he requested. It was easier to get him the information than put up with his constant inquiries.

The car registered to Nathan had left the country occupied by three people when it crossed the border. Records revealed one was Alice Bradley, who made periodic trips to Canada visiting an Aunt. The others were a cousin and niece, both holding Canadian passports. From border cameras the cousin looked like Nathan and the niece Andrew's remaining twin daughter Sandra.

Another neighborhood car registered to Barry Bradley, who had recently retired, was at a rural location in Iowa and a recorded occupancy permit indicated he had leased a house in the country. Indeed aerial vulture sightings had identified his face in the backyard. All Bradley's documents appeared in order, but his moving within a few miles of the suitcase in Julie's possession was cause for suspicion. Julie or her suitcase that is, had not traveled on to Connecticut as expected

It took him two days to get an appointment with his supervisor after he had sent her the new information. She was not pleasant but became more interested as he laid the information before her.

"So what do you suggest?"

"That I be allowed to follow the lead to Iowa with six agents accompanying me in order to completely stake out the targets and get some answers."

"Do you realize that area of the state is a level one on the security index? There are only three other areas in the country other than DC with that classification. It is not like the area is without observation."

The regional director studied her options. The proper avenue would have been to notify the ATF supervisor in Iowa of their suspicions. Doing so would have resulted in one of two outcomes, either the suspicions would not be borne out, in which case she would be embarrassed at the least, or illegal activity would be uncovered in which she would get minor credit compared to the local ATF people.

Sending her people would either be a waste of time that no one need know about or they would find something and she would take full credit. Given that the area was a level one, the risks and rewards were heightened. She chose the prudent avenue for her.

"Okay. Here are the conditions; you won't notify ATF or anyone there what you are up to, or even that you are there. It is absolutely for our knowledge only and you can take one agent with you. You can take the one you have been in most contact with."

Seeing his face flush, she knew she had made a point, "Yes, I know what my agents are up to. Having said that I assume you trust her.

You are to go separately and be back in ten days. She is not to know you are going and you are to have no contact with her there. As far as she is to know, you remain here. Neither of you are to have any contact until you are back here; in fact, I want you staying in different towns. At her return she will report only to you. She will not know I authorized this operation. Later you will report both of your findings to me and only me.

Neither of you will do anything other than observe the targets in stakeout mode. If you find one of the subjects is even an active serial killer you will not arrest them, understood?

I assume you can both write by hand, correct?"

"Yes, but we have seldom need today."

"Well you will now. You may take your grapes, but they are to remain in your hotel rooms. Nothing goes on them. You will hand write logs of your stakeouts and the targets' activities. And you will protect those with your life.

I will see to it you are both provided special cars from the motor pool and neither of you are to get within a mile of either the NSA or the FDA facility even if your subject does. Is that understood?

Do you understand why these precautions are necessary?" Before he could answer she did, "Sending one agent outside of my region would cause enough problems. But sending two and risking being found out without previously clearing it. It could destroy both of our careers."

The next morning the blond agent picked up a special car from the ATF motor pool. Shortly after she left her supervisor also picked up a car and headed east on a different route than the blonde agent.

"There is far more danger in public than in private monopoly, for when government goes into business it can always shift its losses to the taxpayers."

Thomas Edison

Chapter 15

Julie utilized a number of search engines researching nano-technology mass production methods and who the leading innovators in the field were. Barry aided her by searching outside her reach to collaborate and extend her quest. They identified eight experts in the country who normally worked in the public arena. They concluded six were not in the Midwest. One was at the University of Chicago but his schedule, which they verified, left him no time to spend in Iowa. That left one woman, perhaps the most capable, unaccounted for since she left MIT two years ago. Her name was Melinda Rhoads.

Eric's research started with what he knew. His wife had been hospitalized with the flu at Mahaska County Hospital which served a population in the area of 25,000. He heard reports while he was in the hospital with his wife that 15 people had died there of the flu. Rumors were that 8 had died in nursing homes around the county. He stopped at the hospital under the auspices of his wife having left something in her room and asked a nurse he had come to know about the flu death tally. The nurse said that they had been instructed not to talk about it but six more had died in the last two weeks. The tally was 28 out of a service area of 25,000 or over a tenth of a percent.

He contacted a confidant in Houston whose husband was a hospital administrator; they had a higher rate of 0.20 percent. His sister in Seattle whose daughter was a registered nurse gave him some rough numbers that he calculated the fatality rate at 0.18%. The weighted average was just over 0.18 % which, if a representative sample, would translate to over 630,000 flu deaths in the country's 350 million population. His statistical background was a little weak to calculate the significance of the sample in probability, but he knew it was high.

Julie was waiting at their previous meeting place on the path. Eric noticed she held a hair brush in her hand, strange he thought not knowing its alternative use. She thought it was precautionary. He led her to the same place they had stood two days earlier but she suggested a fallen log further into the brush behind wild raspberry bushes. They sat beside each other facing the path.

"Well?" Julie asked.

"The flu fatalities appear to be considerably above what is being reported. If fact I didn't need to look very hard to draw those conclusions. Years ago when the press had a healthy curiosity, they would have been all over the discrepancies."

"And the name of the nano production expert?" she asked.

"Melinda Rhoads."

Julie's skepticism started to melt. "So we both confirmed the information we shared."

"So can we trust each other?"

"Stand up and raise your shirt."

He did.

"Take your shoes off and toss them beyond the oak tree."

He did, and then hooked his thumbs in the elastic of his running shorts.

"That won't be necessary," she said as she put the hair brush in her fanny pack.

They both laughed nervously at first, but gradually relaxed. "I can't blame you for being careful," he said.

"Neither can I you. Let me show you a video. Have you ever been to the town of Knoxville?"

"No."

Julie pulled her grape out and inserted a video chip. "This is what happened at a flash rally there."

She then switched to the airport transfer. "Do you recognize the airport?"

"Sure it's the one officials use here, I've been in and out of there numerous times. Oh, my God!"

"It's my turn now," Eric said as he handed her a written list of various disciplines of people working at the NSA facility.

Stimulation of GABA, the feel-good hormone
Behavioral genetics
Rejection antibody suppression for non-organic objects
Radio wave transmission to nano-technology
Mass production of nano-technology
Vascular physiology
Glucose conversion to electric energy

Julie studied the list and started to put the pieces together. "I suspect the confluence of this is what someone wanted you to warn Andrew about. What do you make of this?"

"Well, I'm not a rocket scientist, although many once worked under my direction, but the most reasonable conclusion is there is an effort to build a hormone producing machine to place in people on a mass scale."

As a young girl Julie loved to put puzzles together. She first put the border together, then started filling in from there, the matching colors and objects were next, but there came point when euphoria set in as she got to the last pieces. The same feeling came in algebra class as the route to the answer became apparent. It was a Eureka moment for her.

"I know what they are doing and how they plan to do it."

They sat on the log for over an hour as she told what she knew of the flu, the vaccine and Guantanamo Bay connection. The proposed tunnel fit the hypothesis. He explained how his work on glucose conversion would power what they concluded would be the complete suppression of dissent. They explored alternative conclusions, but nothing else made sense.

They parted after agreeing they would confirm their conclusion, learn as much as possible about the implementation and meet again.

Andrew was alarmed noticing three missed calls from Julie on his SP. He knew she hadn't been caught or she wouldn't have tried to call him but he remained concerned until she reached him that evening. Julie explained what she had learned but avoided her take on it and let Andrew draw his own conclusion. He soon did. She was not surprised. He was aghast.

"My god, they plan to squelch all liberty."

At the cabin-center

Software engineers on the island-boat developed an encryption system they were confident with. It relied upon input by a smart phone to daily change the codes. Completely separate links would require access to both links for anyone to crack the code.

Julie was with Andrew in the cabin control room when they first made contact with island-boat. Torrence and Melissa's picture was clear on the 50 inch 3-D wall screen.

"You two look great, but tired," said Melissa.

"Thank you. We're so glad to see you again."

"Now we're sure everything is working well, I'll get someone else who wants to see you."

"Mommy, Daddy. You're there."

"Hi sweetie. You look so good. Do you like it on the ship?"

"Yes, everyone is so nice. They all know you. That's neat."

The family had a long reunion together. Jim and Barry were at the farmhouse and would need to wait until the gate camera went through an hourly recycle before entering the compound.

After Sandy left, but before they started with business, Melissa said they had news of a personal nature for Jim. Julie suggested that the news wait until they discussed very important matters. Melissa agreed knowing Julie didn't understand.

Julie had requested the presence of all seven island-boat council members which included Melissa and Torrence.

"It's not fatigue I see on your faces. What is it?" asked Melissa.

Julie walked them through what she had learned from Eric Hansen. "We need to know everything possible about the names on the list I received from Eric which I just sent you."

"Did you get the video chip of the abduction?"

"Yes, we got it. It is pretty graphic and definitive."

"I know. With this link we don't need couriers. What about the Russian video?"

"We shared the video with them, but they are maintaining their position they won't release the Guantanamo Bay video until the time is right. Releasing it will expose their connection in Cuba and they don't want to jeopardize the intelligence until they are sure it will make a difference."

"Obviously we have more important problems than the Russian holding the video. Any preliminary thoughts from there about our first response?" asked Andrew.

"I expect as you built the system you can delay the transfer of nano-machines to the vaccine production line at the FDA plant."

"Yes, I can but we need more. At the best if I completely disabled it, they could use trucks and get it moved although it would blow cover."

Julie interjected, "I think our approach must be two fold. First we must confirm our suspicions and learn as much as possible about the operation of those two plants. We have Adana and Ethan in construction and remodeling at the FDA plant and Caridad in the vaccine development department. At the NSA plant beside myself in security and Andrew overseeing installation of the transport system we now have Eric Hansen.

At the same time we must start formulating plans to stop the operation. I think our emphasis should be to destroy the operation rather than delay it."

Torrence asked, "Can we trust Hansen?"

"I staked a lot on it and we don't have a choice now."

"Andrew, do you remember Rod Ballanger?"

"Yeah, he worked with the Wichita division of Atlas in aeronautical software development."

"Yes, and when he was with Atlas he also had his own company doing drone work. Since Atlas, his company has grown and now they do most NSA drone repair and software upgrade work. We have been in contact with him through secure phone. He is to be trusted and has connections in Oklahoma City and Texas. Anyway the point I'm making, he is one of us and his knowledge of the vulture drones is valuable. He wants to head up your direction and meet you."

"We'll trust your judgment," answered Julie drawing a skeptical look from Andrew.

"We are ready to download software to make your grapes usable," Torrence said leading to a technical conversation with Barry. The crux of it was he had downloaded a program which could be transferred to their grapes. The application which would allow communication with a grape within 15 miles of the cabin-center using a random oscillating piggybacking on old AM radio frequencies once Jim and Barry strung a long loop of fine antenna wire high in the railroad pile.

"How will this work?" asked Julie.

"You will be able to contact each other by voice activated text message routing it through the center. The radio transmission app will replace the GPS tracking capability of your grape. They can't track you and you can text within 15 miles safely. In order to use the system speak, "Text Green" and you will be put on the radio wave mode, key in your code, same as the secure phone-the inverse of the temperature, your personal 4-digit code and the inverse of the date. If the code is entered wrong or the voice recognition system doesn't match your voice, all the battery power is sent to the SIM card frying it."

"And all the inner and outernet functions will be the same?"

"Yes, but remember surfing, tweeting and regular calls will be tracked as always. But the 'green text' function will be secure because the radio waves randomly skip between frequencies every fraction of a second.

"Anything else we should talk about?"

Melissa spoke, "I want you to all know our contacts throughout the country are increasing. We are getting more Secure Phones out all the time and they are running on different circuits so if anyone flips and gives the bad guys a phone, the damage will be contained. The connection goes through Holland, Ukraine, and Australia before it ends up in Costa Rica. They can not be linked to this ship. Our movement is growing, although from the flashes Washington doesn't know. We'll let them think that.

The point I'm trying to make is two fold. First what's going on near you is of primary importance; it must be stopped. Secondly, your upload station is the only one we have in the country, you are the hub. Although we can assist however possible, I think it is important that activities be directed from inside the country. Otherwise they will blame any resistance on foreigners. There is no galvanizing figure in the country for resistance, but our patriots know what Andrew Collier and Atlas did about the asteroid.

"Julie and I and all of us will do what we need to."

Julie checked the time. "We're all getting out of here before the camera cycle changes. Jim you stay Melissa wants a word with you."

As Jim remained inside the cabin, Barry had Andrew hold a ladder for him and he opened up the security camera directed at the gate from the backside. He replaced the chip he had put in it earlier.

"I downloaded a chip from Torrence that will eliminate us needing to alternate by the hour when we use this gate. Our people on the island-boat are getting better at these software things. Keyed from a grape in 'green mode' the camera will now recycle footage for five minutes allowing us to use the gate safely anytime.

"What's up," Jim asked Melissa.

"I want you to sit down Jim. I've someone I want you to meet and it will be shocking."

Jim sat down without any idea what was happening.

A very timid looking Nathan entered the screen from the right side. Jim could feel his heart racing but couldn't say anything.

"They unplugged the machine but I had already started back. I heard you say goodbye and leave, but I couldn't respond. I'm still trying to sort it all out."

"But why didn't you..?"

"Contact you? I needed time. You were headed away, doing what you needed to do. I understood. I didn't want you turning around and running back. And when I found out Orlando was gone, there was nothing for me in Boise. I hope you understand, I had to deal with the experience of being in limbo between worlds and the loss of Orlando and I knew you were okay."

"So how did you get to Costa Rica?"

"I came down with Alice and Sandra. Don't be upset with Alice. She wanted me to contact you, but I wanted to wait."

"Does anyone here know?"

"No."

"I'm so overwhelmed... glad, you... well... and I shouldn't have left."

"Don't go there; you did the right thing."

"What about the future?"

"There's a lot going on, I'm sure I'll be back or you'll eventually be here."

Later Jim joined Barry and Andrew at the farmhouse. They were as shocked as he was at the news.

White House

The Secretary of State informed the President that Poland had officially demanded the release of a national.

"What is this about?"

The NSA director answered, "We picked up a guy in Minnesota driving a car with an altered black box. He has joint US and Polish citizenship and was driving across the country with no stated reason. We also found the remains of some kind of electronic device he destroyed before we apprehended him."

"What was the device about?"

"We don't know but it was rigged for quick destruction. Our people believe it was a communication device."

"Well that's great. Do we have any indication that more of these are around?"

"No, but if it is a communication device and there is one, there are more likely more."

"Here's the question. Who is communicating with whom? What did you do with the joint citizenship guy?"

"We sent him to Guantanamo Bay."

"How do we answer the Poles?" asked the Secretary of State.

"Let's push back, I understand the vehicle he was driving had a black box retrofit made in Poland. Do we know where the possible communication device was manufactured?

"No, we don't"

"Let it be known and have all our embassies distribute the message that we consider any foreign complicity in trafficking communication devices in the country an act of internal interference contrary to the United Nation's recognition of sovereignty. We will consider any interference very serious.

And file a complaint with the Polish embassy here that we will consider sanctions if they persist on allowing the manufacture of devices specifically made to hamper monitoring of the highways. Insist that it is a highway safety issue. And follow that up with a formal complaint at the United Nations. I am tired of playing the punching bag."

"Understood, Mr. President."

"The TIP project can't come soon enough," said the President looking at the NSA director.

The Secretary of State had no idea what he was talking about but decided not to ask.

"That's all," said the President looking at his Secretary of State.

Alone the President asked the NSA director, "Speaking of Guantanamo Bay, are you working on the project we talked about?"

"Yes, Mr. President it is moving forward."

"How soon might we expect results?"

Not understanding the President's uneasiness and urgency, the director said, "When we get the mole in place, hopefully we will have leads quickly, but it seems more prudent to me to let the mole go and see how many contacts he will make."

"I guess that makes sense, I will just feel better knowing we are keeping the pressure on these people. If they are worrying about us they aren't up to mischief."

"Democracy is not a good thing people can enjoy without trouble. It is, on the contrary, a treasure that must be daily defended and conquered anew by strenuous effort."

Ludwig von Mises

Chapter 16

William was outside on a warm spring day at the grille. It was not the first use of the grille in the spring, but it was the first with meat. He had pork ribs marinated in barbecue sauce slowly simmering. On a trellis a few feet away he watched the resident Mourning Dove perched on her nest. Whether it was the same dove or succeeding generations he did not know, but they had developed a cross-species bond. He looked forward to the mournful cooing; it was soothing to a 98 year old man.

Something caught his eye on a post the trellis was attached to. At second glance he saw a bull snake in the process of winding his way up the post, undoubtedly toward eggs in the nest. With barbecue utensils he ended the snake's quest for dinner. As he headed for the garbage can with the snake in his pinchers William heard the hum of an Aerial Citizen Protective Unit. He lost little sleep that night wondering whether his termination of the snake had been recorded. He had little to lose, but the violation had been dully recorded and was attached to his folder somewhere deep in NSA storage.

Guantanamo Bay, March, 2047

Tony Johnson, former KMRT reporter, now inmate at Guantanamo Bay was escorted into the warden's office. Normally such visits took place before solitary confinement in the hot box. Tony tried to fathom the infraction that caused him to be singled out. Nothing serious came to mind.

"Have a seat, Mr. Johnson."

The warden's use of his formal name heightened his anxiety.

"How has your treatment been here?"

It was a question he didn't expect and any answer had downside, so he spoke candidly. "Why are we here without being charged or representation and not allowed any contact with the outside world?"

"We can sit here and debate what is or isn't, but it will not get either of us anywhere. The question is do you want to get out of here?"

"What do you want?"

"Mr. Johnson, your tone is so pungent. Life is full of tradeoffs. Its part of what we call civilization. I have a proposition that would be of great value to you, that is your freedom."

Tony responded with a "go-on" stare.

"You would like to be out of here, we would like information. You and your group are locked up here while many of your cohorts run free and continue to dream up trouble. Where's the fairness in that? Do you see any of them coming to help you?

"Again, what do you want?"

"I think in exchange for your freedom you would resume your regular life which would include having contact with your regressive friends. That isn't asking too much is it?"

"Contact them and what?"

"All we would expect you to do is make your previous contacts and we would take care of the rest."

"Most the people I know who had similar ideas are here."

"But not all you admitted. If you just made contact with them, we would monitor the contacts and no one would ever know."

"But I would."

"I'm sure you are lonely for your family. Let me break the rules and reacquaint you with them."

On the wall screen behind the warden's desk appeared video recently taken of Tony's parents in Urbandale. It was taken through the front picture window in their home. They looked uncomfortable sitting on the sofa watching TV. Following the video clip were backyard videos of his sisters' families in Clive and Marshalltown.

"It looks like they are doing okay, but they could be better or worse," coyly the warden put an exclamation mark on the videos.

The warden could detect Tony's blood pressure rise. Tony held his tongue until his simmer lost some of its edge. Given the methods he had witnessed at the prison, he knew the threats were not idle.

"I will need to think about it."

"I understand. I wouldn't expect you to make any hasty decisions. For your own safety, of course, you will need to go to the box. We wouldn't want the other prisoners to get the wrong idea, that you were getting special treatment, would we?"

Forty-eight hours later after four bottles of water that had not replenished half of what he had lost and two meals Tony was again in front of the warden.

Tony had made a decision. What right did he have to cause his family suffering? They were his ideals, not necessarily his family's, particularly his nieces and nephew's. What was anyone doing to help? And why was he here, but for most likely a lost cause?

"So what, do you want me to be wired?"

"In a sense, we have an implant for you."

"To forever being your snitch?"

"Not at all, the battery life is but sixty days, once it is dead you will have fulfilled our deal."

The warden lied. The implant would utilize new technology developed by subcontracting biological engineers who Eric Hansen was managing. Blood glucose would power the implant indefinitely.

The next morning a small implant was put in the loose skin below Tony's elbow. Rumor was spread that he had become sick in the box. In the middle of the night he was escorted out the employee entrance to the prison. Two days later it was announced that after intense medical care Tony had succumbed to his illness.

The images from the 360 degree convex camera Adelmo Perez passed on to the Russians never caught the extra person dressed as a NSA guard leaving the prison.

Julie and Andrew stayed the night in the cabin-center as they came to call the hidden railroad tie cabin with the maze of sophisticated communication equipment powered by solar cells strewn about the complex. Earlier they had finished an extended conference call with the island-boat giving them much to digest.

"Torrence was adamant that we meet with Rod Ballanger and Mason Trotter tomorrow. How dangerous do you think it is?"

"I met Rod a few times at Atlas. I know Dan thought highly of him. Torrence believes his expertise and connections with vulture spies could be invaluable to us. So I think we should go with it. And the Dallas group led by Mason is by far the largest, most active flasher group in the country."

"Yes, I guess you're right. We can't get reckless but neither can we pass opportunity. And they are driving a long way from Dallas and Wichita."

"We haven't been reckless, but unless someone comes up with another explanation for the activity at the NSA plant other than the obvious, we must take some risks. Until we find otherwise we have to assume they plan to impregnate the population with an ultimate control device."

Andrew continued with Julie's thoughts, "Let's call it what it is, technological rape. It must be stopped, whatever it takes. If this nanotechnology gives them anything close to the control and manipulative power we suspect, any future resistance is doomed. No longer do we have the luxury of a tactful retreat until conditions improve."

"That's why I want you to meet Eric the next time I talk to him. He is doing more investigation at the facility and through other sources about the potential capabilities of this machine. Perhaps he has an idea for stopping this from an inside perspective."

"I will. We need to start fabricating plans for how we stop it. Some people on the call talked of exposing the operation. I'm skeptical of that. It wouldn't guarantee stopping the operation, but it would expose what we know and how deeply we are into their operations. Even if we were successful in cancelling their effort, where would it resurface? No way could we pin it on them politically; they're much too astute with too many allies in the media."

Jim and Barry talked about sabotaging the nano-machines to make them ineffective. "We can get Eric's ideas on it. But how? We don't have people in the right places. Maybe Eric could alter the glucose to electricity conversion such that it wouldn't work, but with the controls that are in place, I doubt it. You said they have doubled the ATF presence at the plant. How would we get people in and out? We have to assume Eric would need help, even if he would participate."

Andrew interjected, "We certainly don't have the people to storm the place. Pondering alternatives brings to mind something Torrence talked about today."

Julie reflected, "Yes the way he brought the subject up was seemingly out of the context of our discussion, but I'm sure it was not."

In the conference call Jim had asked about the security of the island-boat. Torrence said from the time the former Atlas people purchased the old cruise liner their biggest fear had been the US Navy. The ship had no protection and could easily be boarded by the Navy at will.

As many nations had discovered the best deterrent against US interference was a nuclear capability. The Russians, feeling indebted to Atlas employees for their warning and help averting the asteroid, provided the ship with three tactical nuclear weapons. The weapons were designed to be artillery fired and similar sized to the US Davy Crockett artillery projectile with a yield of 0.02 Kiloton or 20 metric tons of TNT. They were miniature compared to the Hiroshima bomb at 15.0 Kilo tons. The tactical weapons' radiation yield was low because they were intended to be used in close troop support.

Although the Russians offered cruise missiles which could deliver the nukes, the island-boat council declined as the purpose was defensive and cruise missiles were too easily shot down. Engineers at the island-boat dismantled the three weapons and miniaturized them into twelve payloads each with a 5 metric ton payload (11,000 lbs of TNT equivalent). The projectiles weighed 20 pounds and could be delivered three miles by mortars on the ship.

The effectiveness of hitting another ship wasn't a priority, but if the need arose the ability to demonstrate a nuclear capability could be instrumental in their survival.

Andrew made sure Julie understood his position, "We estimate half a million people are dead from their flu, which was the price they were willing to pay to set up their quest for control. Yes many old, perhaps with not much life left, but many including our Daniel with full lives in front of them. Moral constraints will not be appropriate if we are to preserve liberty."

After some thought he added, "We mustn't take any tool off the table."

"I agree. And I noticed your addition to the décor in this center earlier," Julie said looking toward the walnut framed drawing of the founding fathers he had brought from Boise. "They espoused and represented no timid behavior or limited goals and neither shall we."

The sun was at ten o'clock as the vehicle driven by Mason Trotter pulled into the farmhouse driveway. Mason had picked up Rod Ballanger in Wichita in route from Dallas. They switched drivers and drove straight through the night. Air travel would have been easier, but airports tracked people; the new Polish black box retrofit avoided that.

Jim was at the log center, Barry and Andrew had been awaiting the visitors. They watched the car pulling into the driveway and Barry headed for the door before he was stopped by Andrew.

"Look," Andrew pointed to the sky. Barry pulled back also seeing the mechanical spy vulture. They were surprised as the last one buzzed around only an hour ago.

Andrew opened a window and hollered toward the visitors while pointing up, "Vulture, get back in your car."

The Arial Citizen Protection Units had come to be called vultures, not only as a derogatory term because they collected information for the NSA. They resembled the common Turkey Vulture in many respects.

Both biological and mechanical vultures used thermals in flight seldom moving their wings to conserve energy. And they were black and of similar size with a wingspan of six feet and weight of 2.3 kg (5 lbs). Both were cold, the biological version was able to lower its body temperature to conserve heat, not a common trait in birds, and the mechanical version was cold by definition.

Although the biological forms estimated numbers were 4.5 million in the U.S., they were a protected species, protected against hunters as was the mechanical version. The biological's primary form of defense was regurgitating semi-digested meat on its enemy; the mechanical's was regurgitating harmful information.

While the biological version dined on carcasses, the mechanical version had solar cells on its wings and an energy cell. On a sunny day they could sail all day and into the night. Without sunlight the energy cell would keep them afloat up to 8 hours without strong winds. When the mechanical vulture's power neared depletion it landed at one of hundreds of fueling stations around the country for a 12 hour battery recharging.

Rod continued to stretch after his long ride oblivious to the warnings. Barry opened the door and warned them in a volume they couldn't miss.

"Don't worry," Rod finally replied pulling a device from his pocket and pressing keys.

Rod watched the vulture glide downward and come to a stop in the driveway a few feet from him. Barry and Andrew's fear was replaced by curiosity. Rod and Mason summoned them outside.

After introductions were made, Rod talked about the vultures.

"As you have witnessed I control this critter. I know that you are aware while I was with Atlas in Wichita I started a repair business when they first started deploying these creatures. My business grew as their numbers increased. They have gone through a number of upgrades which involve replacing microchips. For the upgrades they fly to our facility in Wichita and we replace a chip.

On the microchip embedded in a tiny corner is an override that allows us to take control of the vulture as I just did this one. It did not record this vehicle in your driveway nor its landing."

Rod gave a gesture of a kick, entered something on his hand held device and said, "Get out of here". The vulture took off, caught a draft of air and was soon sailing away.

"We have our micro-circuitry in 90% of them. And I have programmed the 90% to not capture any new images within a three mile square area centered here. In other words when they fly over here they will record the place as it was a year ago.

"But why capture images anywhere?" Andrew asked immediately knowing the answer.

"We must let them capture enough information to avoid tipping our hand, but we can be selective in what they get.

The country has three million square miles and around ten thousand of these things, five thousand in the air at any one time. That's about one per 600 square miles. But whatever is happening around here has caused them to employ ten-fold the coverage, one per 60 square miles.

But enough about what we are doing, Torrence has told us wonderful things about what you guys are putting together. First though, we want to hear about this potentially catastrophic plot you have uncovered and see how we can help."

"Let's head for our log compound and we'll talk," said Andrew leading them.

Andrew and Barry walked Rod and Mason through what they knew about the flu epidemic and the circumstantial evidence indicating the NSA facility's purpose.

"Unfortunately it makes sense; far more of our people contacted the flu than the general population, because we are skeptical of their directive to get vaccinated. We knew they… well had no scruples… but I never imagined. Torrence said you have a video of a flash," asked Mason.

It was the first time the visitors had seen the video of the flasher roundup in Knoxville and their transportation out of the country. They had heard Torrence describe the video on a Secure Phone, but they were taken back by the realism of actually seeing it.

"No disrespect, but if they try that in Texas, there will be civil war," said Mason.

Jim piped in, "We're at that point. It must be stopped whatever it takes."

"You've heard of the Guantanamo tape the Russians are sitting on?"

"Yes, we have, and frankly some of our people are working on contingency plans to rescue the prisoners."

Andrew trying to bring the focus back to the NSA plant said, "As a diversionary tactic it could be useful but the focus must be on stopping what we have here."

"Can you get Torrence and the island-boat up anytime?" inquired Rod.

"Sure. They were soon on a video conference."

"This is amazing, so much better than our secure phones."

"It is," Torrence answered, "but too risky to have more than one download/upload facility in the country."

"I understand; that's why we must protect it. Did you get the control software for the vultures?" asked Rod.

"It's downloading as we speak."

Rod accessed the computer terminal and soon had a map of the country on the wall screen showing 5,000 vultures in the air. He zoomed the focus on the Midwest to show the fleet. About 10% of them were represented by red dots.

"The vultures in red are not under our control. Those are the ones that should worry you. I see one over Galesburg, IL, one in the Omaha area and another around Kirksville, MO. The software

Torrence downloaded will allow you to see where they are and it will send an alert if any get within ten miles.

I assume with the jumble of railroad tie debris around here it wouldn't be hard to hide a couple vultures. I'll dispatch two here for your use. If you have a need to see something, use them. If fact I suggest you have one up all the time.

"What if a red invades our space?"

"Then you'll need to hide, unless it is deemed important enough to take it down."

Andrew asked, "How would you take it down?"

"Simply kamikaze one of the 90% into it."

Rod spent most of the afternoon training Andrew, Barry and Jim to use the vulture software.

Later Julie joined them and inquired about what if any repair work Rod's company did on the larger version of the vulture called the Carrier Pigeon. It was used to transport up to twenty-five pounds of cargo.

"We repair them. They are basically the same machine."

"Can you control any?"

"Only about five percent of the carrier pigeons. We never saw as much of a need, but we are retrofitting about one percent a week."

"So if we ever had a high priority to deliver a package, could they?"

"We could deliver a twenty-five pound package anywhere in the country with a few days notice. And our numbers are increasing. Do you have a need?"

"You never know. By the way what is the name of your company?"

"Salta," he said and saw Julie's look of recognition.

"I don't get it," said Jim.

"Turn it around," offered Andrew.

"Atlas, I like that."

Before the night was over the group was solidifying their mutual bond with Andrew's Glenfiddich. He poured the remainder of the bottle and observed, "There is something invigorating about knowing we're not alone."

The sentiments were shared.

At midmorning Rod and Mason stood by the vehicle. "If necessary we can get a thousand armed people here to storm the NSA facility and destroy it," offered Mason.

"Let's hope we can come up with another way, but it would be prudent to make those plans," answered Andrew.

They shook hands around and Rod offered, "We trust your group and certainly trust the Atlas contingent on the island-boat. We're in this together. The respect you and Julie earned with the asteroid make you natural figures to rally around. I consider our group as important as those represented in the picture of our founding fathers hanging in the log cabin center. We are their descendants and as such we have responsibility. We will be successful."

On a slight rise behind a clump of giant foxtail nearly four hundred yards away lay the bald-headed ATF agent in a prone position. Using his own 10 X 50 wide angle binoculars the agent peered at the driveway farewell. He wished he had brought a high-powered sighting telescope, but he needed to leave before his supervisor changed her mind.

He checked into a motel in a nearby town the prior night to avoid running into the blonde agent. His car was parked partially hidden in a corn field a mile away and he had been observing the farmstead since daylight.

His clothes were wet with morning dew, but the discomfort had been rewarded beyond his expectations. Within an hour he had not only observed the former Boise resident, Barry Bradley, but also his two nemeses, Andrew Collier and Jim Harding. He contemplated pinching himself to verify reality. No doubt they were up to something outside the realm of permissible activity. The temptation was strong to contact his supervisor. Against her orders he had brought his grape but pulled the battery. It was in his car; however he would follow her instruction and wait. Before the week was over he would have the goods to bring them down, he thought as he contemplated his stature in the agency rising as Jim and Andrew got theirs.

He had no idea who the strangers were but recorded the car license number on his paper pad with pen before they left. He wondered if he had brought a big enough pad for all the information he would get this week. Having another six days to observe he didn't move but cased the place to establish their routine. They headed toward a distant wood stack and tracked back and forth throughout the day. Tomorrow he would move closer.

The blond headed ATF agent sat outside an apartment building that contained a suitcase with a tracking device. She sat and waited watching people enter and exit the building seeing no one she recognized. At 11:00 pm she was about to leave when a blonde approached the door from the parking lot. At first she didn't recognize her, but having spent a good deal of time sitting in a car with her supervisor observing Andrew Collier and his wife, the walk was familiar as was the body confirmation. It was the wife of Andrew Collier with blond hair, Julie was her name. She was supposed to be at ARC company headquarters in Hartford, obviously she wasn't.

In an hour the ATF agent was in her hotel room struggling to make notes of her activities for the day in hand written form. She knew Julie most often jogged early, she would follow her.

"Everything government touches turns to crap."

Ringo Starr

Chapter 17

Julie left the apartment at 5:30 am wearing her fanny pack. In ten minutes she picked up a jogging partner at a college dormitory parking lot on the North side of town.

"Maybe you should have met me closer to the meeting site," she asked her husband.

"Oh, I think I can handle it."

Julie stopped later, more to alleviate a feeling they were being followed than to give Andrew a rest. They soon continued.

At 6 am they were seated at the meeting place. It was none too close for Andrew as he had just regained his breath when Eric approached. Without words they headed for the place where Julie and Eric normally left the trail and checked to make sure no one was within sight. The three all noticed a vulture making a pass overhead and headed for the safety of their decaying log seat hidden from the trail by brush and the sky by overhanging lush maple branches. Julie and Andrew knew the vulture was theirs, Eric did not and they would keep it that way.

"Glad to finally meet you again," offered Andrew.

"Likewise, I hope our past is… well past."

"Have you made anymore contacts with Melinda, the nano production authority?"

"I had lunch with her yesterday and discovered she is coming in late and staying late to work alone. At lunch she had just arrived and said she would stay until midnight. I asked her why the hours and she said it allowed her to work alone with fewer distractions. I couldn't ask more with raising suspicions."

"Do you have any suggestions?"

"If we can catch her exiting the production section alone after hours, we or you with your hairbrush, could immobilize her, get through the security door and spend the evening corrupting and deleting software. In a few hours I'm sure we could make sure the production doesn't meet deadline. And if they can't meet deadline it will be delayed a year until the next round of flu shots."

Julie was interested but skeptical of plan. "I assume entry into the section requires the standard protocol, entry of a five digit code followed by a security authorized iris print."

"Yes and it would need to be done as she leaves when no one is around."

"That would require that we have the code beforehand, enter it and hold her eye to the lens. I'll start fashioning a plan."

"Hopefully our plan will delay the project, but I assume you are working on other plans."

"You may assume so," answered Andrew in a manner discouraging further inquiry.

"I would hope so; let me know how I may assist."

Observing most of the conversation just outside of earshot and well hidden was the blond ATF agent. She employed the discreet trailing skills she had learned in surveillance classes at the ATF academy. Arriving at Julie's apartment shortly before Julie left, the blonde agent wore a camouflaged hooded sweatshirt and hunter green shorts.

The agent was surprised when Andrew joined Julie. The blond wished she was allowed to contact her supervisor and roommate back in Boise with what she knew he would consider good news. It was a shame, she thought, he was not here to conclude his quest for the man who had been an obsession.

When the trio broke up the agent carefully made her way back to an oak tree beside the trail. Julie had decided it best for Andrew and her to head back separately. Andrew passed within a few feet of the oak tree that hid the agent. Knowing Andrew was a higher priority than Julie and still feeling a bit of scorn at his refusal of her advances she fell in safely behind him.

ATF training for foot trailing of targets stressed the need to keep such distance that you only occasionally caught a glimpse of your target. This required focusing your eyes at a distance. The downside was you sacrificed the ability see what was immediately in front of you. It was the time of year walnut trees dropped their fruit. The agent's ankle twisted severely as it rolled off the hard green walnut ball lying on the trail.

She was wrenching in pain on the gravel path when Julie approached.

"Is it bad?" Julie asked standing over her. The blond agent looked up at Julie causing her hood to fall from her face.

"I'm okay, it's just a sprain." She quickly got up and attempted to walk it off without sounding frustrated by her major blunder.

"Let me help you."

"No, no. I'll just sit back down and rest. If necessary I'll notify a friend, I'm sure it'll be okay, but thanks for the help."

Barry and Jim were in the cabin center playing with the vulture they had airborne over Julie and Andrew's morning jog. They were starting to get the hang of it when a warning sounded from a motion detector they had placed in the machine shed by the farmhouse. Jim grabbed his 45 combat commander and headed out. Last week it had been a deer, but better safe than sorry, he thought, besides he needed a walk.

Jim quietly approached the shed and peered around the corner of the open south front. Once his eyes had adjusted to the darkness, he saw a hooded figure at the back of the truck trying to pick the lock. He flirted with the hope that whoever, was but a prowler and would soon leave, but he dispensed with the thought.

Jim was four steps away when the intruder turned to find a handgun with a large hole in the barrel pointed at him. He froze and mumbled something about being lost.

Thinking he looked familiar, Jim said, "Lower your hood and keep your arms out."

Jim was shocked to find the bald-headed ATF agent who had long tormented him standing in front of him.

"You just as well let me go. Others are coming in."

Jim secured the agent's hands with a plastic tie and searched him. He found only a grape battery and car keys. Thinking he had nothing to lose Jim tied him to a farm implement and left.

"I'll be easier for you if you let me go," pleaded the agent as Jim left.

Jim entered the cabin center.

"Find anything?" Barry asked.

"Yes, our bald headed ATF friend. Where is the vulture?"

"You're kidding; I've got the vulture back over us."

"No I'm not kidding; he's tied in the shed and says others are coming."

They took the vulture in two expanding circles around the farmstead and saw nothing unusual except a car partially hidden in a corn field a mile away.

"Let me get Torrence up and see if there is extra ATF chatter."

Once they were satisfied no help for the agent was imminent, Jim headed for the car to see if it belonged to the agent. It did. Torrence was instructed to initiate the emergency warning to Julie's grape. Andrew was back in the cabin from his meeting with Eric when Jim returned.

"Was it his car?"

"Yes, but I didn't move it, someone most likely is tracking it. All I could find in it were an entry card for a motel room in Sigourney, a notepad and a grape without the battery. The handwriting on the notepad indicates he was watching us the entire day yesterday."

"Why use a notepad instead of the grape?

They were still trying to sort out what it all meant when Julie entered. After considering it strange he had the battery out of his grape to prevent tracking, hand written notes suggesting he didn't use his grape, no chatter on ATF circuits and no activity recorded from the vulture, they decided he might be a lone wolf.

"How long has the vulture been monitoring the area, did it pick him up?" asked Julie.

"No. We had it on your meeting this morning, followed you after you left, then followed the woman who sprained her ankle. We only brought it back and monitored the area after Jim caught him."

"Pull the feed up of the woman on the trail."

"There she is. The first we have of her is when you approached her."

"There, her hood falls down. Zoom in for a close-up of her face."

Andrew who was watching the feed with others on the large wall monitor sighed, "Oh, no," and shook his head. They all looked at him.

"That's the blonde who worked data entry in Boise and made the pass at me."

"Co-incidence no way; did you guys get any more of her?"

"We did later. We followed you until you went past the college, saw red lights a few blocks away, moved the vulture there and saw police cleaning up a car accident. Moved back to the trail, you were gone of course, but the camouflaged hooded walker had reached the trail where we left you. Understand we were trying to learn handling the vulture. She wasn't moving very well and seemed to get slower until she entered a room at the corner of this building." They saw her enter a motel room on the recorded video feed.

The blond sat off the trail on cut grass with her legs in front of her massaging her ankle for a few minutes after Julie left. Deciding it best to move before the ankle stiffened and finding the ground cold she started to get up.

The fourth generation reptile from the species reintroduced to Iowa was startled when a large mammal shook the ground within a foot of its hiding place. Slowly warming in the morning sunlight the offering of a warm-body to speed its warm up lured it closer. The agent was distracted by ankle pain and didn't notice the heat seeking creature slide close to her body. It had warmed enough for the suddenness of the agent hoisting herself to cause an instinctive reaction. Its two fangs sank into the blonde's thigh below the hem of her hunter green shorts. At an inch of depth yellow venom which had been built up for a week oozed through the snake's hollow fangs.

Thinking at first a thorn had pricked her she brushed her shorts to feel the three foot timber rattlesnake wind itself free. Now she wished she would've brought her grape. For the first quarter mile it was the ankle that caused her the most discomfort, but gradually the burning in her thigh increased. She almost stopped a couple who passed her for help, but remembered the admonition to not be seen or heard at whatever cost.

The pain was intense when she reached her motel room, but she knew few died of snake bites and the snake was small as rattlesnakes went. When sudden nausea hit her she never made it from the bed and dizziness overcame her.

Julie was as surprised as Andrew to find that a data entry worker in Boise who had come on to her husband was now in Iowa following her. Julie's attempt at levity, insinuating that the blond must have been following her in hopes of knocking her off giving the blond better access to Andrew, failed to lessen the seriousness of the discovery. Andrew agreed that Julie was better equipped to find out the blonde's motivation.

Julie waited until well after dark before she knocked with hairbrush in hand at the first floor corner room of the motel. With no answer she scanned the area again for anyone watching, swiped a universal entry card and carefully opened the motel door. Hoping to find a vacant room to search she was startled to find the blond laying on the bed with a melted ice pack at her thigh. Julie held the hair brush near the agent's neck and shook her only to discover she was dead. A quick examination revealed a swollen ankle and a highly inflamed thigh under the remains of an ice pack. In the middle of the inflamed, swollen thigh were two puncture marks. Julie had seen snake bite marks before although none deadly. Normally the small timber rattler wouldn't have killed a person, but the blond was allergic to its venom. Only rest, instead of exercise, and anti-venom within an hour would have saved her.

Julie's mind worked quickly. She gathered the plastic liner of a waste basket which had crumpled tablet paper in it and proceeded to fill it with anything of the blonde's. She found a grape, battery, notepad, toiletries and clothes. But finding an agent badge of the Alcohol, Tobacco and Firearms Agency with the blonde's picture on it brought it altogether. Although unlikely, a jilted stalker would have been a preferable discovery.

She pulled her car to the room door put the bagged items in the trunk, rolled the thin bedspread around the lifeless blonde and added her to the trunk. After thoroughly wiping the room of prints, she headed for the farm.

Ethan's grape buzzed. He looked at the caller ID, the source surprised him. "Hello."

"Ethan, how have you been?"

"Alright, I haven't heard from you for a long time Tony."

"Well I got detained for sometime, but it didn't amount to anything. Let's get together."

"Well, I don't know," Ethan answered wanting to play neutral. How did Tony get out of Guantanamo Bay? But Ethan couldn't reveal he knew about the prison. Neither could he sound skeptical; it smelled.

"I mean, sure to say hello, but I'm kind of stepping away from activities."

"What do you mean stepping away?"

"You know, I just don't have the feeling anymore. It may be part of getting older; doing so gives a person a different, bigger perspective. But yeah, let's get together."

"Great. I'll be back on the air tomorrow morning."

"I'll be watching."

—m—

Ethan and Caridad pulled into the farmstead after Julie had and joined the group in the machine shed. Ethan explained Tony's reappearance. He soon learned more than he revealed.

Andrew drew a deep breath and summarized, "Let's see we've got a snake-bit dead ATF agent in a trunk, another ATF antagonist tied up outside, God knows how many people soon chasing us and an escaped prisoner who smells of traitor trying to trap us. Is that it?"

"At best we better hope they have room at Guantanamo," observed Jim.

"Yes, but we have no reason to believe they have made contact with anyone. Grapes disconnected, making hand notes, no activity in the agency, I think they are acting alone or on the QT," added Barry.

"What about the cars?"

"The one a mile from here we've got to move," said Jim.

"Do you still have two of those early model Polish black box retrofits like the courier who was caught used? asked Julie.

"Yes, why?"

"I've got an idea; perhaps we could roll these disparate parts to our advantage.

"Could you retrofit those black boxes tonight?"

"Yes,"

"What do you have in mind? Asked Andrew.

"The problem we will have with sabotage at the NSA facility is the multitude of ATF agents stationed there. From NSA people I work with I know there is friction between the agencies. If we can bring suspicion on the ATF, we might rid the facility of one level of security."

Jim lay underneath the bald-headed agent's car and carefully detached three wires to the black box. Breaking contact out of order would send an alarm to NSA headquarters as would the wrong sequence in attaching them. With the back plate removed he reached in and detached the mini-mother board. He was stunned finding the car had been retrofitted with the latest Polish version. He replaced it with an earlier compromised version.

He drove the car to the motel parking lot and made the same switch to the car the blonde agent was driving. Barry picked him up. They all breathed a sigh of relief to learn the two ATF cars had not been tracked.

It would be the next night before they executed the plan Julie was still working on. As no ideas had arisen on what to do with the bald-headed ATF agent they moved him to a remote corner of the railroad tie pile and left him for the night. Although he had seen the others through binoculars Jim was the only one who made contact with him.

"You know other agents are watching you."

"Yes, I know about your blond accomplice."

"How do you know that?"

"We just know."

"What are you going to do with me?"

"Honestly, I don't know."

As the night wore on, the tied agent came to believe the rag tags had no choice but to silence him. The thought caused him to work harder scraping his nylon rope constraint across a railroad tie. The hard fiber of the special nylon rope wore the wood more than the nylon. But he was able to move enough to bring the nylon in contact with a steel railroad spike remaining in the tie. By daylight he was free. Having seen his hidden car driven by the farmstead the previous night, he hid in the machine shed waiting to jump someone and steal a getaway car.

—⚉—

The next morning Andrew and Jim from the control cabin, Barry from the farmhouse, Julie from her studio apartment and Caridad and Ethan from their one bedroom flat tuned to the KRMT morning news show.

Promos of the previous day had talked of Tony Johnson's return to the station. He started his segment by telling viewers how thrilled he was to be back on the air in his home community. He talked of contacting a debilitating illness that from which he had only recovered with the innovative help and passionate care of the National Health Service.

> "...Indeed fellow citizens my experience has allowed me
> a different perspective on the truly wonderful society in
> which we live. The balance we have achieved between a free
> society and the provisions of fairness to all is a masterpiece
> which we should celebrate each and every day..."

Ethan flipped the TV off, thinking disgustedly he would not meet with turncoat Tony.

Barry and Jim thought Tony joining the cheerleader ranks of fellow quasi-journalists was not of consequence.

Andrew questioned whether this was a useful ploy if Tony's purpose was to lure others into a trap. Using less than attractive bait with his unnecessary speech would keep people from his trap. Perhaps Tony was trying to protect them.

Julie saw an opening to fold another element into a plan she was working on.

Tony had done what he could to shelter his family while protecting his liberty-loving comrades.

The NSA director of counter intelligence work was furious. Tony had made himself radioactive to those he was supposed to lure, and had done so in a way that insulated him from retribution.

"I predict future happiness for Americans, if they can prevent
the government from wasting the labors of the people
under the pretense of taking care of them."

Thomas Jefferson

Chapter 18

Jim had come from dirt-working stock; he had ancestors who were miners. His Father owned a trenching business and specialized in sewer placement and repair. After years as a navy seal, which Jim considered as far away from earthen work as possible, Jim met Nathan and they started a nursery with Jim's navy severance and Nathan's savings. Again the family genes were working with soil.

His father taught him to take pride in his tools and keep them in top working condition. To put a tool away dirty was to draw the ire of his father. Although he didn't admit it, Jim had acquired the same proclivity to neatly polish his tools. He never realized his father's example would someday save his life.

Jim lifted the back roll up door of his truck and leaned in looking for a light chain. Until they decided what to do with the prisoner he needed to be tied more securely. He had located the chain and reached for it when movement caught his eye. A dirt shovel lay on the floor of the truck with the business end toward Jim. He had cleaned it well before he had put it away such that it had a mirror-like finish. The convex side of the shiny metal blade was up revealing an approaching shape behind him.

The bald-headed ATF agent had found a three foot broken ax handle and remained hidden until Jim leaned into the truck. With two hands on the handle he brought it down from over his shoulder with payback force he had too long contained. In the last fraction of a second Jim plunged himself onto the truck bed. The ax handle grazed his scalp and struck the truck floor producing noise like a gunshot.

With a kick like a mule Jim landed both feet on the agent's chest knocking him to the ground. Only momentarily stunned the agent swung the ax handle like a baseball bat as Jim dove for him. The swing connected with Jim's left arm just above his elbow. Jim ignored the pain that seared into his arm.

Lying side by side Jim drove his right fist into the agent's jaw loosening three teeth. The agent retaliated by pommeling Jim's midsection with swings of the ax handle, but the agent was too close to do much damage. Jim was quick to rise to his knees and nailed his right fist between the agent's mouth and nose driving a front tooth to the back of his throat and breaking his nose, but as the blow did not damage the agent's right arm he delivered the weight and hardness of the ax handle to Jim's temple.

Jim fell to the ground dazed. The agent spitting blood from his mouth with more running from his nose straddled Jim and with a hand on each end of the ax handle and brought it down on Jim's throat. Jim defensively put his hands outboard of the agent's hands and struggled to prevent the handle from crushing his larynx. If Jim could have caught the ax handle with his hands closer to the middle his bench pressing strength would have allowed him to dislodge the attacker. But with no leverage, a partially disabled left arm and fatigue setting in, hope was dismal.

Feeling secure in his position the agent said, "This is pleasant payback for what I've put up with from you?"

Jim answered struggling to keep the ax handle from exerting too much pressure on his throat, "How did you find us?"

Seeing no downside to disclosure at this point and giving him some pleasure the agent answered, "The bug in Julie's suitcase."

Jim could feel strength gradually seeping from his arms. He knew it was now or never. "The blond agent, we had pleasure killing her."

The effect was as Jim hoped. Infuriated the agent leaned nearly all his weight into the ax handle intent upon crushing Jim's larynx at once. Involuntarily Jim's fight-or-flight mechanism kicked in releasing reserves he desperately needed. With all that was left in his arms Jim held off the thrust and used his legs to flex his lower body upward. He caught the agent off balance and catapulted him over his head.

They separated, regained their footing and stood facing each other for what both knew was the finale. Jim's arms were depleted of strength as he faced the ax handle wielding opponent. The ATF agent confidently but cautiously approached his prey with the ax handle readied to hit a home run.

Before the agent was close enough to do damage with the handle Jim charged the agent, leaned back in an airborne horizontal position, drew his legs up and let his body's momentum carry him within the distance to flex his legs outward into the agent's chest.

The ax handle landed hard on Jim's side knocking the wind from him. Jim's legs had also knocked the wind from the agent, but that was the least of his worries. The agent plummeted backward. His fall was broken by hardened steel tines of a farm implement's harrow ground to a sharp edge by friction with the soil.

One tine entered the agent's back between his ribs skewering his right lung. A second tine finished the battle entering his heart's left atrium. He slowly released his grip of the ax handle.

Once Jim had recaptured his breath he stood in front of the agent whose mouth oozed blood from a source other than his nose or tooth cavity. Jim studied the agent's condition. The agent's mind seemed to be elsewhere.

"Is there anything I can do for you?" Jim asked.

"No," the agent mouthed as his vision blurred into darkness.

Time nearly stopped as a serene silence filled the machine shed interrupted only by a fading internal gurgling sound.

It was not the outcome that Jim would have preferred, but given the alternatives it provided a solution to a problem. At the edge of the pile of ties close to where the agent had been tied for the night Jim used the polished shovel that had saved his life and buried the man and the mutual hostilities they had harbored.

The others stood quietly as Andrew said, "He was caught up in the circumstances of his situation. Who is to say we might not have acted the same? I'm a firm believer that 99% of us do what we think is right given our genetic ability to interpret events and what we know, which is colored by our life experiences. That doesn't mean he was right but we have no reason to believe he was motivated by other than what he thought was right. We respect him for that and we will do the same."

They covered the loosened soil with errant railroad ties and continued implementing a plan.

Jim drove the bald-headed agent's car to the far corner of the NSA facility parking lot. Julie drove the blonde's car with her body in the trunk and Julie's suitcase carefully cleaned of prints and hair in the backseat. Andrew parked beside the agents' cars in Julie's car which now had an updated ATF-supplied retrofit in the black box.

Once all were set Jim put the battery in the bald-headed agent's grape and texted Tony Johnson by keying the words rather than using the voice activated system, *Got your note that you are bugged, will contact shortly. Glad you still with us.*

Julie's grape buzzed with a green warning text as Jim and Andrew were about to join her and leave. It was from Barry, *Don't move, picked up bogy vulture overhead.*

She returned, *Can't stay long, ATF text will be picked up very soon.*

While they were nervously waiting Julie pulled the blonde's ATF badge from the glove compartment. She pulled the stamped metal piece from its case, turned it over and with a green marker in her left

For the COMMON GOOD

hand inscribed a large letter S and brought two vertical lines through it, the sign of resistance. It was a mark she had always wanted to make and would attribute it to the blonde agent. The final touch brought a smile to her face.

Torrence, at the island-boat who had been monitoring the parking lot from another vulture green texted all, *Hold on, take care of soon.*

Overhead a vulture under the direction of the island-boat off Costa Rica sacrificed itself bringing down another vulture. They both plummeted to the ground outside the parking lot.

As Tony's grape was under close surveillance ATF and NSA agents from the facility surrounded the grape that generated the text before Julie and the guys were back at the farmstead.

White House Video Conference

The President had weekend plans that did not involve video conferencing with his director of the National Security Agency (NSA), but he had been told it was urgent.

The NSA director was at his office in the 3 million square foot NSA headquarters situated on 68 acres in Fort Meade, Maryland more than halfway toward Baltimore.

"What's up?"

"We have a major development at our facility in Iowa, the heart of the Tranquility Insertion Project (TIP). Unfortunately it confirms my worst suspicions, the ATF has been compromised."

The director went on to inform the President that two vehicles belonging to an ATF motor pool in Boise had been found abandoned in the NSA facility's parking lot. Both ATF vehicles had an illegal black box retrofit. One ATF agent out of the Boise office had been found dead in the truck of snake bite. In the car was also a suitcase with a tracking device authorized by the regional ATF director. A grape belonging to another agent was found in the other car. The grape had texted a message to the TV reporter we attempted to flip from Guantanamo Bay. The message indicated the TV reporter had alerted hooligans of his being monitored and expressed joy that TV reporter was still with them.

"That's not good news and it happened at a place that is instrumental in our long-term plans. I thought you had control of the situation there."

"Mr. President the ATF is out of my administration. As I have indicated in the past it was always a concern of mine. We need complete control of the area under one command."

"What do you suggest?"

"That all ATF personnel be expelled from the facility immediately and be forbidden from coming within ten miles."

"How will you compensate for the loss of security? Such a move would be drastic."

"Mr. President, there is something else you should know?"

"Don't lead me around I don't have the time or patience for it."

"The dead ATF agent's badge we found in her car. On the back of the badge she had a green dollar sign."

"How do you know she did it?"

"The green ink was from an ATF issued marker and our experts say the pressure points indicate it was written by a left-hander."

"And I assume she was left-handed."

"Yes. We can transfer NSA agents from around the country there. But we need more."

"OK," the President commented in a tone that meant continue.

"I strongly suggest that you assign a light infantry brigade to replace ATF at the facility and secure a perimeter around the facility. And also I think it would be prudent to assign an air defense company, because of something else that happened. Two Aerial Citizen Protection Units collided over the parking lot around the time the ATF agent texted the TV reporter. It could have been a coincidence but the timing was certainly handy for whoever perpetrated this act."

"How many incidents have there been of ACPUs colliding?"

"Only two sir."

"So you request employment of one of the new laser air defense companies?"

"Yes, Mr. President. We can not assume what happened was an accident. We know top people in ATF were involved. If we err it should be on the side of caution."

"How many soldiers are you talking about?"

"A light infantry brigade of 2000 and an air defense company of 200."

"There is danger in questions raised about the need for such measures but we can control that. As far as the need to know goes, it is a platoon training exercise for guarding an embassy. And I will see to it that they will report to the NSA manager of the facility."

"Yes, sir."

"What else do we know about the Boise ATF link in this?"

"Our agents entered the ATF motor pool yard this morning and found black box retrofits made in Poland of course."

"My god, an agency spying on an agency; we must set an example. I want the regional director of ATF and the national director taken into custody at once. And I want the director of ATF brought to my office tomorrow morning. Also arrest anyone between them down to the motor pool. It's a national security issue."

"Yes, sir."

"And what about your guy who failed to flip the TV reporter?"

"He has been called into headquarters, for immediate consultation. The consultation will include his demotion."

"And the TV reporter?"

"He is in custody and will be sent back to Guantanamo."

"One more thing, any reports of whatever it takes for TIP implementation as too stringent or aggressive I can handle and deal with; any compromise or set back in the program I will not tolerate."

"Understood, Mr. President."

Boise

The regional director of ATF was interrupted by her receptionist on the speaker. "There are men here who insist upon seeing you immediately."

"Tell them I'm in a conference. I said no interruptions."

Three men burst into her office.

"I say what's going on."

"By directive 23846b under the National Security Act you are hereby placed under arrest for acts endangering national security."

"This is ridiculous."

"You will come with us."

They took her to a lower level of the building. Because the NSA had no facilities in Boise and had used ATF facilities when necessary, they sent the ATF staff home and directed her to a holding cell.

"May I please use the rest room before we get this straightened out?"

After searching her purse and making sure the rest room was clear they allowed her entry. She squeezed a chip, which contained all the information she had received from the supervisor she had sent to Iowa, from her purse's lining. She watched as the floating silicon chip was caught in the downward vortex of water, sensing her career was on the same path.

—◊—

Video conference cabin-center

"I've never seen as much chatter from the NSA as they have put out in the last few hours. And strangely enough ATF chatter was high but has now died out. Your ploy certainly shook things up," observed Torrence.

"The question is for good or bad," wondered Andrew out loud.

"Many groups around the country are suggesting a meeting to plan strategy," Melissa said.

"How would they link up with you?"

"What many are proposing is a meeting here."

"When are you thinking and how many people?"

"We can not accommodate all groups and certainly not without drawing attention to our location. The thought is to have two delegates from each of seven areas in the country plus yourselves. Once we agree on a strategy the fourteen delegates can distribute the message to their respective areas. I think the meeting should be as soon as possible."

"Perhaps they should go ahead and meet, while we work on a solution here."

"Andrew they consider you the De facto leader. We see no need to meet without you."

"Julie and I will get back to you soon."

While Julie and Andrew stepped outside, Alice appeared in a side conference with Barry. They finalized plans for her move to Iowa. It made sense as another legitimate occupant of the farm house would ease covering the comings and goings of others. Alice reentering the country from an extended visit with her Aunt in Canada to be with her husband would lessen suspicion about a single guy living alone.

The opportunity to see Sandy was a strong influence in Andrew and Julie's discussion, but they agreed otherwise meeting did make sense.

Andrew reported later that the endeavor Julie and Eric Hansen had devised to set the nano-machine production back a year would take place next week. And knowing the success of their sabotage would be important to any conference at the island-boat, he proposed the meeting be held two weeks out.

"One of the things the government can't do is run anything.
The only things our government runs are the post office and the
railroads, and both of them are bankrupt."

Lee Iacocca

Chapter 19

Bringing Eric Hansen to the cabin center for planning the effort to sabotage the nano-machine production line would have been easier, but Julie chose to keep the location and information from Eric. Eric knew much was being withheld. Their meeting venue, which had proven to be safe, would not be changed. They sat on the half rotten log away from the recreation trail and hidden from the spying eyes of a vulture.

The nano production section was on the third floor of the NSA building. Entry could only be gained through a five digit code and an authorized iris print. Barry and Torrence had found no way to bypass the entry system, so they would need someone authorized to lead them in. They had deducted the only plausible way was to tranquilize Melinda Rhoads as she left the section usually around midnight, put the code in and hold her eye open for the scan. This would allow six hours to play havoc with hardware and software.

Two problems needed to be overcome. They didn't have the five digit code and there would be a security camera pointed toward the entry. They might hope the person monitoring the camera would ignore what appeared to be a normal entry, but not someone holding a body to the scanner.

Julie had never been to the third or fourth floor; her authorization was only for the first two floors. However, she had noted the code others used in the elevator to get to those floors. Barry was able to find blueprints which indicated the third floor was laid out exactly as the second floor. If this was the case, a woman's rest room was nearly across the hall from the entry door.

The plan they finalized had Eric watching for Melinda's arrival which was usually around noon at the security check-in. He would immediately move to where Julie standing around the elevator could see him while Melinda went through security. Julie would take the elevator to the third floor and wait in the rest room with the door ajar for Melinda to arrive and enter the code. Julie would get the code Melinda used watching her with a small eyeglass. Once the hallway was clear she would attach a small camera lens to the security camera pointed in the same direction.

The next night Julie would enter the hallway, take down the small camera she placed earlier beside the security camera and attach it to a small screen that fit over the security camera lens. It would cycle a video of the entry door from the previous 24 hours. Julie would wait in the rest room until Melinda left for the night, hairbrush-tranquilize her, enter the code, show her eye to the scanner and enter with Melinda. When Eric got the all-clear message he would join her for a few hours of pillage.

Andrew and Julie sat in the cabin center the evening before her trip to the third floor of the NSA building. They had spent a good deal of time talking to Sandy. She was growing up so fast. It was amazing she would soon be 6 years old. Given the education she was getting on the island-boat they agreed she had knowledge of a 12-year old.

"If our plans work out we should be with her on her birthday," Andrew observed.

"Yes, I was thinking of that when we originally agreed to go. Let's make it happen."

The timetable was set. July 15 was the deadline NSA had given ARC to have the underground transfer system operational. Controlling the installation completely off site, Andrew had just made the first successful run of a tube between the buildings. However, it would take another three weeks to complete the intra-building legs of the transfer system and Andrew would assure that completion would not be done early.

Melinda Rhoads had hinted to Eric over lunch that her schedule would lighten once the week was over. He interrupted the remark to mean by week's end her set-up services would be completed and they would be ready for full production. Tomorrow Julie would get the code and Friday night they would destroy as much as possible. It would give NSA as little time as possible to recoup and perhaps the weekend would delay their recognition of the damage.

Andrew looked at Julie pensively, "At least you take the blond wig off when you come here, but one of these days you are going to scare the bee gees out of me wearing that black NSA uniform as you are now."

"Do you want me to take it off?"

The next morning Julie made her jog short and looked into the mirror adjusting her blond wig before she left for work. She was wearing a clean carbon/acrylic fiber NSA black smock, no use to stand out wearing a wrinkled uniform. The smock hung over her fanny pack which she double checked to make sure contained her fully-charged hairbrush. In the lining of her bra she had a computer chip that was designed to immediately desecrate any hard drive it was attached to. Although she had increased her consumption of protein for two days, she put energy bars in the smock's pockets. She would be busy all night and have a full day of work tomorrow. She was ready.

Barry arrived and drove Julie to work in her car. Leaving her car in an empty parking lot until morning could draw curiosity.

Security had been increased ten-fold since the ATF was booted, particularly so with the arrival of an army brigade. A twelve foot high chain link fence with six-foot cylinders of a barbed wire on both sides of the fence encircled the entire compound including parking lots.

The only gate in and out of the facility was bracketed by metal towers obviously made for quick deployment. The tops were enclosed, but it was easy to imagine what lurked behind the tinted glass. Armored personnel carriers parked on either side of the road were intimidating, particularly with their machine guns pointed outward.

Julie gave the explanation that Barry was dropping her off at work and planned to repair her car. Barry presented a fabricated ID, Julie showed her NSA ID.

"You know you can't drive her in the parking lot."

"I know. I'll walk from the gate. It'll do me good."

"Have a good day."

Julie presented her ID again to enter the parking lot on foot. And walked across the parking lot wondering if the road block sergeant would remember that it would be a day earlier that Barry dropped her off when he picked her up tomorrow afternoon.

At the building entrance she showed her ID the third time, had her right index finger and iris scanned, emptied her fanny pack, and walked through the body scanner. A screener picked up her purple hair brush, turned it over and put it back on the belt. A small camera of endoscope size was taped to the underarm of her uniform and the screen that would cover the security lens was inside the cover of her grape.

At her locker she strapped a 4-inch silicon knife above her ankle that she had smuggled in before the security crackdown and put a miniature can of spray paint and a small eyepiece in her fanny pack.

The morning security briefing contained nothing new in information but the number of agents attending kept rising. Now twice as many attended, no announcements were made about staff additions and no one asked. As normal Julie tried to be inconspicuous.

At 11:00 she walked through the lobby and saw Eric sitting, as planned they made no contact, and she took her normal post at this hour on a stool between elevators intimidating people more that monitoring traffic. Melinda most often came closer to noon, but they were ready.

At 11:40 Eric came down the hallway. Julie let an elevator go with two people in it and took the next one. She carried the stool in the elevator, entered the code for the upper floors and got off on the third. The layout was as they expected with the camera pointed toward the entry door and at a height she could reach with the stool. It seemed to take Melinda a long time to reach the floor.

With an eyepiece Julie easily read the code Melinda entered while holding the rest room door ajar. She was ready to bring the stool from the rest room and attach the camera when she saw a pair of armed NSA agents above her grade coming down the hall. She heard them trying to open doors as they came down the hall and hurriedly put the stool in a stall and assumed a primping position in front of the mirror. A female agent entered.

"What are you doing on this floor?"

"What do you mean?"

"The chip in your uniform doesn't allow you access to this floor."

"I've come up here before for a little more privacy."

Her partner entered the room. "Whatever, you can explain it when we get downstairs."

In the elevator he asked her, "How did you get the elevator code to get to this level?"

"I don't have a code. I just hit the button for the third floor." Julie, unable to dispose of the camera recorder she intended to use, knew her explanations would not hold up to the scrutiny she would soon endure. She positioned herself in a corner of the elevator so the other agents couldn't stand on both sides of her.

With her left hand grasping the hairbrush in her fanny pack and the agents both on her right side she asked while glaring into the opposite corner of the elevator floor, "What's that?"

Before they could think the agents turned their attention to the corner where Julie was looking. The man never saw the brush coming at him. As he fell Julie had to reach across him for the other agent who had just touched her gun when she too collapsed from a dose of Antisolo.

Julie hit the stop button on the elevator. The first floor had been entered where security was located. She canceled the selection and hit the lower level button. In the basement Julie stepped out, entered the code for the upper floors and pushed the button for the 4th floor. The bodies would cause havoc on the administrative floor, but there would soon be havoc everywhere and they would not know from which floor the elevator came.

All hope was lost now to sabotage production; her only hope was to get out. She had long considered an emergency escape route via the delivery and garbage area. It was down a hallway. She wrapped a scarf around her head concealing as much face as possible and headed down the hallway. Two security cameras pointed to office doors. As she approached the cameras from behind their pointed direction she hit the lens with a burst of focused paint spray.

The bay doors for delivery of large parcels and garbage pickup were always open during the day. She would exit and make her way to the parking lot, hopefully find a car she could get into and leave. The security camera in the bay area was pointed toward the doors and at a height allowing her to stand on the railing and blacken it without being seen. The open doors were a hundred feet away. She put her scarf away and walked normally. Halfway there an army personnel carrier pulled into each door.

Six helmeted men jumped out and yelled at her, "This place is under lockdown."

"I'll go shut the doors," she replied acting like the NSA agent she ostensibly was. "Make sure your vehicles are inside."

Her second planned escape route would not be as pleasant if available, but pleasantness was not a concern. She turned left at the hallway intersection and headed for the garbage dumpsters. She would hide buried in garbage and hope when it was picked up it would be among the first pickups avoiding compaction. Cracking the door to the dumpsters she saw four armed agents were searching the area. She had exhausted her escape routes.

Julie knew her time was dwindling fast. From drills she knew security's priority was blocking all exits. Having done so, they would soon start searching the building.

She retreated back down the hallway toward the elevator and crossed the hallway intersection heading for the maintenance section. A camera was pointed away from her; she walked under it pointed the paint can up and took it out to create a diversion. From the maintenance area she backtracked across the elevators and entered the janitorial section. Under another camera which pointed away was a door to a stairwell leading to the first floor, she entered it. Reaching under a two inch angle iron frame that supported the metal stairway, she retrieved a key. The key unlocked a storage area under the stairs. It was a storage area she had discovered some weeks ago that would make an emergency hiding place if ever necessary. She pulled the door closed behind her and was able to relock it with some effort.

The storage area was as wide as the stairway, four feet, and was five feet high at the door tapering down to the height of one step at the back. The cleaning crews used it primarily for storing toilet paper. They were stacked in packs of twenty-four. With her small flashlight she moved to the back of the space and stacked the packs in front of her leaving her just enough space to hunker down.

Confusion reined throughout the building. Army personnel had entered the building creating more confusion. Within an hour eight suspects had been brought into the building security center all to be cleared. Finally the army was put outside to watch the perimeter and completely search every car in the lot. No car had been allowed to leave the lot or any person the building.

Through a process of elimination they discovered it was Julie Archibald (the alias name she had been hired under) who had invaded the third floor and put two agents out. They knew she had been in the basement by the blackened cameras but couldn't track her. The lost cameras indicated she entered the maintenance area and took out three cameras getting to the open bays. The most likely scenario was she had gotten out through the bay doors before the army secured them. Consequently the search focused on the parking lot and exterior. But they would leave no stone unturned. The good news was that no one had entered any section of high security clearance and nothing was missing the facility manager told the NSA director.

By late-afternoon agents were searching her studio apartment. They found nothing of significance. The agents who she hair-brushed came around but the effects of the Antisolo prevented them from remembering anything from a few hours before they were struck until they regained consciousness.

Julie pulled her grape and green-texted Andrew. By the immense amount of chatter from the facility Barry had picked up, they knew something had happened. Andrew was glad she had not been captured but understood her situation was perilous. She gave them her location in the building and indicated that she would remain hidden until she could devise a plan of escape. She knew the cabin-center people would work on ideas to retrieve her but she didn't know how.

In the middle of the night someone tried to open the closet door, she heard voices, but they gave it up and walked away. Julie knew it was but a matter of time before they checked every hole and crevice in the building. She contemplated the interrogation she was likely to encounter. A quick trip to Guantanamo Bay was probably not likely. She knew herself to be strong-willed, but in the end how much could she take? If any hope remained to stop what was happening at this facility, the cabin-center could not be compromised. She opened the end cap on her hairbrush and turned the miniature dial to full deadly dosage.

Before morning her grape vibrated with a green text, *Have plan, will create diversion with explosions.* After a series of texts, they decided Julie would stay at least another 24 hours. Unbeknownst to the others Jim had an amount of Semtex, a variety of the C-4 plastic explosive hidden in his truck. They determined each vulture could carry 12 ounces of the explosive. One vulture would hit the parking lot entry gate, the other would tear a gap in the fence on the opposite side of the building from the delivery door Julie would need to exit through. Jim would be waiting at that perimeter with wire cutters. If all went well the diversion would allow them enough time to get Julie through the fence. But it all depended upon her remaining unfound.

The plan depended upon Julie getting outside on her own. And limited stretching in her confinement was not enough to keep her flexible. She carefully opened the door and stood somewhat wobbly. With a keen ear on the stairs above her and the door into the stairwell she fed the lens she had intended to place on the security camera under the door. The other end was attached to her grape. The door faced the elevator hallway. A TSA guard with an automatic weapon slung over his shoulder sat perched on a chair beside the elevator. She retreated, did a few quiet jumping jacks and stretches and buried herself back in her hiding place with a protein bar.

It was mid-afternoon she heard approaching steps and voices. "Yes, this is the door we need keys to."

"I've got them here somewhere."

"What is in there?"

"Just toiletries. Here they are."

Julie tensed with the brush held close to her neck thinking of Sandy and Andrew as the door was opened..

"It's all toilet paper."

"We've got to store it somewhere."

A second TSA guard stepped forward with a powerful infrared detector. It could sense body heat easily through drywall. Neither recognized the insulating properties of multiple rolls of the paper.

The second guard looked at the first, "No heat, should we empty the closet?"

"I didn't take this job to move toilet paper."

The door closed and Julie laid the hairbrush down and relaxed thinking she was probably safe in her hiding place as long as she could remain there. However, it wasn't long before her grape vibrated with another text, this one from Barry.

MUST GET OUT SOON, DOGS COMING.

Barry had picked up an urgent request from the NSA to other law enforcement agencies for a tracking dog. The Chicago Police Department was flying one in. It would be there before midnight.

With scent from Julie's clothes in her apartment, they would find her in short order.

IS ANDREW THERE? Julie texted.

HE AND JIM ARE WORKING ON ANOTHER PLAN, WILL CONTACT SHORTLY.

Julie's grape battery was about to go, she hadn't been moving enough for kinetic energy to keep it charged. She placed it in her palm and rotated it until, as her wrist became weary, Andrew contacted her. She learned Jim and Andrew had decided security still remained too concentrated outside of the building for the first plan to work.

They summarized the alternative escape plan. It would involve exiting the building via the pneumatic system through the tunnel. The route to get there wouldn't be easy but she agreed it offered the best chance of escape.

After her last instructions she suggested that they devise an escape of their own.

Andrew replied: *WE'VE THOUGHT ABOUT THAT*

AND?

WE ARE NOT GOING TO. IT WILL GIVE YOU MORE MOTIVATION TO SUCCEED.

"If you have ten thousand regulations,
you destroy all respect for the law."

Winston Churchill

Chapter 20

Knowing at 8:00 pm security guard numbers would be as low as they would usually get for the night; Julie stepped out of the closet. She stretched and flexed her muscles in place to limber her body after the long sit careful to stay behind the focus of the camera above her. She slid her lens under the door to find a different armed NSA guard but sitting on the elevator guard stool. She also saw no one on the stool down the hall at the service elevator door.

Julie readied her brush and lightly tapped on the door three times. After the second three-knock tapping the guard spoke, "Is anyone there?"

She waited and tapped lighter drawing him nearer. He asked again if anyone was there. She tapped no more and waited. Slowly she saw the door knob turning. Cautiously he opened the door. She saw his rifle barrel poke through the door before she saw his forehead break into view, but she was concentrating on where his neck would be. Her arm holding the brush quickly shot around the door to where his neck should be. The hair brush had no needle; a high pressure air burst delivered the Antisolo tranquilizer as it made contact with skin. Fortunately for him she had dialed the dosage back down.

Julie caught him from falling and put him and his gun in the closet. With her blond wig under her smock and her bra tucked in her slacks she walked confidently into the hallway like she knew where she was going, passed the main elevator and grabbed the stool sitting outside the service elevator as she entered and closed the door. The camera captured her walking past the main elevator but not entering the service elevator. The woman monitoring the screen saw a brunette in NSA uniform calmly walk down the hallway after a guard stepped away, no alarm. Her primary concern was a blond.

In the service elevator Julie stood on the stool, tied one end of her bra around the top of the stool, lifted a ceiling panel and pulled herself above the ceiling. Holding the other end of her stretched out bra she hoisted the stool and replaced the panel. As Andrew had said on the side of the elevator shaft was a ladder. Climbing to the third floor was easier than she anticipated even with the stool tied around her waste. At the third floor level was a half door 90 degrees to the right of the elevator exit door, but beside the ladder. A twist of the latch and it was open. She flung the stool into another closet-sized room. She had insisted to Andrew that her route would be compromised if she left the stool in or above the elevator.

The room was to house the first leg in the transport system ARC was installing. The packaged nano-machines would be put on a conveyer to be moved to this room, from there mechanically sent downstairs and whisked 9 miles to be mixed with vaccine.

This part of the system was a work-in-progress but a 24-inch PVC pipe led to the basement room that connected to the pneumatic transport system. When operational the nano-machines would be moved to the basement via the PVC tube. To avoid employee scrutiny technicians used the PVC pipe to pull parts from the basement into the room. Normal entry into the basement pneumatic transport room was not possible for Julie as it required two cleared iris prints and now also required an armed guard. A hundred foot rope was coiled neatly by the pipe

Julie threaded the rope through a pulley used to hoist parts, made a loop and put it under her arms. She knew thinking about it wouldn't make it easier. She held the other end of the rope as a mountain climber and descended down the tube. Soon she was in the basement transport room.

What looked like a plastic capsule lay on a rail. A dozen capsules were stacked on a wall. Her grape vibrated.

I SEE YOU MADE IT.

She replied, *YES, SO FAR.*

YOU LOOK GOOD.

In the corner of the room she saw a camera. Of course Andrew was monitoring work daily. She waved.

The capsule looked incredibly small 20 inches in diameter and 60 inches long. She wasn't big at 5'3" and 120 lbs, but could she fit in there? She had slid down the tube but now claustrophobia gripped her. Nine miles underground crunched into a space shorter than she was, she knew she should have jumped into capsule before thinking like she did the tube.

In a flurry of texts Andrew tried to calm her. She was concerned whether she would have enough air in the capsule for 20 minutes the nine mile trip would take.

It wasn't lack of O2 that would be a problem; it would be a buildup of CO2. Barry had done research and found if she was completely relaxed 30 minutes in the tube was the limit, excited and stressed it was 10. Andrew did his best to calm her, texting her that if she relaxed she would be fine but viewing her on the wall screen he saw her in an excited state.

Years ago Julie had explained the operation and range of Antisolo effects on a person. Her hairbrush set on high was lethal; the lowest was a short peaceful sleep. Andrew suggested she use the tool to calm herself. She knew he was right as she could not voluntarily calm herself.

Without thinking further she lay in the capsule with her hairbrush in one hand, the silicon knife and grape in the other.

WHAT'S THE KNIFE FOR? Andrew texted.

TO OPEN THE DOOR IF ROBOT FAILS, she replied and brought the hairbrush to her neck on the lowest setting.

A robotic arm reached out and shut the top of the capsule. When the air pressure reached operating level she was propelled away.

Andrew was confident in the system he had designed, it had been tested; nevertheless it was a long 20 minutes. Jim, Barry and he watched the green dot move across the nine mile route on their screen.

On time the capsule slid onto the unloading platform in the basement of the FDA building near Eddyville. A metal arm reached across and opened the capsule. Julie lay quietly for 10 minutes, very slowly rolled out of the capsule and lay on the platform for another 30 minutes before awakening.

GOOD MORNING, vibrated her text as Julie started looking around the unfamiliar room. Her eyes searched for the camera and smiled when she found it.

HOW WAS THE TRIP?

They exchanged texts with her learning that it would be morning before Ethan came to get her but he would have an inspector with him; she would need to hide until the inspector was gone.

She conveyed remembering the sensation that she was traveling and how good it felt to roll out and stretch her legs. Water bottles the workers had left seem to interest her more than describing her experience. Barry and Jim headed back to the farmhouse. Andrew stayed the night and watched her sleep.

The NSA building manager was on hand when trainers let the dog familiarize himself with Julie's scent from her clothes. They started in the basement. The dog ran to the shipping dock, and back and forth the hallways until he sniffed at the door to the stairwell, then pawed and barked at the locked closet door. They didn't wait for the keys; a crowbar opened the door to find a guard that had not yet been reported missing. They brought the dog back out of the stairwell and it

For the COMMON GOOD

ran down the hallway to the service elevator but promptly came back to the stairwell door. Trips to other floors found nothing.

The guard was interrogated for three days including hypnosis, but never remembered anything.

Julie was well hidden behind a large tool chest and boxes when Ethan and the inspector entered the room while the armed guard stayed in the hallway.

"I was thinking about another pheasant sighting like we did two years ago, are you game?" asked Ethan.

"Sure, I'd love to. Let's talk about it later. I've got to head to our morning briefing. I assume you don't need me."

"Thanks for letting me in early."

"It's clear," Ethan said sure that the inspector and guard had gone.

Julie hugged Eric overjoyed to see a friendly face.

"You had us all worried you know."

"Yea, you weren't alone."

Ethan pulled a white lab coat from his tool bag. "Put this over your NSA uniform. Caridad will be in the hallway shortly; you'll look like one of her chemists and she'll walk you out.

Julie and Caridad walked out from the basement across the parking lot to Adana's construction trailer.

"Slow down let's not look in a hurry," Julie advised.

"Are you okay?"

"I'm fine, but a shower would be nice."

"I don't think you want to go to your studio apartment."

"I assumed not."

Andrew and Adana were waiting. Andrew hugged his wife. "You can't believe how worried we all were."

"I can't say I was confident I'd get out of there either."

Adana encircled the pair with her arms. "Well you did, and be assured there was a reason you escaped."

Julie and Andrew both knew she wasn't referring to either Andrew's escape plan or Julie's execution of it.

When Julie pulled the lab coat off her altered bra and wig fell to the floor.

"Dare I ask?" inquired Andrew.

"You're not the only one who can make do with what's available."

—⁂—

Jim and Andrew started to build another smaller cabin away from the cabin-center in the railroad tie dump. They had considered doing so giving them another hideout, but with Julie now with them, it would be another place to spend the night away from the farmstead. They anticipated authorities would start a house to house search.

Eric had nearly given up on Julie meeting him at their regular fallen log under the maple limbs when she appeared. Barry and Andrew had scoured the area well before they had given her the go ahead to meet him. At first he didn't recognize her with short brown hair and green eyes. Although she now looked like she did at the Evanston conference, he had gotten used to the blond wig and brown eyes.

"I can't believe you made it out, but I was about to give up on you meeting me with the vulture overhead,"

"That's right. We have to be more careful now."

"Is it still locked down as tight?"

"Absolutely, we can forget entering the production section. It now takes a pair of cleared iris prints plus an armed guard to get in the door and a minimum of three people are allowed to be in the section. Now that Melinda must have two people with her at all times, she doesn't work at night."

"I expected as much."

"Are other plans in the works?"

"Of course, we'll let you know on a need to know basis."

—⁂—

It was nearly midnight at a 20-something bar in Oskaloosa. The band, as some would call it, and a vocalist put out sounds that would send shivers up the backs of any earlier generation. But it kept older people out of the bar. As preceding generations were shocked by the

Charleston, the jitter bug, swing music, rock, heavy metal and rap, so 40-somethings were shocked by the screechers.

A 28-year old engineer temporarily stationed in Iowa had been observing with interest a 25-year old administrative assistant sitting with friends. His attention was intercepted more than once by her. She leaned somewhat further over the bar exposing the open back of her top to her waistline, turned quickly and met his eyes. He embarrassingly diverted his eyes. Having turned the other way he had his mug raised and was emptying it when she startled him.

"I've seen you watching me. How about buying me a drink or do you just want to look and not talk?"

He nearly choked. She laughed and joined him. She was glad he could laugh at himself. They talked until 2:00 a.m. She found out he worked for ARC and he discovered she had a government job. Sharing more information he discovered her father was the building inspector on his project. By the time they parted both knew they were attracted and would see each other again. They did.

Alice arrived from her supposedly long visit with her Aunt in Canada without difficulty. Barry had received an occupancy permit for Alice at the farmstead.

As rumors continued of house-to-house searches Julie, Andrew and Jim prepared to leave earlier than they had planned for the island-boat meeting. Jim altered the black box in a rental car with the retrofit from the ATF agent's car. Andrew and Julie would take Julie's retrofitted car south on interstate 35.

With Salta's government contracts and necessary, but distasteful, political donations Rod Ballanger had private air privileges allowing his safe crossing of the border on business. He offered to take the trio from Wichita on the company plane. Julie thought better of it.

In a conference call through the island-boat with representatives from the districts connected by secure phones, Julie urged everyone to travel separately as a precaution. Given her background in security, her successful escape from NSA clutches and the fact that she made sense, they agreed. Mason and the other representative from Texas decided not to ride with Rod but cross the Mexican border separately.

Torrence planned for Julie and Andrew to stop at speakeasies in Kansas City, Wichita, Oklahoma City, Dallas, San Antonio, and Laredo on the route down I-35. The speakeasy in Orland Park, Kansas was busier than normal when Julie and Andrew arrived. They had expected to meet a few people from the area but, as the place filled, they became concerned and left. In Wichita they skipped the speakeasy and spent the night with Rod Ballanger as they did with Mason Trotter in Dallas. Between Wichita and Dallas they stopped at a speakeasy in Oklahoma City, it had a larger crowd than Orland Park.

Many at the speakeasy knew Julie and Andrew would be arriving. It made them nervous, particularly Julie. Julie and Andrew answered few questions. They were surprised to hear rumors of a major state activity in Iowa, but no details. People believed they still lived in Idaho, they left it that way. But the size of the crowds, though somewhat scary, built their confidence.

They arrived at the appointed speakeasy in San Antonio at 2:00, early for much of a crowd they thought. They were right, only two couples met them.

"We understand you both like to walk, and we imagine after the long ride you're ready. Let's go for a walk."

Halfway into the twenty minute walk Andrew knew where they were headed. Julie expected a speech at some point about how the group had to muster the courage of those who had fallen at the Alamo. It never came and wasn't necessary as they gazed at the old mission. By the time they returned to the speakeasy it was packed.

They arrived in Laredo about sunset. They were not scheduled to meet the guide who would skirt them across the river until morning. After some discussion they skipped the speakeasy, although they enjoyed the crowds both Julie and Andrew felt uneasy about taking any more chances. They were looking forward to seeing Sandy.

　　　　　　　　For the COMMON GOOD

All major movements in history are compilations of a multitude of minor happenstances, so was Julie and Andrew's trip out of the country. With a missed connection here, missed timing there, the chain of events can be altered. However, the main thrusts of history may be delayed, or the route might be diverted, but the outcome is destined. As pressure builds in molten rock below the surface, the when and where of the first breach through cracks in the earth may yet to be determined but the relief of pressure is not to be denied.

So it was that three NSA moles, who had spent years infiltrating speakeasies, and attending flashes, encouraged by rumors of a couple heading south without a permit, attended a speakeasy in Laredo. They anticipated quietly making an arrest as the couple left, they were disappointed.

Already two of the three moles were suspect, and with their persistent questioning about the couple who didn't appear, they blew their cover. Whether their plan to quietly subdue Julie and Andrew would have succeeded, no one would know. They spent the night in a hospital.

Jim headed West on I-80 purposely with intent upon at least driving by the TSD facility Orlando had been taken to. Deciding he had nothing to lose he tried to get in the only entrance he could find and pleaded to see his son. He was sternly denied access and had to leave before they discovered the arrest warrant out on him. Depressed he reluctantly headed west on I-80, veered down to Denver on 76 and South on I-25. He stopped at the same rest stop they had seven years ago in the ice storm south of Denver. Then they had two nukes for the asteroid, now he had two pounds of plastic explosives hidden above the gas tank for what he did not know. His earlier visit to the rest stop had been the first time he met Ethan. Ethan had learned much since then.

He stopped in Santa Fe for the night and headed for a speakeasy, drinking and talking more than he should have. Two ATF moles, who pumped him for information at the speakeasy, followed him to the motel and checked his car. They found it was a rental and the black box signature was of a different car. They placed a magnetic tracking device under the car. Jim was up early and headed south before they were able to gather enough ATF agents. Backup agents were coming from Albuquerque, Jim was headed for them.

Jim's old 223 caliber AR-15 laid across the passenger seat covered with a blanket and his 45 Combat Commander was under the seat as it had been since he left Iowa. His mind was in another place as he couldn't get past Orlando's predicament. Suddenly he noticed a carnival-like spectacle of lights in front of him; it was a road block. He slowed looking for a place to turn around when his review mirror showed two cars following him join the light show.

Without thinking he pulled into a rocky dry grass cow pasture and headed across it for red rock cliffs half a mile away. His attempted escape found him in a U-shaped canyon with 100-foot red rock bluffs on three sides. With his 45, secure phone in his belt and carrying the AR-15 he left the car and headed into the rocks which tapered up to a high chaparral above the bluffs. Quickly up thirty feet into the rocks he turned to see two cars parking to block his car's exit and lights from another three cars bouncing halfway toward him from the road.

Below him with two cars parked around his and the other three close; it looked like an unnatural island on the landscape. Ten agents were soon out of their cars looking into the rocks. The leader yelled, "Lets make this easy, come on out."

He could hide, perhaps make his way undetected over the bluff or surrender and make the best of it. But with a retrofitted car, guns they would find and an arrest warrant, his hopes were dim. Strangely, a sense of relief came over him.

He drew a breath and yelled back, "I've not wantonly hurt anyone or restricted anyone's freedom." The echo of his words bouncing back and forth in the canyon surprised him. It gave the agents a haunted feeling as if he were more than one man.

"It'll be easier if you come out," the leader said less boldly than earlier.

For the COMMON GOOD

Jim responded in a louder voice than before, "Here's the deal, you leave me alone, I'll leave you alone."

"Search his car," the leader ordered.

"You have no search warrant," Jim yelled.

"Don't need one. I'm charging you with illegal alteration of a motor vehicle."

Jim was well hidden while five ATF agents closed in on his car as if it were a snake and might bite, while the others opened the trunk of the leader's car and each took a short-barreled automatic assault rifle.

"I'm warning you. Leave my property alone," Jim yelled. They ignored him.

Jim really gave it no thought with five ATF agents surrounding his car. After calmly keying the access code on his secure phone, he hit a four digit code. The rental car and five ATF agents were immediately engulfed in a ball of fire. It should have caused him a glimmer of guilt, but it didn't. He struck improper keys and the secure phone sizzled as he dropped it and moved behind another rock on his right amidst the confusion.

He heard gunshots and saw chips of rock flying from the rock he had just abandoned, one rock chip hitting his cheek, another ripping a gash in his arm. When the gunfire stopped the five remaining agents were hiding behind open car doors. How stupid, he thought, that they would seek protection behind an aluminum and plastic barrier.

The first two were dazed when the door panel exploded into their chest from the 223 impact. The third was crawling away from the door toward the back of the car when a bullet cut a path parallel to his spine from behind. Another hid behind a car. Jim put four bullets into the gas tank before it exploded. During the placement of bullets into the gas tank the lead agent who had bailed head first in the front seat pulled away in his car lying on the seat and working the accelerator with his hand. He made the mistake of sitting up too soon, for Jim had been and remained a marksman.

With his last shot the action stayed back on the AR-15 meaning the clip was empty. He had another but it was long gone with his car. Before he could think about heading to one of their cars, a caravan of five cars raced across the sparse cow pasture. The ATF replacements obviously knew the situation. As one car stayed out of range in front of him, the others split up and soon their occupants were in the rocks.

He could climb higher but eventually they would find him. It was probably a matter of time before a helicopter came and vultures would soon hover with links to the NSA. He had no way to reach Rod to try to get the vultures blinded. And it was naïve to think the ATF – NSA spat would keep the NSA from helping. They probably expected him to make a run for a car from where he was or climb higher. He would veer to the right and make a run for a car from a direction they wouldn't expect.

Jim was about where he needed to be in order to move down and make a run for the closest of the ATF cars, when he heard a rock slide to his left. His 45 round pounded the bullet proof vest of the agent, knocking him back violently without penetration. Plastered against a rock the agent raised his automatic carbine, but not before Jim put the next 250 grain bullet in his neck.

At first Jim thought the Combat Commander's recoil was just beyond normal until Jim felt the second bullet enter his midsection. He turned to see another agent perched on a rock. Jim's semi-jacketed bullet entered the agent's head between his nose and cheekbone as the agent's third pullet pierced Jim's abdomen.

Jim slid down the rock until only his shoulders remained elevated. Blood was flowing out multiple holes front and back. It was not how he wanted to leave, but it was what it was and it could have been worse. He would not be killed while penned up at Guantanamo Bay; he would not be prodded for information; he would leave with his boots on having fought for something important. He hoped to leave before they came to watch. His answer came as weakness drifted in, Jim drifted out into a tunnel of light.

For the COMMON GOOD

"The natural progress of things is for liberty to yield
and government to gain ground."

Thomas Jefferson

Chapter 21

Julie and Andrew arrived on the former cruise ship anchored off
Costa Rica a day before the other parties were due to arrive. They
had looked forward to seeing Sandy, although the video conferencing was helpful, it was not like actually being with your daughter. It
was a joyful reunion and they soon found Sandy was having a great
time on the ship. With few children living on board, she had made
quick friends and they were a center of attention. It had become a
challenge for many on the ship to see who could contribute the most
to the children's education; consequently Sandy's circumstance offered an unparalleled education.

They were amazed at what had been done with the ship creating an
optimum working and living environment. Many of the rooms had
been turned into offices and laboratories. One of the pools had been
filled in to create a testing area for products. The ship that originally
held 2,500 passengers now had 400 residents who lived in comfort,
had an ample supply of fish at hand and grew many vegetables on the

topside gardens. Those responsible for fishing sold their product to other residents as did the in ship gardeners.

A variety of consulting, design and development work done for many non-US companies around the world provided a monthly cash surplus. The expertise on the ship included rocket propulsion, electronics, communication and software development. All residents contributed their skills and labor and were rewarded according to the value they produced.

Matters effecting the operation of the ship colony were conducted by the colony council. Council members were selected by lottery with no one allowed to excuse themselves. The term was limited to one year. As serving was considered a responsibly rather that a job, the weekly meetings were kept short. With no pay, council members were incentivized to avoid donating their time to create unnecessary rules.

Over the next day representatives from the regions joined them. Each region had sent two delegates. And each region chose their own method of selecting their representatives. The regions were: Northeast, Atlantic coast, South, Midwest, Southwest, Texas and West. Melissa Barnmore, Rod Ballanger, Torrence, Julie and Andrew served as at large representatives. It was agreed beforehand that they would discuss and formulate a plan and any plan would require consensus.

A division of states had evolved over time. Many formerly productive and affluent states had acquired debt and contractual obligations they could no longer service. As they raised taxes to satisfy commitments it forced those paying taxes to leave which only exasperated the problem.

Illinois was first to levy an exit tax. Residents leaving the state were required to pay Illinois state tax for five years after leaving. New York, Rhode Island, and California among other states soon passed similar bills. In a contentious Supreme Court battle the states right to impose exit taxes was affirmed by a 5-4 decision. Defenders of the tax argued successfully that the home states had an investment in the human capital in the state, as a company would in an idea or concept it had invested in. As corporate investments were protected with patents, states had a similar right to reap rewards from their human investments.

The exit tax slowed the deteriorating financial position of some states but did not halt it. Eventually the federal government guaranteed states' indebtedness when many could no longer borrow and neared default. The Department of Housing and Urban Development (HUD) also helped declining states by requiring occupancy permits for any changes in residency and made movement to affluent states difficult.

Obtaining an occupancy permit to move from California, Oregon, Illinois, New York, New Jersey, Massachusetts, Rhode Island, Vermont, or Delaware was virtually impossible. The department argued that restricting movement from those states was a matter of housing efficiency as those states had a surplus of housing and the states most often receiving new residents had a shortage of housing. It was reasonable and necessary central social planning mitigating the market's excesses.

But even the compilation of these measures had not alleviated the problem; hence the President had for two years sought passage of the Regional Fairness Act. The act would give the IRS discretion to adjust income tax rates based upon the state where a corporation or person resided. Proponents argued that precedent had been established for vacating the equal treatment clause by the variance in milk subsidies by state enacted in the previous century.

As there continued to be fewer states needing help than not, the measure had not passed. The President was encouraging the political class to pressure for executive implementation of the Fairness Act. The consensus in Washington was that soon the President would as he put it, "act to preserve the economic viability of the states."

It was under this cloud that the group of dissidents met on the island-boat to halt the erosion of liberty. Although they all agreed that the first priority was stopping nano-insertion via the flu vaccine (they didn't know it was called TIP), there was much disagreement on what else to focus on. They broke their concerns into three segments: the nano-rape project, NSA control and the Fairness Act.

Many argued passionately that the concerns could not be separated and action needed to be taken against all. Others maintained that to take action against the Fairness Act prior to its implementation would be considered an unnecessary preemptive act of civil war. One party suggested that the last preemptive act by unhappy states at Fort Sumter hadn't worked out very well.

The remark prompted a strong comparison by Rod Ballanger, delegate at large and owner of SALTA.

"We would all hope that it will never come to such a thing and I am not advocating such a drastic measure. But be mindful if the worst of our fears comes to pass, no such comparisons can be made. Two centuries ago Rebels fought for what they saw as a freedom, states rights. The Union fought to end the moral abomination of slavery. Both sides fought for freedom by their definition. If it ever comes to pass today, only one side can claim they were fighting for freedom. The other side represents the subjugation of liberty.

In the civil war those bent upon rebelling had neither the manpower nor the economic might to sustain their quest regardless of their fervor. God hope not, but today if it came to us, we have not only the fervor, but also the majority of economic power and numbers. Both the manufacturing base and the centers of innovation have shifted to the producing states. Hopefully we will find another way, but doubt not, we would prevail."

The conversation and passionate debate continued throughout the day. Julie and Andrew took neither side. At dinner the group began to concentrate on two members of the group that had not made it, Jim and a delegate from the Atlantic Coast region.

Nathan was more than concerned as were Julie and Andrew. They had left at the same time. Although Jim had taken a longer route, their arrival should have been only a few hours apart. The delegate from the Atlantic Coast couldn't fathom how the other delegate as impassioned as she was would not be there.

Andrew noticed Torrence had skipped dinner. The rest had just finished dinner when Torrence entered the hall and summoned Nathan, Julie and Andrew to a small conference room. Andrew knew from Torrence's demeanor he had bad news.

News reports talked of a deadly ambush in New Mexico. A man armed with illegal weapons killed twelve unsuspecting servants of society. The Boise killer had skipped bail for assaulting an officer and had been at large for weeks. Officers had no choice but to terminate him to stop the deadly onslaught.

Two news analysts discussed with a consulting psychiatrist the warning signs of anti-social behavior: a partner who had also skipped the area, a son sent to a TSD, a predisposition to violent behavior, and a business owner who in his greedy quest had been cited for violations. One of the analysts observed, "All the signs of violent, anti-social behavior were present. Until we recognize the danger signals and act proactively these are tragedies we must endure."

Julie and Andrew consoled Nathan as the news spread around the group and speculation mounted that the Atlantic Coast delegate also had most likely been caught.

The next morning's session brought a different tone and sense of urgency to the meeting. Gone were the clashes of how far to go. Those bent upon wrapping their grievances together agreed that the nano-machines and government control of individuals would be the priorities.

Specifically they agreed taking out the nano-machine production facility in Iowa and NSA's datacenter in Utah would be the thrust of their agenda.

"We can discreetly move 2,000 armed and trained patriots into Iowa and destroy the facility," offered Mason Trotter of Texas.

A delegate from the Midwest spoke, "Before we discuss any armed action I think we should thoroughly explore other solutions. Can we expose what is happening with the nano-machines and the FDA and CDC involvement with the flu virus last year? If we could effectively make our case, perhaps we could force them to drop the nano project."

Julie spoke, "All we have to offer about the nano-project is a number of suppositions based upon who is there and the disciplines represented. I'm thoroughly confident our analysis of the purpose of the project is correct, but even if we assume we could get our side of the story out, we don't have proof that would stand up in the court of public opinion. And we can bet their response, if they thought any was warranted, would be that the charge is so outlandish it doesn't justify a response. Who would investigate? Congress? Congress effectively gave up their status as a co-equal branch of government a few decades ago when they tolerated a stream of administration officials perjuring themselves before congressional committees.

We would have the same difficulties convincing people of the other half of the equation, the dissemination of man-made virus which they knew would kill. People want to believe the best of their government. How often have we heard them use the phrase *the government is you?*

It would be helpful if the Russians released the tape at Guantanamo Bay, but they won't. Our best piece of evidence is the video of the kidnapping and murder of flashers, but that doesn't directly relate to either the nano project or the flu epidemic.

To effectively stop the project by disclosure to the public we would need to tie the flu epidemic with the nano-machines and unfortunately we can't prove either on its own. But if we could absolutely make a solid case, how would we get it through their well-oiled propaganda machine?"

Melissa asked for responses to Julie's dismissal of applying public pressure as a realistic alternative. There was much murmuring among the group of delegates until the delegate from the Midwest continued.

"Regrettably I agree with the analysis presented. I hoped someone would be able to make a convincing argument otherwise." He looked around the group. "However no one is able to. Mrs. Collier is correct. It appears we have consensus."

"That leaves what I suggested earlier. We can seize and destroy the facilities," said the Texas delegate.

Andrew spoke, "I don't doubt you can, but I see two problems. According to the press releases an army company has deployed at the NSA facility in Iowa. A company is usually led by a Major but this group is led by a brigadier general which usually commands a brigade of 2,000 soldiers. And our vulture surveillance of the area supports the latter number.

If you take the facility it will not be easy and the causalities will be heavy giving the government sympathy as we would be instigating the conflict."

"What do you suggest?"

"We have another idea."

The delegate from the West spoke up, "The NSA data center in Camp Williams is not nearly as heavily defended. We have forces to take it out."

"Again the same problem causalities on both sides, Americans fighting Americans."

Andrew brought up the mini-nuclear option. He discussed in detail how the island-boat had come to acquire the mini-nukes. Torrence joined him giving the yield and minimal radiation characteristics of the weapons. He assured them, if properly placed, damage would be confined to the parking lots, but otherwise complete.

Julie continued, "The biggest advantage of using a small thermo-nuclear device is it will permanently eliminate not only the nano-machines, but also the hardware to produce them and the intellectual database infrastructure that developed them. Nothing will survive the heat. The same can be said for the NSA data center in Utah. It will be gone permanently. Sabotage or storming the facilities as we discussed might shut them down if we are successful, but what will remain if we must leave in the face of a counter attack before all can be destroyed?

We would not intend to kill the scientists that developed the project as the project is compartmentalized to a point they don't know what the ultimate result of work is to be. It's a mistake to consider them enemies. Like much of society they are but pawns being manipulated; their biggest fault is being oblivious to what's happening."

"Nothing unique about that, just like a good part of the population," interjected a delegate from the East.

Julie continued, "In fact the information which led to our discovery of the horrific purpose of the project came from someone managing research at the facility. He received a tip from someone, whom none of us would expect help. The project manager then started a clandestine investigation which led to the project's discovery.

If we used the weapons, a warning would be issued to minimize causalities. There would be no defense against the nukes and they wouldn't know how many other weapons we might have. An assumption of assured mutual destruction would allow us some latitude in the future. It would allow us to preserve your forces for other uses if necessary. Another advantage, if they succumb to our demands it could be called off at the last minute before it was discovered.

The bottom line is we don't need or want to kill people. Doing so would alienate the population. Eliminating the facilities we discussed would handicap the state's quest for citizen control for years."

The sole Atlantic Coast delegate spoke, "I believe we need to go one step further. Let's finish the NSA rather than just eliminate a factory and data center in Utah. The headquarters is in Ft. Meade, Maryland."

A delegate from the Southwest spoke, "I think we should be very hesitant to jump to the use of nukes. Someone mentioned Fort Sumter earlier, the use of a nuke would be a more precipitous act than shelling a fort. The only time we used nukes was against the Japanese who attacked us first. We are not under foreign attack today. Does this rise to that level, on our own countrymen? There must be another way."

A delegate from the Midwest answered, "That's the whole point; there is no other way. You admitted yourself there is not. I also would be happy to find another way, but what is it?"

A delegate from the West took the floor, "I fail to agree with the premise offered by the delegate from the Southwest. Yes, we used a nuke on Japan who attacked us and yes, we would have used a nuke on the National Socialists in Germany a hundred years ago had we developed one before they surrendered. But let's be frank, neither were the Japanese or the National Socialists, as bad as they were, an immediate danger to our freedom. Japan had no plans to invade LA, nor the German's New York. They had more than enough problems with the areas they had already bitten off, and those problems would have compounded.

Maybe I'm getting too deep in history, but doing so puts today in perspective. We armed ourselves with tens of thousands of nukes to ward off the other form of socialists, the communists, although they were destined to fall of their own weight.

Now we have central planners in our midst that are not some far off, possible, maybe, hypothetical, future usurper of our freedoms. They are doing it every day, slowly but surely squeezing liberty from the country's soul. That we would use nukes on a potential threat and vacillate in using nukes on an imminent threat makes no sense."

The delegate from the Southwest replied, "As reluctant as I am, I must admit the merit of your argument."

After another hour of discussion the group seemed to be in agreement on the use of nukes. Andrew asked, "So do we have consensus?"

No one objected.

Trotter of Texas said, "It makes sense and I agree with it but I have a couple thousand men and women who have been in hard training and want to do something useful. I don't want to demoralize them by saying they are not needed."

"I have an idea," said Julie. "If your people could accomplish one thing it could be a tremendous advantage politically. According to Washington, Guantanamo Bay prison has been closed for years. We know it holds flashers among others. The Russians have proof but are withholding it. If we could storm the base and release the prisoners, we would prove its existence. It would be different than fighting other Americans on U.S. soil. It is a base that supposedly doesn't exist. For them to allege we attacked Americans there would be to admit its existence. Also releasing the few hundred Iowans would boost our numbers as well as morale around the country."

"Great idea, we have enough boats to get your people to Cuba and we will add to your numbers," added a delegate from the South.

There was considerable discussion about the Guantanamo rescue but agreement to leave the planning to retired military people. A delegate from the Southwest brought the discussion back to the nukes. "How will the nukes be delivered?"

Rod Ballanger answered, "I will discuss the topic, but first in light of what happened to two of our delegates, I implore you not to discuss it with anyone outside of this circle. As delegates you should know the more people who know, well I needn't say anymore."

His answer avoided mentioning his ability to control over 90% of the vultures in the air. Information gleaned from the vultures that could be used by different groups would be provided through the island-boat. How the information was obtained wasn't important for others to know. He told the group that three carrier pigeons drones could be used to drop the 20 pound bombs.

"They are designed to carry packages up to twenty-five pounds; the twenty pound bombs will appear to be a normal delivery. Hackers here will log the order and schedule delivery of a package."

Seeing smiles sweep the room, he continued with a cautionary note. "I think it would be safer if the route used to get the bombs into the country be kept between the island-boat and the carrier pigeon operators. Would there be any objection to that?"

They all would have preferred to know the plan but no one wanted to breach the trust that had been established in order to satisfy their own curiosity. One delegate asked if they could be informed as to the expected time of delivery. No one saw a problem with giving all a heads up.

A delegate from the Northeast talked, "I thought I had some understanding of the trials that our ideological forefathers worked their way through nearly three hundred years ago when they stepped forward and said "enough". But participating in this group gives me more perspective on what they did.

We certainly have our differences which have eloquently been expanded upon. Nevertheless we are a culturally homogeneous lot

For the COMMON GOOD

compared to the early patriots. Yes, there are regional differences, but nothing today compared the cultural differences between the early patriots of the Carolinas and New England. And yet they bonded together and trusted each other. As they did, so must we.

I believe we need to come together consensually on another issue. We need a leader, someone we can trust to make decisions that need to be made on the spot, particularly when we attempt to negotiate with the powers that be."

A delegate from the West, "I believe the natural person to fill that role is Melissa Barnmore. She has worked with all of us and she is here at the junction of our communications."

"If I was in the States I would be happy to be a spokesperson for our groups, but I believe our leader should reside in the country. I have duel Polish citizenship. This must be seen as a spontaneous movement within the country, otherwise it would give the state a rallying point by claiming foreign intervention. We have one central downloading location in the country which is in direct contact with this island-boat. The country has familiarity with Andrew Collier and he is trusted by us. I think he should be our leader."

Murmurs of agreement spread through the group and all eyes looked to Andrew.

"I have contemplated this. Melissa and I discussed it last evening. Julie told me it was my duty. Make no mistake, I am completely dedicated to this cause; our success will be the measure I use to judge the final value of my life.

But you and I need to evaluate how I came to this. I lost a child because of the despicable actions of the state. Now I've lost a best friend, prior to that a mentor in Daniel Barnmore. So I am dedicated. But after the state killed Barnmore I became complacent. I adopted a get-a-long attitude and frankly closed my eyes to what was obvious to many, including my wife, Julie.

I know I will not waiver again, but because of my earlier vacillation I suggest someone who has been steadfast in recognizing the danger. I agree our leader should have direct access to the upload with this island-boat. The obvious person has all her life been focused on the excesses of the state and the ultimate consequences of its unbridled accent. She nearly lost her life attempting to sabotage the nano-machine project. I thrust her judgment and not only because she is my wife.

Within an hour unanimous consensus was reached. Julie was declared leader.

Mason Trotter, a Texas delegate, stood and asked recognition, "Madame Chairperson Washington," he started in jest.

After laugher died Julie said, "I know that was said with levity in mind but know I consider it as great a compliment as any citizen could bestow upon another. We can minimize our task comparatively with our forefather's, but I think that is a mistake. For us to be successful it will require all the dedication and selflessness we can muster. How ironic it is that in order to preserve the autonomy of the individual we must work as a community, but that we must and will.

That said; did you have a suggestion Mr. Trotter?"

"Given the importance of our link in Iowa and having been there, may I suggest you accept four well-trained new Texas Rangers to protect the cabin-center. With Jim gone they would offer you some security without higher numbers drawing suspicion. They could hide in the jumble of ties and offer a level of protection your electronic measures can't."

Dealing with the personal loss, Julie hadn't thought about the loss of Jim as the only trained defender of the cabin center. She accepted the offer.

Someone else in the group was thinking of Jim and yelled out, "Remember Jim and think 12 to 1. It takes twelve of them to stop one of us."

Some got it quicker than others. The phrase "12 to 1" became a rallying motivator. Nathan said nothing and, although sad, knew Jim would be proud as was he.

Julie recognized that rather than giving power to a failure by talking about Jim's death, they could give it positive power.

It was early morning when cars pulled into the farmstead driveway. Alice and Barry had been expecting the inspection. A ten mile perimeter of the NSA facility had been ordered searched. ATF agents, local authorities and a NSA supervisor totaling twenty in number spread out over the farmstead as the leader inspected Alice and Barry's papers.

"Well your papers and occupancy permits appear to be in order. Why did you choose to move here from Boise?"

"I guess in my semi-retirement we wanted a change of scenery and we always wanted to live in a rural area."

"Do you ever have company?"

"No, not since we've been here other than a periodic visit from the landlord and his wife."

"I see according to the documents Alice that you've been to visit relatives in Canada, do you anticipate going again or having visitors from there?"

"I have no plans."

"You realize this county has been declared a visitor restricted area and you will need a permit to receive visitors."

"We are aware of that."

The house was thoroughly searched, but they found no evidence of visitors. Alice and Barry were questioned about a second bedroom but Alice said it was necessary as Barry had a snoring problem. The location of her clothes substantiated the claim. In the attic the inspectors didn't notice that a false wall had been erected hiding twin mattresses and others' personal items.

Inspection of the out buildings found a truck parked in a machine shed. Its black box was intact and the truck bed contained only miscellaneous tools.

After another hour of questioning about whether Alice and Barry had witnessed any unusual activities or traffic in the area the leader issued a letter of inspection for their signature. Included in the inspection certificate was an affidavit that they had not witnessed unusual activity and were bound by the signature to report any within twelve hours.

The caravan of inspectors pulled to the main gate of the EPA railroad tie dump and drove around the perimeter fence. Upon seeing no activity and a number of signs warning only EPA personnel were allowed inside, they thought better of stepping on another agency's toes and left.

"The true danger is when Liberty is nibbled away, for expedients."

Edmund Burke

Chapter 22

Natalie and her husband felt lucky being granted the right to have two children. As most children had for generations, they loved pizza. Natalie usually ordered pizza by phone for delivery from a small local pizza place in Boise. Little did she know that Jim and Nathan Harding also had the same taste in pizza. Neither did she know that her calls for pizza delivery constituted a twice-removed phone connection with a fanatical killer. The NSA had taken note.

White House

The NSA director briefed the President on the shootings in New Mexico and the capture of a lady from South Carolina who had been under scrutiny for some time. The shootout in New Mexico had made national news and was orchestrated by numerous press releases from the White House denouncing the continued hoarding of guns by dangerous citizens. The South Carolina lady's apprehension was only brought to the President's attention because of the circumstances of her arrest.

She was caught in a fishing craft headed for international waters after an undercover mole had acquired information about her invitation to attend an offshore meeting. The spy was a former participant at flasher demonstrations. His mother had a long history of illness, no dependents and little public investment in her education. Accordingly when she contacted a rare form of cancer, her low Health Care Index, HCI, would not allow her to receive treatments she needed. The son had a choice to make, his ideals or his mother. He chose his mother, but later regretted it and future information he fed his handlers would be false.

The director did not report the incident with the errant security guard at the NSA facility in Iowa to the President. No harm was done and the director did not need to give the President reason to question his control.

But the nature and whereabouts of any offshore meeting NSA needed to discover. At the director's suggestion the President ordered all vessels within a hundred miles of the coast be stopped and searched. The navy was ordered to assist the coast guard. Strong protests were filed by other countries at UN headquarters about the forced search of foreign flagged vessels. The United States maintained that UN Resolution 143845 allowed a recognized nation to use appropriate measures to thwart potential civil unrest. Poland argued that UN Resolution 32758 allowed for free passage in international waters.

Torrence picked up the board and search orders. Delegates from the East and Southeast who had used water transportation getting to the island-boat used an air or land route to return home.

The President headed for an prime time press conference scheduled to reach the largest audience. He was an accomplished hand at using what some might consider bad news to his advantage. The ability had served him well and boosted him to what some still considered the most powerful position in the world. The press had been advised that he would have a statement.

For the COMMON GOOD

"Fellow countrymen, a few days ago a tragedy befell the nation that shocked us all to the core. An unprecedented act of blatant cowardly murder was perpetrated by someone with an anti-social history using tools that disgust us all. Innocent servants of the people were gunned down without warning. Theirs was a higher calling working selflessly for the greater good. What more can we ask of our citizenry...
As your President it is my job, no it is my oath, to protect you...
This horrendous crime was committed with the aid of tools that have long since been illegal. Guns made for killing the innocent were used. We shall redouble our efforts to rid the country of this barbaric scourge. Administratively I am doubling mandatory sentences for anyone possessing a gun...
Also a foreign manufactured device specifically made to hamper instruments intended to enhance road safety was used. I cannot fathom the rationale to tinker with technology that saves lives. Accordingly administratively I am also doubling the penalty for possessing any car safety box alteration.
As my oath requires me to defend the citizens of the country, I am taking another step. Repeatedly we have filed protests against the Polish Republic for manufacturing and smuggling these death retrofits to no avail. Today I am ordering an embargo on all trade with Poland and the seizure of all Polish assets..."

As had long been established all follow-up questions had been cleared by the White House and only questions were taken from malleable journalists.

—⁂—

"What do you think?" Julie asked Andrew after they told Alice and Barry good night and headed for the spare bedroom.

"I think he is the master of spin, but it won't change the political dynamics. My grandfather often said that people tend to believe what they want to believe. Some will buy into what he said, but they already have. Many won't buy a word of it and will be less inclined to as the media vibrates his pitch through their megaphones. But a good part of the public doesn't care or lacks the inquisitiveness to form an opinion.

That is why any attack on their control mechanisms must be co-coordinated with an effort to win public opinion. Your idea of liberating the prisoners at Guantanamo Bay was brilliant in that it will expose a barefaced lie and further erosion of the constitution.

"I don't disagree with you but our priority must be destruction of the nano-project otherwise public opinion will be become irrelevant."

"What do you think Poland will do?"

"I think they can ignore the rants from the White House. It's amazing isn't it that Poland has emerged as the dominant economic player in Europe after being invaded, sliced and diced for centuries. For decades Poland has been the only country in Europe with a growing indigenous population. Birth rates below subsistence for decades in Western European countries and Russia doomed them. Then the invasion of an antagonistic culture to fill their medial job needs hastened their downfall."

Their conversation ended with those thoughts as Julie turned out the light in the spare bedroom.

Although often slow to connect the dots, with urgency and sufficient pressure from Washington, Jim's former neighbors in Boise came under investigation. A neighbor couple now living in a priority one secure area was reason for further scrutiny. At 2:00 am a vulture Barry had in the sky as precaution gave warning that vehicles were approaching the farmstead from both directions.

Julie and Andrew hurriedly grabbed clothes, an insulated camouflaged blanket and headed out the back door. They had practiced the maneuver often.

Alice got into the bed Julie and Andrew had vacated; Julie and Andrew were out the backdoor running covered by the insulated blanket within two minutes without a house light.

For complete surprise vehicles from either direction parked about five hundred feet from the house. Dressed in black with helmet visors lowered carrying automatic weapons swat team members rushed the house and without warning tore both the front and back doors from their hinges.

In such an operation the vulture had to transmit realistic video of the area. To do otherwise would uncover Rod Ballanger's control of the vultures. Hiding from infrared cameras on a cool night by staying under the blanket was imperative to avoid detection. Julie and Andrew's destination was a cave about a thousand feet from the house they had prepared for this eventuality. Actually it was not much more than a hole in the ground near a fence with a moveable sod entrance.

Peeking from under the insulated blanket Julie spied the intruder first and sank to the ground with Andrew. A dozen night-vision equipped soldiers converged on the farmstead from the West perpendicular to the road. One soldier walked within a few feet of the blanket. Although its camouflage blended well with the ground cover, under the crescent moon the soldier would have noticed them had he not been focused on a further distance with his goggles.

The intruders caught Barry and Alice in separate bedrooms as they had told the earlier inspectors. The few personal items of Julie and Andrew's he was carrying in a bag on his belt. Infrared detectors showed no warm spots in the house other than the two beds. Alice and Barry were informed they would have guests for a few days and confiscated their grapes. A software expert later found nothing out of the ordinary on the grapes as the green mode application was scrubbed the instant it was turned on without the code.

Julie and Andrew reached the cave, pulled back the sod cover and lowered themselves into a hole until they were knee-deep in water from recent rains. The hole in the ground was seven foot deep and four foot in diameter. It would not be a pleasant stay but hopefully safe.

Hidden in the hole, with no possibility of her grape light being detected, Julie put the grape in green secure mode and accessed the vulture feed. She saw at minimum twenty hot-spots west of the farmstead. A few were moving toward the farmstead, others were stationary. One hot spot moved within a few feet of the sod-covered opening and headed east. They decided standing knee deep in water for days if they were lucky enough to not be found wasn't an option and they needed to move before daylight. They were a thousand feet northwest of the farmstead, the cabin center in the Railroad tie dump was a quarter mile south of the farmstead.

At 4 am they detected no hot spots within two hundred feet and rose from the hole covered with the blanket. They headed north before breaking west to avoid numerous hot spots spread west of them. Although some of the hot spots could have been deer they couldn't differentiate. A large half circle brought them to the railroad tie dump gate just prior to daylight.

In the command center they advised the Texas volunteers to take up hidden positions and prepare for an inspection.

It was mid-morning when five vehicles including an armored personnel carrier approached the gate of the railroad tie dump. The search team was led by two NSA officials with a commandeered ATF team and soldiers. The NSA leader approached the gate and examined the lock on the chain securing the gate.

"By the rust on this lock no one's been in here for ages. The key might not even open it." (Jim had replaced a chain link away from the lock which with practice could be opened and closed without using the lock and he had periodically rubbed salt on the lock to speed its oxidation.)

The leader summoned the ATF electric surveillance expert, "Feed into your grape the download from this camera." The camera showed them standing as they were.

For the COMMON GOOD

"We have gone through past feeds from this camera and found nothing happening, except this." He showed a deer cautiously sniffing the lock and licking salt from it.

"And nothing unusual from drones, correct?"

"That's right sir."

"I thought the EPA was supposed to be here and unlock this gate," he asked his NSA assistant.

"That's what they were instructed but they tend to be very uncooperative and guard their turf. Everything checks out, no activity here let's move on."

"No, we were instructed to physically search this place and we will and we'll leave the EPA lock alone."

He sent two ATF agents back to the farmstead they had inspected to retrieve a ladder he had seen and instructed others to walk the perimeter fence and look for any signs of entry. The agents walking the fence saw no signs of traffic. One escape route tunnel existed under the fence but Jim had concealed it well with sod.

With the ladder and a tarp to cover the barbed wire on top of the fence, the NSA leader and four others were soon inside the fence and walked the perimeter of railroad ties.

Four Texans who preferred to be called the 'new rangers' were well hidden high in the pile at strategic observation locations. They followed the intruders with the scopes of their rifles; two had been sharpshooters in the military. For them if the worse came to pass, the standard had been set it was twelve or more each would take out.

Hurriedly, since Julie and Andrew got to the command center at daylight, they had been in contact with the island-boat to assure delivery of the nukes and implementation of the plan in their possible absence. They watched the breach of the fence through hidden cameras and decided it was time to put the command center in fail-safe mode.

Jim had wired the entire complex with explosives to be used in the event of capture. In fail-safe mode detonation would be automatically initiated every succeeding hour unless a delay was received three minutes before the top of the hour. With a delay the destruction of the complex would only be delayed by one hour, which would need to be delayed again. This would continue until it was deactivated.

The invaders circled the pile finding nothing unusual and were headed back to the fence when the leader saw something unusual toward the top of the pile. All the railroad ties he had seen were lying haphazardly, but from one angle he could see four ties stacked tightly together. Four ties appearing to be non-randomly stacked among millions would be expected he thought, but he would make sure.

He started climbing up the pile careful not to step on ties that might roll and unaware that cross-hairs of a rifle never left his midsection. He had not moved up ten feet when he heard the unmistakable rattle of a snake. He very carefully retreated and took another route. Again he heard the warnings of a deadly serpent. Taking a quick step backward a tie rolled and his leg slipped through a crevice in the ties. He nearly freaked out jerking his leg up. Back on the ground he realized his boots would not have protected his leg dangling in a hole if he had been closer to the snake.

He pondered the situation. If he was snake bit chasing something that was very likely nothing, what would it be for? Some would consider it bad judgment. Would he be spoken of in the same breath as the traitorous ATF agent who died from snakebite? In the unlikely event that what he saw represented illegal activity, it was possible cross-hairs could be on him from any of multiple locations. But, he thought, human activity in this snake-infested refuge pile was unlikely. He was not a coward, but finding no other evidence of activity, he was neither a fool. His mind wandered to his beautiful wife and children.

"All right, there's nothing here. Let's move on."

With a vulture showing all had gone except a dozen soldiers hidden around the farmstead Andrew deactivated the fail-safe system.

"I haven't seen any rattlers around the ties," observed Julie.

"Well there may be some, but a couple of tape recorders strategically placed is an old Texas trick," observed a ranger.

In the middle of the night a Mexican started his familiar half walk, half swim across the river between Eagle Pass and Laredo. He had made the 90 meters to the other side of the Rio Grande many times. It was an easy swim with little current this time of year, but the nylon rope he dragged behind made up for the lack of current. On the US side of the river he crawled out of the water under a Coyote willow tree and handed the rope to a friend.

They waited until the all clear signal was sent and pulled the rope until they retrieved five packages tied on the rope. Couriers left with the packages. The excess rope was then pulled back across the river. Normally they would then leave, but tonight they were instructed to wait an hour for another crossing. With the couriers safely away and no sign of being followed a second transfer of another five packages was made.

Neither knew what was in the packages and didn't care. Often the packages were Polish-made black box retrofits. That wasn't the case this night. The first set of five packages contained nothing but a few rocks. After the decoy packages had safely crossed without being intercepted, the second set of packages containing something else crossed. The packages were soon in Crystal City, Texas and two days later were delivered by the US Postal Service to a non-descript warehouse in Wichita, Kansas.

Melissa asked on a video conference call, "How are Alice and Barry doing?"

"Barry and Alice are still confined to the farmstead, or rather they still have company. It's been four days now and they have no idea how long the company will stay."

"Have you thought more about what kind of a message we want to deliver? I believe you are right. If we strike without giving them any idea of who we are, they may think Poland did it." And they need to realize it is home resistance."

"Well there will be no downside. Security couldn't get any tighter than it is. We know we can't just send the President an ultimatum. For it to even get within one level of him, we'll need something to catch their attention. This will be a one step at a time process. Are you absolutely sure a message can't be traced to the island-boat?" asked Julie.

"Absolutely, the route with be through five countries and seven servers. In the process there are two non-linked connections. By that I mean the message will appear on a server monitor and a camera will capture it, digitalize it and it will be hand carried to another server leaving no electronic link," assured Torrence.

"Send this to the President and the director of NSA on all routes we have to contact them: *We know about the prisoners at Guantanamo Bay and your plans to use nano-machines in flu vaccine. You will be hearing from us shortly.* And sign it *DCDBJHGB*"

"Ok, but what do the letters mean?"

"Daniel Collier, Daniel Barnmore, Jim Harding and untold numbers at Guantanamo Bay."

—⟋⟋⟍—

An assistant to an assistant to the NSA director received the note. She had been charged with randomly passing on five percent of the prank messages to her supervisor for review in order that he get a sampling of the whacko traffic. The message, passed upward by chance, would have been tossed as a prank had not the assistant known about Guantanamo Bay.

"I thought you should see this sir," the assistant said to the director.

"Well, we shouldn't be that surprised something leaked from Cuba. It was bound to happen eventually, we'll deny it of course. Forget it and destroy the message."

The director was much more concerned about the note than he let on to his assistant. As he told his assistant the Cuba leak wasn't a big deal, but knowledge about the Tranquility Insertion Project, TIP, was, and knowledge of both was most unsettling. Although many people were involved in components of TIP, only a handful knew the total scope of the project. Those who knew of Guantanamo and TIP were less. Ordinarily he wouldn't have mentioned it to the President. It would not instill confidence from the President and it was another task he didn't need on his plate. But the President had yet to release the laser air defense unit to the Iowa facility. This would be a tool to that end.

"This is bothersome, director. How could anyone have knowledge of both?"

"I'm not sure Mr. President, but they indicated whomever it was will be contacting us again. I've got some teams set up to trace the message, but that entails danger of more people hearing of TIP."

"This is troublesome at the least. I think it is best to make sure others do not see any future messages from whoever it is. Can you route any correspondence from this signature directly to you?

"Yes sir, I've already done that."

"Is there anything else?"

"As a precaution, I believe we should move the laser air defense unit to the facility ASAP, sir."

"Yes, you are probably right; I'll issue the order today."

In the home of the inspector of maintenance and construction at the FDA plant in Eddyville a drama that had played out for millennia took place. The inspector's daughter had yet another date with a project engineer who worked for the other side, a private company. She was breaking her curfew with him regularly and now was waiting for him in attire not fit for public exposure in her father's opinion. He would draw the line and he had a strategy. She was the couple's only child as one child was the socially correct number of children and they lived a life for which he was proud.

"Honey, I'm very pleased with the direction of your life. You got into and did well in a great college, and excelled in social awareness post graduate work. All your hard work and connections have earned you a great job as a public ombudsman at the vehicle licensing bureau. You have a wonderful future."

"Thank you dad, but I think you underestimate the political and union connections you have."

Her acknowledgement caused him to think this would be easier. "I have to ask you, given the future you have, why would you want to spend time, and I mean this with no disrespect, but with a worker bee?"

"I can't believe you would think like that dad. He is a very nice man and respects me. One of the things I learned in social training is everyone has potential and should be treated fairly, which means making none of those judgments."

"I know, I know honey, but we are…, well different. I don't mean… He is a nice young man but he will never get where you will. He just doesn't have the credentials."

"But he is very good at what he does. Doesn't that count for anything?"

"Of course honey, but for greater fairness we dispensed with judging people by what they produce years ago. It only led to cut-throat competition which left many behind."

"He's here, I'm leaving and I don't know when I will be home. I'll see who I want to and for your information he and I may become permanent. Get used to it," she said as the front door shook a window pane.

The inspector didn't sleep much that night. It was three in the morning before she came home relieving him somewhat. He was not ignorant of the mistakes other parents had made trying to push their children away from those they had developed a hormonal attachment. He devised a plan. The next day he called the young corporate employee and invited him to a local bar after work.

"What are your intentions with my daughter?" he asked directly. The project manager expected the question to be asked but more tactfully.

He would be as frank as her father. "I plan to establish a life with your daughter. We have much in common and find ourselves in love."

Well goodie, goodie, I'll buy a round for celebration in the bar, the inspector sarcastically thought but instead responded, "You know I'm going to retire soon and my daughter is on a similar path, how will that work with where you are?"

"Sir, I adore your daughter and will do what I need to make her happy."

The conversation had traveled where the inspector hoped it would, giving him the opening he sought. "If you are absolutely serious about doing what you can to be with my daughter and share a great life with her, I have a proposition to help you."

The project manager listened. It was three drinks and an hour later they both left the bar happy.

"The natural progress of things is for liberty to yield
and government to gain ground."

Thomas Jefferson

Chapter 23

Melissa Barnmore used a number of connections to get a face to face meeting with the Cuban foreign minister. She had flown into Cuba the night before through Mexico City. As far as the Cubans knew she was from the States, which she still considered her primary citizenship. It was only through her friendship with Vicktor Davidov, owner of the Russian space transportation company who worked with Atlas to divert the asteroid, that the meeting was arranged.

Cuba, after following Russia's experiment with collectivism, tinkered with it for many years before abandoning the system. Now Cuba also followed Russia into a strange mixture of just enough capitalism to keep their economy from collapsing, authoritarianism to control the masses and thugocracy to protect the privileged. The nearly century-long embargo of sugar by interests in the United States continued to irritate the Cubans. Although the country harbored a strong distaste for the United States, the ideological differences were minimal.

"It's a pleasure to meet you Mrs. Barnhouse, what do I owe the pleasure? asked the foreign minister true to his reputation as a man of few words.

Matching his disdain for small talk she dove into the purpose of the meeting.

"I want to confirm, however distasteful it may be to your country, that whatever happens among Americans at Guantanamo Bay is not considered a threat to your country."

"I guess I don't follow."

"Let's say a fight broke out among Americans at the base which posed no threat to you. Would that concern you?"

"Not as long as it didn't affect us."

"And what if once this fight was over the Americans who won the fight let the base revert back to Cuba?"

"Well, Mrs. Barnhouse, you have my attention."

"For that to happen we would need help."

"We cannot do anything to risk war with your country."

"We would not require active help, but perhaps turning your head. If boats were to enter the harbor, say private boats, your people might not check them. And if a few people landed close to the base heading for the base, perhaps you might not notice."

"There are strong UN reprimands for interfering with the internal affairs of another country."

"Mr. Foreign minister you are wrong on two counts. Strong and UN reprimand is an oxymoron and what I am suggesting would be staying out of the internal affairs of the United States, not getting involved."

After discussion and the intent to quiz Vicktor Davidov further on the lady's credibility the foreign minister ended the discussion, "Let me get back with you tomorrow."

Late the next morning Melissa received a hand delivered note in her hotel room.

"*Next week home guard forces in the Guantanamo Bay area will be called to Havana for training as will Navy personnel patrolling the bay area. Training will last two weeks.*"

For the COMMON GOOD

White House

"Mr. President we have received another message from the long DC signature, DCDBJHGB. You told me to notify you, I'm mailing it now."

The President read the message.

As the sixth amendment clearly states:
"A criminal defendant has the right to be informed of the
nature and cause of the accusation against him."
We recommend prisoners held at Guantanamo Bay be
released immediately.
Yours, DCDBJHGB

"Well that confirms it. It's a kook. Please don't bother me with such nonsense again."

Regardless of what he told the NSA director the message disturbed him. It wasn't his style to hope problems went away. He took them head on before they festered.

That evening a shrimp boat pulled into Guantanamo Bay for repairs. In its belly were former seals who took control of the harbor naval watch control center. Their leader had worked in the building. Shortly after another shrimp boat entered the bay with fifty former rangers and seals. Under the cover of darkness some headed for the perimeter fence west of Leeward Point airfield, others headed for the eastern fence of the 45 square mile US leased base. Many of the insurgents had served at the base and knew the security installations. Those that hadn't had been trained in the layout for weeks. They soon deactivated security sensors in key locations.

Before midnight a thousand marines and soldiers landed west of the airfield and another thousand near Puta Barlovento to the East. They made their way through the fence opened by the rangers and seals.

Electronic gear on the shrimp boat put out jamming signals over a multitude of frequencies that shut down communications within a ten mile radius. Land lines from the marine base and the prison were also cut.

The colonel in charge of the 800 marine contingent was awakened by his orderly to receive a Brigadier General who had unexpectedly arrived. The colonel was told trouble was expected from the Cubans and communication had been compromised, hence the additional attachment without his notification. The armed soldiers accompanying the general dressed in uniform, speaking English and showing American military discipline soon had control of the unarmed marines in the barracks. Before the colonel discovered otherwise, it was too late. No shots were fired.

"I don't know who you are but this is treason. You could be shot."

"Actually I am in uniform; this is my uniform. I'm a retired brigadier and I don't think you are in position to shoot anyone."

"Why are you risking your pension and everything? Are we prisoners?"

"No, you'll be sent home with your men. And I'll cooperate in any way I can to alleviate you of responsibility for this. I don't consider this treason, but the opposite; I'm defending the constitution of the United States. We are here to release American citizens who have been secretly held as prisoners without being charged with any crime. The only reason we've secured this base is to prevent you from assisting the NSA at the prison."

A similar scenario with a retired admiral played out as control was taken of two Zumwalt-class destroyers docked in the harbor.

Construction engineers with the invading party using backhoes from the airport maintenance building on the Leeward Point Airfield began cutting trenches every few hundred feet in the runway.

There would be no stealthy taking of the prison with retired NSA guards. And three fences, machine guns and poison gas separated over a thousand liberators from 150 guards and 300 prisoners.

With lines cut to the prison and with the jamming of electronic communication, only direct communication was possible. A retired

Marine Captain placed a white flag on an armored personnel carrier and approached the prison fence. With a bull horn by the outer belt fence he asked for the warden. His message from outside the fence startled the prison staff. They woke the warden.

"We have you surrounded. The marine barracks are under our control as is the harbor. Open the gates and surrender."

Confused the warden answered. "And why would I surrender to a personnel carrier and a guy with a bull horn?"

Before an answer came a guard told him all communications were down.

"That can't be, get word out someway immediately."

The answer from the outside came when another half dozen armored carriers and two old M1A3 Abrams tanks driven by former crews pulled within view of the warden's tower.

"You can't be serious. The weekly relief shift of prison guards is due to fly in early this morning." The warden addressed the Marine Captain on the speaker system immediately regretting his release of information.

"That won't happen. The landing strip has been destroyed."

"They can't be serious," the warden said to an assistant. Toward the marine base they heard explosions as a munition dump was set off.

To the captain with the white flag, "What do you want?"

"I told you. Throw the gates open and come out."

"What about the prisoners?"

"We are freeing them."

Prisoners who had picked up the conversation cheered the news. It had the opposite effect on the warden.

"Our job is to keep this prison secure and we will do so."

The captain had heard enough. Their window of time didn't allow for negotiations. His personnel carrier spun around and he tossed the white flag on the ground. He was followed by the other personnel carriers. The warden was convinced he had been successful and was of the belief that it had been a test.

Within an hour the personnel carriers returned, each with a 50 caliber machine gun pointed at a tower, and lay in wait with orders not to fire until they heard fire. Suddenly one of the Abrams tanks that had been sitting at a distance stormed toward the gate at 40 miles an hour. Its track shook the hard soil such that the vibrations could be felt in the Warden's perch. The tank never slowed as it rolled through three consecutive gates until it reached the center of the prison yard and sat amidst a cloud of dust it had generated.

For a reason no one knew, a guard in the Northeast tower decided to try his machine gun on the tank. All the towers were immediately shredded with fire from the personnel carriers, except the main warden tower. It disintegrated receiving a 105 mm round from the second Abrams tank sitting half a mile away. Liberators wearing gas masks burst through the open gates. They were met with sporadic gunfire until the guards surrendered. Three liberators were injured. Forty-five guards and the warden were killed and sixteen injured.

With assistance from the captured guards the prisoners were released.

"Who are you guys?" asked one of the prisoners.

"We're mostly Texas volunteers. How ya'll do'in? We're takin ya'll home."

One of the Texas volunteers heard a "God Bless Texas" come from a prisoner. His pride didn't allow acknowledgement, but he never forgot it.

"You can't believe the things that happened here. Nearly a hundred have been murdered and others died of sickness," was the message the Texans heard from many prisoners.

The marines stationed at the base and the NSA guards were taken to the destroyers in the harbor. Once ammunition on the destroyers was dumped in the harbor they were allowed to head for the states.

After destroying as much hardware as possible by noon the invaders and the former prisoners boarded boats from shrimps to yachts and left Cuba for good.

The Cuban/US Guantanamo Bay lease agreement stipulated that continuation of the lease depended upon the continued use of the base by the United States. As it was abandoned, Cuba reclaimed the base.

—m—

For the COMMON GOOD

The loss of communication with Guantanamo Bay was only known by lower level NSA employees until the weekly air transport carrying a changing shift of NSA guards was forced to return. Without any communication from the base tower the converted passenger plane made a pass over the runway. Its destruction was obvious and it returned to the states. Once the plane was outside the jammed area it reported what it saw. The information reached the director of NSA the same time returning destroyers notified the Pentagon.

Late in the afternoon a meeting commenced at the White House with the Joint Chiefs of Staff, the Secretaries of Defense and State and the director of NSA. The Chairman of the Joint Chiefs of Staff briefed the President.

"Our overview of reconnaissance craft confirms Cubans have secured the base, but they did not invade and evict our people. Reports from the destroyers that left the base are that an American force of some unknown origin took the base, released prisoners and destroyed most of the munitions on the base. The Cubans merely came in after they left."

"Do we have a coup d'état in play here?"

"Absolutely not, sir, all personnel and units are accounted for."

"Okay who were they, where did they go?"

"By the time we got surveillance in the air all we were able to find was the normal domestic air and sea traffic. But initial reports indicate a number of retired members of the armed services were involved; only people knowing the layout of the base could have accomplished this. We will begin debriefing our people immediately. But again the Cubans could not have had the information required to orchestrate this."

The President was ready to ask the location of the prisoners but stopped himself. Too many people without knowledge of the prison were in the room.

The chairman of the Joint Chiefs continued, "Sir we have a number of marine units ready to deploy for the base. We await your command."

"What will that entail?"

"The Cubans are taking up fortified defense positions, but we are confident we can soon have the base back within days."

The Secretary of State injected, "Sir, the Cubans are diplomatically maintaining that the Guantanamo Bay lease is void as we have abandoned it."

The President stifled a desire to burst out *we didn't voluntarily abandon it* and calmly stated, "I'm going to need some time on this, thank you. You are all excused." He gave the NSA director a "you stay" look.

Once the others were gone the President asked, "Have you determined the source of the messages with the capital letters signature?"

"No, we haven't."

"It's too much of a co-incidence."

"I agree. What are you thinking about Cuba?"

"My inclination is to clear the Cubans out of there and take it back, but it would be a major skirmish that would draw a lot of international attention. If the base invasion is linked to the warning about the prison, retaking the base is probably what they expect us to do. We don't want to be forced to publicly admit we were holding Americans there. Let's not let them back us into that corner.

Let's focus on the big picture. We get a message that someone has knowledge about the prison and the nano-project; then a group of armed men take the prison and release prisoners after we're warned to release them. It certainly gives more creditability that someone of means has knowledge of TIP. I think it is more important to get in front of this group of whoever they are rather than react to them.

The nano project is what will define the future. No longer will people of good intent be hampered from helping humankind by superstitious throwback ideas. Generations from now the morally attuned will thank us."

The President spun in his chair and gazed out the window. The director of NSA knew him well enough not to interrupt his thought. A decision was coming. Turning back to face the director the President announced, "The prison situation in Cuba will be easier contained if we do nothing."

"How do we handle it if the former prisoners start talking? And the guards killed in the fight?"

"We compartmentalize and isolate the information and ultimately deny it. It's a ridiculous charge trumped up by our opposition. Put people's pensions at risk if too many questions are asked or anyone talks to the press. I'll pull some strings in that area. It's a national security issue after all.

If you have a gas fire, you can throw water on it, but the best way to control the fire is by containing it and eventually shutting off the gas. Let's work on prevention rather than being reactive. Are we absolutely sure no one or group can stop the production of nano-machines?"

"The laser air defense unit is deploying as we speak. But we should insulate the command there against a pseudo-higher officer take over as happened in Cuba."

"I'll have the pentagon send another thousand soldiers and up-grade the command to a major general. They'll give me static on having a general report to the NSA official there but that is how it needs to be."

"And Cuba?"

"If necessary we will let it be known the base is no longer necessary for our armed forces and we have negotiated a deal with the Cubans for the base's return."

Moving on the President asked, "When will nano machines start being shipped to the FDA vaccine line?"

"It is scheduled to start in ten days, sir."

"In the meantime let's appear amenable, could you send a message to this anonymous messenger?"

Before the director could answer he continued, "Ask them who they are and what they want."

"Yes, sir."

Within an hour Julie read the message after it had traveled around the world a few times and twice been passed on after a photo was hand carried in its delivery.

"What do you think?" asked Melissa.

"Julie typed an answer.

We are concerned citizens and we want the nano project for the flu vaccine permanently scuttled.

Within another hour they received a reply.

We have no idea of what you refer. Please enlighten us.

"What do you think?" Julie asked Andrew.

"I think we have their attention, but I suggest that we set the agenda and let them fester for twenty four hours by not answering. And in the meantime make sure Rod is ready with what we discussed."

The last boat to leave Guantanamo Bay with volunteers and former prisoners waited for the final passenger. His arm was bandaged. Doctors with the invading force had hurriedly expunged Tony Johnson of a chip under his skin. He boarded the ship with a lighter step; for it was as if the miniature chip had weighted a ton on his body and spirit.

Later in the week a letter was delivered to Tony's parents home in Urbandale, Iowa informing them that their HCI scores had been cut in half. The letter was never opened as the parents had left for Texas the previous day with no forwarding address.

The expeditionary force returned and dispersed throughout Texas and the South. With a taste of success in Cuba they anticipated their next mission. But preservation of the force was paramount to training for another mission. Reluctantly guns were again hidden. Doctors, dock workers, lawyers and brick layers returned to their normal routines encouraged with firsthand knowledge that the onward march toward central control was not inevitable.

The prisoners fearing an immediate return to Iowa were taken in by the new Texas Rangers. An international camera crew led by the expatriate Bret Wilson, who had interviewed Melissa Barnhouse after Daniel's arrest, documented the prisoners' ordeal. Editors splicing the interviews with video taken of their abduction made a compelling documentary to be used when the time was right.

Although the documentary would be held from distribution in the US until the right time, it was shown to the Russians. The hope

For the COMMON GOOD

was the Russians would allow their video to augment the evidence. Seeing the documentary the Russians agreed to reconsider releasing the video they had of the massacre after the escape attempt.

—ɯ—

After days of being under the scrutiny of soldiers and NSA agents, Alice and Barry were relieved at their departure. The soldiers had been called back to the NSA facility to further beef up the perimeter. Alice headed for town in her none-altered black box car. She bought all the groceries she thought possible without causing alarm. At a location on the farmstead and another inside the railroad tie dump fence, canned food was buried with bottled water. She had gradually added to the supply. The goal was to have a 60 day supply on hand.

The soldiers who had been at the farmstead were surprised at the new activity at the NSA facility. With more soldiers arriving daily a second beltway was being constructed with a second security gate. Portable trucks with huge generators coupled to other trucks also surrounded the area. Rumor had it that they were part of an air force air defense unit.

The lieutenant back from the farmstead asked his captain, "What are we preparing for, any idea?"

"No, but someone is concerned about something; the command has been upgraded, I don't get it, but orders are what they are. Frankly, invading the US capitol would be easier than this remote facility."

Workers at the NSA facility soon learned to leave for work earlier as lines developed at both exterior security checkpoints before the final one inside the building. Security that most considered ridiculous soon became the subject of an ever expanding rumor mill.

"Things in our country run in spite of government, not by aid of it."

Will Rogers

Chapter 24

Two days of light drizzle dissipated. Julie had previously canceled her meeting with Eric. It was too dangerous with the low cloud cover preventing a vulture from making sure all was clear. Operating a vulture below low clouds would have scared Eric.

With the sun out Julie ran the recreation trail after parking at the college. Any normal traffic on the trail wouldn't have recognized her without the blond wig. She met Eric at their normal meeting place.

"Glad to see you made it today."

"Sorry about yesterday something came up at the last minute and I couldn't notify you in time."

"You had me worried there."

"Sorry again, anything new happening at the facility?"

"Yes, I don't know where to start. You, I expect, know about all the outside activity, more soldiers, another checkpoint to go through entering the place. And rumor has it that a top-of-the-line air defense unit has been deployed. Would it be presumptuous of me to think someone was expecting an attack from the air?"

With obvious coyness she responded, "I don't know what they might expect."

"Okay," he acknowledged her evasion.

"What can you tell me about deliveries and out-bounds?"

"I've heard complaints about timeliness because of changes in mail and package delivery. Everything incoming is delivered outside the perimeter. Anything bigger than an envelope is opened, repackaged then brought in by hand. No drones can deliver mail or fly close to the building."

Carrier drones had for many years taken over delivery of letters and parcels up to 25 pounds. In buildings of size carrier pigeon drones would land on the roof, unload the cargo into a delivery chute which would robotically send the mail to the basement for distribution throughout the building. It was a completely automated process. No hands touched a letter or small package from the time it left an office until it was delivered to its destination.

"That must cause a nightmare?"

Eric attempted to answer a question that hadn't been asked, "I have no clue how I would get something in the building without carrying it. And I don't know how that would work. My briefcase was causing me so much trouble getting it through security I quit carrying it. But the good thing is, not nearly as many people are going through security."

"What do you mean?"

"The workforce has gone down. The individuals with special areas of expertise, we discussed, are gone. I can't ask many questions but I no longer see them and traffic in the cafeteria has dwindled."

"Would it be reasonable to assume they have completed their work?"

"Yes and that obviously would fit our speculation on the product timetable."

Julie said nothing but nodded her head, yes.

"I don't need to... you know... but I assume there are alternative plans somewhere in the chain?"

Again she said nothing for some time, but finally said almost to herself but knowing he would hear, "I have always had a healthy respect for fire drills, one should always pay attention to them."

Eric stood and gave her a light hug, "God's speed."

"Thank you."

—ᴍ—

On the cabin-center wall screen, "Julie, are you ready? I'm going to link you with the director of NSA. At best it will take five minutes to move the messages back and forth through our communication chain."

"Any time, Torrence."

"Mr. President, are you there?" asked the NDA director.

"Yes, I'll watch and send suggestions to you, but they are not to know I am monitoring this message exchange."

"Understood, Mr. President."

Message exchange between the NSA director and Julie:

> Director: *Where does your concern about connection of NSA and flu vaccine come?*
> Julie: *That is not important. It is important that the project be stopped immediately.*
> Director: *Such a connection would concern us, but I can assure you after personally reviewing operations at the NSA facility no connection exists.*
> Julie: *As there were no American prisoners at Guantanamo Bay I'm sure. Perhaps this conversation is a waste of your time.*

The President sent a message to the NSA director which appeared on a second screen.

> *"Give them something to get information from this exchange."*

Director: *Although your charge of NSA linkage to the flu vaccine is unwarranted, if we were to reduce operations at the NSA facility, would that sooth your concerns?*

Julie: *There might be less inclination to make public considerable testimony by former American prisoners at Guantanamo Bay of the massacre which took place there.*

Director: *I am neither aware of a prison there or any alleged massacre.*

Julie: *Then this conversation is a waste of your time.*

Director: *Hold on, regardless of those allegations, we don't want to fuel any ridiculous ideas about the NSA facility. In order to quell domestic turmoil we may be amenable to shutting down the NSA facility you are concerned about.*

Julie: *How soon would that take place and would all products and contents of the building be destroyed?*

Director: *I'll need to get back with you on that, but I'm sure something can be worked out to your satisfaction.*

The message exchange ended. Andrew was the first to speak. "Amazing how quickly the exchange validated what we know. I find it hard to believe they are that scared about us leaking the Guantanamo Bay prison story. They will deny and marginalize the sources. But they certainly want to placate us about the NSA nano-project."

"I agree," said Julie. "We need to define what the minimum actions they would need to take for us to be confident the nano-project is dead."

"They will stall us but they will not stop it."

At the same time the NSA director and the President were analyzing their moves.

"I'm not worried about whatever they put out about Guantanamo, and we have beefed up the NSA facility such that no one can touch it. Frankly, we have enough fortified troops in place to hold off two army divisions or an air force wing until the little machines are delivered. I say let's call their bluff," advised the director.

"I do not doubt you about staving off armed interference, but we don't know what else is out there. In fact we don't even know who these people are, where they are located, what they know or what is motivating them. Far too many unanswered questions to be playing hard ball when we don't need to.

As long as we don't give up TIP, most anything else we can negotiate. We are 9 days from the transfer of the nano-machines. Let's stall, give a little at a time and run the clock out. Open the facility up to the public and turn it into a museum if necessary, just get the nano-machines delivered first."

"With due respect Mr. President, I think it is setting bad precedent to give into whomever, perhaps a group of hooligans. Where might it stop?"

"You miss the big picture. The CDC is reporting people are clamoring for early flu vaccination. Once the population has been placated by the insertion of the control devices these difficulties with an unruly population will become mute. Let's not use cannons on fleas when a little repellent will do the job. Let's let them think their escapade in Cuba has them in a good negotiating position and stall."

Eight days until nano transfer

With Rod Ballanger, Mason Trotter and other delegates patched in on secure phones across the country the director of NSA messaged Julie. She was an unknown person to him, a person who, given his background, he would have viewed with contempt, but given a full understanding of her, he would have feared.

> Director: *When I took this post as director I pledged to myself, I would do my utmost to build public confidence in our national security apparatus. Accordingly, although I find your concerns most unwarranted, we are undertaking plans to abandon the NSA facility in Iowa. We are going to completely meet your request. I suggest we meet at a place of your choice to work out the details.*

Julie chose to ignore the play to her perceived ineptitude for a meeting.

> Julie: *If that is the case why are you continuing to beef up the security force there?*
> Director: *The Pentagon is using the facility as a training area for future contingences, which was a mistake as it has caused alarm. It will take a few days to get them to turn around. I hope you can understand the wheels of government take time.*

Julie typed, *that's part of the whole problem* but thought better of it.

> Julie: *We are pleased you have agreed to end activities there. In order to validate your actions we request that the facility be emptied only of people and destroyed within three days.*
> Director: *Frankly that is not necessary or possible. We will vacate the premises.*
> Julie: *Oh, I think it is. As director you could order the facility emptied within hours and the military group around the facility has ample firepower to reduce the building to rubble. I think 48 hours would be a more appropriate timetable if you are committed to building public confidence.*
> Director: *I shall get back to you.*

Julie asked Andrew, "What do you think?"

"I think they will come up with every trick to lure us into hesitation while they stall."

—ɯ—

Cole and Ryder had both been out of the Army for over ten years. Their specialty had been mortar deployment in an infantry unit. Neither had ever fired a mortar at an enemy target, but they had set up and fired thousands of mortar rounds fine tuning their aiming skills. They were both accomplished in setting up the mortar, calibrating the target's location, factoring altitude, wind velocity and temperature.

The mortar round of choice, which they had used in the service, was the U.S. M30 whose ammunition had a sub-caliber expandable ring which enlarged when fired allowing greater accuracy. The ring allowed the projectile to easily slide down the barrel but grip the rifling when fired. Obtaining the mortar barrel and ordinance from military supply depots in the U.S. was daunting and dangerous because of close tabs on weapons inventory. Such was not the case in a number of countries that had purchased surplus U.S. military supplies.

They had both spent time staking out a park a mile and a half from a major electrical grid junction and distribution center for the DC, Northern Virginia and the Maryland area. More than once they had set up the mortar, dialed in the coordinates and reloaded the barrel into their vehicles and left the park. It could be done in minutes.

Seven days until nano transfer
Julie had requested the next message conference with the director of NSA convene at 8:00 pm.

> Director: *You will be happy to know I talked to the President today and he is agreeable to destroying the NSA facility in Iowa as you have requested. We will immediately begin work on achieving the goal of having the facility destroyed within a few weeks.*
> Julie: *That will not suffice; we requested that it be destroyed in 72 hours yesterday. That leaves 48 now.*

A message from the President appeared on the director's second monitor, "I'm taking over this conversation."

The President: *This is the President of the United States. Please tell me why we should negotiate with you people? Who are you and where are you? Are you US citizens? This we need to know at a minimum.*

Julie: *Respectfully, Mr. President we are a group of concerned citizens. We are from Peoria, Knoxville, Bakersfield, Waco, Dodge City, Sarasota, Roanoke, Skokie, Tucson, Fargo and Buffalo.*

The President: *I get it. You realize that political protocol suggests we shouldn't even talk to you people, but I'll think about your terms, but don't push it."*

Julie: *Mr. President, I hope the White House generator is in working condition.*

Julie then disconnected the link while nodding to Barry.

A delegate from the Atlantic Coast district was situated with a clear line of site to Cole and Ryder who were a half mile apart. Upon receipt of the code on his secure phone he gave both Cole and Ryder three flashes from his high powered light beam.

Cole and Ryder each retrieved a projectile with a short wing on the tail from their vehicle and dropped it into the tube which they had pre-positioned. With a woof and a flash of light the projectile was thrust airborne. In less than a minute with gloves they tossed the tube in the vehicle and were gone.

The two projectiles landed in a concentrated web of electrical transformers, boosters and high voltage lines that channeled through a manifold of circuits to be spread out over miles. The explosions destroyed the heart of the oversized electrical junction box causing a blackout over the greater DC area.

The exchange of messages had been scheduled by Julie at 8:00 pm to make a point. It was the time of maximum electrical usage. It was dark, people were up using electricity and most electric cars were recharging at that hour.

In the White House the lights flickered and went out. Soon the President heard the hum of a generator and the lights were back. It

For the COMMON GOOD

took thirty minutes to re-establish contact with the NSA headquarters in Ft. Meade, during which time the President went to a window and looked out over the darkened DC area.

"Tell me you have some idea of where these people are and who they are?"

"No sir we haven't."

"How bad is this power outage?"

"Good news, Mr. President. Electricity is being rerouted and all users should have power by mid-night."

"Well, they made a point, didn't they? Do we know of anyone close to a likely source of this insidious activity we can use to pressure them?

"If the guy who assaulted an ATF agent and killed twelve was part of this, he has a son at a TSD in Omaha."

"But the father is dead and one kid is not enough to give them a message. Can we get the timetable moved up to start the nano transfer early?"

"We've been putting pressure on the makers of the nano transfer system, Amalgamated Robotics Company, ARC, and quite frankly they are on schedule which is usual as our projects go, but if they finished today it wouldn't help. We are producing the nano-machines but none will be ready to ship before the transfer system is ready."

"Ra, Ra, a federal project done on time. Use any incentive you have to get started earlier, if only a day or two."

The director hadn't mentioned a potentially better bit of news to the President wanting to wait until he could verify the information, but given the President's mood he changed his mind.

"Mr. President, I may have better news. We have been working diligently to find the source of the alphabet signature. We have a lead. We have identified a remote location in the country that is generating encrypted radio signals and receiving the same from outside the country. It appears to be a sophisticated version of the old ham radio. The location has been transmitting signals during our message conferences with the mysterious entity."

"That's great news. Use whatever forces necessary to capture the group."

"Mr. President, we really need to verify this information first."

"Find out all you can, but let's not hesitate. It is illegal activity. Communication outside the country is not allowed without a permit and encrypted communication is a violation of the National Security Act. You can bet this alphabet signature is moving the signal around outside the country before it gets to us. We need the military involved in this. It can't be screwed up. Get back to me as soon as possible. In the meantime I'm getting the Chairman of the Joint Chief's here early tomorrow. If hooligans can put a thousand troops in Guantanamo Bay, hard to tell what they have guarding the location you found. We can't go in with a few hundred of your local yahoo NSA agents."

The director cringed at the insults to his agency but answered, "Yes, sir I'll be there in the morning," while regretting that he had brought the subject up before it had been checked further.

"Government is essentially the negation of liberty."

Ludwig von Mises

Chapter 25

Six days until transfer

Air transport planes filled the lighted runway at Fort Bragg. The 82nd Airborne division had never deployed directly from the base. The division's 2nd brigade of 2200 men had been given only an hour notice to be ready. They were standing on the runway with parachutes and equipment ready to board. No one except officers above Captain knew where they were headed. But all knew it was not a drill.

Out of the ear shot of others a company commander, a Major, questioned the colonel who commanded the brigade.

"This division has landed at Normandy, South Korea, Vietnam, Grenada and Iraq, but never would I have thought, ever in the country, in a remote part of the Midwest. May I be frank sir?"

"Yes, but watch your volume."

"I'm not comfortable conducting an operation inside the country. It is not what I signed up for."

"We have our orders Major; we are told it is a national security situation, and we shall proceed. If you have a problem let me know and I will relieve you of your command," the Colonel said dressing the Major down, but harboring the same concerns.

The first few planes that took off contained many NSA agents. They transferred to helicopters at a base close to the target and were to land close to the target area. The planes of paratroops would secure the area around the cabin first.

—m—

Cabin-center, Mahaska County, Iowa
Video conference with the island-boat

"Delivering a package as planned through normal channels into the NSA facility is out. All deliveries go outside the security perimeter and only enter after being opened, inspected and repackaged.

However, I've been working on another method of delivery. Actually Julie knows about it first hand," teased Andrew.

"I don't know that much. I drugged myself remember?"

"Simply, we ship the package to ARC at the FDA building; it gets delivered to the pneumatic transfer construction area in the basement. And I direct the robot to load it in a tube and zip it inside the NSA building 9 miles down the tube…

Torrence interrupted him, "I've got something here. Just a minute… are you sure… Yes?… How soon?"

"Cabin center, we just picked up chatter and confirmed Fort Bragg is sending a brigade of paratroops due West. They took off an hour ago and our information says it is not a drill and they are headed for a cabin. I think we have to assume they are headed for Iowa. It could be raining white chutes there in an hour. Go to fail-safe mode and get out of there now."

Barry headed for the farmhouse to stay with Alice. They would appear to be spending a quiet evening at home. Once fail-safe was set Julie and Andrew tried to budge the Texas rangers but they would not leave saying they would be far enough away from the explosion and buried so deep in the railroad ties no one would find them.

"Besides," one of them said, "If the thing doesn't blow we'll set the railroad ties on fire."

Julie gave one of them the fail-safe bypass and explained its use. "Remember keep calling the code before each hour, unless you get company. Unlikely but maybe it's a false alarm."

In a black-box altered car Julie and Andrew headed for Des Moines with the intention of getting lost.

Aiden was more nervous than normal in a parking place with his girlfriend at the Springfield Conservation Nature Center 15 miles Southeast of Springfield, Missouri. It had been over a month since Olivia and he had gotten out alone. It was not just high school activities that had kept them apart. Olivia's mother had objected to their going out and had threatened to have them followed. Between kisses he kept a lookout around the car. The moon was just rising when he saw light reflecting from an object in the sky. One object soon became many and his mind immediately leaped to Olivia's mother's warning of her connections and the bad things she could bring down on him. Other fears gradually replaced Olivia's mother when hundreds of white chutes dangling armed soldiers descended upon them.

"We're not doing anything," Aiden pleaded as paratroopers surrounded the car.

"Yeah, yeah, out of the car buddy."

The night was much more ominous for Liam. He had moved from Springfield months ago after his divorce. His wife had kept the two-bedroom home and he moved to a one room cabin in the woods. With the move he had brought all his amateur ham radio equipment. In the solitude of the isolated cabin his company for most evenings, other than a family of raccoons he fed, was people around the world who he conversed with by a simple encryption system he had developed. Once a week he attended a local speakeasy but wasn't involved in anything remotely political. He just wanted to be left alone. Tonight he was in conversation with an Estonian and would not be left alone.

Initially he was convinced a tornado had unexpectedly arrived or a bomb had exploded outside his cabin. Glass from all three windows shattered across the floor at the same time the front door of his cabin burst across the room plunging into his shoulder and battering his head against the desk. He woke to find his cabin filled with black-shirted NSA agents and his hands in cuffs. His next week became a bewildering trip through an unimaginable hell.

Similarly a speakeasy on the outskirts of Springfield was entered and ransacked. Thirty-five occupants were taken as prisoners.

—⚏—

White House

"You are telling me we sent 2000 paratroops halfway across the country to arrest some aberrant miscreant. What were you thinking?"

"Mr. President, with due respect, we are on a priority basis to find the people responsible for this extortion. Accordingly, we aren't double checking our sources. I was under the impression to err on the side of being proactive was preferred."

"Yes, you are right but again they've made us look like fools."

"As far as anyone knows sir, the 82nd went on a training mission and the NSA picked up a guy breaking the law in cahoots with foreign governments."

—⚏—

Wednesday, Five days to nano transfer
Conference call with delegates on secure phones through the island-boat

"Sorry about the false alarm. It certainly looked ominous and we couldn't tell until the last minute that they were headed south of you."

"Okay, Torrence, better safe than sorry."

"From what we can tell they were after a ham radio operator, whom I suspect they thought to be you. I can't imagine what he thought came down on him."

"Rod, how are you on delivery of the packages?"

"Tomorrow carrier pigeons will deliver a package to our Western friends near Camp Williams, Utah, and to our Atlantic coast friends close to Ft Meade in Maryland. Our delivery to Iowa will need to be picked up in Des Moines as security is too tight around the target area for chancing a closer flight."

"Thank you Rod, lets hear about our Utah plans," asked Julie.

The delegate from Utah spoke, "The initial delivery will be to Orem, just north of Provo around 25 miles from our target. Only five people in our organization know about the package and only two know what it is, the other delegate and me. We have a carrier pigeon drone already hidden away ready for flight. The married couple who have the drone hidden will be available to send the package for final delivery within ten minutes of orders. They do not know what the package contains, although I'm sure they would be elated if they did."

"What about the target?"

"Saturday night has the least activity at the Data Center. Primarily maintenance and janitorial crews but even they are lighter than on a week night. We did deliver a dummy package last Saturday night to make sure the package receiving system operated as we expected. Our tracking device showed the package being taken into the belly of the beast. Ten minutes to launch, flight time of thirty minutes and ten minutes for robotics to unload the package and get it into the basement package receiving room. We need fifty minutes notice to have the package in place."

The Utah Data Center was the shorter name used for the Intelligence Community Comprehensive National Cybersecurity Initiative Data Center. The data storage facility went into service in 2013 at Camp Williams near Bluffdale, Utah. The center had been located at the Utah location because of its proximity to a military base for protection and the low cost of electricity in the area for its original 65 megawatt demand.

When it went into service in 2013 it had 1.5 million square feet of data storage, data analysis and administrative space, more than the

100-story John Hancock Center in Chicago or 30 times the space of the U.S. Capitol building. Since its opening the facility had been expanded many times, but the later numbers were classified.

Before the numerous expansions after 2013 the center was estimated to hold as much as 5 zetabytes of information, which at the time was the equivalent of 62 billion stacked iPhones 5s, the most sophisticated communication device of the time. In another comparison the location had the capacity to store 1000 times all the words ever spoken by human beings or 100 million times all the words in printed material at the Library of Congress.

Information on every phone conversation, e-mail, twitter post, voicemail, social media communication, grape file transfer, inter and outernet browsing history, Aerial Citizen Protection Unit (vulture) observation, stationary camera observation, vehicle location history, airport personal traffic data, individual health care records, credit transaction card activity and nuances of 350 million citizen's DNA structure were buried somewhere in the mountains of information kept at the center. All the information lay in waiting of the state acquiring the analytical ability to piece it all together.

"How are we looking for the Maryland target? And you guys pulled off the electric grid shutdown brilliantly. It certainly got their attention."

"Thank you, I talked to the mortar guys last night and they are certainly available if needed again. I was tempted to tell them about the impending package delivery but thought better of it. We have the package outside of Clarksburg, Maryland around 35 miles away. If we synchronize with the Utah people we should send our carrier off about ten minutes sooner. I personally will be there to send it off, but there will be two of us available just in case one of us gets detained or doesn't make it. As a precaution we are not going to be together until then to assure we both don't get picked up.

There does seem to be more activity at the NSA headquarters here on Saturday night than our friends say there is in Utah. Activity has picked up since you've started communicating with them. I suspect they are burning the midnight oil trying to locate you."

"Well they better get at it," Julie quipped.

The headquarters of the National Security Agency sat on a huge complex at Ft. Meade, Maryland. The nation's covert intelligence gathering organization was housed in two high-rise office structures built and dedicated by Ronald Reagan in 1986. The huge complex included at least 10 acres of underground facilities. The last known numbers from 2012 showed over 20,000 people worked there, making it the largest employer in the county and one of the largest in the state. At that time the complex was also the largest employer of mathematicians in the country and housed the most powerful supercomputers in the world.

The National Security Agency originated as a code and cipher decryption unit during World War I. During World War II the Signal Security Agency was created to intercept and decipher Axis communication. In 1952 President Truman officially formed the units into the NSA under the direction of the Defense Department and the Director of National Intelligence. It soon became the largest U.S. intelligence organization in terms of personnel and budget.

"Okay, that's all for now. Again I warn everyone to keep your head low and take no unnecessary risks. I would certainly recommend that you stay away from speakeasies. We don't know what happened to the speakeasy occupants in Springfield, MO."

"At least we know that they are not at Guantanamo Bay," added Mason of Texas.

"As we heard, the NSA is doing everything to identify where we are and who they are dealing with. Although they mistakenly apprehended folks in Missouri, I think we should realize any of us could go down before Saturday. Accordingly, since we are all together on this conference call I think we should again come to consensus that our plans are to be implemented Saturday night. Do we have a clear understanding that if some of us or part of our means is compromised, the remainder of the plan will be implemented?" Julie asked.

There seemed to be general agreement, but Julie insisted that all delegates state their position. It was unanimous.

"Next I would like authority to have complete latitude to negotiate with the President. Don't misunderstand me we will not accept promises, anything less than destruction of the facilities before we can will not deter us. And I don't think anyone believes that will happen, but I need your consent to deal and put things on the table. I also need authority to time and orchestrate our reply to their expected propaganda after we act."

The chorus of response to her request was varied but Rod summed it best. "For practical reasons you should be able to make the calls. As you said we don't know what will happen in the next few days. We might not be able to meet again. And don't take this wrong because we trust you, but we have mistakenly trusted many people in this country who we shouldn't have. So, although it makes sense for you to make the decisions, we reserve the right to disagree with your decisions or withdraw our support."

"I not only accept that, I understand that."

—❧—

Thursday, four days until nano transfer

Analysts at the Ft. Meade NSA headquarters were in a dilemma. They were under tremendous pressure to identify the source of a high volume of encrypted communications moving in and out of the country. The analysts did not know the content of the communication but knew that they were of great concern to the top levels of government. Leaves and vacations had been canceled and quotas for the spectrum of communication avenues gleaned had increased to a point many were forced to work extended shifts. Some employees were beginning to question their choice of what they thought would be easy, low pressure work in government service.

Two anomalies were passed to the director although neither lead was as clear as the Springfield ham operator's signature. An encrypted signal had been picked up about once a week from Bangor, Maine sent to the hundred-year old Ramstein U.S. Air base in Germany. The mathematicians estimated the probability of the source being responsible for the messages at less than half a percent.

The other detection was short micro bursts on random frequencies originating from an old EPA hazardous waste dump in Iowa. Their best estimate placed the location at only a tenth of a percent probability as the source.

The director not wanting to go through the Springfield scenario again flipped the leads back to the analysts with a mandate to investigate and have a report increasing or decreasing the probability of the two possibilities by 6:00 pm.

Further investigation of the Bangor source by encryption cracking experts found the communication was image transmissions of a personal nature. Nevertheless, as sending messages in code was illegal, they seized the computer of a serviceman's wife in Bangor and brought her husband, who was stationed at Ramstein, in for questioning.

For the Iowa location to be the source of the mysterious messages, analysts explained it would be similar to one car part from every junk yard in the country being dropped from the sky and miraculously falling together to make an operable vehicle. They also found that the EPA site was a thrown together small mountain of rail road ties, all lying at different angles which could theoretically reflect radio beams in a haphazard manner. They also discovered that the EPA site had recently been inspected by NSA.

The NSA supervisor received an e-mail requesting a call about his inspection of the EPA Railroad dump. It was marked urgent. Urgent did not speed his call to NSA headquarters. Urgent meant he needed to contemplate what was going to be asked and his answers.

It bothered him that he backed off inspecting the suspicious stacking of ties when he heard rattlesnakes. There would have been other ways to get to the suspected ties. Nevertheless he was faced with a dilemma. To admit he failed to inspect something suspicious would be disastrous for his career. The risk this time was more ominous than a rattlesnake; he chose to minimize the risk.

"Yes, we checked the EPA dump thoroughly and no, we saw absolutely no irregularities or signs of any activity."

Given information that the dump had been thoroughly inspected, analysts rated the Iowa EPA dump source probability as nil, but they would continue to investigate.

"When all government, in little as in great things, shall be drawn to Washington as the Center of all power, it will render powerless the checks provided of one government on another and will become as venal and oppressive as the government from which we separated."

Thomas Jefferson

Chapter 26

Friday, Three days until nano transfer
White House

The President asked, "So make sure I understand you correctly, we will start transferring the nano-machines to the FDA facility Monday and the process will take two weeks. Is that correct?"

Attempting to make it better the NSA director said, "We have built in a couple days for unexpected trouble. If everything works flawlessly we'll be finished in twelve days or less."

"Okay, let's get the link up with those anarchists."

The President disgustedly looked at his director and gave a partial shake of his head and a half smile which flared his nose. "Dealing with these people, I'll wash my hands when I'm finished."

President: *Can I be confident you will adhere to any deal we make?*
Julie: *Of course, Mr. President.*

President: *I've given this much thought and it isn't easy being pressured, but as always, I must place the greater good of the country before all else. And for you to expel a lot of propaganda, no matter how ridiculous, doesn't serve the country. If you will agree to refrain from releasing what you discussed, I'll start the process to dismantle the NSA facility in Iowa and have it destroyed a week from Monday."*

Julie: *That doesn't meet our timetable, but if you can guarantee the date we will compromise, Mr. President. Like you, we wish to do what is best for the country. I'm glad we've rectified this situation.*

With all signed off the NSA director spoke, "You know we can't complete the transfer in a week."

"I know, but we've bought some time. Of course it will take more time to dismantle than I expected, if it happens at all."

Andrew could read Julie and knew better but Barry was confused, "We can't wait a week. It will be done in two weeks and there are no assurances he will carry out any of it."

"Of course we can't trust him or wait a week, but if the lie will buy us time and lessen their pursuit of us, it was worth it. I prefer not to lie, but when dealing with those whose Alinsky playbook directs them to lie, we shall fight fire with fire. The conversation has served its purpose. They know we are the internal resistance. "

Adana was in the construction trailer early as usual and finished going through the daily task scheduling for her employees before she opened her e-mails. There was mail from the FDA delivery and shipping department that she first ignored then returned to. It said deliveries to the construction contractor could no longer be picked up at the main shipping station in the building, but would be delivered directly to the construction trailer.

Caridad arrived and as usual stayed with her mother an hour before she left for the laboratory.

For the COMMON GOOD

"There's construction going on outside the parking lot that your company is not part of, I think I know what it is about. Coming in this morning I saw a carrier pigeon landing with a package and two people from shipping were there. I suspect they've off-sited the shipping here as they did at the NSA plant."

Adana fed Ethan a message on her grape's green app, "Get here immediately." She was still explaining the significance of the change in shipping to Caridad when Ethan entered the trailer. He was soon headed for the cabin-center.

Barry had just entered the cabin center when Andrew informed him that Ethan would be there shortly with important information. Barry was concerned, "We agreed we need to limit activity around here as much as possible."

"I know but Ethan says it is urgent," Andrew told him as they watched a vulture feed of Ethan pulling into the farmstead driveway with his construction work truck. They sent their second vulture on a wider search of the area to make sure he wasn't being followed as Ethan made the quarter-mile walk to the cabin-center.

Before he could say "hi" to Julie and acknowledge the others, Ethan said, "We've got a problem." They soon understood his reason for coming and the magnitude of the problem.

"I've already placed the order in the system for a package scheduled for delivery Saturday evening. Isn't it possible; they won't repackage it, or suspect nothing, repackage and deliver it anyway?" Barry said partially hoping out loud."

Julie responded, "Possible, but unlikely. If they have gone to the trouble of moving deliveries off-site, they most likely will use the same procedures of opening and repackaging everything. As inept as they are in many ways, you can usually count on them sticking to a pattern. And besides, if they repackage, a package delivered Saturday evening may not get delivered to the building until Monday."

Barry, "I know you are right. We've got to come up with another way."

Andrew, "Earlier Rod and I discussed dropping a package from a carrier pigeon and setting it off like a bomb. We rejected the idea because a detonation on the roof might not do the damage we need deep inside the building and would cause more collateral damage. But I don't know how we would get a carrier pigeon there given the air defense system."

Barry, "What if we saturated the sky with vultures over the NSA building? Hopefully they would tie up the laser defense and allow a carrier to bring the package in for a roof top detonation. Not the best but better than nothing."

Julie, "That could be the last resort, but we've got to do better."

Ethan noticed an aerodynamically shaped container in which carrier drones delivered packages sitting in the corner of the room. While the others were exploring options, he opened the container and lifted out a metallic cylinder 5 inches in diameter and 16 inches long. It weighted 20 pounds. He turned it over in his hands and studied it.

Julie noticed him. "I know it's safe to handle but the rest of us grip that cylinder with caution."

"I've got an idea," he said and left the center before anyone could ask.

The others continued to explore options, none of which seemed to have much merit as the vulture feed remained on the wall screen. They saw Ethan looking for something in his construction truck, then walk back to the center carrying something.

Andrew, "Why the fuel cell pack?"

Ethan laid a package of six bundled electrical fuel cells that powered tools and offered back-up power to robots on the table made of hewn railroad ties. He laid the thermo-nuclear cylinder beside the fuel cells.

Andrew got it first. "It makes sense for the pneumatic tube terminal to have a backup supply of fuel cells, right?"

"Exactly."

The grouping of six fuel cells held together by a commercial plastic wrapping with bar code was approximately the same diameter and only two inches longer than the package they needed to deliver.

"We paint the device the same color as the fuel cells, add a black delineation line every three inches to make it appear as though the package has six components and carefully put the fuel cell wrapping around the device," continued Ethan.

Andrew finished describing what Ethan had started, "And you, a construction supervisor, the only one in our circle who has access to the room under their watch, put the spare fuel cells in the construction tool box in the tube terminal room. If any questions arise you are going the extra measure to insure success."

Ethan continued on the emerging plan, "I lock the tool box as they require, but I leave a key in the room for your robot to find, retrieve the package and set in a tube at the appropriate time."

Julie, "Brilliant, so we sneak the bomb in disguised as fuel cells; let's go to work."

Barry, "Alice has an acrylic paint set. I'll go get it."

At 3:00 in the afternoon Ethan pulled his construction truck up to the company trailer headquarters and entered carrying his toolbox. Caridad, concerned over what was happening and where her husband was, waited with Adana. He explained the alternative plan.

"I've called the inspector and told him I have tools that must be delivered. He is meeting me at 3:30 to let me in with a security guard before they leave work."

"Is he the inspector whose daughter Andrew's project manager is dating?"

"Yes."

"You've got to be careful. He is by-the-book only guy."

"Remember he's the inspector who wants to go pheasant sighting on the farm again this fall. He's looking forward to it. I'll get it delivered."

Adana who had been eyeing his tool box asked, "Is it in there?"

His eyes told her it was. "Get it out I want to see it."

Ethan pulled out the mislabeled package and seeing his Mother-in-law with her arms out to receive it, handed it to her. She instructed him to pull a real fuel cell package from the storage shelf. He laid the fuel cell package beside the well-disguised thermo-nuclear weapon.

She put the two non-carbon devices end-to-end, held her hand on one and reached for Caridad's hand with the other. "Touch the other device and hold Caridad's hand," she instructed her Son-in-law.

Ethan didn't understand what Adana was doing, but knew better than ask. Soon he was keenly aware that tension he had felt building inside him subsided. He met the inspector and security guard with confidence.

The building inspector and a security guard met Ethan outside the check-in inspection area, "I hope this is important, we've both weekend plans and this is a twenty minute delay we didn't expect."

"Well, I just got to thinking as the priority level of the tunnel project has been raised so high, I don't think we should chance not having back-up fuel cells on hand this weekend for the testing."

"I suppose it makes sense, but I thought all the fuel cells were changed mid-week."

"They were, but we've seen about one in a hundred fail, do we want to take that chance?"

"Okay, here is the key to your tool box."

"And we can talk about the pheasant sighting trip. How would next week work?"

At the building security checkpoint Ethan emptied his tool carrier. The checkpoint security guard inspected the energy cell bundle closely on a table turning it over with his hands and scanning the barcode.

"It's an energy cell bundle. He brings them in all the time," the inspector started to protest a delay.

"How many cells are in this package?"

"Six."

The checkpoint security guard thought about opening the package of six, then thought of the lateness of the day, "All right, go on."

When the computer matched Ethan, the inspector and security guard's iris prints the entry door to the tunnel room unlocked. Ethan quickly hunched to his knees, unlocked the lower door of the tool storage cart and placed the mislabeled fuel cell bundle inside and relocked the door.

Immediately after Ethan pulled the key from the lock the inspector was standing beside him with his hand out expecting the key to be given back to him as normal protocol. After he gave the inspector the key, Ethan started to rise up from his knees. Halfway up he gasped and fell to the floor with one hand holding his left knee. His other hand inconspicuously reached under the tool box and attached a spare key coated with a sticky substance beside a coaster wheel on the tool box. Months ago when security was less stringent Ethan had copied the key not knowing what use it might be, now he knew.

"Are you all right?" the inspector asked as the security guard and he helped Ethan to his feet.

"Yes, doesn't happen often, but my knee just gave out."

"You need to rest it before our pheasant sighting trip."

"I will."

Watching it unfold from the ARC camera in the cabin-center Andrew gave a sigh of relief, "He got it done."

Julie observed in jest, "Yes, and as slick as he is we better watch our pockets." Everyone in the cabin-center and the island-boat laughed in relief.

"We the people are the rightful masters of both Congress and the courts, not to overthrow the Constitution but to overthrow the men who pervert the Constitution."

Abraham Lincoln

Chapter 27

Saturday morning

Andrew went over the final checklist remotely with the ARC project manager who was on site at the NSA facility, "I tried to reach you earlier."

"Yes, I came in later today as I'm staying late tonight."

"Why would you stay on site late tonight?"

"I'm going to run the final live systems check tonight."

"But that is scheduled to be done tomorrow."

"I'm going to do it earlier. It will give us more time to work any glitches out."

Andrew trying not to show any alarm, "I want it done tomorrow and I'm doing a final go-through on the software today, your check needs to be run after I finish," he lied.

"That wouldn't impact what I do."

"What's going on, why can't you stick to schedule?"

"I've always been honest with you Andrew. You know I'm seeing an FDA building inspector's daughter. We're making plans. The inspector is retiring next month at 51 and will recommend me for the position. He has invited me to the regular Sunday meeting of the Public Mechanical Overseers Union (PMOU). I need to be there. It is an opportunity of a life time I can't pass."

"Well, you weren't honest earlier when you said you were running the test early to allow time for glitches."

"You are right, I'm sorry. I should have been upfront."

Andrew put aside his own deceptions, among them that he was in Iowa, not Idaho. But his slight was not for personal gain or security, and he earnestly lamented the prospect of losing someone with productive potential.

"But I don't understand. Why would you? You are one of our top new engineers. You are inquisitive, bright, and resourceful. You have the tools to move technology in robotics to the next level. Why wouldn't you want to be part of that?"

"Again being straight with you, I want to have a future with the inspector's daughter. The inspector has made it clear he doesn't want his daughter with someone like me, but it's more than that. He has offered a solution that offers more than his daughter.

What are you now Andrew, 62, and still working? I've been working 8-10 hours a day here, more than 5 days a week. The inspector works seven hours four days a week and makes more money than you. I'm 27, with the new public allowance of my college years counting toward pension, I can retire at 48."

Andrew didn't want this young man or any person needlessly killed. But on another level, the potential loss of an industrious member of society to non-producing work frustrated him. "But what would be the point? What will you produce? Were we put here to ride a lazy raft down the river, or to stir the current? I didn't think you were a rider. How do you justify your existence without producing?"

"My mind is made up."

Julie hadn't heard all the words of their conversation but could tell from the tone of her husband's voice that he was frustrated. She realized how disturbed he was when he tossed his grape on the table popping the back off and sending the battery flying.

She walked to him and put her arm around his waist. "What is it?"

He explained the situation and looked at her, "We don't have a choice, do we?"

"Perhaps he will leave with the fire alarm. You have a few hours to fabricate a reason why he should, if not you've done what you can."

At a noon conference call with the island boat Andrew explained the alternative method for delivery of the package to the Iowa NSA facility through the FDA complex. Julie and Andrew were relieved to learn that shipping and receiving procedures had not changed at the other NSA buildings.

Only a few delegates were on the conference call via secure phones. Most had decided as close as they were taking further chances were unnecessary.

The conference call centered on plans to counter the propaganda that loss of state's eyes and ears database would precipitate. Although they had been successful in hijacking news programs during the aftermath of the asteroid diversion, many layers of government security had been added. Work attempting to regain the ability to hijack media feeds in the country had gone on for years by Barry and software technicians on the island-boat.

They expected that their actions would cause a shift of opinion toward the state. But given the cost of inaction and the long term advantages of blinding the state to internal opposition, a temporary loss of popular support could be accepted. The focus now at the island-boat was to minimize any negative shift in opinion.

"You know the final decision is yours," stated Melissa seeking a measure of Julie's mindset.

"I know and given that one package is irretrievably in the belly of the beast, the decision has been made."

With business finished, Torrance, Melissa and others left the island-boat communication center and Barry joined Alice at the farmhouse. For the next hour Julie and Andrew connected with their daughter, Sandy.

The conversation covered nothing serious, but nevertheless important subjects from school, friendships and how they missed each other.

"I miss you Mommy and Daddy, but everyone here says how important your work is."

"Well you remember we do our work for you, Danny and countless others."

"Will I understand someday?"

"I'm sure you will, honey."

At a 5:00 early dinner Andrew, Julie, Barry and Alice dined on venison, boiled potatoes, and green beans in the farmhouse.

"What a delightful meal, Alice. Where did it all come?"

"The potatoes and green beans are from my garden and the venison is complements of the army troops who stayed here. They got tired of chasing hotspots thinking they were you, which turned out to be deer. A sergeant from Kentucky shot a deer saying his lieutenant had ordered the area cleared. A corporal from Texas had experience dressing deer. Funny no one seemed curious about from where he obtained his butchering skills. Anyway, I fixed them venison and have some left. Don't kid yourself, politically correct or not, they love meat.

So we can thank the army for this meal. Most of them are good people. If given a choice they would be with us. I'm confident if they had their rathers, they would be glad you are eating compliments of them."

Walking back to the cabin-center, Andrew asked Julie, "Are you still considering sending a last message?"

"Yes, I think it's important for them to absolutely know this is coming internally and not blame a foreign government."

"Is there anything going on at the White House tonight?"

"Yes, according to Melissa, it is a party of the celebritiocracy."

White House, Saturday 7:00 pm EDT (6:00 CDT)

The President dressed in one of his three tuxedos was waiting for the first lady to finish for their grand entry down the staircase. It was an event held quarterly with an assortment of celebrity guests. There would be a collection of Hollywood stars, professional athletes and

For the COMMON GOOD

corporate executives who had become wealthy exploiting their government connections. The parties were held under the auspices of an exchange of ideas among the successful. In reality they were exercises in recycling money crony capitalists had obtained from government favors back to the politicians who had made it possible.

The President held no lofty illusions about the function, "Honey are you ready for the mutual kiss-fest of egos?"

"Give me 5 minutes, dear."

"You're looking good tonight. Too bad it's not the 10th of the month."

A secret service agent knocked on the door, "Mr. President, the NSA director is on line. He says it is urgent."

The President logged on his grape to see a message from DCDBJHGB.

> Good evening, Mr. President. We have to inform you our deal is canceled.
>
> The president entered: What do you mean canceled? What do you want?
>
> Julie: We want the Iowa NSA facility destroyed before Monday, and the Idaho and Ft. Meade NSA facilities abandoned and destroyed within a week.
>
> President: Is this a joke, is that all?
>
> Julie: You should know we represent citizens demanding a restoration of liberty and prosecution of those responsible for murder.
>
> President: For civility, I won't tell you what to do with your requests. I've more important duties to attend. Contact me no more.
>
> Julie: Have a good evening.

The President messaged the NDA director as the first lady approached:

I no longer deal with rubbish.

She held his arm and they started for the stairs, "Still working, I see. Maybe we could pretend it was the 10th later tonight."

The President realized, given the alphabet group's prior actions, he shouldn't have lost his temper and didn't hear his wife's invitation. Her irritation at his perceived snob would soon be the least of his concerns.

—∽—

7:00 CDT (8:00 EDT)

Julie sent the code to a delegate waiting for the signal at Clarksburg, Md. Within ten minutes a carrier pigeon drone lifted off with a twenty pound package, on which someone had painted a liberty bell.

—∽—

7:10 CDT (6:10 MDT)

A couple in Orem, UT received the same signal and acted according to plan.

Andrew logged into the ARC robot control software and moved a robot that he had designed toward a construction tool box. With the robot facing the tool box he maneuvered a set of pinchers until it retrieved a key held precariously by the wrong end.

Alarm started to grip Julie. She thought of boys in middle school who had tried to woo her at carnivals by picking up a toy from a glass cage with mechanical pinchers. They most often failed. That was a game, this was not.

Andrew was neither a boy nor a failure; he dropped the key, picked it up by the right end with learned dexterity, unlocked the cabinet door and soon had the decoyed package in the pneumatic tube. Before he closed the tube the robot placed the key also in the tube for incineration.

—∽—

7:20 CDT

With the door closed on the tube and the air system engaged, Andrew held his finger above the SEND button. Julie nodded and the tube left the FDA building.

Earlier in the day the director of NSA instructed a team tracking the mysterious messages to give him a report before he left the building in Maryland. He had been told they were making progress.

The team leader knocked on his office door earlier than expected.

"Come in. Any headway?"

Beaming with pride the analyst reported, "Yes sir, I am happy to report we have found the source of the messages and an offshore communication center the messages have been going through. The messages originate at the EPA dump in Iowa we looked at earlier and go through a ship off the coast of Costa Rica."

"Great work. I'll get the President and we'll strike immediately."

"Thank you sir. Our work done, the team is ready to leave for the night."

Thinking of security, the director stopped him before he got to the door. "As delicate and high priority as this is, I want you and your team to stay here until I reach the President."

"Are we being quarantined sir?"

"Just being cautious, it won't be long and don't worry your work will be noted at the highest levels. I'll personally see you highly rewarded."

8:05 CDT

Julie received a message from the Island-boat that all packages were in the belly of a beast. They opened a video link with the island boat. Melissa, Torrence and the rest of the island-boat council were in the room visible on the wall screen as Barry, Andrew and Julie were to them.

"Activate the fire alarms," commanded Julie.

Fire alarms at the three NSA facilities went off. Those few employees and maintenance staff working left the buildings obediently as they had been drilled by state protocol. Most were happy for a chance to escape work and mingle with friends. The ARC project manager at the Iowa NSA plant had nearly finished his final run-through when the fire alarm went off. He was distracted when the air system charged and a tube arrived from the FDA building. His grape buzzed. It was Andrew.

"I understand there is a fire in the building, are you still there?"

"Yes, about done. Funny thing though, a tube was just sent from the FDA building."

"Yes, I'm working on the problem now," said Andrew as he watched the Project Manager standing ten feet from the tube. "You better get out of there now."

"I don't smell smoke, this baffles me." He was walking closer to the tube.

Andrew looked over at Julie. She was motioning to him holding five fingers in the air.

"I know it does me too. Let me check out the software while you wait outside. No use you taking chances with that pretty girlfriend in your future. If it's a false alarm, by the time you get back I'll know more."

"Okay, catch you later," answered the project manager causing Andrew to breathe a sigh of relief.

8:07 pm CDT

At both the Ft. Meade and Camp Williams buildings vultures crashed near major exits to the buildings. They carried a very small C-4 charge that had replaced the camera. The explosions did no damage but succeeded in moving those who had left the building further away to the far corners of the parking lots.

In the White House the Chief of Staff whispered in the President's ear that the director of NSA wanted him and it was urgent. The President said it could wait until the party was over.

8:10 pm CDT

Julie typed DCDBJHGB on the keyboard. She looked at the group on the wall screen from the island-boat.

She drew a deep breath and read from her notes:

"As other shackles controlled the less connected in past times, whether they were considered lesser by class, race, or origin, we are controlled by a shackle of information.
The shackle of information is no less restrictive than chains of iron, for it controls the individual through taxes, the right of movement and speech, and life itself through healthcare access.
As people throughout history have justifiably thrown off their chains when the weight became too oppressive, so shall we."

Julie put the notepad down and said, "For both Daniels, Jim, those at Guantanamo Bay, and liberty seekers everywhere."

She turned and looked at the walnut framed sketch of the founding fathers hanging on railroad tie cabin wall and said, "We too," as she lowered her finger on the ENTER key.

The director of NSA was still in his office after putting the message tracking team in the office next door. Hearing the fire alarm then a small explosion outside, he called building security. "Is this a drill and what about the noise I heard?"

"Sir, a vulture crashed by the front door. But we have no reports of damage."

"Call me if anything changes."

He shortly received reports of fire alarms in other NSA buildings. He smiled thinking if this was a feeble attempt by a group in an EPA dump and a boat off Costa Rica to cause havoc, they would soon learn real havoc. He again contacted the President's chief of staff.

"Yes, director, what do you want?" the chief of staff asked.

The line went dead before his question was answered as did the director.

The few nighttime workers at the three National Security Agency buildings were conditioned to follow guidelines; they waited at least 500 feet from the building as fire drill training dictated. Explosions at various entries to the buildings served the purpose and pushed them further away.

Light as bright as the sun erupted through windows of the facilities soon to be followed by sound, heat and concussion. The temperature at the core of the buildings approached the temperature of the sun, as 70% of the explosion's energy was thermo, 30% blast and less than 1% radiation. Roofs of the buildings were thrown in the air creating a cloud of debris. The interiors of the buildings were incinerated leaving only the lower portions of the outside walls standing.

Surprisingly within a minute only small wisps of smoke trailed upward from the remaining partial skeleton of the buildings as the initial incineration left nothing to burn. Cars in lots close to the buildings were overturned but most employees were far enough away to experience only cuts and scrapes from falling debris.

Gone forever was information that:

Sophie had used a sick day to shop at a mall
Avery had used an illegal animal repellent to rid her garden
of rabbits.
Joshua had bartered services with neighbors without report-
ing to the IRS
Lois had attended two college classes with Aaron Hamil
Jayden had three flashers on his call log
Liam had smoked cigars only after his annual medical
check-up
Lucus had his car within two miles of five flash
demonstrations
Addison had watched foreign news feeds on her grape
William had killed a bull snake threatening a Mourning
Dove
Natalie had bought pizza from the same place as Jim
Harding.

At the White House the chief of staff approached the President who was in a flirtatious conversation with the last Oscar winning blonde, her mesmerized by his power, him her looks. "Mr. President, I've numerous people trying to reach you."

The chief of staff received a response in a *"go-away"* look rather than words and left the President to his party.

Shortly thereafter some among the partiers were seen checking their grapes. *Insulting,* thought the President. Soon more were and he stepped over to his chief of staff.

"What?"

"We've got a problem, sir."